Can't
LET GO

GENA SHOWALTER

Can't
LET GO

HQN™

HQN™

Recycling programs
for this product may
not exist in your area.

ISBN-13: 978-1-335-14337-2

Can't Let Go

This edition published by arrangement with Harlequin Books S.A.

For questions and comments about the quality of this book, please contact us at CustomerService@Harlequin.com.

www.HQNBooks.com

Printed in U.S.A.

This book would not have been possible without three amazing ladies:

To Jill Monroe and Kresley Cole for the invaluable brainstorming. And laughs. And fun. And, heck, for being you.

To my amazing editor, Emily Ohanjanians, for incredible feedback. I love that you just get me! Even better, you get my quirky characters.

And I have to give a second, special shout-out to Jill Monroe, who spent eight hours holed up in a hotel room with me one day, helping work through the kinks in the story.

I'm blessed!

Can't
LET GO

CHAPTER ONE

He was back.

Ryanne Wade poured her world-famous fruit cocktail moonshine—affectionately known as CockaMoon—into a small mason jar and, as discreetly as possible, watched as Jude Laurent prowled through her bar. And okay, the moonshine wasn't exactly world famous but regionally famous. Okay, *almost* regionally famous; made from her personal recipe, it was distilled at a local brewery and sold exclusively at the Scratching Post.

Jude had once called the drink Downfall in a Glass. Or DIG. Like, *you're digging your own grave, Wade.* Just to get a rise out of her, she was sure.

The former army ranger was a new resident in her hometown, and one of three co-owners of LPH Protection, a security firm. Sometimes he looked like a brawler from the maddest, baddest streets, yet other times he looked like a businessman fresh from a boardroom negotiation—and he'd won. Tonight, he was a bona fide brawler, ready to throw down and heat women up. He wore a black T-shirt, ripped jeans and combat boots. Leather cuffs circled his wrists, and three silver rings glinted on his fingers. His version of brass knuckles?

No matter his persona du jour, he was always as gorgeous and tempting as sin—and an all-around pain in Ryanne's backside.

He really churned her butter.

Usually he only blessed the Scratching Post with his exalted presence when one of his two friends required a designated driver. He never ordered anything but water, and never spent a dime or even left a tip for the waitress unlucky enough to serve him. Namely Ryanne. Not even the insulting kind of tip: a note on a napkin. *Fetch my drinks faster next time, and you'll get cash.*

The worst thing about him? He liked to stand at the jukebox and intimidate patrons with a death-ray glare. Oh, and let's not forget how he sometimes attempted to police the door, commanding people to sit and stay as if they were dogs, simply because they'd had a sip of something—*anything*—alcoholic.

The nerve of the man. And the body on him...

Ryanne fanned her flushed cheeks. Time to crank up the air conditioner. Because no, her boiling blood had nothing to do with Jude's sexy, muscled, delicious, sexy, mouthwatering, sexy good looks.

Not too long ago—okay, okay, soon after meeting Jude—Ryanne had decided to nix her ban on romantic relationships and pick someone to date. The timing was purely coincidental, of course, but her hormones had been out of whack ever since.

Besides, even if she did want Jude, she wouldn't go after him. Despite his surly attitude, females young and old continued to approach him in droves, stealthily or not so stealthily dangling their bait, but he never even nibbled. He might as well have Off Limits tattooed on his forehead.

Was tonight the night he relaxed and had a little fun?

Shivers rained over her as he cast a dark, brooding glance in her direction. He had collar-length blond hair with the slightest wave, eyes bluer than a morning sky, and the body of a surfer: lean, muscled and bronzed. But he also had a perma-frown. To her knowledge, he'd never smiled, joked or laughed, and he'd always radiated scary-hot menace and aggression.

If he ever smiled…goodness gracious, her hormones might explode from lust overload!

Of course, he had a good reason for his bad attitude. A few years ago, he lost his entire family in a terrible car accident; his wife and twin daughters were gone in the blink of an eye. Talk about the ultimate heartache. Ryanne reckoned guilt and grief ate at him on a daily—hourly—basis. And she absolutely 100 percent empathized.

But come on! His troubled past didn't give him the right to accuse her of duplicitous flirting practices in order to boost return visits, and oversalting snacks to ensure patrons remained thirsty. First, she wasn't a plain, ordinary flirt; she was flirtish, and there *was* a difference. She wasn't after conquests but smiles. Second, how would Jude know anything about the food? He hadn't tasted a single dish she served.

For some reason, he'd pegged Ryanne as a villainess at their first meeting, and his opinion of her hadn't changed.

Dang him. I'm as sweet as sugar, and probably tastier to boot!

When he turned on his heel and headed her way, a frisson of electricity raced through her. Their gazes locked once again, and his step hitched—so did her breath. The sight of him, drawing nearer while fully focused on her…

Keep your cool, mi querida.

Impossible! Her heart thudded against her ribs, and sweat glazed her hands.

Attraction gave way to irritation, but irritation gave way to compassion when she noticed his limp. Poor guy. It was more pronounced than usual.

On a mission overseas, he'd lost the bottom half of his left leg. Now he wore a prosthesis.

Fingers snapped in front of her face, and she blinked. Cooter Bowright, one of her regulars, stared at her with concern. "You all right, Miss Ryanne? You've been spacing while I've been foaming at the mouth. Dehydration is deadly, don't you know."

Ugh. Caught ogling a man who despised her. Feigning nonchalance, she topped Coot's CockaMoon with a sprig of mint and slid the jar in his direction. Since she'd begun selling the fruity specialty, her nightly revenue had increased over 20 percent. Maybe because the cocktail consisted of strawberries, blueberries and grapes, a tribute to the three Oklahoma towns that surrounded the bar: her childhood home Strawberry Valley, Blueberry Hill, where the Scratching Post was located, and Grapevine. Or maybe because the cocktail utterly rocked.

"I'm all right enough to know this is your last moonshine of the night," she said. "If you get to feeling dehydrated again, I'll pour you a sweet tea."

Coot took a long swig, draining half the glass, then wiped his mouth with the back of his hand. "Come on, Miss Ryeanne." He sometimes drew out the syllables in her name when trying to make a point. "Don't cut me off just yet. The night's barely even started."

"You know the rules. Three CockaMoons, no exceptions." No one got blackout drunk on her watch. Actually, if anyone slurred their words or staggered while walking, regardless of the limits, she pulled a Jude and stole keys. One, it was illegal to sell alcohol to anyone who appeared intoxicated and two, no, just no.

Safety first, sales second.

The difference between her and Jude? She called a cab afterward and never judged.

"I'd say you suck rotten eggs, but I love you too gosh dern much," Coot muttered, only to brighten. "Hey, you gonna be singing tonight?"

Sometimes she enjoyed performing a couple sets with the band, but she couldn't sing, mix drinks *and* make snacks. "Not tonight. I—"

Jude reached the bar, and the rest of her response died in her mouth. *Sex made flesh.* He leaned against the polished wood and—shocker—glared at Coot. "Public intoxication is a crime."

Coot withered. "You're right, Jude. I'll be more careful next time. Honest."

Hoping to lighten the mood, Ryanne winked at Coot and said to Jude, "Your *shirt* is a crime." The black cotton was far too tight and likely to cause riots. She wiggled her brows. "How about you do us all a favor and take it off?"

See? Flirtish.

He frowned at her and, right on cue, she withered just like Coot.

The old man patted her hand in a show of camaraderie. "I ever tell you two about the night I let the wife use zip ties in the bedroom?"

Yeah, he'd told her about a dozen times. Mrs. Bowright had tied him up all right, only to fall off the bed and knock her head on a side table. Cooter had to crawl bare-butt naked across the floor to get to the phone stuffed in the pocket of his discarded jeans. He'd ended up using Google to find a way to free himself from the ties before the paramedics arrived—something about spreading your elbows, raising your arms and slamming your joined hands into your torso—but not before he'd mistyped and found himself on a zit-popping site.

Ryanne listened, anyway. She loved the old man.

For once, Jude refused to be ignored. He stepped into her line of vision, their gazes tangling together. Blood fizzed in her veins as her stomach performed a series of flips.

How did he affect her so quickly and intensely?

Easy: her romantic past was basically a blank slate. She had no experience, so she had no means of fighting her attraction to this—*any* man.

Bottom line, she'd gone two and a half years without dating. Before that, she'd only gone out a handful of times, too distrustful of the male species to offer more than a handshake at the door.

Why bother doing more? In high school, her mother slept with not one but two of her boyfriends, and Ryanne had feared it would happen again (and again).

Just wanted to know if they'd cheat on you, cariño.

Yeah, right. You don't betray your "sweetie."

Ryanne's trust issues had only gone downhill when she'd started working here. Before taking over ownership, she'd balanced the books, bused tables and waitressed. Every night, someone had propositioned her, pinched or swatted her butt, or groped her breasts. Supposedly devoted husbands had picked up singles, and women who'd left with a man one weekend had cried a week later when he'd gone home with someone else.

As a child, some of her mom's "special friends" had gotten handsy. Once, Ryanne had overheard one of those special friends laughing with coworkers, bragging about easy conquests and sneering about "clingy bitches."

It was a miracle Ryanne had gotten over her issues, and a bigger miracle someone as cranky as Jude had set her fantasies aflame. He really, *really* wasn't her type.

Was anyone?

Surely! She would find a candidate sooner or later, and he would be everything she'd ever wanted, everything she'd ever needed. Honorable, loyal to the bone. Kind. He would prize and cherish his significant other, no matter how long or short their relationship.

He would be like Earl Hernandez, who'd had a heart of gold.

When Earl died of pancreatic cancer a few years ago, her entire world had come crashing down.

Only recently had she cracked open the journals he'd written throughout his life. His devotion to his first wife, who'd died before him, had shone as brightly as a star in the darkest of night. If those two had lived, they would still be together.

"I need to speak with Ryanne privately," Jude said to Coot.
He did? About what?

"Course. No problem, Jude." Coot blew her a kiss before
wandering off.

"So…how are you?" Jude said, now looking anywhere but
at her.

Going to exchange pleasantries, were they? Okay, fine. "I'm
well. How about you?"

He shrugged and said nothing else.

Oookay. Exchange over. "What can I get you? Liquid Viagra?
Blowjob on the rocks? Screaming Orgasm?"

"Water." His voice was a little hoarse, and she fought a grin
as she filled a glass with his beverage of choice. "And add a
lemon," he said.

Ooh la la. Lemon. She wedged a slice on the rim. "That'll
be two dollars and fifty cents."

His gaze zoomed back to her, his lips pursed, pulling his scar
taut. "Two fifty for water that's never before cost me a dime?"

Was he such a miser at other businesses or just hers? "My mistake. Tonight I'm charging you for my time and energy. And if
you think you're getting a bargain, you're right." While everyone else tiptoed around him, afraid of making him unhappy—
well, unhappier—she often bristled like a porcupine.

Unfortunately, she'd inherited her mother's hair-trigger temper.

He stroked two fingers over his beard stubble before placing
a five-dollar bill on the counter. "Do *not* keep the change. And
since we're on the subject of time and energy, you'd do well not
to waste mine by admitting you need me."

You need me.

Was this an attempt to ask her out? "Excuse me?" she said,
and grudgingly handed him two dollars and fifty cents.

"Your *security*—" air quotes "—wouldn't stop an accident

much less a deliberate crime. You need me to fix the problems before someone gets hurt."

Nope, he wasn't trying to ask her out, and she wasn't disappointed.

"No one's going to get hurt." Her "duplicitous flirting" helped maintain the peace, preventing fights. When one happened to break out, she handled it.

"You're too trusting," he said.

What! "Too trusting? Me?"

"You must think the best of people. Otherwise you'd fix your ancient locks, and better watch your customers. You have four employees, and there's no way the five of you can keep track of everyone at once. What if someone steals money from your register? How will you know, until it's too late? Plus, there are too many dark corners in and around your bathrooms. What if a woman is assaulted? And do you have any idea what's going on in the parking lot?"

The thought of anyone being assaulted in her establishment sickened her. "Just so you know, I'm not responsible for the decisions others make. And my locks do their job, which is all that matters. But what do you suggest I do about the dark corners? And what's going on in the parking lot?"

"Add motion sensitive lights, as well as hidden cameras." He said no more, ignoring her second question.

"Lights, yes." Even though the constant on and off might be annoying. "Cameras, no way. They're a violation of privacy."

"It's perfectly legal to put cameras in the hallway outside a bathroom. Also, you need at least two men at the front door. Someone to monitor who enters, and someone to monitor who exits. The latter can issue Breathalyzer tests to anyone planning to drive."

A customer signaled her from the other end of the bar, but Ryanne held up a finger, asking for a moment. "Hello. *I'm* a walking Breathalyzer. And as much time as you've spent here, you should know it. The things you're suggesting will only tick off loyal patrons, costing me business and money."

Every spare cent she made went into her travel fund.

As a little girl, she'd escaped her rocky home life inside the pages of travel books, imagining she was somewhere—anywhere—else. Now she longed to visit those places for real.

Last week, she'd purchased her first ticket. In two months, twenty-eight days and seven hours, she would be on a firstclass flight to Rome, where she would spend four weeks biking through the city and its surrounding countryside, touring the Vatican, oohing and ahhing over famous artwork, eating fresh cheese and homemade pasta, and tasting wine at different vineyards.

Muscles jumped beneath Jude's navy blues. "For Ryanne Wade, monetary profit comes before other people's lives. Got it." He turned on his booted heel and stalked away.

Dang him! He always had to have the last word. But…was he right about something bad happening in the parking lot?

She hustled to the waiting customer and, for the next hour, managed to push Jude from her thoughts as she mixed drinks. It was Saturday, but only 6:30 p.m. Still, the bar was crowded, her waitresses rushing from table to table.

After her full-time bartender, Sutter, clocked in, Ryanne made the rounds, making sure customers were happy and no crimes were being committed. The regulars smiled and waved at her.

Most came from Strawberry Valley, where she'd lived the bulk of her life.

Her mother, born and raised in Mexico, had moved to the United States to marry a Texan. However, the two soon divorced, and a pregnant Selma Wade—once Selma Martinez, now Selma Wade-Lewis-Scott-Hernandez-Montgomery— moved to Oklahoma City, where she later met and married a prominent Blueberry Hill businessman. Like husband number one, he hadn't kept her attention long, and she'd divorced him in favor of marrying a pillar of the Strawberry Valley community. When those two divorced, Selma married Earl, another Strawberry Valley resident, only a far less reputable one. All too soon she'd divorced him, as well. She dated around before marrying her fifth husband and moving to Colorado, where she still lived.

That's when newly minted eighteen-year-old Ryanne made the quality decision to move in with Earl, her third stepfather. He'd owned the bar, but he'd had trouble running it after his cancer diagnosis. And though she'd come here to help him, the wonderful man had helped *her*, supporting and encouraging her the way a father should, even when people accused him of falling for a "cheap Lolita."

A pang in her chest, Ryanne blew a kiss to his picture, which hung above the bar, right alongside postcards of every country she'd ever dreamed of visiting. Greece. Egypt. Finland. Iceland. Actually, all the lands! Ireland, Greenland, Switzerland, the Netherlands, Thailand, and England. Australia. Africa. Costa Rica. France. Germany. Israel. China. Mexico. Russia. The Virgin Islands. Basically, she planned to travel from one end of the earth to the other, and everywhere in between.

Throughout the rest of the building, she'd preserved Earl's country-western motif. The walls had patches of exposed brick, and above the dance floor were the words *Wild West*, every letter surrounded by colorful neon lights. For bar stools, saddles were welded to metal bases. In the corner, swinging saloon doors partitioned off the bathroom hallway.

Do you have any idea what's going on in the parking lot?

Jude's words rolled through her mind, and curiosity got the better of her. With her favorite .44 holstered inside her boot, she marched to the rear exit. In the alley, cool night air couldn't mask the pungent scent of garbage due to be dumped. The overripe smell hadn't driven away the people who sat along the wall.

At the end of every shift, she liked to give leftover food to the homeless, and word had spread.

"Hey, guys," she said with a wave. "Anyone seen anything suspicious going on out here lately?"

A man known only as Loner stood to wobbly legs. Dirt streaked his skin and caked his hair while stains littered his ragged clothing. Her heart ached for the man. She didn't know his story, only knew his eyes were dulled by hopelessness. Life had given up on him, and he'd given up on life.

"There's been a young man skulking through the shadows," he said. "Tall, blond. Looks constipated all the time. We thought he worked for you 'cause he paid us to report any drug sightings or—" Loner tugged at his collar "—flesh peddlin'."

Constipated? Only Jude. The man hated every second of his existence.

Why did Jude care what happened on her property, anyway? Why did he think people were selling drugs and sex? Oh…crap. What if people *were* selling drugs and sex? Acid churned in her stomach, quickly burning a path up her throat.

"And did you have to report anything to him?" she asked.

Loner shifted from one foot to the other. "Past few nights, different men have climbed inside a van and, uh, it started rocking soon after. Those men took off about fifteen minutes later." Again he pulled at his collar. "Not sure if no money was exchanged, though."

Poo on a stick!

Ryanne had heard so much cursing on a daily basis, she'd decided to keep her words and thoughts, like, superclassy. Snort.

She sooo did not want to call the cops about this. While she loved the hardworking, honorable men and women who worked for the Strawberry Valley PD, she didn't fall under their jurisdiction. Instead, Blueberry Hill PD would be sent out, and one of their officers—Jim Rayburn—wanted her shut down by fair means or foul. Sometimes he showed up at the bar to card and question her patrons. Other times he pulled them over for suspicion of drunk driving. Ryanne suspected Jim was the one who'd written "Ryanne Wade is a slut" and "For a good whore call Ryanne Wade" on the men's room wall.

He despised her, all because she'd helped her friend and ex-stepsister Lyndie Scott leave her husband, Chief Carrington, Jim's former boss.

The abuses the chief inflicted on the delicate Lyndie, turning a buoyant young girl into a woman with crippling shyness and constant panic attacks… For the first and only time in her life, Ryanne had contemplated cold-blooded murder.

A jealous husband did it for her, giving the beater and cheater a taste of his own medicine. In Jim's mind, Lyndie and Ryanne were responsible. What if he blamed the sex and drugs on Ryanne? What if he *jailed* her?

Can't risk calling for help. "Thank you, Loner. Please report any other shady activity to me instead of the constipated man. Okay?"

He nodded. Determined to hunt down the van, she surged into the crammed parking lot. As she wove in and out, peeking into windows, the loud wail of a jackhammer registered. Her gaze zoomed across the street, where halogen lights were posted around a construction site.

Not too long ago, a man named Martin Dushku had come to see her. Though he'd had violent tattoos on his neck and hands, he'd worn a sophisticated suit that probably cost more than her SUV.

He was opening a strip club nearby, he'd said, and hoped she wouldn't mind having competition.

She'd smiled and said, "What competition? I run a bar, not a strip club." Besides, economic theory suggested two competing businesses being located right across from one another was actually better for each business, because the competition fueled more activity and therefore more business.

He'd laughed. "And your place is low end while mine will be

high end. But," he'd added, "I'd prefer to buy you out and run both businesses, which would free you up to travel."

Her desire to travel wasn't a secret, but he'd still managed to creep her out. She'd refused his offer. She wanted to travel, yes, but she also wanted a home to return to, something she hadn't had as a child. More specifically *Earl's* home. Also, she enjoyed providing meals for the homeless. Mr. Dushku struck her as the type of man who would treat the less fortunate like dirt.

She'd expected a fight, but he'd accepted her refusal gracefully and taken off.

Mind on the task at hand. He's not my worry tonight.

Right. Almost done. Only a few more cars to check. In fact, she was about to breathe a sigh of relief that there was no sign of the van or foul play when she came to a shadowed corner in back, with only two vehicles. One—a van. The other was a sedan. Her stomach sank. Both vehicles had tinted windows and, just as Loner reported, the van rocked back and forth.

What should I do?

Light suddenly flooded the sedan, allowing her to lock eyes with the man behind the wheel. He was smoking a cigarette, casual and unabashed. Beside him sat a man with a snake tattooed on his jaw.

I should...run? They had to be pimps or bodyguards, because their charge was clearly doling out goods and services in the van.

Run? No! Fury sparked inside Ryanne, tempered only by dismay.

Calling the cops was no longer a should-she-shouldn't-she situation. She should. She would. First, she needed proof of her innocence, just in case Rayburn tried to turn the tables on her. So, despite possible dangers, Ryanne withdrew her phone and took pictures of the men and the license plate on both vehicles. No one would be pinning a crime on her.

When she stood at the rear, the passengers decided now would be the perfect time to emerge. Well, crap. She began to stream a live video on her phone. A weapon in and of itself: it proved her innocence, while ensuring the guys couldn't do anything violent without a boatload of witnesses.

"Say hello to the world," she said, and grabbed her gun as a just in case.

Cigarette was over six feet tall while Snake topped out at about five-five. Both males were muscled, heavily tattooed and glaring at her.

Ryanne stood her ground. How many times had she been forced to break up fights involving big, scary men? Countless.

Cigarette slapped a hand against the van, once, twice, and it stopped rocking.

"You and your crimes aren't welcome here." She was proud. Her voice, like the rest of her, held steady. "Leave, and don't come back."

Snake looked her over slowly, leered and licked his lips. "You might want to watch your mouth, little girl. You don't, and bad things are likely to happen."

"Please," she said, "threaten me again. I'm not sure the camera captured your best angle."

The door in back of the van suddenly swung open, a man wearing tighty-whities falling out. With the rest of his clothes clutched against his chest, he sprinted past Ryanne and down the street. The alleged prostitute—blonde, pale and thin, with wide eyes full of fear—remained inside and shut the door.

"You okay in there?" Ryanne called.

Silence.

Cigarette took a menacing step toward Ryanne.

"Stop! Anything happens to me, and the world will know who's responsible." As a tremor swept through her, the phone fell from her grip and thudded on the concrete. Crap! At least she still had her gun.

"We know who you are, and we know the cops hate your guts. They'll blame you if anything happens to *us*," he replied.

How did he know about *her* fears?

Thumping footfalls sounded in the distance, growing closer by the second. She tensed, unsure what was about to happen, when—

Jude appeared in front of the vehicles, his hands balled like sledgehammers. He squared his shoulders and braced his legs apart, his posture rigid. A precombat stance. He wasn't panting, but he *was* making some kind of low growling noise, as if he were a rabid animal who'd finally found a meal.

Commando likes the taste of blood. And oh, wow, *she* liked this side of him. In the moonlight, he was a god. A warrior without equal.

Still, her tension spiked. If he were hurt...

To her astonishment, Cigarette and Snake immediately backed up. Cigarette slid into the sedan, and Snake climbed behind the wheel of the van. All without a word. One after the other, the vehicles shot out of the parking lot.

Ryanne lunged forward, intending to follow. On foot? Idiot! But the girl...

Jude latched on to her wrist, keeping her in place. "Don't," he snapped. "You'll only get yourself killed."

Was he mad at *her*?

No, no. Couldn't be. He was mad at the world. Always.

She swiped up her phone, intending to dial 911. Instead, she paused. "Who are they? Were they selling that girl?"

"They work for a man named Martin Dushku, and yes. They were selling that girl. Have been for the past two weeks."

The answers hit her like twin jabs to the gut. Why would Mr. Dushku sell a girl on her property rather than his own?

To blame Ryanne and get her shut down? Why not call the cops on her, then?

Maybe he only wanted to scare her so she'd sell?

"Why didn't you tell me?" she demanded. "And why didn't you call the cops? We need to help that girl."

"I know all about your history with the Blueberry Hill PD. And I was handling it. You can't help someone who doesn't want to be helped."

Had he tried and failed? "Clearly you weren't handling it well enough."

Malice radiated from him as he bared his teeth. The fact that they were straight and white made him no less intimidating. "You know there are Eastern European gangs in Texas, right? I dealt with them when I lived in Midland. They've migrated into Oklahoma, and like I said, the two assholes you threatened work for Martin Dushku, the guy building a club across the street. He isn't known for his sharing and caring but his fervor to own *everything*. He'll try to force you to sell or shut you down, whichever comes first."

Gang members? Here? No freaking way.

Maybe Mr. Dushku wasn't involved at all. He might have been a little creepy when he offered to buy her out, but he hadn't been pushy. "How do you know this?" she asked, one brow arched. "Let's face it. *You* could have arranged this little show in an attempt to scare me into hiring you."

He stepped toward her, far more dangerous than Cigarette or Snake, and yet she wasn't afraid. "I don't want your business, Ryanne. I'll never be your biggest fan, and I despise your bar. Frankly, I'd rather let it burn to the ground. If you weren't friends with my friends, I would. And I know about Dushku because I investigate everyone who moves to my town."

She believed him. One thing she couldn't doubt—his loyalty to his friends, Brock Hudson and local hero Daniel Porter. The three had served in the military together, and had each other's backs without fail.

And she wasn't hurt by Jude's *I'll never be your biggest fan* crack. The man had terrible taste.

"I'm sorry," she said, fear suddenly clawing at her insides. A gang had come to Oklahoma, and the leader wanted her bar. Her home.

She'd taken care of Earl here. Happy memories abounded. If something happened…

Who was she kidding? Something *would* happen. Martin Dushku and his associates were bad people, willing to do bad things. What if they hurt her patrons, innocent people who'd done nothing wrong?

Biting the inside of her cheek, she sheathed her gun and extended a shaky hand to Jude. "Congratulations, Mr. Laurent. You're hired."

CHAPTER TWO

Jude Laurent ignored the delicate hand being offered to him, his mind remaining on high alert. He'd provoked two predators tonight. At some point, both men would return, and they would act out in an attempt to save face.

"I'll be back tomorrow," he told Ryanne. "Nine a.m. We'll go over details and prices then."

Sputtering, she dropped her arm to her side. "Nine a.m.? No way, no how. I don't go to bed until four a.m., and I'm never up before noon."

"Nine a.m., Miss Wade." When their meeting concluded, he'd have to make a two-hour drive to the city to purchase whatever equipment they'd agreed upon. And, to be perfectly blunt about the matter, he didn't care if she got her beauty z's or not. "Not a minute later, or you'll be on your own with Dushku."

A cool breeze blew in, caressing strands of inky hair over the delicate rise of her cheek. Motions clipped with irritation, she hooked the strands behind her ear. "Remind me who will be paying whom."

"Remind me who will be *saving* whom."

Now she anchored her fists on her hips, the picture of feminine pique. "Well, this is just freaking perfect, isn't it. We're not going to drive each other crazy *at all*."

"If you do what I say, when I say, we'll get along fine, guaranteed."

She bristled, pricklier than a porcupine. Perhaps she believed he was acting like a hard-ass. Too bad. He wasn't acting. People could take him or leave him. He didn't care about that, either.

"How about we split the difference and meet at ten thirty?" Once again she offered him a fine-boned hand. "Deal?"

This time, ignoring her hand proved more difficult. Her nails were square-tipped, painted soft pink and glittered in the moonlight. A surprise. As tough—and sexy—as she was, he expected bloodred or jet-black.

A series of calluses marred the tips of her fingers, and on her wrist was a small but elaborate tattoo. An antique lock without a key, surrounded by emerald ivy, as if her arm had a hidden doorway to paradise.

His wayward gaze traveled over the rest of her, unbidden, as if drawn by an irresistible force. Her hourglass figure sizzled with carnality, and he suspected everyone who'd ever looked at her imagined her stripped naked and spread over a bed. Or any flat surface, really.

He certainly had, and he hated himself for it. Desire Ryanne Wade? No. Hell, no. The twenty-five-year-old single woman was the bane of his existence: a bar owner who threatened his control. But he'd told her the truth. His friends loved her. She was close to Dorothea Mathis, who was engaged to one of his buds, Daniel Porter. She was also close to Lyndie Scott, who was desired by Brock Hudson, Jude's only other bud.

That made Ryanne Wade a double whammy.

At the end of the day, Jude would do anything for Daniel and Brock, who had served with him overseas, saving his hide more times than he could count. Which was why he'd added their names to the massive tattoo on his chest.

They, along with a rare few others, were the only people who mattered to him.

Jude forced his gaze to lift at last, meeting rich brown eyes so often filled with joy he could no longer understand. Those eyes were framed by curling dark lashes somehow sweet and sultry at once. Long raven hair surrounded a face that belonged in a movie. She had smoky eyes, high cheekbones, a pert nose and pouty red lips.

Beauty, brains and bravery. The whole package.

"Well?" she demanded. "Judging by your silence, I can only guess you're blown away by my brilliance."

"I'll meet you at nine a.m. and not a minute later," he croaked. Then he backed away, and motioned for her to get her ass inside. Any time she brought her "sassy tone" into a conversation, he had only one option: retreat. That tone twisted him up, and sometimes even hollowed him out.

She stood in place for a long while, different emotions sweeping over her exquisite features. Anger, irritation, frustration, but finally resolve. Decided his services were worth the hassle, after all?

When she trudged into the bar, he followed close on her heels. As he moved, phantom pains shot through the calf he no longer possessed. He should go home, remove his prosthesis and relax for the first time in…never mind. He didn't know how to relax. He should work, the best distraction from his toxic thoughts.

Ryanne maneuvered through the crowds, being sure to give her hips an extra sway. Witch. Whistles preceded her, and catcalls trailed her.

Jude cursed the circumstances that had brought him here. *Ignore her. Ignore everyone.* He had work to do, and a very short time to do it.

The Dushku motto: Don't Bend, Break.

As soon as the family had moved into Blueberry Hill, only minutes from Jude's home in Strawberry Valley, he'd done background checks on every member. *His* motto? Can't Be Too Careful.

Ryanne was in serious danger. Years ago, Dushku moved to a small town in Texas. He offered to buy out every bar, restaurant and liquor store in the area. Soon after, anyone who'd refused to sell suffered a tragic fate. Some were arrested for a crime they swore they'd never committed while others were injured in some kind of accident.

Dushku was never charged.

On edge, Jude counted the number of cameras and lights he would need, and tested the reliability of every lock. Something he'd done several times before, as he'd waited for Brock to finish drinking and say the magic words: *take me home.* He repeated the process, checking and double-checking his findings. His analysis remained the same. Anyone with a tire iron and a couple minutes to spare could break in without difficulty.

How had Ryanne survived so long?

His gaze sought the beautiful brunette unbidden. She'd settled behind the bar, her attention locked on Daniel and Brock.

Daniel had dark hair, though not as dark as Ryanne's. His eyes were light brown and there was a slight bump in the center of his nose. That nose had suffered one too many breaks.

Overall, he looked like the soldier he was: rough, tough and solid as a rock.

On the other hand, Brock looked rougher and tougher with multiple piercings and arms sleeved in tatts. His jet-black hair was cut close to his scalp, and a thick five-o'clock shadow darkened his jaw, a complete contrast to the pale green eyes that often reflected skepticism, disdain and warped cheerfulness.

Brock had grown up filthy rich, but as the old saying went, money hadn't bought him happiness. Just like a lack of money hadn't been the source of Jude's problems. Wealth had nothing to do with emotion. Both he and Brock had parents who never should have had children.

Daniel hadn't been rich *or* poor, but he'd had the kind of childhood most people only dreamed about. He'd been born and bred in Strawberry Valley, Oklahoma, adored by his parents, cherished for the boy he'd been as well as the man he would become.

He was the reason Jude and Brock had moved to the speck-on-the-map small town. Any time their military unit had gotten stuck in a shit storm, waiting for escape or death—whichever came first—Daniel had spun fairy tales.

Dude. Check it. Strawberry-scented air.

All the peace of a beach without sand in your ass-crack.

Magazine perfect. If there's heaven on earth, it's Strawberry Valley.

Unwilling to go back to Georgia, where Jude had been stationed after joining the army, and equally unwilling to return to Texas, where he'd grown up—where beloved and hated memories waited to torment him—he'd moved to Oklahoma with his friends.

Ryanne's eyes flashed with merriment, and *Jude* almost smiled. Had anyone ever loved life with such abandon?

Part of him hated her for that abandon.

Damn it! When had his focus slid back to her?

Daniel spotted him and waved him over. "There you are."

Ryanne smiled with feline satisfaction, as if she'd discovered a particularly juicy secret.

A muscle clenched low in Jude's gut.

Though he would rather avoid the bar owner until he'd calmed from whatever she continued to do to his emotions, he closed the distance between them.

The scent of strawberries and cream filled his nose, courtesy of Ryanne. Every time he neared her, he was reminded of his favorite dessert, strawberry shortcake, and his mouth watered. When his mouth watered, his teeth gnashed, because a wave of crackling heat always followed, as if—

No. I do not *want her.*

Daniel patted him on the shoulder. "Ryanne said you'd taken off."

"Ryanne isn't always aware of her surroundings," he replied, flicking her a cool glance. "She's usually too busy flirting with customers."

She puckered those red, red lips and flipped her glorious fall of hair over her shoulder. "If I can convince just one more man to buy another penny beer, I might be able to afford that solid gold *bi-deet* I've been wanting. Fingers crossed!"

Brock snorted at her—purposeful?—mispronunciation of bidet. "What are you doing here, anyway, my man?" he asked Jude. "I thought you were staying home tonight."

"Changed my mind." More and more, he'd had trouble avoiding the Scratching Post, knowing Dushku could strike at Ryanne at any moment. "LPH will be taking over security here."

"Well, it's about time," Daniel said with a nod.

Ryanne batted her lashes at Jude. "Can I get you another water with lemon, Mr. Laurent?" Her voice was sugar sweet, but strangely, also as mean as a rattler.

"And let you charge me another two fifty for roughly five seconds of your time?" He shook his head. "At your rates, I'll owe you nine thousand dollars for an hour of our meeting tomorrow."

She winked at him, sensual, erotic—so beautiful it hurt to look at her. "Trust me. I'm worth that and more."

Raising an empty bottle, Brock told her, "Before you guys go and drag me into this odd little mating dance you're doing, I'll have another of those penny beers. Please and thank you."

Jude bit his tongue in an effort to remain silent, annoyed by both the comment and the request. Mating dance? Hell, no. He and Ryanne argued, nothing more. And though he'd never asked his friends to give up alcohol, he'd wanted to, which made him loathe himself a little more. Their pasts were as painful as his own, and they needed an outlet.

"Daniel?" Ryanne asked. "Another ginger ale?"

"Yes, please," Daniel replied with a grin. "I'm Brock's designated driver tonight."

"Well, then, I'll make sure your sacrifice is rewarded and add a cherry and a lime wedge free of charge." Slowly, languidly, she leaned toward Jude. "You see anything you want, Mr. Laurent?"

Another clench of muscle low in his gut. "No, thanks. I'm good."

"Oh, sugar. I'd bet my unmentionables you're very, very bad." Hooded gaze locked on him, she flattened her hand on his shoulder. He had to hide a jolt of surprise, the warmth of her skin burning through his shirt, the scent of fresh strawberries and cream strengthening.

"What do you think you're doing?" he demanded.

"Don't think. Know. I'm wondering why you look so hungry. Positively ravenous."

He stiffened in places he shouldn't. Had she just insinuated that he hungered for *her*?

He didn't. He wouldn't.

She winked at him, all coy femininity and smoky charm—and he did hunger, shit, he did. "Stay right there. I'm going to satisfy your appetite." With another wink, she took off.

Those hips swayed with more vigor, and his hands curled into fists.

Brock whistled under his breath as he watched her go. "That is one mighty fine woman."

Of course he would think so. She was exactly his type. The kind of female who would tick off his parents.

Teeth gnashing again…

Don't care who my friend wants to nail.

"She's a trouper," Daniel said with a sly glance at Jude. "We're in a tri-city, right? Between Strawberry Valley, Blueberry Hill and Grapevine. In all three towns, her mother was known as a get-around girl. Remarried a couple times, but in between marriages she stole the husbands of other women. Even slept with one or two of Ryanne's high school boyfriends."

Having done his homework, Jude knew a lot of people disdained Ryanne for her mother's behavior, and he sympathized. Back in Midland, his mother had been the town pariah. Poor as dirt, so desperate to keep her family farm going, she'd sold herself to any man willing to fix tractors, repair barns or feed cattle.

But Daniel wasn't done needling Jude. "When Ryanne moved in with one of her former stepdads, hot damn. Even the residents of Strawberry Valley went a little crazy. Earl Hernandez used to own this bar, and Ryanne was seventeen, I think, maybe eighteen. Countless people called her a whore. Parents forbade their children from spending time with her, fearing she was just like her momma. Fact was, she'd moved in to care for the guy. He had cancer."

Yeah. Jude knew that, too. *Damned if you do, damned if you don't.*

Not that he would allow Ryanne's past to matter to him. He would keep his eyes off her curves and on the prize: her survival.

He'd already briefed the guys about Dushku's move to town, so he used their minutes alone to explain his plan for camera placement inside and outside the bar, with twenty-four-hour monitoring. A necessary component, considering Ryanne lived upstairs.

"The Scratching Post falls under Blueberry Hill jurisdiction, so we shouldn't involve the cops just yet," he added. "There's serious bias against Ryanne, Dorothea and Lyndie."

"It's true," Daniel said. "Lyndie was married to the former chief, and Ryanne helped her leave him. I wasn't here, but I remember my dad's shock when the seemingly happy couple split. Apparently Carrington was beating the shit out of Lyndie."

"Where is Carrington now?" Brock's words were laced with so much rage, Jude had no doubt the ex would be beaten to death if he ever walked through the door.

"Dead. Which saves you from killing him and being sent to prison," Daniel said. "As for Dushku, we don't want to stay on the defensive. We need to go on the offensive as soon as possible."

Jude rubbed the back of his neck, unable to alleviate the tension coiled there. "The Dushkus are merciless, even the ones who are in prison."

"We put the fear of God in Martin Dushku now," Brock said, "and we'll save ourselves a lot of trouble later."

Or start a war.

Who was he kidding? The war had already started.

"I'll take care of this," Jude said. He'd keep his friends—and their women—out of it.

"We'll *all* take care of it," Brock corrected. "Together."

All for one, and one for all. The story of their lives. Even still, Jude would take the lead on this. When things got bad, and they would, he wanted to be the sole target.

Unlike the others, he had nothing to lose.

He said none of that, however. His friends would only argue. What they couldn't do? Stop him.

Ryanne arrived with drinks, a bowl of popcorn with sesame-glazed pistachios, soft pretzel sticks with beer cheese fondue and a plate of bacon-wrapped french fries. "In case you want to order another, this is the One Night Stand. Expect an orgasm in your mouth. This is the Horizontal Tango, and this is the Porking. If you'd like to add a plate of Thai-coconut chicken wings, aka the Boneyard, just let me know." Smiling as Jude nearly choked on his tongue, she presented him with a bill. "Enjoy," she said with a wink.

He expected her to leave, but once again she leaned toward him. "Well? Taste everything, and tell me again about the amount of salt in the food."

Daniel snagged a french fry, and Brock grabbed a pretzel and shoved one end into the dip. Jude hadn't had a real appetite since…in a long time, but he couldn't stop himself from tossing a handful of popcorn and pistachios in his mouth. The sweet and perfectly salted flavors hit his tongue, and he nearly moaned.

Next thing he knew, he'd emptied the bowl.

"Guess my snacks are delicious, after all." Ryanne laughed, the magical sound turning the food in his stomach to rocks. "Tips are encouraged or the next round might come with an extra special topping."

With one more of those annoying winks, she wandered off to do what she did best: charm absolutely everyone.

Before his brain registered his intention, Jude found himself on his feet, stalking after her, finally jumping in front of her. "You're being nice to me." Not just flirting with him but enchanting him. "Why?"

"I realized I'm now your boss." Cheeks glowing a lovely shade of rose, she beamed up at him. Whether she was flushed from the temperature of the room or pleasure, he didn't know. Didn't *want* to know. A devil never appeared with horns and a tail, holding a pitchfork. A devil appeared looking like everything you'd ever secretly wanted but knew you shouldn't have. "My word is law, no matter how much you protest."

Fighting her allure, he crossed his arms over his chest. "You actually think you're in charge."

"You said you were doing this for your friends. I know how much you love them, how much you don't want to let them down." In the muted light, her dark eyes glittered like jewels, threatening to hypnotize him into submission, tempting him to—nothing. "I'm willing to play the part of happy employer, but it's going to cost you."

Blackmailing him? "The price?" he grated.

"Praise. One compliment a day. Two if you're being particularly snarly."

You've got to be kidding me. "An unearned compliment is a lie."

"And you never lie?"

"Never." Truth was too precious.

Her head canted to the side, her study of him intensifying. "So you can't think of anything positive to say about me?"

"I—" *Could.* Denying it would have been a lie.

She'd well and truly trapped him, an impressive feat. One worthy of the compliment she desired. Unwilling to give up an inch of ground he'd won, however, he said, "If you want your business to come out of this alive, you'll do what I say. End of story."

She took a step toward him. Her breasts brushed against his chest, earning a gasp from her and a hiss from him. Like a coward—an aching, throbbing coward—he took a step back, severing contact.

"I think I'll be okay. Forgot to tell you I streamed a video of Mr. Dushku's men tonight."

"A video won't save you in the future." Another step back.

"Are you afraid of me, Jude?" She followed him, voiding his retreat, suddenly so close her warm breath rasped over the racing pulse at the base of his neck.

"No!" His spine bowed as the denial roared from him. Over the years, he'd been shot, stabbed and had part of an appendage blown off. Fear a slip of a woman? "No," he repeated, doing his best to sound calmer.

"Well, I'm sorry to hear that." As graceful as a ballerina, as erotic as a pole dancer, she turned and glanced at him over her shoulder. "I think I would have enjoyed soothing you."

Had she just…come on to him?

Jude pulled at his collar, skin growing clammy. Ryanne Wade was too hot, and so was his blood. His body was in serious danger of overheating, a physical reaction he hadn't experienced in a long time, thanks to another woman.

Constance Laurent. *My Constance.*

Memories fought for his attention. The way she had smiled at him each morning when she'd woken in their bed, as if overjoyed to find him home. The way she'd somehow ruined every meal she'd ever cooked, but had looked at him with adoration whenever he'd cleaned his plate. The way she'd cried during Hallmark movies.

The air might as well have turned to syrup; it was too thick to pull into his lungs, his chest too tight. His limbs shook.

Time to go. He didn't bother saying goodbye to Ryanne as he rushed past her, didn't even wave to his friends. He flew out of the bar, never once looking back.

Jude threw his truck in Park. Half the vehicle was in grass, the other half in the driveway. At least he'd made it to the cabin he leased with Brock rather than stopping in the middle of a road.

Each breath more labored than the last, Jude headed for the porch. Midway, he fell to his knees. Pain and grief exploded inside him, filling him, *killing* him.

A lie. He wasn't dying. Not even close. Death would have been a mercy, and mercy wouldn't touch him with a ten-foot pole.

Screaming obscenities at the sky, he punched his fists into the grass. Crickets quieted, and fireflies vanished. Hanks of dirt flung this way and that. A rock sliced into the side of his hand, the sting a minor inconvenience compared to the fire seeming to pour through his chest, ashing his heart, charring his lungs.

This was his life now, a series of minutes and days bleeding into months and years. He existed, nothing more, except for moments like this, when the pain and grief overtook him— then he agonized.

Why? Why did he continue to agonize? He should rejoice. Pain and grief were his friends. Pain had been there for him on the worst day of his life. Grief had hugged him close and kept him focused on what he'd lost: his entire fucking world.

He knew the answer, though. Deep down, he resented every second he spent on this earth. And yet, still he fought to survive.

I don't want to fight anymore.

Must.

Long ago, he'd made a promise to Constance. Shy, sweet Constance, his high school sweetheart.

They'd met on a double date he'd attended only because his friend had begged. One look at Constance, and he'd been a goner. She'd been as pretty and delicate as a cameo, and she'd sent his adolescent hormones into a tailspin.

She'd wanted him, too, willingly shucking convention to go steady with the poorest boy in town. The boy who'd once nailed more tail than Brock on his best day, all in an effort to prove he was wanted, or worth something.

You're worth everything, Jude Laurent. Do you hear me? Everything!

They'd married the week after graduation. Determined to provide a better life for her, he'd joined the military.

Before he'd shipped out the first time, she'd wrapped her arms around him and said, "Promise me you'll never give up, no matter how hard it gets and no matter what happens."

"I promise. I'll never give up. Now give me a kiss. Remind me of what I'll be missing."

If he could have lived inside the fabric of his happiest memories, he might have had a halfway decent chance of becoming the man he'd once been. But reality was a determined foe, as unstoppable as the pain and grief, clawing and kicking at his mind, demanding its due. Dreams offered no succor; any time his subconscious took over, he relived a moment he hadn't actually witnessed—a night forged in blood, fire and death.

The night his wife and twin daughters had died.

In the present, hot tears poured down his cheeks, leaving raw, stinging tracks in their wake. Two and a half years ago, a frat boy had drunk too much at a local bar, climbed into his car and driven away. No one had cared enough to stop him. Only nine minutes, twenty-three seconds later, he'd crashed into Constance Laurent's car, ruining Jude's life forever.

Constance died on her way to the hospital. The twins, Bailey and Hailey, died on impact.

The entire world should have ceased spinning that...very...second. The galaxy should have mourned the loss of such beauty, laughter and light. Rare treasures, his girls.

Dance with me, Daddy. I found my moves and *my grooves!*

Daddy, I'm not joking and I'm not playing. I need chocolate right now or I'm gonna lose it.

Lose what, little sweet? he'd asked.

I don't know. Whatever it is.

Children changed you the moment they were conceived. Made you softer and harder all at once. You learned to play defense and offense simultaneously, protecting your kids while warring with anyone who dared to threaten them.

After the accident, people had offered him what they thought were words of comfort. *Meant to be. No stopping fate.*

More lies. Fate hadn't poured alcohol down Frat Boy's throat, or put car keys in his hand.

Besides, *nothing* comforted Jude. The only arms capable of offering him solace were now rotting in a grave.

All he had left were memories of a life he'd once adored. Memories he both adored and despised. He remembered the way Bailey's nose had crinkled when she'd giggled. The way Hailey had twirled a strand of hair around her finger when she cried. The way Constance had blown him a kiss every time he'd walked out the door, whether he'd been headed for another mission or to the grocery store.

Memories would never keep him warm at night.

Only pitying yourself. He had friends who'd swooped in the moment he'd called. *Gone...they're just...gone.*

Now he lacked a purpose. And family. He supposed he could do something about the purpose. Or maybe he already had?

Maybe he'd found one in the Scratching Post. At least temporarily. By saving Ryanne and the bar he despised with every fiber of his being, he would save Daniel and Brock from losing someone *they* loved.

Through the trials of war, they too had already walked hand-in-hand with enough pain and grief, sorrow and loneliness. Enough…or far too much. Overseas, they'd lost friends in a hundred different ways. They'd overcome great odds to save Jude on the bloodiest of battlefields; as gunfire rained around them, they'd risked their own lives to carry him away when he couldn't even crawl.

As his breathing normalized, Jude wiped his face with the bottom of his shirt and fell back on his haunches. He loved his friends so deeply, he would willingly die for them, but he missed his family more than he missed his leg. Sometimes he experienced phantom pains, allowing him to pretend the leg was still there. At no time did he ever forget he was a family man without a family. A father without a child.

He was essentially alone.

He wished he could be more like Ryanne. She lived in the moment, enjoyed the highs, basking in her triumphs, and rolled with the lows. He thought she might even embrace those lows, choosing to learn from her mistakes rather than wallow.

Irritation pricked at him. Be like a bar owner? A person who served alcohol to potential motorists? Never.

He would go on as always, pretending to live, breaking down, then pretending to live again.

I'll never give up.

CHAPTER THREE

Mental note: *never tease Jude Laurent.*

After Ryanne's "I think I would have enjoyed soothing you" crack, he'd stormed away as if his feet were on fire, his expression a mix of horror and dismay.

Okay. Revise: *sometimes tease Jude Laurent.*

Despite her former ban on romance, flirting had always come easily for her. Bottom line, she'd inherited her mother's gift, though not to the same degree. Selma could pop the top off a man's biscuits with only a wink and a smile. Ryanne had to work at it, maybe because the guys knew they wouldn't get anywhere with her. But, with a little time and a lot of banter, she could charm the uncharmable. A necessary skill in her line of work. People tended to treat bartenders like therapists, and Ryanne wanted everyone who left the Scratching Post to feel good, or at least better than when they'd entered.

Not my biggest fan? Get ready, precioso. *You will be.*

The guy clearly had a stick up his patootie and yet, for one too-brief moment, he'd looked at Ryanne as if he wanted to devour her. And she'd liked it. A lot.

She wanted him to look at her with hunger again and again.

Jude was the one, she decided. The man who would break her amorous fast. Despite his surly attitude, he was the only guy her body craved. The only male her mind trusted. He might dislike her—presently—but he was still determined to save the people and things she cared about.

How sexy was that?

In order to win him over, she suspected she would have to teach him how to relax and have fun. In order to teach him how to relax and have fun, however, she would have to learn more about him.

Quickest way to gain info: covertly question Daniel and Brock. The perfect plan—until they finished their drinks and took off without saying goodbye. Disappointment delivered a swift one-two punch to her determination. Then she rallied. Jude would return tomorrow morning, and she would get her info straight from the source.

Then she could begin his training—uh, teaching him to relax.

After the bar had emptied for the night, the staff cleaned up and Ryanne fed the homeless. That done, she locked the back door, then the front...and thought she spied Jude in the parking lot, sans his truck.

Had he returned? When she blinked, he was gone.

I'm exhausted, that's all. She checked the windows, making sure they were locked as well, and trudged upstairs. How much would Jude charge for his services? How much of her precious savings would she lose? Enough to turn a first class trip into economy? She shuddered. To live her childhood aspirations properly, she required luxury.

She also required surviving Mr. Dushku, so, there was that.

What measures would Jude the Ice Man take against the mob boss? For that matter, what kind of trouble would her new neighbors attempt to cause?

Would Jude use legal means or push boundaries? He struck her as the boundary-pushing type.

With a dreamy sigh—*I'm turned on by outlaws?*—she stripped to her underwear, set her alarm and crawled into bed. To her dismay, sleep proved impossible, her mind continually flashing on images of the prostitute. The fear on the girl's face when those van doors had swung open...

Fear of arrest or fear of her guards?

Either way, Ryanne pitied her. And sympathized. As a kid, she'd often found herself under the iron rule of whichever man Selma happened to "love" at the time. Some had been kind, others cruel...like Harold Scott, Lyndie's dad. Mr. Hit-and-Blame.

The mental and physical abuse he inflicted on poor Lyndie had continued long after Selma divorced him. When Lyndie turned eighteen, she moved out, finally free. Only, she'd started dating Chief Carrington soon after.

He'd been a regular at the Scratching Post, and she'd heard Ryanne complain about the monster lurking beneath his good ole boy veneer more than once. Even still, Lyndie accepted his marriage proposal without hesitation, as if she felt she *deserved* to be slapped around.

A high-pitched buzz sounded from Ryanne's phone, and she groaned. Her alarm. It was already time to get up?

Hey, why was she complaining? Soon she would have to— *get to*—face Jude.

Well, well. Her nerve endings awoke in a hurry, tingling with anticipation. She stretched and grinned, her heart leaping, her blood heating. For so long, her body had felt frozen, hormones nonexistent. Now the ice was gone, fire in its place, desire as much a part of her as her lungs. She breathed, and she wanted... burned. It was ecstasy, and it was agony.

Her grin faded as she felt the full weight of her inexperience. Oh, she'd made out with the boys she'd dated before her ban on romance, but in her brief attempt at being a femme fatale, she'd never, well, gone all the way.

Yep, good ole Ryanne Wade was still a virgin.

She wasn't embarrassed about it, but she *was* nervous. Years had passed since her last date, and times had changed. Vanilla was no longer the norm; guys expected varying shades of gray.

What did Jude like? What kind of women did he prefer?

How could she break through his icy reserve?

On some level, he reminded her of Earl. Strong, competent and concerned about her well-being. And he was nothing like the playboys who frequented the bar. He never hit on women. Heck, he barely even seemed to notice them. Difference was, Jude had only ever insulted Ryanne while Earl had only ever supported her. But then, Earl had loved her unconditionally, valued her and built her up, never tearing her down. He'd taught her that family didn't have to be flesh and blood, or have legal ties.

Rubbing her burning eyes, she stood. Wobbly legs managed to get her into the bathroom, where she brushed her teeth, showered while sitting on a special bench she'd had made for times just like this, when she was too lazy—uh, *tired*, she meant *tired*—to stand. She applied lotion and dressed in a tank, a pair of faded jeans and flip-flops. She opted not to spend time drying her hair or applying makeup. Mornings sucked. No reason to dress up for one, even to attract a man.

If Jude didn't like the look of her when she dressed-down, well, he wasn't the one for her, after all. No matter how much she wanted him. Better to find out sooner rather than later.

After eating her favorite breakfast—Chips Ahoy! dipped in coffee—she tidied up her apartment, then slung a bag of trash over her shoulder. She made her way outside. Ugh. The sun! Too bright!

Eyes watering, she quickened her pace. As she turned to head back inside, a bottle rattled behind the Dumpster, and she paused, her brow furrowed. "Hello?"

As usual, the homeless were gone. Mornings and afternoons were often too hot here, despite the shade. Loner and friends would return in the evening, after the sun had set and the bar had opened.

Ryanne padded forward, searching...there! A morbidly obese cat was curled into a ball. He was black with white markings, his fur matted and dirty. Spotting her, he lumbered to his feet. Then he whimpered and sat back down, because "he" was actually a "she," and very pregnant, her nipples distended.

Mierda! The little darling looked ready to pop.

"Something wrong?"

Though she'd detected no footsteps, the masculine voice came from directly behind Ryanne, and she yelped, her hand fluttering over her hammering heart. Jude.

She spun. When her gaze landed on him, her breath snagged in her throat. Okay, so, the sun wasn't the enemy today but a welcome companion. Light illuminated him, painting him in shades of amber, gold and bronze. He looked like a fantasy come to startling life, a punk rock Prince Charming who'd stepped from the pages of an erotic fairy tale. His pale hair possessed a hint of wave this morning, and his jaw had the shadow of a beard.

Once again he wore a black T-shirt, plain and simple, dark jeans and combat boots. Those boots had a slight bulge on each side, a bulge she recognized. Holsters for guns.

A leather band circled each of his wrists. One hand held a duffel bag while the other held a briefcase. He was both street hardened and business savvy, the sexiest combination on earth.

"I don't mean to stare," she said, "but my hormones are busy giving you a standing ovation. Gold star for today's wardrobe selection, Mr. Laurent."

He shook his head, as if he wasn't sure he'd heard her correctly. "Excuse me?"

"Why?"

"Why what?"

"Why do you want me to excuse you?" she asked, feigning

innocence. "Were you thinking inappropriate thoughts about me…the way I was thinking inappropriate thoughts about you?"

His frown contained notes of confusion and uncertainty. "Let's go inside. We have a lot to discuss."

Any other time, she might have pressed. *Ignore me? Get asked more invasive questions.* This morning, seduction had to wait. "Do me a favor and use your big, strong man-muscles to bring this cat inside." She motioned to the feline even as she planned her next move. *Call Brett Vandercamp, the only vet in Strawberry Valley, and convince him to give the cat a home. Call Lyndie. She's a schoolteacher, and today is Sunday; she'll be home. Request any supplies she'll need before Dr. Vandercamp is able to take the cat.*

Food…but what else? A litter box? Ryanne had never had a cat. Or a pet of any kind. Not even a goldfish.

Jude approached her, his limp less pronounced than it had been last night. After taking in the situation, he foisted off his bag and case on Ryanne and carefully gathered the cat close to his chest. "Only you would have a bar named the Scratching Post and a pregnant cat hiding in your alley."

Okay, *this* was the sexiest combination on earth. A surly man with a soft heart for animals. Her ovaries joined her hormones, clapping and cheering.

With a gulp, Ryanne led Jude upstairs and into her apartment. Along the way, she phoned Brett. He promised to swing by on his lunch break but, to her dismay, he turned down her plea to keep the cat. His facilities were overcrowded.

"You can take her to a shelter in Oklahoma City," he added. "It's only a two-hour drive."

Force the cat to have her babies in a cage? "No way."

"There's nothing either of us can do to help her, anyway," Brett replied. "Nature will take over, the cat will have her babies and no human intervention will be necessary. You'll see."

So she should just twiddle her thumbs? *"Tonto del culo,"* she spat, and hung up.

"Fluent in Spanish," Jude muttered. "Good to know."

"Do you know what I said?" Translated literally, the words meant *an idiot of the ass.* It was her mother's favorite curse.

"Don't care. Tell me about the vet."

Through clenched teeth, she relayed Brett's cruel shelter idea, then set Jude's stuff on the couch. Nervousness set in, and she chewed on her bottom lip. What next?

Ugh. She knew how to take care of herself. Broken down car? No problem. Leaky pipes? She'd grab a wrench. She'd always rolled with the punches life delivered. But this? Caring for a pregnant cat? Shudder.

"Make a pallet on the floor," Jude said. "Use blankets or towels, whatever you have available and don't mind ruining."

A bed. Duh! She hurried to obey, selecting blankets—they were softer. When she finished, he settled the cat in the center.

"I grew up on a farm." Jude rubbed his temples, lines of tension branching from his eyes and mouth. "I can ensure this beautiful little girl has a safe delivery here in your apartment."

Oh, thank the good Lord! And oh, wow, it was difficult to imagine rough, tough city-boy Jude as a farmer. "Thank you."

"She's got a few days to go. Maybe even a week." Jude gave the living room a single visual sweep.

She suspected he'd taken in everything at once, noting any changes since his last visit, when he'd helped her take care of a drunken Brock. What did Jude think of her furnishings and embellishments? She'd picked pieces to represent different cultures throughout the world. A throw from India draped a Victorian settee. A French side table displayed a Moroccan vase, an Egyptian bowl filled with blown glass fruit and an elephant figurine hand-carved in Africa. A landscape of the Scottish Highlands hung on the wall.

Nothing really fit together and colors clashed, but she loved every piece.

He remained on the floor, petting the now purring cat, a

faraway expression on his face. She sat across from him, trying not to be envious while wishing she were the one being stroked so gently.

"She needs a name," Ryanne told him. "The cat" and "feline" were already old. "Since she'll be staying at your place—did I mention I think you should take her home?—I'll let you have the honors of choosing—"

He choked on his own tongue. "Hell, no. Finders keepers."

"But you said you'd ensure her delivery—"

"No, no, a thousand times no. I'll ensure a safe delivery *here*."

"Fine," she grumbled. "She can stay here." For now. "I'll call her... Ali Cat?" No. Too on point. "Kitty Poppins? Kitkat?" Argh! Same problem.

"Names are important. They define who we are and set the stage for who we become. So choose one with care."

"Wow. That's a lot of pressure for a single word." She traced a finger over her lock tattoo, her curiosity too great to ignore. "What does Jude mean?"

There was a slight hesitation before he admitted, "The praised one."

"Seriously?" She snickered, and the corners of his mouth might—might!—have twitched. *So close to success, but still so far away.* "I wonder what Ryanne means."

"It's the feminine form of Ryan, which means little king."

Had he known already...or had he looked it up after meeting her?

Warmth settled low in her belly. "So. Ryanne means little queen. You're right, our names set the stage for who we become. But I'm not calling you the praised one. Do you have a nickname?"

A pause, a clipped nod.

"Well," she prompted. "Don't hold back. Tell me before I start calling you Gollum or Spanky McSparkle."

"Spanky McSparkle?" He pursed those beautiful, scarred lips. "In the military, my teammates called me... Priest."

"Seriously?" she repeated. "Why—"

"Nope. No more sharing. Name the cat and move on."

Someone sure turned cranky superfast. Oh, wait. Cranky was Jude Laurent's default setting. "We'll call her Belle." Decision made. "And yes, you did, in fact, name her. You called her beautiful."

He glowered, and yet the expression lacked heat. "All right. It's 9:03. Let's get down to business."

"All right. Let's."

Over the next hour, he explained the complex camera system he intended to put into place. Once, only once, she accidentally touched him. He jolted, as if she'd burned him. A bad reaction, or a really, really good one?

The next time she touched him was on purpose. Again, he jolted.

Focus. Business now, play later.

Basically every inch of her bar and parking lot would be filmed twenty-four hours a day, with the exception of the bathrooms and the inside of her apartment. A panic button would be added to her apartment, and with a few tweaks, the closet in her bedroom would become a safe room. She would hire three bouncers, though he'd suggested four, and all three males would be big, burly and fearless; they would enforce her rules and eject anyone who acted out of line. And if ever she held a big event, he had employees in the city who would drive down to help with security. Finally, she would hire a full-time night watchman, who would patrol the parking lot, stopping any outside mischief before it had time to enter the bar.

"You do realize all these changes and additions will eat up my profits, right?" Thousands of dollars would be spent on cameras and installation, plus the ongoing salaries of four new employees.

"If something were to happen to your bar, you'd make zero

profits. But, to supplement your income, you can begin hosting daytime events. Think about it. The bar is closed mornings and afternoons every day of the week. You can offer private parties, showers, whatever. The possibilities are endless."

The Strawberry Valley book club *did* need a bigger place to get together. And the local matchmaker wanted a venue for the meet and greets she was hoping to host. But everything Jude suggested meant more work for Ryanne, and she was already overtaxed.

Still, he was right. What if she made enough money to pay for all the security additions, salaries *and* upgrades for her travels? Excitement sparked.

"The panic button you mentioned," she said. "It will be linked to Blueberry Hill PD? Strawberry Valley PD? Grapevine PD?"

A muscle jumped underneath his eye. "None of the above. The signal will go to LPH Protection. We have monitors in place 24/7. Someone there will notify 911 as well as call Daniel, Brock...or me."

Delicious, drugging warmth spilled through her. Getting personal with Jude Laurent... "Are you saying you'll drop whatever you're doing in order to save a damsel in distress?"

His nod was immediate. "I will. So will they."

"Well, hiring the right employees will take time." *Am I really going to do this?*

"I know. That's why I'll be acting as a bouncer in the meantime."

Her heart leaped, a thousand butterflies taking flight in her stomach. Jude...nearby every night... "There's a slight problem with your plan. You make my customers uncomfortable."

"Good. They'll be on their best behavior."

"Or they'll leave and never return."

His wide shoulders hiked in a shrug.

Such a contradiction, this man. Helpful, but indifferent. Kind, but aloof. Smoldering, but standoffish.

"All right," she said, and sighed. Safety first. "You have permission to proceed. With everything." She couldn't help but add, "*After* I hear my daily compliment."

One brow arched. "Rescuing your cat wasn't enough?"

"*Our* cat. We're co-owners." She'd almost said coparents, but had stopped herself in time. No reason to remind him of the daughters he'd lost.

"Fine." His lips compressed, and he gave her his patented *I disapprove* look. "You want a compliment, you get a compliment. You are a...singular woman."

She waited for him to say more. He didn't.

Well. "Singular woman" was as good a compliment as any, she supposed, and maybe kinda sorta better than she'd anticipated. "Just so you know, I'll expect something a lot more personal tomorrow."

"Why?" he grated. "Why do you care what I think about you?"

Make a man laugh, and he'll have a good day. Teach a man to have fun, and he'll have a good life.

Remembering her plan, she twirled a lock of hair around her finger and batted her lashes at him. "Don't be silly, praised one. I just like to watch you squirm."

CHAPTER FOUR

For the next week, Jude did his best to avoid the too flirtatious, too happy Ryanne. An impossible task, considering he worked at the Scratching Post each of the seven days, installing cameras in the morning, checking food deliveries in the afternoon, acting as a bouncer in the evening and helping care for Belle every minute in between. The pregnant, very grumpy cat hadn't yet given birth.

Ryanne had texted him a few times, too. Random invitations to do ridiculous things.

Let's go to a finger-painting workshop! We've GOT to improve our employer-employee relations.

His response? How will finger paint help us?

Duh! Our bodies are the canvases and we get to paint each other. (You know, a little hands-on learning. Or big. Yeah, probably big.)

No.

Not just no, but hell, no.

Her next text had read What about a petting zoo in the city??? (I promise I'm not the animal you'll be stroking.)

Again he'd replied, No.

Movie? I'll pay AND share my popcorn w/you.

Another solid No.

She texted him a gif of a cartoon character sobbing.

Avoiding this woman had begun to prick at his pride. He'd once been part of a military unit known as the Ten. Ten soldiers sent on the most dangerous missions—secret missions that would never be talked about in history books. They'd killed the enemy and rescued other soldiers amid impossible odds of survival. Amid it all, Jude, Brock and Daniel had seen and done things no human should have seen or done. It changed them.

Brock now tried to make everyone he met fall in like with him, since he couldn't like himself. Daniel kept all newcomers at a distance, too afraid of losing another person, and Jude…he tended to numb-out, and live life on autopilot.

He *craved* autopilot. But Ryanne had twisted him into a million little knots, and none of those knots helped him stay numb.

Despite her—or *because* of her—he pushed himself to his limits, wanting to get the job settled as soon as possible. As soon as he finished installations, he would make Brock front man. That way, Brock would receive a notice when something went wrong at the bar, and Jude could finally wipe Ryanne from his mind.

Already he'd spoken to Martin Dushku, who'd thrown more shade than a decades-old oak. He'd lied with a smile, misdirected with ease and hid his threats behind false concern.

Jude felt sorry for the man's wife. The pair had been together for thirty-one years and had two adult children. A twenty-seven-year-old son named Filip and a twenty-three-year-old daughter named Paulina; they also had a four-year-old grand-child named Thomas.

Filip, Thomas's father, was in prison for manslaughter, with only a year left on his sentence. Interestingly enough, Jude had been unable to find any mention of Thomas's mother.

When Jude had first walked onto the construction site, two goons had closed in fast to frisk him, as he'd known they would. Of course, they hadn't found the small metal pins sheathed in the heels of his boots. More than that, Jude himself was a weapon. He could turn any innocent object into a weapon, as well. An ink pen, a keyboard. A paper clip. A chair.

After coming up empty, the men escorted him into a luxuri-ous trailer, where Dushku perched behind a desk. The conver-sation had been short and anything but sweet.

"Both the Scratching Post and its owner are under my protec-tion," Jude had said. "You won't like what happens if you harm them. And keep your stable off Ryanne's property. The next time someone sells a ride at the Scratching Post, a live stream will be the least of your troubles."

Dushku had chuckled, not the least bit intimidated. "You must be mistaken. I value women and would never take part in prostitution. And I certainly wouldn't do so on Miss Wade's property. I've heard about her problems with the local PD." He'd sighed, as if weary. "If sex and drugs *are* being sold at the Scratching Post, I'm sure authorities will believe Miss Wade is the one responsible."

"I didn't say anything about drugs," Jude had grated.

The man's amusement had bloomed into a smirk. "I've al-ready looked into you, Mr. Laurent. You were a good soldier once. A husband and father. Now you're a cripple with nothing to lose—except another leg."

Behind him, one of the guards had snickered. "What do you call a man with one leg? A pogo stick."

Laughter had abounded while Jude simmered in his seat. Rage

and grief had bubbled in his chest; the two emotions were always there, rooted deep in his heart, but some days were worse
than others. How dare this scumbag mention Constance and
the twins!

"If you take me on, Mr. Laurent, you will fail." For a moment, only a moment, Dushku had allowed his true demeanor
to surface, his features cold as ice. "I promise you."

Mere seconds had passed as Jude struggled to control his
breathing, though it had felt like an eternity.

"Did the truth hurt your feelings?" Dushku had shaken his
head. "I'm not sure why. You *are* a cripple without a family, and I
won't hesitate to ruin this new life you've carved out for yourself."

More rage. More grief. At the best of times, Jude felt like only
half a man. What if he *couldn't* protect Ryanne?

He'd mimicked the man's smirk. "I don't think you searched
deep enough into my background, Mr. Dushku. I'm a hunter,
born and bred. When I was just a boy, I learned to stalk and kill
deer and wild hogs. As a man, Uncle Sam taught me to stalk
and kill men. I'm very good. My victims are never found." He'd
stood. "Again, I suggest you stay on your side of the street, and
we'll stay on ours. I won't stop you from running your business,
but I will stop you from hurting innocents."

Dushku had said, "I, too, would hate for any harm to come
to innocents, especially someone as kind and beautiful as Miss
Wade. If she decides to sell the bar within the next couple of
months in order to travel the world as she dreams, I'm willing
to help her. If not… You might be a hunter, Mr. Laurent, but
I'm a ghost. You'll never see me coming."

Jude had left, before he broke down and showed Dushku the
error of his ways.

So far, there had been only one attempt to strike at Ryanne.
Blueberry Hill PD raided the bar, harassing customers as they
checked IDs and asked questions about "reported suspicious
activity." Jude had admired Ryanne's calm in the midst of the

chaos, and he'd been surprised by the support of her patrons, almost everyone rushing to her defense, forcing the officers to leave without making an arrest.

"A little help, please." Ryanne's sex-drugs-and-rock-and-roll voice stopped him in his tracks.

Behind the counter where he'd watched her mix drinks was the entrance to the basement. He watched as the gorgeous woman lugged a large box up the steps. Mason jars clinked together, her infamous fruit cocktail moonshine sloshing inside. Beads of sweat glistened on her forehead, and he almost—almost—rushed to her aid. While he was good with protecting her and her home, he avoided anything related to the actual buying, selling and marketing of alcohol.

"Is this a test?" he finally asked. "This seems like a test. The moment I help you, you'll accuse me of setting back feminism a hundred years."

"Yeah, that sounds *exactly* like me," she muttered as she lumbered past him.

He kind of wanted to grin. Usually she was the one teasing him.

No wonder she did it so often. Hello, fun. Long time no see.

For the next hour, Jude worked like a man possessed, installing motion-sensitive lights in the bathroom hallway. Soon the bar would open to the public, and he would have to walk the room for eight hours, on the lookout for any signs of wayward activity. Guaranteed, he would irritate people tonight. His leg had pained him all day, darkening his mood. He needed to rest, but he needed to work and remain distracted more.

When he entered the main area, he found Ryanne doing what she did best, mixing drinks for Lyndie and Dorothea. Considering Brock had a secret thing for Lyndie, a delicate strawberry blonde, and Daniel was almost always attached to Dorothea's side, Jude expected *his* friends to be nearby, but...no.

"—negotiated. Said I could have three orgasms a day or one

more dog." Dorothea rolled her big, blue eyes. She was a pretty woman with dark, corkscrew curls, and the soft curves of a '50s pinup model. "I demanded four orgasms a day and two more dogs, of course."

Ryanne threw back her head, laughing with abandon.

Lust punched Jude straight in the gut, shocking him, waking once deadened nerve endings. Tingles exploded throughout his entire body, followed by heat and hunger, such clawing hunger.

He gnashed his teeth as he fought the sensations. Want a bartender? No! And yet, the hunger persisted.

"Did he protest or thank you?" she asked. She looked good enough to eat, her silken hair falling in a haphazard braid over her shoulder—a shoulder bared by a lacy pink tank top. Short shorts revealed the long length of her legs while cowgirl boots adorned her feet, stretching up her calves.

Made of sugar, spice and vodka poured on ice.

"Well?" Lyndie prompted.

"He protested...*and* thanked me," Dorothea replied with a proud grin.

Ryanne gave her a thumbs-up. "Good girl. Always up the ante."

Jude bit his tongue to stop a rush of protests.

Ryanne had once claimed she liked to make him squirm, and she'd proven it every day since. Her hips swayed enthusiastically any time she walked past him, creating a sultry, powerful rhythm. Often she cast him coquettish glances and blew him kisses. And she touched him constantly, a brush of her fingers here, a squeeze of his hand there. She cracked jokes, and made lewd innuendos—and he wasn't sure how to handle her.

Right now, he was sure of only one thing. A relationship with Ryanne wasn't possible. If his body had finally woken from hibernation, he would maybe think about considering being with a woman, scratching an itch. But he wouldn't pick *her*. He would pick someone easily forgettable, someone as uninterested in a relationship as he was.

The moment he did, Constance would no longer be the last woman he'd slept with.

He rubbed the almost debilitating ache in his chest.

He'd never cheated on Constance, even when offers had been made. His teammates, the other members of the Ten—everyone except Daniel and Brock—had mercilessly teased him about it, and had ultimately given him the nickname of Priest.

Ryanne's gaze landed on him, and her smile fell, confusing him. His mood affected hers?

In a flash, her smile returned and widened. "Jude." Only she could say his name and sound as if she were moaning in pleasure, delivering another punch of lust to his gut.

He wanted to hate her, but more and more he actually... liked her.

Not only did she have a drink limit for the ultra-potent moonshine, but she cut off anyone who appeared drunk. A legal requirement, yes, but she also kept a cab company on standby.

She made zero exceptions to the rules, even when customers protested, loudly. No one could charm her from her refusal, though some people did—cough Brock cough—manage to get wasted regardless, fooling the seasoned Ryanne into believing he was sober. When that failed, he convinced others to buy drinks for him.

Something else Jude had discovered. Ryanne truly cared about her customers. Her kindness wasn't for show. She treated everyone with respect and affection, whether they ordered drinks or not. When someone told a story, she listened. When someone flirted with her, she flirted right back. If anyone had a craving for something that wasn't listed on the menu, she headed to the kitchen to see what she could do.

Smiling again, Ryanne waved him over.

He settled in a chair on the other side of the bar, avoiding her friends.

"I owe you a huge thank you for the list you left me this morning," she said.

He nodded, his version of *you're welcome*. He'd written up a To Do list in case Belle went into labor and he wasn't nearby.

"Are you hungry? You look hungry." She leaned toward him and whispered, "Come upstairs later, and I'll heat something up for you."

His stomach twisted. "Excuse me?"

"Why?"

Not this again. "What are you planning to heat up?" *Do not say* you.

"A pie, of course."

Disappointment hit him. No, no. Relief. Only relief.

"I owe you a thank-you, remember?" Her gaze raked over him. "Or did you want me to heat something else up?"

Fire in his blood, a tightening in his jeans. Too late. He was already burning. "Stop flirting with me," he grated.

"Hey, what are you guys whispering about? And did I hear you thank him for leaving a list this morning? You don't usually rise before noon." Dorothea wiggled her brows. "Or was Jude the one who did the rising?"

Ryanne chuckled behind her hand.

Lyndie snickered. "You don't have to answer her, Jude." Even amused, the petite beauty looked like she'd break with the next gust of wind. "We'll just let our imaginations run wild."

Knowing anything he said could be misconstrued as an innuendo, he pressed his lips together and sat a few seats away. His patella momentarily rolled out of place, and he had to hide a wince.

"Ignore them." Ryanne leaned over the bar, and her magnificent cleavage beckoned his gaze... *Look at me, look how pretty I am...*

He gulped. The scent of strawberries and cream wafted from her and, this time, lust didn't punch him in the gut; it washed through him like a gentle rain. A far more dangerous occurrence. The punch had mixed pain with pleasure. The rain promised something he wasn't sure he'd ever feel again: peace.

"Are you parched? Let me satisfy you," she said, and he knew she'd used those particular words on purpose.

He gripped the bar to stop himself from adjusting the growing problem behind his fly. He wished Ryanne would act like the girl he'd first met. The one who'd enjoyed sniping at him.

"I am parched," he finally said. "I'd like to drink the tears of my enemies."

A laugh burst from her, her features glowing with amusement. "I'm out of tears. How about sweet tea?"

He gave a brusque nod. "Thanks."

Motions fluid, she filled his glass then lifted a small plastic tub from behind the bar. A tub she opened and sat in front of him, revealing a club sandwich and hand-cut fries.

Had she reserved both for him?

"Eat now, *and* later," she said, and he realized yes, yes she had.

The ache returned to his chest. "I'm not hungry." Not for food. *Not for anything*, he told himself.

"Eat anyway," she insisted. "Boss's orders. You worked through lunch."

She'd noticed?

The ache worsened. "Fine." Determined to end the conversation, he bit into the sandwich—and groaned. The flavors were incredible. She'd used strawberry jam instead of mayo and the combination of salty and sweet blew his ever-loving mind. "This is good. Thank you."

"You're welcome." She flattened her hand over his in what should be a simple, friendly gesture. With her, it was a sensual assault, more than his long neglected body could tolerate. "If you ever want another sandwich, it's called the Do Me Baby One More Time."

Yes. I'll do her so—

Wrong.

Inhaling sharply, he yanked his hand from hers and flattened his palm on his thigh.

This was Ryanne. A flirt. Born seducer. Good time girl. But…if ever she'd followed through on her come-hither glances, he didn't know it. What he did know? He'd escorted a Blueberry Hill resident from the building for calling her a "slut." Afterward he'd ejected three guys for trying to pick her up. She had no idea he'd done it, and he refused to think about his reasons. Although his mind was more than happy to provide a suggestion: *falling for her…*

Sometimes his mind was a dumb-ass.

Jude *would* resist Ryanne. If he had to pick another woman to do so, he would. Anyone but Ryanne Wade.

Thousands of curses suddenly bellowed inside his head. He wasn't interested in a one-night stand, or a long-term relationship, and he damn sure wasn't willing to risk an unplanned pregnancy. Children would never be part of his life. No children, no possibility of loss.

In fact, he should make an appointment with a urologic surgeon and have a vasectomy. Then, if ever he had a moment of weakness, he wouldn't have to worry.

The food in his stomach seemed to turn to lead. He pushed the Tupperware away, saying, "I've had enough."

Ryanne sighed, the enchantress persona evaporating like smoke, leaving a concerned…friend? "You've been working so hard but eating so little."

"Don't worry. I won't fall down on the job." He'd lost his appetite years ago and now fueled himself with protein shakes.

"That's not— Never mind. Why don't you take the night off? You can nap upstairs with Belle."

"I don't nap."

"Ever?"

"Ever." He rarely slept at all. When he did, he dreamed of the car wreck he hadn't witnessed, watching, helpless, as Constance's SUV rolled over at least a dozen times, glass and metal shards cutting at his girls.

"I'm sorry." Ryanne's nails lightly scraped the pulse in his wrist, jolting him from his heartbreak.

Damn it! When had he placed his hands back on the bar? "Don't be."

"If you don't want to eat, how about you give me a compliment instead?"

"I'm not in the mood to be nice."

Rather than leaving him alone, as he'd hoped, she studied him with compassion in her beautiful dark eyes. "Is your leg paining you?"

He scowled. Was she making excuses for his waspishness, or had she watched him so intently, she'd recognized the signs of his distress? "Be honest. You're trying to make me squirm again, aren't you, Wade?"

"Wade?" She snorted. "Let me guess. By using my last name, you put a little emotional distance between us."

Yes. Exactly. Nicknames mattered, created a bond. He'd rather die than create a bond with Ryanne.

He'd called Constance "sweetheart" and his girls "Daddy's little sweets." He'd settled arguments about who could ride an imaginary pony first. He'd fielded questions about where babies came from when the girls were far too young to ask about such things, and battled monsters in the closet.

When I grow up, I'm gonna be a mom. Bailey had grinned a mischievous grin. *Moms are the boss of everyone.*

Well, I'm gonna be a dad. Hailey had hugged him. *Dads are nice to everyone.*

Even when I'm a big girl, I'm gonna love you best, Daddy.

My friend Sally doesn't have a dad. Will you be her dad, Daddy? I told her you build the biggest fort-castles in the world.

He remembered the day the girls threw pennies in the wishing well.

"What did you wish for?" he'd asked.

Bailey had gazed at him adoringly. "I wished for you to be handsome, Daddy."

He'd tried not to laugh. "Thanks, little sweet. I appreciate your thoughtfulness."

"I wished for you to stay home forever, Daddy, and never leave again," Hailey had said.

He rubbed the sudden burn from his eyes, then pinched the bridge of his nose.

He didn't like that Ryanne had guessed his intent. But then, he shouldn't be surprised that she'd done so. The woman had a knack for reading people.

"Well." She fluffed her fall of ebony hair. "Aren't you *precioso.*" Her sassy tone somehow contained both a Spanish and Southern accent. "By the way, I'm calling you *cowboy* because you always look like you're ready for a ride."

Walk away. Walk away now. No good can come from this conversation.

He stood, but remained rooted in place. Her gaze slid down his chest, making him regret—and extol—his immobility.

"Jude, wait!" Lyndie raised her hand like a student in class. "Dorothea, uh, she has a question for you."

"I do?" Dorothea asked, then cleared her throat. "I mean, yep, I do."

Not wanting to frighten Lyndie, he forced his posture to soften. The elementary schoolteacher spooked far too easily. He'd noticed her tendency to leave a room whenever an argument kicked off.

He even forced himself to smile at her, and hell, it felt weird to lift the corners of his mouth. Weird, wrong on every level and stilted. As soon as he looked away from her, he returned to his normal expression, the one that said *I don't want to be here, or anywhere.*

His gaze landed on Daniel's fiancée. "Ask," he said, knowing she didn't actually have a question for him. He wasn't sure why Lyndie wanted him to stay, but he wasn't going to call her out.

Dorothea looked at Lyndie, then Ryanne. Frowned. Opened her mouth, closed it. Finally she said, "Yeah, so… I'm going to be picking bridesmaid dresses soon. Ryanne, of course, is a co-maid of honor with Lyndie. Lyndie is wearing pink chiffon but thinks Ryanne should be forced to wear a trash bag. Do you agree?"

His gaze zipped back to Ryanne, who was now watching him with a thoughtful expression…and upset? "A trash bag won't detract from her raw sensuality." The primal admission left him before he could stop it, wiping her upset away.

A grinning Lyndie pressed a hand above her heart. "If you guys were in a movie, female viewers would be sighing dreamily right now, and male viewers would be throwing popcorn at the screen. You just set the bar *very* high."

Ryanne peered at him, her lush lips gaping open. "You claimed you were too grumpy to be nice, but I swear I just heard the best compliment of my life."

"Truth is truth, not a compliment."

"Well, then, that's even better." She beamed at him, so radiant he wanted to take her in his arms and—

Nothing.

Ryanne wasn't his type, would *never* be his type. Forget her job. She was too bold, too brash. Too…everything. She drew attention and loved it. Nothing slowed her down. She sizzled with passion and marched through life with no care for the obstacles thrown in her way.

Jude craved solitude, which meant he wasn't Ryanne's type, either. Actually, he had no idea what type of man she actually preferred. She was an equal opportunity flirt, charming young and old alike. Hell, charming large and small, tall and short, rich and poor.

Always irritating me, and I don't know why.

The front door opened, saving him from having to think up an appropriate reply, and the members of Power Trip—the band she hired on Friday and Saturday nights—strode inside.

Daniel and Brock came in behind the drummer, and both males pulsed with a palpable air of anger and frustration they couldn't hide behind cheerful waves.

Something had happened out there.

The women sensed a problem, as well. As soon as the guys reached the counter, Dorothea threw her arms around Daniel. Lyndie inched away from Brock and glanced at the door, as if planning an escape route.

Ryanne reached out to latch on to Jude's wrist, the softness of her skin momentarily paralyzing him. *Can't force myself to pull away this time...*

"What's wrong?" she asked.

No doubt Dushku had struck.

Daniel gave an unconvincing laugh. "Who said anything was wrong?"

"Someone trashed the alley outside, spray-painted vile things on the wall, that's all," Brock said, and Daniel glared at him.

Dorothea and Lyndie gasped with horror.

Ryanne stiffened. "Show me."

Jude wrapped *his* hand around *her* wrist; she'd held him, and now he held her. It was an intimate pose, and one he wasn't emotionally equipped to handle. Did he let go? No.

"Stay in here. Please." He knew his friends, and knew a trashed alley wasn't the only problem out there. "Let me make sure everything is safe. That's what you pay me the big bucks for, after all."

At first, she opened her mouth to protest. Then she looked

at her friends. If she insisted on going outside, they would insist on going with her, and they would be in danger, as well. So she nodded, released him.

Silent, he, Daniel and Brock headed outside. His friends led him to the back alley, where he saw *bitch*, *slut* and *whore*, and an assortment of other vile words, spray-painted on the walls. His molars gnashed again, and he wouldn't be surprised if they turned to powder.

The boys kept going, stopping when they reached Ryanne's SUV, parked behind the building. Rage sparked.

The tires had been slashed, and the words *YOUR NEXT* spray-painted over the windshield.

"Idiot," Jude muttered. "*You're*. Not *your*."

This was a scare tactic, nothing more, meant to intimidate Ryanne into doing whatever Dushku wanted.

"What do you want us to do?" Brock asked.

"For now, we clean up the mess. Later we'll give Ryanne the bare minimum of facts." The less she knew, the better. He would do the worrying for her.

A woman like her should only ever smile.

CHAPTER FIVE

Mondays were usually Ryanne's favorite day of the week. She got to sleep in, drink wine, play video games and relax in a bubble bath. Today, however, she hadn't slept in. Belle had done her cat thing, somehow climbing on the desk, despite the size of her belly, knocking over a coffee mug, pens, a book and even a laptop. During the loud *bang* that had followed every downed item, Ryanne had lain in bed thinking about the smile Jude had given Lyndie. A kind smile. Humorless, yes, but kind nonetheless. A smile he'd never given Ryanne.

For a moment, she'd been eaten up with jealousy, and she'd hated herself for it. Lyndie deserved all the kindness in the world.

After giving herself a kick in the pants, Ryanne had gotten up, showered while standing for once and dressed in a hurry. The Scratching Post would be hosting the Strawberry Bookcakes today, and she would be serving tea, finger sandwiches and cookies. Despite the twenty-dollar cover charge, a whole gaggle of retired matrons had signed up.

Guaranteed the sweet old biddies would start off discussing their book club selection—a scandalous paranormal romance titled *The Darkest Night*; it was chosen because Lincoln West, a beloved resident of the town, had designed a video game based on its mythology. Once the discussion ended, everyone would start gossiping about nonfictional people.

Ryanne had a few hours to run a million errands. Still, she texted Jude an invitation to join her.

Want to be my sidekick today? (I know what you're thinking—your job comes with perks, like spending time with your favorite person. Hint: me!) Pick you up in twenty?

At some point, he had to say yes and their fun times could finally begin.

This wasn't that point.

His no had come in so fast her head had spun.

Dang it, why? Last night a guy had flirted with her while she'd mixed drinks behind the bar, and Jude had come over like a heat-seeking missile.

"Leave," he'd snapped at the guy. "Leave while you can still walk. In thirty seconds, you'll only be able to crawl."

Ryanne had watched, flabbergasted. "Uh, he did nothing wrong."

"I didn't trust him. He could have been one of Dushku's men."

Or maybe Jude didn't want other guys hitting on her?

She ignored a little thrill and checked her extra stash of moonshine in the basement. Time to place a new order. She shot off a quick email to her contact at the brewery and drove into town to check her account at Strawberry Savings and Loans. Every night at closing, she took all the cash from the register, minus the next day's float, which she left in a safe, and put the money in a special deposit bag with the bar's account info. Then she deposited it through an after-hours slot at the bank. Last night Jude had insisted on doing the chore for her, not wanting her to drive around with that much cash. She'd finally relented and let him do it. While she trusted Jude—for the most part—money could do strange things to people, turning the honest into thieves. With Jude, she should have known better. Every cent was accounted for.

Next she visited the grocery to buy cat food and kitty litter. From there, she went to the bookstore to pick up a detailed traveler's guide to Rome.

Every time she climbed behind the wheel of her SUV, she experienced a twinge of disconcertment. Something was different.

Her windshield was clean, not a single speck of dirt or a dead insect in sight, but there *was* a small crack in the right-hand corner, one she hadn't noticed before. And she had brand-new windshield wipers. Also, her tires were immaculate, cleaner than the windshield, and taller than usual.

When Jude first returned to the bar last night, his posture had been rigid as steel. "We're going to clean the alley walls," he'd said, "but I need to buy a few supplies. I'm going to borrow your car, all right?"

Now she wondered if yesterday's vandalism "in the alley" had involved her car as well, and he'd fixed it for her?

Yeah. That. Most definitely. How like the man.

Could he *be* any sexier?

No, no, he couldn't. Dang him, he always looked like sex and smelled incredible, like dark, aged rum—which was ironic, considering he'd never even sipped her alcohol. As grumpy as he was, he cared about people, helping ensure the intoxicated never got behind the wheel of a car.

Every hour she spent with him, she wanted him more, wanted to know him better. Why had his military buds nicknamed him Priest? When he'd served, he'd been married with children.

More than anything, she wanted to make him smile. The desire had become an addiction, an obsession. His innate sadness hurt her heart.

Over the past week, she'd learned he never rested and rarely ate, relying on protein shakes for energy. The only time he lost his temper? When an intoxicated person resisted aid and said something akin to "I'm okay to drive."

He would shout about the dangers and end every speech with the same world-rocking question. *Do you want to murder an innocent family?*

Ryanne had begun to suspect a drunk driver killed his wife and daughters, and a little online research had confirmed it. The college boy who'd crashed into Constance Laurent's car, killing everyone inside, had gotten a ten-year split sentence. Five years in prison, five years on probation.

At last she understood Jude's disdain for the Scratching Post. It was a miracle he worked so hard to save the place, and a true testament to his loyal heart.

Loyal…but also broken.

Two nights ago, he'd left his cell phone at the bar. She'd followed him home, intending to tease him, maybe flirt a little before returning his property. Instead, she'd sat in her vehicle, watching as he'd sat in his, banging his fists into the steering wheel, his tears glinting in the moonlight.

He missed his family. Of course he did.

She could empathize—after all, she missed Earl. He'd been more of a father and mother to her than her bio parents ever had.

Sometimes she still expected to see Earl behind the bar, mixing drinks, or hear his booming laughter when she "got her Spanish on" with a customer.

Loved ones left marks on your soul, and when they died, those marks became scars.

As Ryanne's SUV eased along Strawberry Valley's town square, she forced Jude the praised one and his loss out of her mind, and focused on the majestic scenery, a true gift from God. Antique lampposts lined the sidewalks, the perfect complement to both the historic and modern buildings. The Strawberry Inn—Dorothea's home and business—was a sprawling antebellum estate with an array of massive white columns. The local grocery store, Strawberries and More, was housed in a metal warehouse with a tin roof.

On the next street, box-shaped homes had been turned into a café, a hardware shop and a dry cleaner. A whitewashed bungalow contained the Rhinestone Cowgirl, the only place to buy handmade jewelry. The theater was Ryanne's favorite building, with a copper awning and multiple gargoyles perched along a balcony. Actually, the theater tied with Strawberry Community Church, a white stone chapel with spectacular stained-glass windows. Reminded her of pictures she'd seen in a book about Holland.

Wild strawberry patches grew along the sidewalks and between the shops. During the summer, she could pluck the sweet fruit straight from the plant for a quick snack, any time, any place.

How she loved the charm and enchantment of the town. One of the many reasons she opted to move in with Earl rather than go to Colorado with her mom and brand-new stepdad. Or stepdouche.

When she turned the next corner, she caught sight of a petite blonde walking beside a hulking, tattooed giant Ryanne recognized. Cigarette! The blonde...could she be the prostitute from the van?

Ryanne pulled over a little too sharply and parked at the sidewalk. Both Cigarette and Blondie glanced in her direction. His eyes narrowed, while the woman's widened. He grabbed her by the arm and picked up the pace, soon disappearing around a corner.

Trembling, Ryanne palmed her phone and fired off a text to Jude. Guess who I just found? Our friends from the parking lot. I'm going to follow them.

She added a thumbs-up emoji and pressed Send.

His reply came only a few seconds later. Do not pursue. I repeat, just in case I wasn't clear. Do not. NOT. If you do, there will be consequences.

Well, well. Commando was back in action, and more delicious than a bag of Chips Ahoy! *I could eat him up.* Still, encouraging his power play would only end badly for her and their upcoming sexlationship—because yes, they would have one.

She jabbed her fingers into the keyboard, typing, Aren't you precioso. Consequences, cowboy? Try. Please.

Then she added a gif of two people jumping up and down, laughing and clapping.

No way Ryanne would do what the big, strong man had told her. How many times had her mother obeyed every whim, command or request of a husband, boyfriend, lover or even potential lover, losing her own identity? Lyndie, too, had lost her identity in her father and husband. Though Dorothea loved Daniel, she had given up a promising career as a storm chaser in order to be with him.

I'll give up nothing.

Would Ryanne be in danger? No!

Okay, maybe. But probably not. This was a public place. Even if Cigarette decided he didn't care about their audience, he couldn't come within ten feet of Ryanne without getting shot. Having gotten her conceal and carry license at Earl's insistence, she never left home without protection. What truly motivated her to get out of her car, however, was the thought that Blondie might be a sex slave in need of rescue. The way Cigarette had grabbed her...

Determined to ferret out the truth, Ryanne marched down the sidewalk. Cool air stroked her bare arms, causing goose bumps to sprout. In September, or any month, really, Oklahoma weather could change from one hour to another, from sizzling hot to ice cold. Picking up the pace, she snaked around the corner, tense and ready...

Dang it! No sign of Cigarette or Blondie. She checked between the buildings and inside a few of the shops. Still nothing.

With a sigh of frustration, she pivoted—

And smacked into a brick wall. Or at least what *felt* like a brick wall.

Big hands settled on her hips, pinning her in place. Her mind reacted before her eyes had time to assess the situation. Cigarette? On instinct, she drew back her fist and punched. Pain exploded in her knuckles, but she swallowed a yelp, determined to maintain a strong persona.

Nope, not Cigarette. Jude Laurent rubbed his jaw. "You hit like a girl," he grated.

Deep breath in, out. Meanwhile, her heart continued to race. "If you put a little more strength behind *your* blows, you could hit like a girl, too," she retorted.

The corners of his lips twitched. Rays of sunlight spilled over him, framing him in gold, and oh, wow, he looked good. Like a fallen angel. His hair appeared lighter today, and his tan darker. A storm brewed in his navy blue eyes.

The urge to soften against him was insistent, but she somehow found the strength to step backward rather than forward. Now wasn't the time for romance.

"How'd you get here so quickly?" Wait. "How'd you know my location?"

A muscle jumped beneath his eye. "I was following the pair before you spotted them."

Of course he was. *Sexy warrior.* "Were you able to learn anything about the woman?"

"Nothing. A shameless flirt spy-blocked me." He flicked a lock of hair from Ryanne's shoulder, his knuckles brushing against her skin. Warm tingles erupted.

She gasped while he peered down at his hand, as if shocked by what it had just done. Was he experiencing tingles of his own?

Was she getting to him at last?

Little fires ignited in different parts of her body, until every inch of her burned. "Why would I ever entertain shame, cowboy?" A breathless note stole into her tone. "Flirting is fun for everyone involved."

Before he could respond, Virgil Porter and Anthony Rodriguez rounded the corner.

Virgil—Daniel's dad—tipped his baseball cap in greeting as he passed. Anthony, owner of Style Me Tender Salon, waved. The two were best friends and daily checkers partners, and while they didn't stop to chat, they *did* slow down to eavesdrop.

"Very subtle, Mr. Porter." Jude threw the universal sign for *I'm watching you* at Virgil. "But I'm on to your tricks."

"I told you to call me Virgil, son. And FYI, I have no tricks. I just wish you'd use your outside voice so we could hear your conversation better." He never even glanced over his shoulder, just kept moseying along. To Anthony he muttered, "Did I use that there acronym right or not?"

"Yep, sure did," Anthony replied, "but really the only acronyms you need to know are WTF and GOML. *Wait! Too Fast* and *Get Off My Lawn.*"

The two disappeared around the next corner.

Adorable old bears.

"I need to speak with you. Privately," Jude said to Ryanne.

Uh-oh. "Why?"

Determined, he clasped her hand and hauled her into the nearest alley. Then he backed her into the brick wall, looming over her, his narrowed eyes glaring daggers at her. "I told you there would be consequences if you followed a man in Dushku's employ."

She tried to focus on his anger, she did, but her brain short-circuited. This was the closest she'd ever been to Jude, and she was having trouble catching her breath. Her blood heated another thousand degrees, and her skin tingled worse than ever before, little quivers rocking her on her feet.

Just then, she didn't want to make him laugh; she wanted to make him hot.

Led by desire, logic nowhere to be found, she wrapped her arms around his neck and combed her fingers through his hair.

He didn't jump away. "What are you doing?" His ragged voice was as potent as a caress.

Why not tell him the truth? She licked her lips, reveling as his eyes followed the motion. "I think I'm...seducing you."

"You *think*?" he croaked.

"I've never done this before." Others had tried to seduce her, but this was her first attempt. "For a long time, I had serious trust issues and didn't date. When I decided there *were* good guys in the world, I wasn't attracted to anyone...until you."

He gulped. "How long since your last date?"

"Two and a half years," she said, toying with the ends of his hair.

He stiffened but still didn't jump away. "Were you cheated on?"

Growing bolder, she plucked at his collar, her nails lightly scraping his heated skin. "Twice my mother slept with my boy-friends. And the things I've seen at the bar..." With a nibble on her bottom lip, she asked, "What about you? How long since you—"

"Two and a half years." Another croak.

Ohhh. They had more in common than she'd realized. And the fact that they'd remained alone for the exact same amount of time, well, the odds had to be astronomical.

"Jude?" Wait. What did she want to ask him?

For a moment, he ceased moving, perhaps even ceased breath-ing. Then he took two steps back. Oh, heck no. He wasn't leav-ing her, not now. She fisted his shirt and tugged him forward, and the impromptu action caused him to stumble.

She opened her mouth to tell him she was sorry, but suddenly found herself plastered against his chest, speaking a talent beyond

her. Their gazes clashed. His eyes sizzled with molten awareness. Again he stopped breathing. And this time, so did she...

"I should go," he rasped, even as he braced his palms flat on
the brick, caging her in. A predator who'd just captured prey.

This prey wanted to be *devoured*.

Her pulse points hammered and throbbed as his body heat
enveloped her. Scorching waves of agony and ecstasy swept over
her, destroying her but also making her into a new woman.

Jude's woman.

This man had suffered for years. He deserved pleasure. While
Ryanne couldn't replace his beloved wife, and didn't want to,
she *could* help him forget the past, if only for a little while.

Shouldn't she at least try?

"Don't freak out, okay?" Her whisper caressed the air. She
cupped his face and, not giving either of them a chance to
think, pulled him down while lifting on her tiptoes. Her lips
pressed against his scar, once, twice. The softness...the sweetness of him...

More.

He stiffened and wrenched from her hold, but again, he didn't
storm off. He glared at her, panting now. She was panting, too,
the scent of him teasing her nose. Spiced rum with oranges
and a subtle floral note; it wasn't feminine but strangely—deliciously—masculine.

A whimper escaped her. She was so hungry for him. "You
freaked out," she accused.

He closed his eyes for one second, two, before focusing on
her with fury...and fiery lust. "You surprised me."

If she continued with this, she would stoke both the lust and
the fury? Probably. He might like it, but he might not forgive
her, either.

She had a choice. Stay here, and risk ruining their relationship before it ever began, or leave, never knowing what could
have been.

No contest. Great risk, great reward. If she walked away, she would always regret not taking a chance.

Seduce...

"Did I also turn you on?" Slowly, giving him time to process her intention, she leaned forward to nip at his lower lip. "Because I turned *myself* on."

"Ryanne... *Wade*."

He had to force himself to put distance between them, didn't he? It no longer came quite so naturally. "Yes, cowboy." *Yes.*

With a growl, he dove down and devoured her mouth, his hunger a perfect match to her own. Their tongues dueled, creating a hot tangle of desire. Her nipples crested, needy, and the apex of her thighs ached, liquid need pooling there. As her bones melted, passion surged through her, flooding her. Move, she had to move. She arched her hips—contact! Her throbbing core rubbed against the long, thick length of his erection, and a groan spilled from her.

In the midst of the earth-shattering kiss, his aloof veneer shed like a winter coat he no longer needed, because the sun had peeked from behind storm clouds at long last. With a hiss born from raw frustration, he seemed to shed a thousand pounds of anger, sadness and pain. She *felt* their absence, the temperature of his skin heating, arousal ashing everything else.

"More." He stepped closer to her, forcing her spine flush against the brick wall while smashing his chest into hers.

Ice cold behind her, searing heat in front of her. The warring temperatures bombarded her with sensation, a tornado of lust ravaging her. Inhibitions were the first casualty.

She and Jude were outside, in a public setting, but so what. And so the heck what if this man disliked her most of the time. He kissed her as if she were his last meal or the air he needed to survive.

As if she alone held the key to his happiness.

"Ryanne." He kicked her legs apart. The action lacked finesse, and yet it electrified her from head to toe.

Can't get enough of me...

A cry of abandon split her lips as he ground his shaft between her legs. Currents of passion whisked through her bloodstream. She trembled. She craved.

How desperately she wanted to strip and ride him, to feel him deep inside her, moving, thrusting, pounding. Finally she would experience everything a man had to give—everything *this* man had to give.

"Jude." She pulled at the hem of his shirt, her knuckles brushing the blistering skin that covered his rock-hard abs. Her knees threatened to buckle.

She might have gone two and a half years without a kiss, but she couldn't go two more weeks...two more days...two more minutes without Jude Laurent.

"You taste like strawberries," he rasped. "You smell like strawberries, too. How is that possible?"

"I've lived in this town most of my life. I'm shocked I don't taste and smell like pineapples. Dummy," she teased, and nipped at his bottom lip.

He chuckled. A husky, rusty chuckle that was ragged at the edges. It shocked them both. In unison, they stilled. Once again their gazes met, clashed. His pupils were blown, what remained of his irises glittering wildly. His cheeks were flushed, and his nostrils flared every time he inhaled.

So beautiful. I'm not ready for this to end. Ryanne traced a fingertip along the seam of his lips. Such soft lips for such a hard man.

"No." His eyelids narrowed, and he stepped back, leaving her bereft. A scowl darkened his features.

Was he about to blame her for what just happened? Would he vow never to come near her again?

She braced for whatever vitriol he planned to unleash, determined to roll with the punches. She'd known a kiss would upset him, but had plowed full steam ahead, anyway, because she'd wanted him.

She wanted him still.

But all he did was take another step back and wipe his mouth with his hand. Then horror replaced his scowl and he took another step back, and another. The silence cut deeper than a knife.

"Jude," she said. "Care enough to talk to me about what you're feeling." *Please.*

"I...won't. I'm sorry, but I won't talk about feelings, and I won't let myself care." He spun on his heel and stalked off, soon disappearing around the corner.

Ryanne remained in place. Her heartbeat refused to slow, and her bones refused to solidify; they were too hot.

Deep breath in, out. *Won't let myself care.*

Harsh words, and yet she took no offense. Part of him *did* care, or he wouldn't have to fight it.

Did he feel like he'd betrayed his wife? Maybe. Probably. Constance had died two and a half years ago, and he'd gone two and a half years without kissing or touching another woman.

The poor man hadn't *wanted* pleasure. Actually, he'd done everything in his power to ensure he couldn't, wouldn't, enjoy his life, she realized. Misery had become a treasured friend.

Been there, hated that.

Whether he knew it or not, Ryanne had helped him take a step in the right direction. His body had new life—she'd felt every inch of it. He'd been long, hard and thick. *For me. Only me.*

Already addicted... One kiss had been too much, obsessing and possessing her, but hundreds...thousands would never be enough.

Hope joined the festivities. All was not lost. If she could turn Jude on once, surely she could do it again...

CHAPTER SIX

What the hell did I do?

Jude burned rubber, hauling ass to the home he shared with Brock. Unfortunately, the thousand-square-foot log cabin in the heart of five wooded acres offered no solace. Nor did the winding creek that split the property into two sections. *My half, your half*, Brock often joked.

The wealth of pecan, hickory and oak trees surrounding the property offered a private, tranquil escape from the rest of the world, yet Jude only felt turmoil.

Granted, he only ever felt turmoil, period. Especially at the Scratching Post. Or anywhere Ryanne Wade happened to be.

She hadn't dated a man in two and a half years.

The timing wasn't lost on Jude, and it threw him for a loop. *We waited for…each other?*

No. Absolutely not.

Why did she want him? He'd done nothing to lead her on.

Idiot! Of course he had. Constantly he watched her. He stared at her lips, riveted, when she spoke. He sought her out, and cock-blocked anyone who flirted with her.

Damn her. The woman had tied him into knots, and he wasn't sure how much more he could take. Soon he would break.

Wrong. He'd already broken. That kiss...

To his utter shock, he hadn't felt a shred of guilt—until the kiss had ended. Now he knew Ryanne's sweet taste. The feel of her silken skin, and the little mewling sounds she made when pleasured. How was he supposed to resist her?

Easy. If he couldn't resist the owner of a bar, he wasn't a man deserving of Constance's love.

The bartender who'd served his family's killer hadn't been charged for serving an obviously drunk man or for allowing that man to drive away. And really, Frat Boy hadn't received much of a punishment, either. His ten-year split sentence—five years behind bars, five years on probation—was a joke. Soon the murdering asshole would be out on the streets, ready to murder another family.

How was that okay? The most ridiculous crimes sometimes came with a severe life sentence, but kill a mother and two young girls and you'd only have to push the pause button on your life for five too-short years.

Cursing, Jude slammed his fist into the steering wheel again and again. As his knuckles bled and throbbed, his cell phone buzzed, signaling a text had come in.

If Ryanne had messaged him, expecting to talk about what had happened, he would—what? Say something terrible he could never take back.

Angry, uncertain—hopeful?—he checked the screen. The anger and hope drained as the name Carrie Jones flashed. Constance's mother.

I found a baby book Coni made for the girls, and I think you should have it. When I saw the pictures inside, well, I laughed through my tears, and I think you will, too. Please, Jude, tell me where you're living so I can send you the book.

With another curse, he tossed the phone on the floorboard and smashed his fists into his burning eyes. After the car wreck, he'd packed up everything he and Constance owned and shipped the boxes to her parents. When he moved to Strawberry Valley, he'd left his own belongings behind to be sold or tossed, and hadn't told anyone back home. Too raw to handle anyone else's grief, he'd simply cut all ties.

Through it all, his love for the Joneses had never faded. He'd never known his biological dad, and his mother had washed her hands of him as soon as he could take care of himself, just as she'd done with his sister and three older brothers, each of whom had moved out or run away by Jude's thirteenth birthday. Russ and Carrie had welcomed him into their family with open arms and, through example, taught him how to be a good father to his own children.

He'd wanted to be a better parent to his girls than his mother had been to him. And unlike his dad, Jude had planned to be there any time his babies needed him. A monster under the bed? Dad to the rescue. Got a hankering to give a makeover— lipstick, hair bows, nail polish, the works? Dad's your man, or model. Can't reach the cookie jar on the kitchen counter? Dad will lift you up so you can pretend to fly.

But in the end, Jude *hadn't* been a better parent than his own. He hadn't been there for the girls when they'd needed him most. No, he'd been in bed, recovering from the bomb blast that had taken his leg.

Not your fault, so many had said. But it *had* been his fault—he had made the decision to join the army. He had fought to join the Ten against Constance's wishes. He had wallowed in self-pity, refusing to work harder to leave the hospital sooner.

He was so ashamed. And he was ashamed of his desertion of the Joneses. The past few months, Carrie had contacted him at least once a week. Her grief had eased, he supposed, and she'd found the strength to go through her only daughter's things, and probably assumed he had the strength, too.

Maybe he should fly to Texas…where his relationship with Constance had begun. Where memories lurked in every corner. He shuddered.

Can't leave Ryanne. Not with Dushku nearby.

But Jude *could* reach out.

He swiped up his phone, sent his new address to Carrie and ended with, I'm sorry I've been out of touch. Thank you for thinking of me.

Send.

What he would do with the baby book when it arrived, he wasn't sure.

After a moment's hesitation, he sent a second message. How are you guys?

Her response came quickly. We're good. As good as can be expected, anyway. We miss you like crazy. We lost Coni and the girls, and feel as if we lost you, too. Come visit us soon?

Rather than reject her offer outright, he opted for radio silence. At least for now.

Next he called a surgeon he'd met while serving, a guy who was now a urologic surgeon for civilians. The first available appointment was a month away—though Jude suspected the good doctor wanted to put him off, thinking time would change his mind. He asked to be notified if an appointment opened up sooner.

When he looked up, he found Brock lazing in a hammock, shaded by a portico they'd built together. His friend appeared relaxed, completely at ease, but Jude knew better, knew the chaos and pain trapped inside his head. Most nights the guy woke up soaked in sweat and screaming. Sometimes he broke down and cried. Other times he hopped on the treadmill and ran until his knees gave out. Jude understood.

During their years of service, they'd killed a lot of men and lost a lot of friends. That kind of loss did things to a man—ruined his ability to live a "normal" life, leaving stain after stain on his soul.

Jude exited the car and closed the distance, his stride long and strong despite the pain in his knee.

"Dude." Brock rocked back and forth. On every inward swing, Jude saw the fatigue etched into his face. "You look like you could use a good cuddle. What put your panties in such a twist?"

"Everything." He scrubbed a hand down his face. "Nothing."

With his chin, Brock motioned to the cuts on Jude's knuckles. "In other words, Ryanne Wade. Go on."

Jackass. "She's only part of the problem." He reached over and tipped the hammock, dumping his friend on the wood planks beneath. A heavy thud shook the entire porch.

Sputtering, Brock jumped to his feet. Once steady, he barked out a laugh. "You suck, my man. Big-time."

"I know. Sadly it's one of my better qualities." He pressed a shoulder against a post and crossed his arms. "What are you doing here, anyway?" The guy spent every night with a new woman.

Brock shifted from one booted foot to the other, clearly uncomfortable with the topic of conversation. "Today is career day at Scottie's school, and she asked me to dazzle her class with my occupation. What am I supposed to say when the only thing I did was kill people? I've only got an hour to come up with something true but also appropriate for innocent ears."

"Talk about the security firm. Tell the kids you're basically a superhero, because you stop bad guys from committing crimes. Now, who is Scottie?"

The indomitable Brock Hudson flushed with embarrassment. "Lyndie."

"Ah. Lyndie Scott. Who is now Scottie. How *adorable*. Are you guys finally on speaking terms?"

"Barely. She's afraid of me."

"You know her father and husband abused her. She needs time to get to know you, to assure herself you've got control of your temper."

"Do I? Have control, I mean." He scrubbed a hand down his face. "I think not knowing me actually works in my favor."

"You've got your faults. Who doesn't? But you're a good guy."

"Please. You're my friend. You're required by bro-rules to think the best of me."

"No, I *get* to think the best of you because I'm your friend." Jude patted Brock's shoulder and made his way to his bedroom.

He could have offered more assurances or even a few platitudes, but to what end? Brock was attracted to Lyndie, but hadn't changed his MO. He only ever had one-night stands, using and losing women as a distraction from his troubled mind. Lyndie was a permanent part of their group; a one-night stand would never work. Brock would have to face her multiple times a week, every week.

Jude kicked off his shoes, then his jeans, and sat at the end of his bed. He removed his prosthesis and, with a wince, massaged the scarred stump under his knee. Sore muscles ached in protest as well as relief.

He'd been patched up on the field and then flown to Germany, where he spent a week convalescing from surgery. Then he was flown to San Antonio, where he spent three months in recovery. Constance and the girls had come to see him as often as possible, staying in temporary housing. With every visit, his wife had seemed brighter, happier, and once she'd even told him that she would love him no matter what, but deep in his heart, he hadn't believed her. He was no longer the man she'd married. He was less. He wasn't as strong or capable as he'd once been. Hell, he had to learn how to walk all over again.

Acid scalded his throat as he wondered how the flawless Ryanne would react to such an ugly sight.

He shook his head. What did her opinion matter? They'd kissed once, and they wouldn't do so again.

No matter how desperately his body longed to possess hers.

A beep sounded from his phone, distracting him from his thoughts. He checked the screen, his tightening grip nearly cracking the plastic case when he spotted Ryanne's name. If this was another invitation—

Wade: HELP ME!!! How fast can you get here??? I need you here five minutes ago. Belle is giving birth, and you probably can't tell, but I'm freaking out!

He sent a hasty reply. I left the list for a reason. Follow it.

Wade: COME OVER RIGHT NOW JUDE LAURENT OR I SWEAR I WILL HUNT YOU DOWN AND—I DON'T KNOW WHAT! BUT IT WILL HURT. IT WILL HURT BAD.

Already on my way.

Wade: Thank you thank you thank you. Sorry not sorry that I threatened you. Still friends?

We aren't friends, Wade. We're coworkers.

No response.

Maybe he'd been too harsh? Guilt prodded him.

Moving with lightning speed, he reattached his prosthesis, pulled on his jeans and shoes, then stood. He palmed his keys and raced outside, calling, "I'll be at the Scratching Post."

He made the twelve-minute drive in six, *without* being pulled over. A true miracle. As he parked in front, he noticed a flurry of activity at the construction site across the street. More men than usual congregated there.

No better time to drive his truck through the gate and scare the piss out of everyone. Mess with Ryanne and suffer. But she'd asked for help, and he'd promised to be there for her and the cat. He would keep his word.

Jude rushed inside the bar and climbed the stairs to Ryanne's apartment, easily bypassing the coded locks he'd installed on the doors. He paused in the foyer, watching as she paced, his chest aching all over again.

She'd anchored her dark hair in a sloppy knot on the crown of her head, but several tendrils had already slipped free. Her wide eyes were windows to her vulnerability, her cheeks devoid of color as she clutched a bag filled with supplies. Never had the spirited woman appeared so fragile.

"Don't be silly," she was saying—to the cat. "I'm not the one in need of a distraction. You are. So where's the father?" She'd either chewed on her lips, or Jude's kiss had left them looking bee-stung and red. "Did he love and leave you, or did you guys have a casual affair?"

"You do realize you're questioning a cat, right?" he piped up.

Her gaze found him and watered with relief. "Yes, I know, but *she's* my friend. And how else am I supposed to find out about her past?"

A fresh round of guilt hit him and, shockingly enough, it was followed by a wave of amusement. Ryanne always found a way to lighten his mood. Something only a friend could do.

Get your head in the game, soldier.

Right. Jude marched into the kitchen and washed his hands. That done, he claimed the bag of supplies. Alcohol, blunt end scissors in sterilized packages, hemostats that were also in sterilized packages, petroleum jelly, gloves, a suction bulb, thermometer and stethoscope. He entered the sunroom, pulled on the gloves. Per the To Do list he'd left her, she'd shut the blinds. The room was darkened, the air warmed by a small heater in the corner. A gram scale waited on the side table. Belle lay on a folded blanket, four kittens already curled up against her belly, each with different colored markings. She panted as a fifth kitten entered the world, the little cutie trapped in a jelly-like membrane filled with clear fluid.

Belle turned her attention to the new arrival, licking the sac from the kitten's face with more and more force until finally the thin membrane shredded, improving the baby's circulation, allowing him to breathe. Then she chewed through the umbilical cord and ate the placenta.

"Um, gross?" Ryanne said.

"Belle needs the vitamins." Jude listened to the kitten's heartbeat, cleared his airways and checked him over before presenting him to his mother.

"Good girl, Belle," he praised. "You've got this."

"You promise?" Ryanne flattened a hand over the racing pulse at the base of her neck. "You're not just being nice? You're being honest?"

"I'm always honest. But I wasn't talking to you, Wade. I was talking to Belle."

"I know." A tremor shook her in place. "Just to be clear, though, you're promising she's got this? That she'll survive?"

Had the tough bartender fallen in love with a cranky alley cat? "So far this is a textbook birth with zero complications."

"Oh, thank the good Lord." The words rushed from her. "Belle might be a small psychotic cream puff, but she's *my* psychotic cream puff. At least for now."

"Tell me about her," he said, to keep her talking and distracted.

"Well, she's ruthless but adorable. Destructive but cuddly. She hisses when I pet her, but glares at me when I don't. More than once she has perched in my lap, purred happily, then bitten my finger when I reached for her."

Her description amused him, which irritated him. Desiring Ryanne Wade was one thing. Constantly being amused by her—*charmed* by her—was another matter entirely. "Basically she's you in feline form," he grumbled.

Her lips quirked at the corners, as he'd intended, and some of the tension left her. "Maybe she is. But unlike Belle, I haven't bitten anyone. Yet."

An image flashed through his mind. One of Ryanne on her knees before him, her straight white teeth nibbling on his inner thigh…as she worked her way up to his shaft.

He cursed and made a mental note to call his doctor, and beg, if necessary, for the surgery to take place this week. No waiting until October.

"Where are your towels?" he asked with a little more force than he'd intended.

"Right here." Ryanne tossed him the desired item.

He cleaned the rest of the kittens, then used the suction bulb to remove any excess mucus from each baby's nose and mouth. While he worked, Belle birthed two more babies, making seven total.

After she expelled the placentas, he took care of the newest additions, then helped the entire group feed from Belle. "They'll want to—and need to—eat a full meal every one to three hours. You'll need to make sure Belle is fed as well, so she keeps up her strength. Wet food will be easier for her to digest."

"Me?" Ryanne squeaked. "On my own?"

"Who else? Unless you have a roommate I don't know about."

"Maybe I'm like Cinderella and live with talking mice."

"Say goodbye to those mice. They'll be a nice snack for Belle."

"Good, then there will be plenty of room for you to move in and help me. Just for a few days."

The thought of spending even one night here…

Every muscle in his body tensed. "Nope. You're on your own."

What little color Ryanne had regained suddenly vanished,

leaving her waxen. He almost shouted, *Never mind, I've changed my mind, I'll stay as long as you need me.*

As gently as possible he moved Belle and her crew to a clean blanket. Then he ushered Ryanne into the living room, where he urged her to settle on the couch.

"Breathe in, out," he instructed as he pushed her head between her legs. Hard to believe this was the same woman who'd so boldly yanked him close for a world-rocking kiss. "Good, that's good." When he realized he was tracing his fingers down the length of her spine, he ended the contact and gripped his knees. "Better?"

"Yes, thank you." Her voice was weak, thready.

He headed to the kitchen, washed up and dug through the cabinets until he found a glass. The first time he filled it, he drained the contents. The second time, he returned to the living room and crouched at Ryanne's feet.

The position hurt his knees, but he hid a grimace and said, "Here. Drink."

Radiating concern, she jackknifed into a sitting position and patted the area beside her. "I'll drink. You sit."

She was so aware of him she'd noticed his discomfort?

He eased onto the couch, careful to maintain a bit of distance—nearing her had been a mistake. Her sweet scent teased him, beckoning him closer. "Tell me about your upcoming travels," he said in an effort to distract them both.

Slight tremors shook her as she drained the water and clutched the empty glass to her chest. "I've never even been to another state, but I plan to travel the world. I'll be starting with Rome. I leave in roughly three months, and I'll be gone for four weeks."

Four weeks without her smile? Something dark razed his chest. *Ignore it!* "Why did you select Rome for your first outing?"

"Honestly? There are so many places I want to go, I ended up spinning a globe and pressing my finger into a random location."

"The globe served you well. You'll fall in love with Italy. The

Colosseum, the Pantheon, the Piazza Navona. St. Peter's Dome. The churches. The Vatican. Museums. The food."

"You've been?" Excitement pulsed from her, and she leaned toward him. "Tell me everything!"

The urge to reach out, comb his fingers through her hair, smoothing the errant strands from her cheeks, bombarded him. No doubt she would misconstrue the offer of comfort. And rightly so.

Comfort? Ha!

"I took my family while I was on leave. Michelangelo's Sistine Chapel blew my mind."

Her dreamy sigh left him breathless.

He added, "Be sure to stand at the top of the Castel Sant'Angelo. There's a spectacular view of Vatican City and the Tiber, and you can see the Ponte Sant'Angelo with Bernini's carved marble angels."

"Sounds absolutely heavenly." Her eyes closed, as if she were imagining every location, a smile playing at her lips.

Desire—and his lack of resistance—nearly gutted him. He'd seen that look once before, after they'd kissed.

His muscles clenched, his entire being ready to give and to take. To possess. For a moment, he let his mind revel in what could be. He would strip her, strip himself and give her everything they both wanted. Passion, pleasure. Connection.

They would stay in bed until she left for Rome.

As if his desire for her could be satiated in three months. Please. It was planted too deeply, the roots too strong. He had a sinking suspicion every touch would only make him want more of her.

In his mind, and this stolen moment, she would invite him to travel with her. He would say yes, and experience her delight as he escorted her to all his favorite places. He would make love to her on hilltops, verandas and, hell, against any flat surface he could find.

Longing joined desire, a double punch to his solar plexus. He popped his jaw, killing a groan. He had no business feeling this way, even in his fantasies, and he wouldn't stand for it. Returning to Italy without his girls would be too painful.

"Uh-oh." Ryanne *tsk-tsked*, watching him through hooded lids. "You're thinking about our kiss, aren't you?" She leaned toward him, as if she had a secret to impart. "Guess what. So am I."

In an instant, his shaft hardened beneath his fly. "I most certainly *wasn't* thinking about our kiss," he grated, only to admit, "Not anymore."

"Too bad." Folding her legs underneath her, she offered him an innocent smile. The seductress knew how to play demure. Noted. "We should probably discuss what happened between us...and how it's going to happen again."

He fisted the edge of the couch—*don't reach for her, don't you dare reach*—and swallowed the barbed lump in his throat. Another mistake. The barbs sliced and diced his stomach. "I don't want to be with you, so there's nothing more to say."

Hurt crossed her features, then suspicion. Her gaze roved over him, seeming to burn through his clothing. Satisfaction radiated from her. "Well, well. The man who says he never lies is lying. You're hard as a rock right now."

Not so demure anymore, was she. No other woman would dare point out the battering ram in his pants. "You're right, so let me rephrase. I don't want to want you." Not her, not anyone. Constance was no longer the last woman he'd kissed, but she *would* be the last woman he'd slept with.

Why are you so determined to get that vasectomy, then, hmm?

The dark *something* returned, only sharper.

"I like you, cowboy, and I like spending time with you." She traced her fingertip along the seam between his lips, then his scar, dragging a moan from his deepest depths. "I'm not looking for anything serious or long-term. I just—"

"Stop." *Please.* Already his mouth watered for another taste of her, and his hands itched to touch her every luscious inch. Need and want clawed at him, his newly awakened body *throbbing*. "You're a bar owner. The bane of the world."

He expected another flash of hurt, or a flinch. A curse or a slap. Instead, she offered him a gentle smile, as if she understood the worst of his pain, and said, "Conversation isn't going to help either of us. We need to act first and think later."

True to her word, she flattened her palm on his chest, the heat of her seeping through his shirt. Jude jumped to his feet. He had to leave. He had to leave *now*. Withstanding her charm had been difficult. Withstanding her touch would be impossible.

Silent now, he stalked to the door.

She called, "Don't walk away from this, Jude. Give me a chance to prove we're good together."

His step faltered, but he didn't look back and he didn't stop.

CHAPTER SEVEN

Perhaps I came on too strong?

Ryanne didn't see Jude for nine days. He failed to report for bouncer duty, always sending Daniel or Brock in his stead.

The first day, she almost called or texted a thousand times to reprimand him. *I'm paying for your services, not theirs!* Like a big girl—or superhero, yeah, definitely a superhero—she controlled herself and only texted him once, and only to return to their light, teasing relationship.

Want to go swimming with me, praised one? The pool at the Strawberry Inn is ready to go. I promise to wear my swimsuit... most of the time.

He never responded. No matter, though. She knew beyond a shadow of a doubt that her absentee employee monitored the bar from afar...and his cameras clocked her every move.

Bad, naughty boy. She decided to teach him a valuable lesson. *You can run from your desire, but you can't hide from it.*

And he did desire her. For him to stay away this long…yeah, he had to be tempted by her, and fear he couldn't resist.

A slow grin bloomed.

Throughout the week, Ryanne did everything in her power to vamp it up for Mr. Peeping Tom. At first, she was a little shy about it. Like she'd told Jude, she'd never tried to seduce a man before. For goodness' sake, she was still a virgin! But honestly? Over the years, she'd seen other women go all out, so she knew what to do—and soon she grew to love the chase. Also, she discovered she had a talent for it. Maybe because she wanted Jude in a way she'd never wanted another man—desperately, madly.

Day one was all about the hair flip. Slow, sensual and just like a shampoo commercial. Day two, she practiced her shimmy. Any time she had an opportunity to shake her butt, she shook her freaking butt. Day three, she focused on her cleavage. Or rather, she made certain *Jude* focused on her cleavage. She wore a low-cut top, her breasts pushed up until she was pretty sure she'd asphyxiate. Day four, she put her finger to her mouth at every opportunity. A lick here, a nibble there. Day five, she forgot to wear a bra. Oops!

A text came in early that evening.

Cowboy: Stop this!

Ryanne replied: Make me.

Cowboy: How can you be so at ease…so happy and carefree when your livelihood is at stake?

I choose to focus on the good. Give it a try, cowboy. You might like it.

Annnd once again he opted not to respond.

For day six, she decided to up her game, and wore a short

skirt but no panties. Walking to her office, when no one else stood in the hallway, she *accidentally* dropped a pen and bent down to pick it up.

Her phone buzzed, but she didn't check the text until she sat behind her desk, no cameras nearby.

Cowboy: I think you dropped something else.

A laugh bubbled from her. Grumpy Jude Laurent had just teased her sexually!

Soon after the exchange, Brock had stormed into her office and snapped, "Whatever you're doing to Jude, stop. He's miserable."

Miserable...without me? A girl could hope. "Sorry, but the blame for his misery can't be heaped on my amazing shoulders. I'm not doing anything wrong." Well, maybe the light torturing wasn't *right*, but it was for his own good!

"Exactly! You're not doing anything. So call him for phone sex. Text him nudes. I'm happy to be your photographer. Maybe wear nothing but a smile and a temporary tattoo—and definitely make sure I'm home when you do. Just get your ass in gear and do *something*. The past has a knife at Jude's throat, leaving him in a constant state of fight or flight. He either needs to be sliced, or released. Limbo sucks."

In other words, he'd gotten stuck in survival mode.

She wanted to help, but how?

When Dorothea first crushed on Daniel, she'd had to overcome his PTSD before a relationship could work. He'd worried about falling for her and then losing her, about being unstable, unable to sleep without having violent nightmares, and disappointing his family if their relationship tanked. Jude had served as an army ranger, too, and clearly suffered from his own form of PTSD, but Ryanne suspected his deepest worries and fears began and ended with the family he'd lost.

Realization slapped her upside the head: being with Jude, even for a little while, would require major time and energy—from Ryanne. Look how much she'd had to give already. Why pour so much of herself into a temporary fling?

Because…just because! Jude wasn't just a pretty face or hot body, though he certainly had both. Actually, no. He didn't have a pretty face; he had an interesting face, and it was sexy beyond imagining. He was smart, witty despite his sadness and fierce about protecting the people under his care. He had a good heart. No, a *great* heart. He deserved to be happy, dang it.

The rest of the day, he texted her on and off, but only ever to ask about Belle and the kittens. Brett had checked on the new family just this morning, and had given everyone a clean bill of health.

As Belle recovered from the birth of her litter, she revealed different nuances of her personality. The little darling was more mischievous than Ryanne had realized.

Eight a.m. was her favorite time to walk across Ryanne's face. Belle loved a certain brand of food, until Ryanne bought a new bag. Then she hated it. She wanted to play with the laptop, but only when Ryanne had to work. If she could knock something down, she knocked it down without hesitation. If the toppled items shattered, even better.

When Belle—or Hells Bells, as Ryanne had affectionately nicknamed her—was back to her pre-pregnancy self, she would destroy everything in her path, guaranteed, the way Jude was destroying Ryanne's peace of mind.

Days seven and eight, Jude opted to ignore her again, so she decided to disregard the cameras…and ended up agonizing about her cowboy. What if she'd miscalculated his desire for her? After all, he'd run away from her like a Victorian maiden afraid of ruining her rep. What if Brock had things wrong, and Jude was miserable because Ryanne had come on to him, and he didn't want to hurt her?

Or did he fight his attraction to her because a drunk driver killed his family, and Ryanne just happened to schlepp drinks?

I don't want to want you. You're a bar owner. The bane of the world.

Yeah. That. Somehow, she had to prove she was more than her job.

For Ryanne, no other man would do.

She took her place behind the bar, helping Sutter serve drinks to the steady influx of customers. It was time to resume Jude's torture. This was day nine.

Maybe she'd call him, strike up a sexy conversation filled with innuendos?

Old Coot approached, saying, "'Nother CockaMoon, please."

"How about a coffee?" The bar had been open only a few hours, but he'd already reached his limit.

"Add whiskey to that coffee and you've got a deal."

"A *splash* of whiskey." She checked the video on the baby monitor she kept with her at all times, allowing her to spy on Belle and her kittens. The little milk mongrels had finally opened their eyes. Soon they would be crawl-machines, causing nothing but trouble. And okay, okay, probably delight.

"Deal. Hey, are you gonna sing?"

"Not tonight, but maybe next week." Her emotions were too raw, her longing for Jude too great, and if anyone picked up on it—especially Jude himself—she would die of embarrassment.

"Well, *sheet*. You don't ever sing no more, which is a cryin' shame 'cause you got the pipes of an angel."

She poured *herself* a shot of whiskey, and quickly downed it. Rinse, repeat. The alcohol burned going down, but settled nicely in her stomach.

A text came in, and she checked her phone.

Cowboy: Stop drinking on the job.

Defiant, Ryanne poured another shot, saluted the nearest camera and drank.

"Miss Ryanne?" Coot asked, and swayed on his feet. "What about *my* whiskey?"

Whoa. He'd had three CockaMoons, and he was wasted? Worse, she'd agreed to give him more alcohol.

No way, no how.

She could guess what happened. He'd brought two marine buddies tonight, and had snuck sips of *their* moonshines.

She finished off the bottle of whiskey. "Sorry, Coot, but I just ran out."

He pouted.

His friends joined him, and they, too, were swaying. Both males were in their late sixties. One had a comb-over, while the other had a full head of silver hair. Deep-seated wrinkles spoke of time spent in the sun, an abundance of laughter and lives lived rather than sidelined.

"Who's the designated?" she asked, filling a mug with coffee.

The three shared a look, all *what's a designated driver?*

Lord save me. Two more coffees, coming up.

"Come on, Twigs. There's another bar about fifteen miles away." Silver ignored the steaming mug she offered him. "Let's go."

Twigs? There was no way she was letting any of these guys get behind the wheel of a car. "Hold up a sec, gentlemen." Ryanne leaned forward, her forearms pressed against the bar, allowing her biceps to smash her breasts together to create more noticeable cleavage. Though the men were not looking at her eyes, she batted her lashes. "Coot mentioned you served together in the military, and I'd love to hear the story behind the nickname Twigs."

Comb-over laughed with a sudden burst of glee. "Woo wee, that a doozy."

"My favorite kind of story," she said.

Another laugh. "See, one night enemy fire pinned in the boys and me. When we ran out of bullets, Coot decided to use twigs to make a crossbow."

Silver almost—almost!—cracked a smile.

"This I've got to see. Will ink pens work?" Genuinely intrigued, Ryanne handed him two of the pens she kept beside the cash register. "Because you're not leaving until you've proven your claim, *pollito*." Little chicken.

"All right." Coot nodded. "But I'm gonna need you to fetch me a rubber band, too. Unless you want me to cut the elastic out of my underwear?"

With a snort, Comb-over pounded him on the back. "Go ahead. Give her the show of a lifetime."

"And let Coot get more tips than me?" she said with a shake of her head. "No, thanks."

Coot guffawed and even blushed, making her smile. She'd had little to smile about since Jude had bailed, which rankled! Her happiness would never depend on a man. She would not become her mother. But…she couldn't deny how badly she missed Jude.

As she searched for the necessary rubber band as slowly as possible without rousing suspicion, the old guys drank their coffees and, thankfully, started to sober up. Steady again, Coot taught her how to make the crossbow, and danged if the weapon didn't actually work.

He bit off the lid of one of the pens, creating a groove at the end.

"Don't hurt yourself!" Ryanne exclaimed.

"As if." He wrapped the rubber band around the other pen and pulled, anchored the other pen in place, then aimed at a postcard behind her. The missile soared overhead and embedded in wood. "See? Easy as pie."

Wow! "You could do serious damage to someone's eye with one of those."

The threesome beamed with pride.

One of the bouncers Jude had handpicked—Bobby Beaudine, a guy she'd met in junior high—stalked across the dance floor, a scowl darkening his face. Her stomach twisted. Something was wrong. Again. Perhaps another visit from Blueberry Hill PD. A pack of officers had come by three times this week to check customer IDs. Among them each time? Her nemesis, Jim Rayburn.

The night Lyndie had ended up in the hospital with broken ribs, admitting her husband had done the damage, Jim called her a bitch and a liar and accused her of paying someone to rough her up in order to make Chief Carrington look bad.

Ryanne had been there, and refused to leave her friend's side. She'd asked Jim why in the world Lyndie would want to make her own husband look bad if he wasn't, in fact, bad, and his response had shocked her.

"Chief Carrington explained the situation. Lyndie wants a new car, but he doesn't have the money to buy it for her, so she decided to punish him."

Bastardo!

He wasn't even the worst of Ryanne's problems. Yesterday, a masked man disabled the cameras in her parking lot and slashed over twenty tires; she wished she had hired a night watchman, as Jude had ordered. It was just, she'd hoped to save a little cash by relying on the security cameras to pick up any problems. Though Jude was alerted and had arrived a mere ten minutes later, the damage was already done, the slasher gone.

The constant harassment had begun to affect her bottom line, fewer and fewer newcomers showing up. Her regulars remained constant, at least.

"To thank you for teaching me a trade secret skill," she said to Coot, "I'm going to give you and your friends a plate of my world famous nachos. Anyone have any dietary restrictions?"

"Dietary restrictions?" Comb-over rolled his eyes. "Do we look like sissies, young lady?"

"No, sir. You surely don't." She winked and walked away without revealing a hint of her inner turmoil. A difficult feat.

By the time she met Bobby at the end of the bar, tremors racked her. "What's wrong?"

"Officer Rayburn is back. He's alone this time, wearing plain clothes, and he's hiding in back, but I have a feeling he's hoping someone, anyone, will cause trouble. Also, there's a homeless guy at the door. He wanted in, but I told him to wait in the alley with the others, that you'd pass out food when we close. He said he has the information you asked for. That—I quote— a *flesh peddler* with blond hair just snuck into the bar through the back alley entrance."

Well, crap. The alley door had a brand-new coded lock, and only a handful of people knew the numerical sequence. Ryanne, Jude and the employees.

The homeless man had to be Loner. "If the homeless man wants in, you let him in, any time, every time," she said, scanning the area for the "flesh peddler." The blonde from the van, she assumed. Why sneak in? Unless Blondie meant to drum up business...while Jim was here?

If Jude was watching the camera feed as diligently as he watched Ryanne, he would have spotted *anyone* doing *anything* illegal and texted her the details.

Maybe Loner was mistaken.

"Are you sure?" Bobby asked. "There's no way the guy is going to spend money in here. He's filthy and he smells. Customers will be—"

"Let him in," she interjected with a firm, intractable tone. "Respectfully, of course. And quickly."

He looked at her as if she were a crazy person before dashing off to collect Loner, who he escorted to an empty bar stool.

Sweet Loner kept his gaze down. He wore the same clothes he'd worn last week, only the garments were dirtier, speckled with bits of grime and...dried blood?

Heart aching for him, she reached over and patted his hand. "Thank you for keeping me informed." Would he spend the night at the Strawberry Inn if she paid for the room? "I owe you."

"You don't owe me nothing, Miss Ryanne," he replied softly, still not looking up.

"I do, and I'm going to pay up. I'm giving the guys at the other end of the bar a plate of nachos, and you're getting one, too. No protests," she added when he shook his head. Later, she would mention the room at the inn.

"You shouldn't, and I should go before I hurt your business." His voice remained soft, barely audible over the thundering blast of music now spilling from the stage. The band had just started its first set of the evening.

"Stay. You're welcome here." Before Earl had met her mom or owned the bar, he'd been homeless. Briefly, but even twenty-four hours was too long. In his grief over his wife's death, he'd gotten involved in drugs, lost his job and his family, and ended up on the streets. The best man she'd ever known had once felt less than human—and he'd been treated that way, too. "You are *always* welcome here, Loner. I mean that."

He nodded reluctantly, then asked, "You going to sing tonight?"

"Not tonight."

"Oh." His features fell with disappointment.

"But one day soon," she added, "and I'll be sure to let you know beforehand, so you can make plans to be here."

On her way to the kitchen, she jotted down a mental To Do list. *Fetch the food, speak with Jim, find the flesh peddler.*

A few days ago, she'd bitten the bullet and hired a "snack specialist." And she used the word *specialist* lightly. In order to continue serving food to her patrons while she traveled, someone had to know how to prepare every item on her menu.

Only two women had applied. Caroline Mills from Strawberry Valley, who once worked in the big city as a masseuse, and a pretty young girl from Blueberry Hill, who had been far more qualified. Maybe too qualified?

Some of Jude's suspicious nature must have rubbed off on Ryanne, because she'd wondered why the girl would want to work at the Scratching Post when she should be opening up her own restaurant in town. So Ryanne hired Caroline instead. The sassy brunette spoke her mind but couldn't boil a cup of water. Still, she'd known Caroline most of her life.

While they'd never been close—Caroline's mom, Edna, had disapproved of Selma—they'd been friendly.

Caroline sat behind the counter, typing into her phone.

"Order up," Ryanne said.

"One sec. I've got to send this text to Pearl. She's in the middle of a crap storm."

Pearl Harris was Caroline's best friend, the owner of Secret Garden, and Lyndie's cousin. The two looked a lot alike. Both had strawberry blond hair and alabaster skin, though Pearl had freckles and Lyndie didn't.

"If you like your job, Caroline, you won't tell me *one sec* ever again. You'll put your phone down and fix two plates of nachos."

"Nachos?" Her new employee jumped to her feet and pocketed her phone, her cheeks flushing. "Slight problem. Hardly worth mentioning. But, uh, I kind of made burritos with the refried beans...and ate them. I'm sorry!"

Deep breath in, out. Ryanne soaked those beans overnight, and let them simmer for an entire day before frying them the next. The entire bag had cost less than three dollars, but customers spent ten on a single plate of nachos. Not that Coot or Loner would have paid; the food was a gift. But without beans, the nachos would suck, and there was no way Ryanne would serve sucky food.

Forget the time and money, though. Caroline had just cost her coveted customer satisfaction.

"Your actions have made a liar out of me," she grated. "I promised two of my favorite customers nachos."

"I'm sorry," Caroline repeated, cheeks reddening further. "Can we, I don't know, turn the bacon-wrapped fries into a *type* of nachos? Maybe top them with the hamburger meat and cheese sauce?"

Not a bad idea. "Yes, we can and we will. But if there's a next time…" Ryanne took a page from Jude's playbook, letting the threat hang in the air, unspoken.

The imagination could be far crueler than reality.

Now the color drained from Caroline's cheeks. She nodded. "Yes, ma'am. I understand."

Ma'am? Ma'am!

Never been so insulted in all my days.

They made the "nachos," and Ryanne left Caroline to deliver the plates to Loner—he'd stayed, as requested—and the former marines, so she could deal with Jim.

She searched the entire bar, but found no sign of him.

All right. She would deal with him later—

Her gaze landed on the prostitute who might or might not be here to cause legal trouble. Blondie had a scarf wrapped around her neck. Hiding a fresh bruise? Having lived with Lyndie and her dad, Ryanne knew all the tricks of batterer-batteree.

Her anger turned to pity. Poor Blondie.

What was the plan? Turn a trick or two, so Officer Rayburn could say he'd witnessed the crime?

Would Blondie claim Ryanne had approved of her trade, had even taken a cut of the profits?

Great!

Blondie sat at a table in back, partially hidden by shadows. She wasn't alone. Two guys who looked like they'd come from a frat party laughed at something she'd just said. Definite city boys. Ryanne recognized the type; they sometimes ventured into small towns to score "easy country chicks."

She did another search, this time on the lookout for Cigarette or Snake. Maybe they were waiting outside? Or maybe
they were with Jim? Either way, Jude would tell her to send a
bouncer over—that was what she paid them for, after all—and
lock herself in her office. No, thanks. Her bar, her problem. If
she needed backup, she had her trusty .44 sheathed in her boot.

Spine rigid, she marched to the table. Blondie spotted her
and gulped.

"Hey, guys." Ryanne faked a carefree grin. "You having a
good time?"

"Look who decided to stop by. Senorita bartender, the hottie with the body." The speaker had a piercing in both of his
brows—brows he wiggled in her direction as he reached out to
pat her butt. "We're having a better time now that you're here."

As she latched on to his wrist and held his arm as far away
from her body as possible, without wrenching her shoulder out
of its socket, her smile never faltered. "The first touch is free,
cabrón." Player. "The next one will cost you a finger." A threat
and a promise, rolled into one.

Grabby McGrabbyhands ran his tongue over his teeth. The
other guy snickered; his belt buckle had a display screen that
flashed the words *Do Me* in neon red letters.

Not in this lifetime.

Blondie watched the exchange with eyes as wide as saucers.

"Why don't you boys head to the bar." A statement, not a
question. She released Grabby to wave in the direction of the
bar in question. "Sutter, the guy with the knives tattooed on
his arms, has recently been promoted to manager. He will give
you both a mug of our infamous moonshine, no charge. Just use
tonight's magic phrase, 'No means no.'"

Her words were met with another snicker from Do Me and
a glare from Grabby.

Alienating her customers was foolish, but stress had removed
her filter.

"I'm happy where I am," Grabby said. "Why don't you be a good girl and fetch the mugs for us, hmm?"

A wave of heat suddenly rolled across her back, the scent of spiced rum filling her nose. A scent she knew well.

Her heart raced, goose bumps breaking out along her nape. Her breasts ached, her nipples beaded and her belly quivered. Need and heat pooled between her quaking legs.

Jude was back.

"You have five seconds to leave," he said, his voice soft but filled with pure menace. "When I get to six, I start whaling."

CHAPTER EIGHT

Jude should have stayed home.

He'd gotten the vasectomy eight days ago. After letting his doctor know he'd be having the surgery one way or another, he was worked in right away. Brock had driven him and lectured him about lifelong mistakes the entire time.

Jude would never regret it.

Of course, he would never again hold a son or daughter against his chest, either. Or watch with amazement as his children took their first steps. Or hear the sweetest word on God's green earth spoken with unfettered joy. *Daddy*.

But then, he would never attend a funeral for babies too young to have truly lived.

He ignored the hollow sensation in his chest. Carrie had sent the baby book as promised, but he'd cracked the spine only once. After a single peek at the photos glued to the inside cover, he'd cried so hard he'd vomited.

So, yeah, he'd made the right decision. Now he could be with a woman without worry.

A woman...or Ryanne?

Both. Neither. He didn't want to be with anyone, damn it! He'd gotten the vasectomy as a just in case.

So why had he counted the days until he would be cleared for sex?

With Ryanne's hair flipping, butt patting, full body shimmying, cleavage showing, finger licking, bra-and panty-forgetting ways, counting had been…hard. Very, very hard.

Day one, he'd found himself staring at a calendar. Day two, he'd nearly kicked his own ass himself for being so desperate. Day three, he'd come close to showing up at Ryanne's apartment, to hell with everything. Days four, five and six, frenzied frustration had set in. He'd paced, wondering when time had slowed to such a crawl.

Eventually, he'd broken down and texted her, asking how she could be so at ease while Dushku was causing trouble. Her response had stunned him. How could she focus on good things? And what did she consider good? Jude? She couldn't possibly.

Deep down, he'd begun to question whether or not she was a cosmic punishment for all of his misdeeds. *A man forever doomed to desire the woman he should despise.*

Had any man ever desired his punishment more?

Days seven and eight, he'd rationalized. Did he really need to hold out all eight days? What was the worst that would happen if, say, he had sex *now*? Still he'd resisted. If he opened the incisions, minute as they were, he would have to wait to have sex another few weeks.

Waited two and a half years. What's one more day?

Finally day nine arrived. Today. D-day—dick day. The small incisions had fully healed, and a record number of hard-ons said, *You're ready.*

He could have sex.

He could have Ryanne.

Damn her! She tempted him as no other. Two and a half years equaled thirty months. Or 130 weeks. Or 913 days. He thought he'd go the rest of his life sustained by memories of Constance, but Ryanne Wade had proven him wrong. Giving in to her appeal would be...

Delicious.

Wrong.

Perfect.

Now that the fear of impregnating a woman was gone, temptation proved stronger than ever. For Ryanne, only Ryanne. Was this his new normal? Growing hard every time he thought about her? Driven by unquenchable thirst and gnawing hunger?

Possessive instincts demanded he stand in front of her to shield her from the gaze of other men. *She's mine.*

This was crazy! His craving for her should have waned. They'd had no physical contact. Nor had he breathed in her sweet strawberry and cream scent. Or looked into her dark, magnetic eyes and drowned over and over again. Or listened to her phone-sex-operator voice and wished they were in bed, their limbs intertwined.

Maybe his craving for her *would* have waned if he hadn't watched her on camera, but Ryanne TV had become his favorite program. He hadn't been able to get enough, had had to know what happened next. It was more than her incomparable beauty and her innate sensuality. More than her attempt to drive him insane. She wasn't just kind, as he'd thought; she was generous, giving and compassionate. She genuinely loved her customers and remained as vigilant about their protection as their enjoyment. She had a secret code: ordering an *angel wing* alerted her and her staff that a patron felt unsafe and needed help.

Jude actually admired her, a bar owner. And though she flirted often and liberally, her dark eyes never turned dreamy, her lips never softened as if preparing for a kiss.

Soft and dreamy happened for him, no other.

"You won't be getting a free drink, but a ticket out of the

bar," he said softly, his gaze locked on the guy who'd dared to put his hand on Ryanne.

"Now wait just a—" Ryanne snapped her mouth closed, going quiet.

Did she hope to present a united front?

Smart girl.

Sexy girl.

"If they grabbed you, they'll grab others," he said, and smiled his coldest smile at the young men. "And if they protest their eviction, I'll happily wipe the floor with their faces."

The two sensed the truth of his words, jumped up and scattered, their bravado gone. Daniel and Brock, who'd followed Jude to the bar, made sure the pair found the exit with ease.

The prostitute stood, clearly hoping to abandon ship, as well.

"I wouldn't," he told her. This was their second meeting. He'd talked to her weeks ago, when he'd first learned of her occupation, before Dushku had known who, and what, Jude was.

He'd bought an hour of her time and spent every second questioning her. She'd answered nothing. Still he'd offered help. She'd refused him.

When he'd told Ryanne she couldn't help someone who wouldn't help herself, he'd meant it.

The girl gulped and eased back into her seat.

Jude was pretty sure Dushku had sent her here to cause trouble. "There's a plainclothes cop from Blueberry Hill hiding in a stall in the men's bathroom," he said to Ryanne. "I have a feeling our friend is supposed to lead those two boys inside and demand payment, allowing the officer to catch her in the act."

"Yeah, I had the same thought," Ryanne muttered.

He stepped around her, ignoring the pain in his knee, and held out a chair for her.

For one prolonged moment, their gazes held. A familiar blast of lust punched him in the gut. His cells caught fire, scorching his veins. The urge to yank her against his body overwhelmed him, worsening as she eased into the seat, the scent of strawberries and cream enveloping him.

Want her now, now, NOW, his body cried. *Give her to me.*

Must resist temptation.

Motions jerky, Jude claimed the only other chair and forced himself to focus on the blonde he'd watched break into the bar. Somehow she'd known the code to the lock, which meant Dushku knew the code to the lock. Really, only one way made sense. Dushku had put up cameras of his own, and observed as Ryanne or Jude plugged in the code.

The cameras must be hidden with expert precision. No matter. Jude would make sure they were found and destroyed before night's end.

Right now, he had to deal with the prostitute. The moment the door had opened for her, he'd raged, and would have trashed his cabin if he hadn't been in such a hurry to reach the bar.

He wasn't sure why Dushku had played his hand tonight, this way, rather than sending a man to break in early in the morning, when Ryanne was alone.

"If you've been forced into this line of work," Ryanne said to the blonde, "we'll help you escape."

There she went, putting someone else's problem above her own.

"I'm not being forced," was the whispered response. "I'm just... Let me go, okay?"

Determined to find out more about her, Jude asked, "What's your name?" Before, she'd told him "Bambee" with double ee's, pronounced "Bam-bay."

A terse pause, then, "Savannah."

The truth? "Savannah what?"

"It doesn't matter." She lifted her chin, her pretty blue eyes going blank. In an instant, she looked hardened by life, completely removed from the situation, a skill she'd most certainly learned in order to survive. A skill he, too, had learned and utilized on occasion. "I'll be whoever you want me to be. Sex slave? Sure thing, lover. Tie me up. Where there's a wallet, there's a way."

He wasn't going to play this game. "Where are your bodyguards?"

"At home, waiting for a call from the Blueberry Hill PD." Savannah smirked at him. "Why? Are you eager to lose a fight? Or are you hoping for a three-way?"

Ryanne snorted, surprising him. Always surprising him. "Sorry, *cariño*, but you don't know men as well as you think you do. One, Jude doesn't lose fights, and two, you and your guards couldn't handle him in the sack. He nearly burned me alive with a single kiss."

Her confidence surprised him further, thrilled him. The mention of their kiss…didn't fill him with guilt but lust.

Shame flashed in Savannah's expression, quickly gone, replaced by resolve. "Leave me alone and let me do my job. Okay? Please. Or better yet, sell your bar to Mr. Dushku and save us all a lot of trouble."

A commotion at the front door drew Jude's notice. The bouncers were denying entry to Dushku's men, the bodyguards Jude knew were named Anton and Dennis. He'd taken photos of the two, and told every employee to be on the lookout.

The men protested. Loudly.

The color leached from Savannah's cheeks. "I didn't text them, I swear."

"I think that honor belongs to Officer Jim Rayburn." Ryanne pointed to the undercover officer who'd been hiding in the bathroom; he'd finally come out to perch at the bar, a smirk on his ugly face.

Enough of this shit. Jude jumped to his feet and rushed for the door, shoving patrons out of his way. A chorus of "Hey" and "Watch out" trailed him, but he was too worked up to care.

"Ryanne told you not to come back here," he snarled when he reached his prey.

"You can tell your bitch—"

Jude threw a punch, taking both men by surprise, knocking one into the other. A fresh tide of fury exploded inside him. Words wouldn't help this situation. Obviously Dushku placed no stock in verbal warnings.

As the pair stumbled, Jude threw another punch, sending both men to the ground. He followed them down and whaled, his audience forgotten.

Time to send Dushku a message that could not be ignored or misinterpreted.

Strong arms wound around his waist and jerked him backward, and Jude got a bird's-eye view of his opponents. Anton had a broken nose. Dennis was missing a tooth and had a knot on his jaw. Blood splattered their faces, the crimson an obscene display of violence.

In a whoosh, the rest of the world came into focus. The music had stopped, Jude realized, and a large crowd had gathered around him.

As he panted, rage like acid in his chest, Brock held him against his chest. "The cop is here, remember?" his friend said. "The difference between assault and manslaughter is years, and people are starting to dig out their phones to record. You get arrested, and Ryanne will be alone. Thankfully Daniel made sure the cop couldn't see what you were doing, and I stopped you before anyone could press Record."

Can't afford to be arrested. Can't leave Ryanne unprotected.

Realizing he'd calmed, Brock released him and patted his shoulder. "The guy without a temper has a temper. Who knew?"

Savannah rushed past them to kneel beside Anton, fear replacing her earlier swagger. Did she think she would be blamed for what had happened tonight?

Next, Ryanne arrived and curved her fingers around Jude's

bicep. The touch, though innocent, only amped him up again. She was so soft and delicate...so breakable. She could be hurt so easily.

"What happened?" The off-duty cop—Rayburn—pushed his way through the crowd. When he spotted the injured men, he stiffened. His narrowed gaze found Jude. "Did you do this?"

"Nope. No way," someone called. The drunk named Coot. "Watched the men do the damage themselves, I did, and Jude there tried to help."

"Is that why his knuckles are bloody?" the cop snapped.

One after another, Strawberry Valley residents stepped forward.

"I saw it, too. Jude definitely tried to help. Repeatedly. That's why he's bloody."

"Yessiree. Someone give that boy a medal of honor. He helped them somsabitches something fierce."

Jude listened in shock. He had allies he hadn't known about. The town had already begun to feel like home, and this... This was just icing on the cake, making Strawberry Valley feel like a *happy* home.

If he were normal, he would have basked in that happiness. Instead, he fought it, proving just how messed up he really was. Happiness led to complacency, and complacency led to mistakes. Mistakes led to disaster.

In other words, mistakes led to Ryanne's bed.

"You're lying, all of you." Rayburn's narrowed gaze slipped through the crowd. "I know you're lying."

Might be time to bring the Strawberry Valley PD up to speed about what had been happening at the bar. Someone Jude could trust to do the right thing, even if that "thing" meant going against a fellow officer.

Probably time to pay an off-duty officer to sit at the bar as well, watching *everything.*

"Why don't you ask Anton and Dennis what happened? When

they wake up, of course." Jude offered Rayburn a cool smile. He would bet his savings the officer was working with the body-guards. Why not turn the tables?

Quietly, for Rayburn's ears only, Jude added, "Or I could check our security feed. We have cameras *everywhere*. If any-one did anything wrong tonight, like, say, hide in a bathroom, we'll know it."

Rayburn blustered for a moment. "No need to do that."

He called an ambulance, but Anton and Dennis awoke be-fore the paramedics arrived. The twosome glared daggers at Jude while lumbering to their feet, issuing a silent but clear warning: *you will pay*. But rather than admit a one-legged man had beaten both their asses—pride more important than orders?—they ex-onerated Jude, claiming he'd done nothing wrong. Then they stumbled out of the bar, Savannah fast on their heels.

Jude called her name, and though she paused in the doorway, she kept her back to him. "Stay here," he said. "Let us help you."

Her shoulders drew in, as if her muscles had contracted spon-taneously. She shook her head and whispered, "You can't help me without consequences you're not ready to face, so don't even try," before marching onward.

Ryanne took a step toward her, stopped and wiped away a tear before it could fall. "You're right. We can't help those who won't help themselves." Trembling, radiating sadness, she turned to face him. "Why don't you go up to my apartment and clean up?"

He nodded and headed upstairs, but didn't immediately wash up. First he spent a little time with the kittens. Staying away from the fur balls had been almost as difficult as staying away from Ryanne. And oh, hell, had they grown.

Belle and the babies had completely overtaken the sunroom. Clean towels and blankets covered the tile floor. Belle reclined in the cradle of a windowpane while most of her brood slept on a pallet, one cutie piled on top of the other. Only two kittens were awake, and they tried to stand but failed. Their eyes were open, but their ears hadn't yet unfolded.

Behind him, the door opened and closed with a snap. Ryanne approached him, two shirts in hand.

Her gaze roved over him, leaving a trail of fire in its wake. "Your shirt is ruined. Take it off."

The command nearly undid him. He hesitated but ultimately reached for the hem and eased the material overhead.

A sharp intake of her breath made the fire crackling inside him burn hotter. Sensual smoke filled his mind.

"Oh, wow," she said, and fanned her cheeks. "Good news for you, bad news for me. I have a replacement shirt for you. Well, maybe this is bad news for you, too. I keep a few clothing items in my office as a 'just in case' for customers. You get to pick between a double XL T-shirt with a bikini printed on the front, or a small T-shirt with the Scratching Post's logo."

"Give me the bikini," he said, doing his best to ignore her admiration of him.

"Is it because your muscles will rip the small one like you're the Hulk? Good thinking." With a smile she tried unsuccessfully to hide, she tossed the requested garment in his direction. He caught it and yanked the material on, then pitched the ruined one in a trash can.

She pressed her lips together. "Who knew you'd look so good in a bikini?"

"I did. Brock and Daniel, too."

Now she snorted. "If you tell me you've worn a real bikini, I will absolutely, one hundred percent, insist on seeing pictures."

"I lost a bet and as my punishment, I had to sport a two-piece G-string on the beach. I threatened to kill anyone who took pictures—so of course both Brock and Daniel have hundreds."

She giggled and the happiness returned. This time, he basked.

"I need to borrow your laptop so I can change the code to every lock in the building," he said. "And if it's okay, I'll work up here tonight to keep an eye on the security cameras." No way he would be leaving her side any time soon. As added protection, he would text his friends and have them begin the search for whatever cameras Dushku had placed inside and out.

"Sure thing." She walked over and gently placed her hand in his. Her skin was soft and warm—it was life. Slowly, giving him time to protest, she lifted his fingers to press his knuckles against her cheek. "I'm glad you're okay, cowboy."

He closed his eyes tight, knowing he needed to man up and fight her allure. But she felt so good. The *connection* to her felt good, and damn it, he was tired, so tired, of fighting.

"I thought you were covered in their blood, but some of it belongs to you." Her voice was infinitely tender. "You injured yourself in an effort to defend me."

A vine of thorns seemed to sprout inside his throat. "I've had worse." He peered at her again; somehow, she'd become even more beautiful. "Do you want to talk about what happened down there?"

Maintaining her hold on him, she shrugged. "You took out the trash. What more is there to say?"

Blink, blink. "I took out the trash *violently*. You should fire me, or at least order me to control my temper." Why wasn't she frightened of him? Of Dushku? This was only the beginning. This battle marked a turning point for the war. "Tell me to apologize to Dushku. Something! Now he's going to up his game. No more minor inconveniences and veiled threats, guaranteed. He'll come after you, as well as the bar."

She arched a brow. "First, an apology wouldn't do either of us any good. Not with a man like him. Second, why will he come after me, but not you?"

Hurting Ryanne *was* the best way to strike at Jude.

Dushku had done his homework. He knew Jude had failed to protect his family from a drunk driver. If Jude failed to protect Ryanne as well, his guilt and mental anguish would never be appeased.

When he remained silent, she sighed. "I'll deal with whatever comes. Thanks to you, I've taken a boatload of precautions."

I'll deal, she'd said. Not *we'll deal*. Thinking you're ready for anything and actually being ready for anything were two different animals. "Your trip to Rome," he grated. "Leave now. Today. *I'll* deal with Dushku and the bar." There was no line he wouldn't cross, no task too dark.

"Jude, honey, there's something you need to know about me. I'll never do what a man commands. Call it a quirk. And even if you were to wise up and ask nicely, my answer would remain no." Silky locks danced at her temples as she shook her head. "I'll be staying here, with you."

"Why?"

"Because."

"Because why?" he insisted.

"Because!" She raised her chin, the picture of feminine stubbornness and sexy beyond belief, as strong and brave as the soldiers he'd once served with. Her grip on his hand tightened. "I don't run from my problems."

The way he'd been running from his desire for her?

A muscle twitched in his jaw. He wanted her, yes, but he also refused to insult his wife's memory by being with someone who sold drinks to potential motorists, even someone like Ryanne, who fought against drunk driving to the best of her ability.

He bit the inside of his cheek. Ryanne wasn't looking for anything serious, so his lack of attachment and attention afterward wouldn't hurt her.

Perhaps they were perfect for each other?

Damn it, the lines between black and white had begun to blur. This woman had well and truly screwed up his head. Well, screwed up his head *more*.

If he took her profession out of the equation, he would already be on her, lost in the throes. Sex could be basic, primal, but it didn't have to mean anything.

If it didn't mean anything to him, would it—he—insult Constance's memory more or less?

Worry about the particulars later. He needed to work Ryanne out of his system *now.* Until he did, she would obsess him.

Rationalizing never helped anyone.

Afterward, he would feel guilt, he was sure of it, but he could deal. He would have to deal, because he didn't have the strength to walk away. Not tonight.

I'll never give up.

I'm sorry, Constance. I'm alive, and I'm going to live.

"You should go downstairs," he said, his tone flat. "And you should hurry."

Her eyes widened—with arousal or fear, he wasn't sure which. Still she clung to his hand. "Or what?"

Arousal. Definitely arousal. Her breathless voice shattered what remained of his control.

"Or you're going to get fucked."

CHAPTER NINE

Ryanne reeled, unable to catch her breath. Jude was in her apartment. Gorgeous Jude, who looked a little shell-shocked by the intensity of his desire for her. Sexy Jude, whose gaze remained locked on her as he removed the shirt she'd given him.

As if she could leave now. The man was cut with muscle, enhanced by sinew. In the light, his bronzed skin appeared dusted with gold, and his plethora of tattoos only added to his masculine appeal. A heart in the center of his chest, pierced by five different swords. On the handle of each sword was a name. Constance. Bailey. Hailey. Daniel. Brock.

Constance, his wife. Bailey and Hailey, his twin daughters.

Ryanne's own heart squeezed. Over and under Jude's tattoo was a detailed countryside, complete with trees and winding roads.

She wondered if the countryside reminded him of home while overseas?

Her gaze followed the trail of golden hair leading from his navel to the waist of his jeans, and she groan-gasped. An odd sound. An *animal* sound. He was already hard, and his erection appeared to be as thick as her wrist, so long the glistening tip stretched above the waist of his jeans.

Something had changed for—and in—him. He hadn't made a token offer. *You're going to get fucked.* He'd meant what he'd said. She could have him. Here and now.

Things had just gotten real.

She'd gone two and a half years without a man…not that she'd ever had one. So. Scratch that. She'd gone two and a half years without kissing or making out or even hand-holding, and now she was dealing with a sexual god.

"I notice you're not running for the door." Jude's voice was low and husky now, setting her blood on fire.

"The only place I'm willing to run to is my bedroom." She walked away, but didn't actually stop in her bedroom. Instead, she ended up in the bathroom.

As she'd hoped, Jude followed.

The large space had counters made of Italian marble, mirrors framed by hand-hammered brass from Scotland and wall tiles that created a beautiful Spanish mosaic of colorful flowers. Beside the Victorian claw-foot tub was a shower stall complete with steamer, rainspout and her beloved bench. That stall was her most extravagant indulgence.

Jude took hold of her hand, as if he couldn't bear to be parted from her. For some reason, the new position was far from comforting. It said: *you are well and truly trapped.*

He was the spider, and she was the fly.

Shivers danced through her as he clasped her by the waist and anchored her against him.

"Jude." So hot, so hard.

He swooped in, thrusting his tongue into her mouth. He conquered. He owned. The heat of him scorched her, the stubble of his beard abrading her cheeks, sending tingles straight to her core.

He kissed her slow, and he kissed her fast. He kissed her as if he had no tomorrow. As if his dying wish had just been granted: Ryanne, in his arms. Warm honey seemed to flow through her, softening her—hardening him further. His muscles bunched underneath her hands, and the shaft he rubbed between her legs began to cover more and more ground.

Desire fogged her head, and for a moment, she felt as if she were in an X-rated dream. Her nails curled into his shoulders, scraped through his hair. He nipped at her bottom lip—approval. When he cupped her breasts, her nipples puckered for him; they wanted his approval, too.

A growl rose from him, and it was pure auditory porn. More shivers danced through her.

About to reach a point of no return...

Okay, she really needed to think this through, maybe weigh the pros and cons. Sex with Jude, here and now, during work hours. A delicious idea. But. Despite all her flirting, she hadn't learned much about the man. Plus, his low opinion of her hadn't really changed.

Did she trust him not to brag to others about nailing her? Strangely enough, yes. Could she trust him not to cheat on—

Whoa. How could he cheat? They hadn't agreed to any sort of commitment, only momentary pleasure.

"Ryanne?" He lifted his head, his warm breath fanning over the lower part of her face. "A second ago, you were eating my face. Now you're stiff and unresponsive. What's wrong?"

Head check! Ryanne jolted from his arms and took a step back, remaining out of reaching distance. "I can't do this. You don't even like me."

His brow furrowed, his eyelids slitting. "I like you. I just don't like what you make me feel."

"Or maybe you like what I make you feel too much?" The question lashed from her.

He glowered but nodded. "Maybe. Probably. Definitely."

His gaze remained steady as he unclasped the button on his fly. "How do *I* make *you* feel?"

Heated breath snagged in her lungs, and goose bumps rose, sensitizing her skin. The tingles returned. Between her legs, she ached. "You make me feel—" *Sexy. Powerful but vulnerable. As if I'm standing in the middle of a storm but also flying.* "—curious. How can you like me? I'm the bane of the world, remember?"

Let's say they hooked up. Would they cuddle afterward, or would he rush out the door, hating himself for what he'd done? Or worse, would he blame her for any perceived weakness in his resolve to avoid her? And like she'd told him, she wasn't in the market for a long-term boyfriend. As a teenager, she'd made a vow. She would not become her mother, and her happiness would never depend on a man.

"Will this be a one-time thing?" she asked.

Jude toyed with the top of his zipper, teasing her with what she wanted but couldn't have. "I like you," he repeated. "Don't make me try to explain why or how. I just do. And yes, this will be a one-time thing."

He'd just told her everything she'd wanted to hear, so why did she experience a flicker of disappointment?

Didn't matter. Two of her worries had been alleviated. He liked her, and they both wanted a one-night stand. Did anything more need to be discussed?

Well, yes. One thing.

Mimicking him, proving she could tease, too, she played with the button on her jeans. "You want me, then you can have me. But first you've got to compliment me. Just one. Tell me something you like about me."

As he watched her, riveted by the movements of her fingers, his pupils swallowed his irises. What he didn't do—lower his zipper. *Imbécil!*

"I'd rather touch you," he said, "and show you the *parts of you* I like best."

Tempting, so very tempting. "Compliment me, then," she insisted.

A vein pulsed in his temple, but he grated, "I'm glad I met you."

"That's not a compliment but a statement of fact." He'd taught her the difference. "*Why* are you glad you met me?"

"You—" A low growl rumbled in his chest. "Damn you, you brought me back to life."

She gasped.

He yanked her into his embrace, crashing his lips into hers.

Swept up in a searing wave of desire, she poured herself into the kiss, tasting him, devouring him, becoming addicted all over again. Their panting breaths blended, his every inhalation marked by her every exhalation, until they survived on the other's air. This couldn't be real. Men only kissed women like this in books and movies.

Anticipation collided with a sense of contentment. There was no man so danged perfect.

Really going to do this?

Yes. Yes! She was going to do it. She was going to give herself to Jude.

Should she tell him she was—technically—a virgin?

"Take off your shirt," he commanded.

New shivers of excitement danced through her. No, she wouldn't tell him. What if he stopped?

She obeyed his command, revealing her lacy pink bra. Cool air kissed her bared flesh, and yet, inside she continued to heat up, her bones seeming to crackle with flames. Her tremors worsened, remaining on her feet a chore. Every fiber of her being longed to stretch out on the floor, his weight pressed against her as her hips cradled his.

"Jude." She flattened her palms on his chest, his nipples hard little points against her skin.

His gaze perused her, aggression radiating from him. "I want more of you. Take off your pants."

He was so fierce, so male, she only wanted more of him, too. But she forced herself to say, "And deprive myself of a show? No way, cowboy. It's your turn to take something off."

She would give, but she would also take.

Without a moment of hesitation, he kicked off his boots. *Zzzzzip.* Down went his zipper. He lowered his jeans, kicked the denim out of the way, and her heart nearly beat its way out of her chest. He wore white boxer briefs, his leanly muscled physique the sexiest she'd ever seen.

"Now it's your turn," he rasped. "Show me *everything.*"

Nibbling on her bottom lip, she toed off her shoes and slipped out of her jeans, revealing pink lace panties to match her bra.

He stopped breathing, his chest no longer rising and falling. "You..."

"Yes?"

"You are exquisite. And I'm...not." He motioned to the sleeve art covering the prosthesis. It had an American flag.

She'd done a little research and knew the metal appendage had a custom-made socket, a pylon and a foot. A pin on the end allowed the liner to lock into the socket.

"This is me," he added. "Broken."

"You aren't broken. You are perfect." And that wasn't a lie.

Maybe he believed her, maybe he didn't. He wouldn't meet her gaze as he said, "Give me a few minutes to shower off the blood. Alone," he said, his voice now hard and uncompromising. "I have to remove the prosthesis. It's sensitive to moisture, and I'd rather not have you—"

"Whoa. You want me to leave when things are just getting good? I don't think you understand. Water is going to drip down your muscles, and that's a show I'd pay to see." Did he think the missing limb bothered her? Or was the strong man embarrassed to reveal a weakness, and didn't want her to see him hop or crawl into the shower? Was he too proud to ask her for help? Well, too bad. "I'm going to shower with you and that's that."

When she twined her fingers with his, he stared at her, silent, for a long while. But he didn't protest.

"Want to know a secret?" she asked. "I've been attracted to you since the second I laid eyes on you. Getting to know you has only made me want you more."

"Ryanne," he croaked.

"Want to know another secret?"

Appearing dazed, he nodded.

She rose to her tiptoes and whispered, "I'm eager to get my hands on you."

He jolted, as if punched. Then he drew in a heavy breath, slowly released it. "You're killing me. You know that, right?"

A slow smile bloomed. "The French call an orgasm *la petite mort*. The little death. I hope I kill you well."

Another jolt. With his free hand, he reached inside the stall to turn the knobs. Water streamed from multiple spouts, and in seconds, sultry steam thickened the air. He didn't enter, but released her to sit on the vanity stool, where he removed the covering from his prosthesis, pushed the lock on the ankle and removed the device from his leg. Next he rolled a thicker piece of cloth from his leg, and she saw his injury for the first time. Scars circled the top while the bottom appeared red and irritated.

Compassion squeezed at her. How much pain did he endure on a daily basis?

Though she longed to kneel before him, massage his knotted muscles and kiss every single scar, she remained in place, several feet away, and played with the straps of her bra. "My turn."

As soon as his gaze lifted and glued to her, she undid the center clasp. He sucked in a breath, tense as he waited for the straps to fall down her arms. A smile bloomed at the corners of her mouth as she held the bra's cups to her breasts, forcing the material to remain in place.

"How badly do you want to see my breasts?" she asked.

"*Badly.* Now stop teasing." He scowled at her one moment, and devoured her with his eyes the next. "I want to see every inch of the body I've been craving."

He craves *me…*

Shivers slid down her spine, a groan of need nearly wrenched from her. "You mean this body?" She let the bra fall to the floor at long last. The kiss of cool air. Her nipples puckered, begging for his attention, ignored too long, now desperate.

He sucked in a breath and gripped his knees. To stop himself from reaching for her?

"How about these? Should I get rid of them?" Empowered by his admiration, Ryanne hooked her fingers in the waist of her panties and pushed the lace down one inch…two…only to pause and draw the material back up. "Perhaps I'll leave them on."

He swiped his tongue over his teeth. "If you were the enemy, Wade, and this were an interrogation technique, I'd be screwed."

"Oh, cowboy. You're going to be screwed, anyway."

He barked out a laugh, a genuine laugh of amusement that made up for his use of her last name—his desire for distance—but he sobered quickly and patted the corners of his mouth, as if smiling felt weird, the necessary muscles somehow atrophied. His next scowl proved darker, and yet a sense of triumph flooded her. *I'm getting to him.*

His gaze darted to the door. Was he thinking about getting the heck out of Dodge?

Message received. He might be ready for sex, but he wanted nothing to do with humor.

"I'm far overdressed in these panties, don't you think?" She played with the sides of the material.

"Agreed." He grated, "Remove them."

Oh, wow, he was so deliciously forceful! Her nipples swelled, and her belly quivered, but she strove to remain calm. The moment she gave into the fever in her blood, the sooner this encounter would be over.

"I will…after you remove your underwear."

In a blink, the briefs were gone, a massive erection stretching from between his legs. The moisture in her mouth dried.

"Now the panties," he croaked.

"Not quite yet." The moment she was nude, the conversation would cease. "We have a few medical matters to discuss first."

He inclined his head in a stiff nod.

"I'm clean, and I'm on the pill. Haven't missed a single dose." She'd gotten a prescription not too long ago, when she'd decided to end her moratorium on men. "Are you?"

"I'm clean, but I'm not on the pill."

Now a laugh barked from her. Maybe he *was* ready for humor. "I'd still like you to wear a condom, okay?" Just to be extra safe.

He nodded, an odd look on his face. "I'd planned to, anyway. I recently had a vasectomy, but sperm remains active for a few months afterward. Anyway. Soon I won't be able to have kids."

What the what! A vasectomy? He really didn't want to have more kids, did he.

One day Ryanne would love to have a family of her own, but only after her travels.

He bent down to dig a condom out of the pocket of his jeans. The fact that he'd come prepared…

Deep down, he'd known his resistance would crumble.

With a slow smile, she wiggled her hips. "I've decided you're going to have to ask nicely if you want the panties gone, *mi hombre hermoso.*"

"My handsome man?" The epitome of wicked desire, he stood with stunning grace despite his handicap, reached out and ripped the sides of the panties. "I think we both know you don't want a nice man, Wade. You want me."

Another use of her last name. When would he learn? Distance

sucked. His gaze more than made up for the slip, however, devouring her, desire a palpable, sizzling current in the air.

No more playing. Ryanne wanted her man.

Unwilling to wait for an invitation, she moved to his side and wrapped her arm around his waist, becoming a crutch to help him walk. He stiffened but offered no rebuke, and together they entered the shower, hot water raining over them both.

After washing the blood from his hands, Jude eased on to the bench and set the condom aside, out of the spray of water.

For several long, protracted seconds, she was paralyzed by an immense surge of uncertainty. This was so new to her. Should she climb onto his lap or remain on her feet? What did he like?

They'd kissed twice, but they hadn't gone on a single date. Actually, all they'd ever done was insult each other. Now they planned to have no-strings sex?

Was foreplay even necessary, considering two and a half years had passed without satisfaction? Despite the pain of being deflowered—was that even the right term?—Ryanne suspected she would come the second he thrust inside her.

"Nervous?" he asked, his features softening. "Don't be. I'm just like every other man."

No. No, he wasn't. He was more. He was better. "I haven't… I mean, I'm not…" Ugh! *Get the first time over with. Next time you can—*

News flash: there wouldn't be a next time.

Right. Despite another surge of disappointment, she waved her hand through the air.

"You're not what?" he asked.

"Just tell me what you want me to do, and I'll do it."

"You want a play-by-play or a few surprises?"

"Play-by-play." Pretty please.

"All right. Straddle me, and I'll kiss you. I'll touch every inch of you, every perfect curve and hollow, and when you beg me to fill you, I'll thrust so deep inside you that you'll feel me tomorrow every time you take a step."

Just like that. Frenzied need overtook her. She straddled him, saying, "Thank you for the play-by-play, but now it's time to follow through, cowboy."

CHAPTER TEN

Skin to skin. Heat to heat. Wet to wetter.

Incredible hardness pressed against the softest part of Ryanne, electrified nerve endings purring with approval. She was careful to brace her weight on her knees rather than Jude's thighs, unwilling to exert undue pressure on him. With only one foot, he might have trouble remaining balanced.

"What are you waiting for?" She glided the tip of her nose over his. "I've done my part. Kiss me." *Kiss me, and never stop.*

"Needed a second to enjoy the view." He tangled his hands in her hair, fisted the strands and drew her down slowly, so slowly, an eternity seeming to pass as the space between them shrank... more...a little more...

His mouth pressed against hers, the contact exquisite.

Eager, she opened for him. His taste tantalized her senses, and reminded her of his scent; spiced rum on her tongue, black magic in her veins. He dueled her for control. The moment she ceded, he rewarded her by yanking her ever closer. Her nipples smashed against his chest, her next breath sparking a glorious friction. Her blood like gasoline, the breath after that starting a fire. Inside and out, she burned.

This is sex, just sex. Pleasure for the sake of pleasure, and a long overdue rite of passage. An experience she yearned to have, her desire for Jude Laurent eclipsing…everything.

Just sex, just sex, just sex.

"I swear you're the human equivalent of strawberry shortcake." He sounded accusatory—and drunk with passion.

"Well, *you* are the human equivalent of honey, and I want you drizzled all over me."

The words drew a moan from him, and with the next sweep of his tongue, the tone of the kiss changed. From exploratory to explosive, the fierceness of his desire feeding hers. Pressure built. They ate at each other, ravenous. The more he gave, the more she wanted, until she feared her appetite would never be satisfied.

With one hand on each side of her spine, he trailed his fingers down, down, then he cupped her bottom and *moved* her. Her aching core met his erection, and she groaned with delight.

"Jude." Biting the cord of his neck, she anchored her nails in his shoulders. "Don't stop."

The sounds he made…like music. An erotic melody. Or a spell meant to enthrall her for all eternity.

As his fingers continued their journey, sliding to her stomach, she began to pant.

"You were made for this, weren't you, shortcake." He cupped her breasts, dragged his thumbs over her aching nipples.

Shortcake. What an adorable nickname! Tears of happiness burned her eyes. Tears Jude might not understand. He might think she was too attached to him, or too heavily invested in their relationship, and leave. At least the water continued raining over her, steam filling the stall, masking the embarrassing development.

With his chest flush against hers, she felt surrounded, every inch of her body sensitized. She glanced down, luxuriating in the sight of his hands—those big, bruised hands—kneading her breasts.

Those hands had beaten two trained fighters senseless earlier, had cracked bone, busted cartilage and ripped out enamel with ease, and yet, those same hands now handled her as if she were priceless china.

Trembling, she grazed her nails over the stubble on his jaw. Jude's inhalations grew as labored as her own, the tattoo on his chest heaving, the inked heart seeming to beat, the swords sliding in and out of the chambers.

Their eyes met, and for the first time, she thought she saw scorching possessiveness in those navy blues. Shivers didn't dance, they consumed.

"Look at you," he said. "Eyes wild, lips red and puffy, even a little pouty. Breasts spilling from my hands. Hips rocking. You are passion incarnate."

She was?

She must be. She couldn't stop grinding against his erection. "I want you." Now. "Foreplay isn't necessary."

"Maybe not for you." He ran his tongue along her collarbone, earning a hiss.

When her thundering heartbeat slowed, she nipped at his lower lip. "Are you telling me you're having trouble with your equipment?" Reaching between their bodies, she wrapped her fingers around the base of his shaft. "Because I would beg to differ."

Peering into her eyes, he pinched her nipples. "There's nothing wrong with my equipment. I like the sounds you make when I touch you, the way you move and touch me, and I don't want it to end."

New shivers, an avalanche of want and need. "Tomorrow we can—" The words *do it all over again* died inside her mouth. *One time. Just sex. No regrets.* "Take your time, then, cowboy. I'll just sit here and enjoy the ride. But don't go too slowly, or

I'll have to shift your gear." As she spoke, she stroked his length up…down…up.

"Problem." He flexed in her grip. "If I speed, I'll get ticketed."

"Don't worry. You can pay my tickets with kisses…and give me a thorough body cavity search."

He chuckled, then nipped the lobe of her ear. After kissing the curve of her jaw, he licked a drop of water from her chin. "You truly enjoy making me squirm, don't you?"

"I do, honey buns. I really do." Nuzzling his cheek, she added in a breathy voice, "But I think I'll enjoy squirming *on you* even more."

With a growl, he bent his head and sucked her nipple into his mouth, his golden hair tickling her collarbone as his masterful tongue flicked one of the swollen buds. His control had snapped.

A ragged cry left her, pleasure stringing her body as tight as a bow; any second now, her arrow would fly.

Want him to come with *me.*

Her grip tightened on his shaft. To her surprise and delight, she realized her fingers weren't even close to meeting. He was too danged big.

Angling her wrist, she rubbed the tip of his erection against the drenched, aching center of her body. Her other hand combed through the silken strands of his hair. When he began to suck on her nipple harder, increasing the pressure, she dug her nails into his scalp to hold his head in place.

"You're right. I think foreplay is overrated. You ready for me?" No other warning as he thrust a finger deep inside her.

She gasped…moaned. The pleasure!

Adding a second finger, he stretched her, but not enough. Not nearly enough. Her body was starved for his, and he'd merely given her an appetizer. She needed the entire meal. "More. Now."

He wedged a third finger inside her, and she cried out, teetering at the brink of agony or ecstasy, she wasn't sure which.

"You're wet. Tight," he said, a sharp edge to his tone.

Too tight? Did he suspect the truth?

Unwilling to risk ruining the moment, she released him to rip open the condom wrapper. Tremors prevented her from successfully rolling the latex down his length. Or maybe it was her inexperience.

Need this man. Need him now.

If only she'd practiced rolling one on a vibrator, or a banana, she might have earned a gold star for her first real-life application.

Finally, exasperation got the better of her. "Help me."

He claimed the latex and expertly secured the thing in place.

"Thank goodness. Snug as a bug in a rug," she said. "Let's do this!"

He snorted and yet tension emanated from him, delighting and emboldening her all over again. She affected him as powerfully as he affected her. And, as much as he hadn't wanted to want her, he couldn't resist her.

His hands settled on her hips and squeezed firmly enough to bruise, but he wasn't hurting her on purpose, she knew. He was swept up in a maddened storm; they both were.

Tremors worsening, she rose to her knees, positioned him for entry…and paused.

"After this," she whispered, "there's no going back."

"It's already too late," he intoned.

Their gazes met once again. The water had turned his sandy hair dark. Skin stretched taut over broad cheekbones, and his chiseled jaw remained clenched. His lips were open, swollen from her kisses, yet his scar appeared softer.

Yes, it was far too late to go back.

She forced her body to accept him by sliding down…down his length. Despite the potency of her arousal, despite being soaked and desperate to climax, despite the fingers he'd worked inside her, his entry burned, and she had to grit her teeth.

Though she hadn't yet reached his base, stars winked in her line of vision. Bad news: the pain was almost too much. Good news: pleasure hadn't abandoned her; it waited at the periphery, ready to return front and center at any moment. She just had to hold on.

"Need a sec," she said between panting breaths. Sweat beaded on her forehead. "It'll get better." Absolutely. No question. No doubt.

Okay, one question: *right?*

"Shouldn't have stopped the foreplay," he said, and cursed, clearly blaming himself for her predicament.

"Not your fault. I've never—" She pressed her lips together, saying no more.

His eyes widened...with horror? "Never what, Ryanne?"

Jude battled the most savage need of his life. Here, now, the past had no chance to intrude. He was too primed for release, Ryanne, tighter than a fist, slick and molten, and so hot he would swear she burned through the latex.

The urge to slam in and out of her bombarded him. Gnashing his molars, agonized by the pressure building inside him, he called on his training. Skills he'd developed when his commanding officer deprived him of food and sleep, or beat the shit out of him in order to better hone his reflexes. *Take a licking, keep on ticking.*

Ryanne needed tenderness, not brutality.

"Never what, Ryanne?" he insisted, afraid to move as suspicions danced through his head.

She was in obvious pain. His possession hurt her physically, as if she were...or had been...

There was just no way. No way in hell this was her first time. She was in her midtwenties. Sensual. Confident. She wouldn't gift her virginity to a piece of shit like him. A man who would walk away as soon as he'd come.

A broken man.

He remembered his first time with Constance. She'd had a boyfriend before him, and the guy had taken her virginity. At the time, the knowledge had disappointed Jude, even though he'd had no right to complain. He'd slept around so much he'd put present-day Brock to shame. The poorest boy in town, unwanted by his parents and siblings, had sought attention and affection from the girls at school. But in the end, Constance's past hadn't mattered. Nor had his. Together, they'd learned the difference between sex and making love.

Still, the irony wasn't lost on him. He'd wanted Constance to be a virgin. She hadn't been. He'd wanted, *needed*, Ryanne to be experienced. She might not be.

For a heartbeat of time, he wasn't sure he'd change anything, his possessive instincts roaring with satisfaction.

Not just broken but twisted, too.

"You know I haven't been on a date in two and a half years," she said. The strain began to fade from her features, and she arched her back, sending him inside her another inch, wrenching an agonized groan from him.

Right. Two and a half years. The same as him. Almost as if they were fated to—

Nothing.

He reached between their bodies and circled his thumb where she must throb. Her hips jerked and she cried out, her inner walls clenching around his shaft. He gnashed his molars *harder*.

He hurt physically, but he didn't stop. As he continued to rub her little bundle of nerves, he fit his lips around her nipple and sucked. Sucked and nipped and licked and flicked with his tongue and then sucked again. Little mewls left her as she writhed against him.

Can't get enough of her.

Falling...

No! Hell, no.

"That's so...so good," she praised.

Only wanton excitement in her tone now. No, she hadn't been a virgin. And he was relieved about that. Of course he was relieved. This hookup wasn't special or meaningful just because Ryanne was the first woman he'd slept with since the death of his wife.

We're scratching an itch, that's all. People do this every day.

But shit. Shit! Guilt flared. For nine years, he'd been true to Constance. Today, his devotion had crumbled, a single wrong deed negating every right one. No longer could he say his wife was the last woman he'd slept with.

His heart stuttered against his ribs, and he stilled, only able to concentrate on his breathing. What the hell had he done?

Ryanne stilled, as well. Her gaze searched his face before she lifted her delicate hands to frame his face. Tracing the rise of his cheekbones with her thumbs, she pulled him closer, kissed the corner of his eye, the corner of his mouth.

"I bet you've never been so clean while being so dirty," she said.

A soft chuckle.

"You are so beautiful," she continued. "So wonderfully rough and tough. I've wanted you for so long. I tried so hard to resist you, but you, Jude Laurent, are irresistible."

The sweetness of her words yanked him out of his head and back into the moment.

"Irresistible, huh? Woman, you just described yourself." *She's more than an itch, and you know it. Why continue to deny the obvious?*

Didn't matter. Deny it again he did. No one had a stronger will than Jude, and in matters of the heart, he would not break or even bend, no matter how great the temptation, or how incredibly perfect. He'd faced and overcome worse obstacles, and he would not falter now. He could have this—have her—accepting a brief moment of happiness, then moving on.

"You ready for me to thrust?" Jude gave her nipple a little nip, then licked away the sting.

"I am. Are you?" Her nails scoured his back, stinging deliciously. *"Pelea contigo mismo mañana. Dame lo qui quire hoy."*

Spanish, spoken in her pleasure-roughened voice...hell, yeah. But the words themselves were what pushed him over the edge. He'd spent time in Mexico and easily translated: *Fight yourself tomorrow. Give me what I want today.*

She knew him well enough to decipher his mood. Must have watched him as intently as he'd watched her.

Precious woman.

Dangerous woman.

"I wish you could feel what I feel. You aren't just irresistible, you are incredible," he whispered straight into her ear.

As she shivered, he licked the delicate shell with multiple piercings. He kissed his way down the slope of her neck—and bit the tendon running through her shoulder, the way she'd done to him.

Just. Like. That. She shouted his name, her inner walls clenching on his shaft as she came. She shuddered against him, and her nipples stroked his chest, making him mindless with desire. Remaining in place nearly killed him, but he did it. For her.

Only when she sagged against him, fully sated, did he press his back against the tiles, arch his hips and drive himself deeper inside her, burying every inch of his erection into her scorching heat.

She gasped his name.

He would have given anything to stand and press her against the tiles, using the wall as leverage while he hammered into her, her beautiful legs wrapped around his waist, squeezing him.

"Jude... I can't...it's...you're... Argh! Why did you stop?" She beat her little fists against his chest.

"Am I hurting you? You're so incredibly tight."

"Well, you're so incredibly big. Am *I* hurting *you*?"

He chuckled. "You're killing me with pleasure."

"You're welcome." She nipped his chin. "And no, you're not hurting me. I'm all systems go, so please, *go.*"

He bit the inside of his cheek to stop another chuckle. Then he shook his head in wonder. How did she do it? How did she make him want to laugh at the most inopportune times? Or hell, how did she make him want to laugh *at all*?

Slowly, so slowly, he pumped in and out of her, propelled to new heights of pleasure every single time. Heights he'd never before known, as if he'd been a boy before and had finally become a man. As if Ryanne Wade had been made for him and him alone. As if he'd lived in the dark long enough and had finally stepped into the light.

Ryanne moaned in sync with his thrusts, only maddening him further. Somehow, she'd become his entire world. He knew nothing and no one else, *wanted* nothing and no one else. She was a tempest without equal, a storm he couldn't escape, and she'd swept him. He would happily drown in her.

He lifted his head to peer deep into her eyes, eyes that were at half-mast as water droplets caught in her lashes. Passion flushed her flawless skin, adding a rosy undertone. The pulse at the base of her neck raced. Plump breasts bounced with his movements, dusky nipples puckering under his gaze. This woman…

In, out. "Ryanne." Her name slipped past his lips. Her body was a masterpiece. Perfect curves, elegant spine, legs for miles. A flat belly that led to a thin landing strip of dark hair. In, out. In, out. "I'm so close."

"Want you closer. Faster."

He grabbed her hips and slammed her down on his lap while lifting himself up, hitting her deep, deep inside. She erupted a second time, screaming his name, her inner walls once again clenching and unclenching on his length.

Unable to prolong the inevitable any longer, he followed her over the edge, coming…coming…coming so hard…

It was the most powerful orgasm of his life.

Strength poured from him and into her, leaving his muscles lax. The same must have happened to her. She collapsed on him, her head resting on his shoulder. Their hearts raced together but out of sync, the pitter-patter of water heralding the return of reality.

He fought it, wanting to enjoy the moment, to hold her and never let go, but reality was as determined to have him as he'd been to have Ryanne.

"We finally had fun together," she rasped. "And, honey buns, it was amazing."

"Yes." Yes, it was, but without the haze of desire to cloud his thoughts, he was left with nothing but raw disappointment—in himself. He should feel satisfied, but empty, guilt ridden rather than blissful. He'd given all his lasts to Ryanne, saved nothing for Constance; but he was far from satisfied and guilt ridden. He already craved another go-round, desperate to claim everything Ryanne was willing to give him.

Now he knew her sweetness, her softness…the breathy sounds she made when she came.

Now he needed more.

He'd gone years without the touch of a woman, despising even the thought of casual contact. Now he couldn't touch this one enough, wanting his hands on every inch of her at once.

How was he supposed to ignore her appeal tomorrow? How was he supposed to live without another hit of bliss?

"This was a mistake, Wade," he croaked.

She stiffened. "Wade again. Well. It's a good thing we decided on a one-night stand, isn't it?"

He'd hurt her. Damn it, that hadn't been his intention. His head, normally a mess, was screwed up more than usual. "I've got to go." He placed her on her feet and removed the condom. Seeing the tattered remains caused the heat to drain from his face. "You had one job, only one, and you failed."

"Hey! I'm not—"

"Not you. The rubber. It broke. Damn it, I knew the water would be a problem." Barely able to breathe, he demanded, "The timing is wrong, yeah?"

"Only if you mean I'm ovulating right now," she snapped. "I had a period two weeks ago, making today the perfect starter-family day. Except I'm on the pill, and you had a vasectomy, remember?"

"Sperm remains active for months after the procedure, *remember*?" He scrubbed a hand down his face. "But you're on the pill, and I'll have to trust its effectiveness. Listen, don't leave the bar tonight or tomorrow, all right. In fact, just stay up here. You'll make yourself an easy target for Dushku. Let Sutter take over again. That's why you promoted him to manager." He stood and lumbered from the stall.

"Jude. Don't—"

"No. We both agreed. This was it, a one-time thing. No need to discuss it to death."

"Did we agree you could treat me like garbage afterward, because I don't recall that particular detail."

Fighting guilt, he toweled off and reattached his prosthesis, then pulled on his jeans, his shoes, and tied the laces.

"I'm sorry," he finally told her. "I'll... I'm gonna go."

"What happened to watching the security feed on my laptop?"

"I'm sorry," he repeated. "I'll watch it from home." Not trusting himself to say more, he strode from the bathroom, the apartment...never looking back.

CHAPTER ELEVEN

What the heck had just happened?

One minute Ryanne was basking in postcoital rapture with Jude, the next she was alone. No longer a virgin. Now a scorned lover.

Over the years, she'd imagined her first afterglow a dozen different ways. A little cuddling, a lot of laughter and talking. Drinking a glass of champagne, perhaps taking a bubble bath together to ease her sore muscles. Lying under the stars, quiet. None of her fantasies had ended with her alone in her shower, aching body and soul.

For however long, she sat on the bench, her knees drawn up to her chest. *Wasted my virginity on a hit and run.* Jude Laurent had to be one of the worst decisions she'd ever made. But then, she hadn't based her decision on logic but feeling.

Just like Momma.

I'm an idiot!

And Jude, well, Jude was a jerk. How dare he abandon her the second he climaxed? How dare he not realize he'd made a huge mistake and come running back to beg for a second chance she would absolutely refuse to give him?

Hot water poured over her, steam enveloping her, almost convincing her the entire encounter had been a dream. Almost.

Despite her inexperience, she knew she'd rocked Jude's world. The look of sublime pleasure on his face every time he'd thrust inside her had affected her on a cellular level. He'd found the ultimate satisfaction in her arms. And then he'd ruined everything by running away.

This is me. Broken.

Considering his unwavering devotion to his wife, it was a miracle he'd come near Ryanne at all. Maybe she was being too hard on him? After everything that had just happened, he had to be emotionally vulnerable, or worse, emotionally destroyed.

Let's face it, Ryanne had been a wrecking ball to two and a half years of intentional celibacy. To him, up had to be down and down had to be up.

Why else would he have gotten a vasectomy? It was such an extreme action—one born of desperation? Because he'd known he couldn't resist Ryanne much longer, and he'd feared getting her pregnant?

Oh, how she would love to shake some sense into the man! He'd screwed up his future, all to appease his fears in the present. What if he fell in love again? What if he remarried and his new wife wanted kids?

Ryanne's nails cut into the pad of her palms.

He wasn't her concern. More than that, she wasn't in the market for love or marriage, and didn't have time for a relationship. But dang him! He wasn't the only one who was emotionally vulnerable right now.

Perched on his lap, spent, great waves of affection had washed over her. The man had taken her virginity—popped her cherry. Whatever you called it, the act would fuel her dreams forever. Jude's attention to her details had set the standard of measure for any other man she invited into her bed.

I don't want another man. I want him. Jude Laurent. Just one more time…

Too bad, so sad, mi querida.

From now on, Jude was off-limits. They would be friends without benefits. But…since they *were* friends, she should probably prove she had no hard feelings about his deplorable finish today. A few minor—cough major cough—renovations in the bathroom, like a grab bar to offer him support in the shower, one on the wall beside the claw-foot tub and one next to the toilet, should do the trick. Just in case he got into another fight and had to come upstairs to shower off the blood, of course.

Would the additions embarrass the proud Jude?

Did it matter? Friends helped each other out, even when it hurt.

Speaking of hurt, Ryanne stuffed what remained of hers into a box, locked it and shoved it in a hidden corner. Out of sight, out of mind. Feeling more upbeat, she shut off the water, dried off, and dressed in a T-shirt and pajama pants, and tried not to wince at the tenderness between her legs. All the while, her skin tingled, as if to tell her *I remember what it's like to be naked and damp, Jude's hands on me. Give me more of that.*

Hello, new addiction.

If only Jude hadn't played her body quite so masterfully. He'd known when to touch and when to retreat, when to slow down and speed up. Part of her wished the experience had sucked, so she could write him off and move on without a problem.

She *hmphed.* Like his expertise really mattered. After a two-and-a-half-year hormonal deep freeze, a strong gust of wind could have given her an orgasm.

Am I bitter? I sound bitter.

No hard feelings, remember?

Oops. Some of her hurt had escaped the lockbox. *Stuff. Click. Shove.*

Time to focus on those support bars.

Taking a page from Coot's book, Ryanne watched instructional videos to figure out what she needed to buy and what she needed to do. Then she called her girls to invite them over and, okay, okay, request supplies.

"You understand me better than anyone," she said to Belle, then pulled her wet hair into a ponytail and gave her sweetie a pet behind the ears. "Your man loved and left you, too. Hopefully mine hasn't left me in the same condition, though."

The odds were astronomical. His little swimmers would have to overcome the formation of scar tissue caused by his vasectomy, as well as her birth control.

Belle gave her a look that said, *You should be so lucky, silly hooman.*

"Easy for you to say. You have the cutest babies in the world." She kissed a little black-and-white beauty, her mind straying to Jude's twins. Had the girls looked like him or his wife? Had they been happy children or somber? Princesses or tomboys?

You couldn't live without experiencing loss, a fact as old as time. Death was hereditary. Ryanne comforted herself with the knowledge that she would one day see Earl in heaven. Because yes, she was going up, not down, and no one could stop her! Did Jude find comfort the same way?

Well, comforted or not, the pain of losing a child, much less two at the same time, *plus* a significant other...the pain had to be unbearable.

Any lingering bitterness over his abrupt departure faded. So. Ryanne wouldn't castigate him by word or deed. She would act like the friend she'd agreed to be...even though she wanted to be more.

There. She'd admitted the truth. She might not have time for a relationship, but she wanted one—with him. He'd introduced her to the height of sensual pleasure, and once hadn't been enough.

He'd ruined her for other men.

She would give anything to be the girl he smiled at, laughed with, and slept with every night. The one he craved under him, as well as beside him.

By the time her friends knocked on her door, Ryanne had convinced herself to make another play for Jude.

If he rejected her, he rejected her. She would let him go, content in the knowledge she'd done everything in her power to win his affections. No regrets.

Also, she would force herself to remain open to possibilities—with other men. No more shutting down her desires.

"You owe me big-time." Dorothea placed a large box on the kitchen counter. "I had to promise Mr. Mumford a free night at the inn just to open the hardware store after hours. The last time he stayed, he partied like a rock star. He literally swung from the chandelier."

Lyndie, who'd come in directly behind Dorothea, covered her mouth to muffle a giggle. Ryanne smiled. She loved seeing her former stepsister at ease. For too long, happiness had seemed unattainable.

After their parents had married and Ryanne had realized the abuse poor Lyndie had suffered most of her young life, she'd done everything in her power to protect the dear one, to offer hope amid a hopeless situation.

One day we'll run away together and travel the world!

Lyndie had sniffled. *I don't want to travel the world. I want to fight back and win.*

They'd taken a self-defense class together, at least for a little while. Only Ryanne had finished the course. Lyndie had a panic attack and dropped out.

To Selma's credit, she'd tried to help, too, staying with Mr. Scott far longer than she'd wanted, doing everything she could to convince Mr. Scott to let her adopt Lyndie, at the same time planning to divorce him after the papers were signed so she could fight him for custody. Somehow, he'd learned of her intentions, and *he'd* divorced *her.*

That's when Selma finally filed a report about the abuse. Of course, gossip had quickly claimed the "man-eater" only wanted revenge, that she'd lied in order to hurt the first man to tire of her.

Ryanne still battled intense guilt over her inability to shield the fragile Lyndie from further harm. But every time her friend displayed some semblance of joy, like tonight, that regret eased a little bit.

"If Mr. Mumford swings from the chandelier again," she told Dorothea, "I promise I'll cheer you on while you buy a new one."

This time, Lyndie's giggles burst forth, as if a dam had crumbled.

"Actually," Dorothea said, wagging a finger at Ryanne, "you'll reward me by coming to my engagement party in two weeks. It's on a Saturday night, your busiest time, but I need you there. My mother decided I absolutely *had* to have one. She wants to let the town know Spotty Dotty has finally landed a man."

"Hey. That man is lucky to have you," Lyndie said.

Saturday was her busiest night, and her employees were always overworked, but they *could* handle the crush and rush without her. And she could wear a slinky dress. As one of Daniel's closest friends, Jude would certainly have to attend the party; he'd never seen her dressed to slay-and-lay.

Anticipation washed through her, leaving goose bumps on her skin. "Yes. I'll be there."

"Why are you installing grab bars in your apartment, anyway?" As soon as the question left her, Lyndie gasped, her amber eyes aglow. "Are you and Jude officially dating?"

"Oh, oh, are you?" Clapping, Dorothea jumped up and down. "Did he pass the Ten Commitments?"

The Ten Commitments. A list of requirements they'd come

up with in high school, for anyone hoping to date Ryanne, Dorothea or Lyndie.

A boy shalt not:

1) Lie to anyone, ever, not even to flatter.

2) Cheat with so much as a look.

3) Steal even when desperate.

4) Harm others in any way.

5) Make excuses for bad behavior.

He shalt:

6) Compliment when merited.

7) Help when needed.

8) Treat others with kindness, always.

9) Consult you when making big decisions.

10) Do his best, not just what's good enough.

Well, no wonder Ryanne had so often demanded Jude give her compliments. The list must have been in the back of her mind the entire time.

You brought me back to life.

She shivered now as she'd shivered then. Sexier words had never been spoken.

Her friends didn't know it, but a few years ago she'd added an eleventh commitment. *He shalt want me for more than sex.* Plenty of boys had asked her out pre-romance ban, but only a rare few hadn't tried to get into her pants at moment one, because *of course* she'd had to be as easy as her mother.

Somehow, she'd convinced herself to settle for sex, only sex, from Jude.

Worth it?

"I'm not dating Jude." She wouldn't mention the orgasms he'd just given her. Dorothea and Lyndie would demand a complete retelling, and there would be no hiding the remnants of her emotional vulnerability. "He's working for me, and I'm kind, caring and magnanimous."

"And *super* humble," Dorothea said with a laugh.

"Such a giver." A sly gleam in her eyes, Lyndie waved a hand in her direction. "And a receiver of hickeys."

What! She had a hickey? Ryanne resisted the urge to cover her neck. "You're lying. I do *not* have a poor girl's tramp stamp on my neck."

The sly gleam got slyer. "I know. I was seeing if *you* knew."

Rat! "Lyndie, dear, would you be a lamb and tell us all about your feelings for Brock? Inquiring minds want to know."

Twin pink circles colored Lyndie's cheeks. "Okay. Enough conversation. We're here to work, so let's get to it."

Do not laugh. "You sure?"

In a rare show of spirit, Lyndie flipped her off. "What do you think?"

Ryanne snorted and carried the box her friend had brought into the bathroom—where she promptly panicked. Had she left any sexual reminders out in the open?

Wet towels—in the hamper.

His clothes—gone.

The condom and its wrapper—in the trash can.

She released a relieved sigh.

"You know," Dorothea said, digging through the box's contents and withdrawing a power drill. "Jude was prowling around the bar, looking particularly stylish in a bikini shirt, and snapping at everyone with a drink in hand."

He hadn't gone home? Maybe later she could watch him on the security feed, the way he'd watched her...

"His hair was wet, just like yours." Dorothea wiggled her dark brows. "Doesn't that strike you as an odd coincidence?"

Poo on a stick! She had no leverage against Dorothea. "All right, detectives. You busted me. I took a shower with Jude. We conserved a little water, had a little sex. Happy now? Great. Help me install the bars."

Both women squealed.

"I knew it!" Lyndie said.

"Daniel owes me five dollars." Dorothea fist pumped the air. "But I'm going to do him a solid and accept payment in the form of orgasms."

Ryanne planted her fists on her hips. "You guys took bets on when I'd sleep with Jude?"

"Of course. Did I mention I won?"

"Wow. I need better friends."

"Too bad. You're stuck with us." Lyndie bumped her shoulder. "So. Tell us everything. Was your first time everything you dreamed? How do you feel? Any different?"

Unable to cut off her dreamy sigh, Ryanne pressed her palm over her heart. "It was better than I'd imagined. *He* was better. I'm still amazed. And probably in shock. Yeah, definitely in shock. I'm pretty sure I left my body, soared through the heavens, danced with angels, came back to my body and died of acute, intense pleasure, only to have my heart shocked back to life."

Her friends shared a look before bursting into laughter.

"So you and Jude are a couple now?" Dorothea asked, her tone happy, as if she was certain of a positive response.

Ryanne pasted a false smile on her face. No one was going to blame Jude for her desire for a relationship, rather than a one-night stand. "Nope. We had tonight, that's all." At least until she convinced him otherwise.

"Oh, Ryanne. I'm so sorry," Lyndie said. "I know you were secretly hoping for more."

Knows me better than I know myself.

Dorothea patted her shoulder, her big baby blues filled with remorse. "If you want more, you'll get more. He'll be back."

Ryanne gulped. Maybe. Hopefully. "Come on. We've got a lot to do, and not a lot of time to do it."

They hopped to, but neither Lyndie nor Dorothea were used to such late hours and soon began to drag.

"Hey. When you came through the door, did Jude ask what

was in the box?" Ryanne asked, then bit her lower lip. "Did you tell him? Show him? How did he react?"

"At first he said nothing, just waved us in without even glancing at the box." Dorothea yawned. "Then he chased us down and demanded to know what was going on."

Lyndie lifted her chin. "You would have been proud. I told him we'd be sure to tell him all about it the moment the information was his business."

Dang, Ryanne loved these girls. "Okay, maybe I'll keep you guys as friends."

They worked another hour. Or rather, Ryanne worked. Dorothea fell asleep with her head resting on the edge of the tub while Lyndie fell asleep on the floor in a fetal position.

When a soft knock sounded at the front door, neither woman reacted. Ryanne left them where they were and checked the monitor Jude had installed last week.

Daniel and Brock stood in the hall, no sign of the third amigo.

Was she ready to face his best friends? Didn't matter. The best friends in question wouldn't leave until they'd collected their women.

Deep breath in…out… Ryanne disengaged the lock and turned the knob.

"Your better halves are asleep in my bathroom," she said.

"I have no better half," Brock replied.

Both men marched inside, only to remain in the foyer, watching her. And oh, wow, they were handsome. Not Jude handsome, of course. No one was. But these two exuded strength and animalistic sex appeal. While Daniel possessed good ole boy charm, Brock had bad-to-the-bone down to a T.

T is for tempting.

If anyone could coax Lyndie out of her self-imposed exile, it was Brock. The woman only left her house to teach at Strawberry Valley Elementary School, and to visit with Ryanne.

Brock winked at her before holding up one hand. "Go ahead. High-five me."

Though she was confused, she obeyed. "Why are we acting like teenagers?"

"You rode Jude out of misery, straight into agony." With a smile, he offered her a thumbs-up. "Well done."

She nearly choked on her tongue. "He told you?"

Brock turned his widening smile to Daniel, revealing a bright red smudge of lipstick on his neck. Dang him. Boning girls in the bar bathroom had become his specialty.

Now that Jude had given celibacy the stinky boot, would he follow in his friend's footsteps?

A curse brewed in the back of her throat.

Okay, so. She was a wee bit possessive and jealous. If Jude turned to another woman, she would kinda sorta want to take a crowbar to the girl's face—then Jude's junk—even though he'd made no commitment to Ryanne.

It would have been nice to know she'd feel this way about her first lover before doing the deed, but no matter. She could deal.

"Don't take this the wrong way," Daniel said, shifting from one boot to the other, "but he told us he'd made a colossal mistake."

There was a right way to take that?

"We worked out the details on our own," he added. "His wet hair…your wet hair. Plus, the last time I saw such a haunted look in his eyes, he'd just lost his family. But don't worry. We're not going to ask for details. Are we, Brock?"

His buddy hiked his shoulders, clearly disappointed. "You take the fun out of funniest."

"So Jude is now in agony?" she demanded.

"You misunderstood." Brock linked his fingers with hers, startling her. "This is a very good thing. He's going to be in a dark place for a while, but that's okay. In the dark, he might finally see the light."

A beautiful sentiment, but what, exactly, constituted light for Jude? So far, Ryanne had only seemed to add to his troubles.

"What are your intentions toward my boy, anyway?" Brock's head canted to the side, his attention on her deepening. "He doesn't give his goods and services away lightly. Well, not anymore."

"Brock." Daniel sighed.

"What?" Brock stretched out his arms, acting like the last sane man in a universe gone to hell. "She needs to know the kind of man she's dealing with. And to Jude, sex equals commitment."

Her heart fluttered wildly. *Sex means something to Jude.*

He waited for me, as I waited for him. We were…fated for each other? No, no. I don't believe in fate. Do I?

"Look, I'm going to ask him out," she said. "If he says no, that's it. I'm done. If he says yes…" She shrugged, feigning nonchalance.

Please, Jude, say yes.

CHAPTER TWELVE

For the next two weeks, Jude was militant about security at the Scratching Post, both physically and digitally.

Dushku's cameras were found and removed; they'd been expertly hidden as Jude had suspected. Every afternoon he dozed lightly in Ryanne's office, a laptop resting on his chest, the screen split to reveal feed from four different areas: three inside the bar, one outside. Every night he worked alongside the bouncers and did his best to avoid Ryanne.

She texted him twice. First she asked him out on a date.

I had fun with you, and would love to see you again. Interested?

He turned her down—and called himself a thousand kinds of fool.

She took his refusal in stride, all *no big deal*, then asked how they could help Savannah.

He'd messed up, hadn't he? He should have said yes.

No, hell, no. He'd done the right thing.

Sex was supposed to end his unhealthy obsession with her

porn-star body, whip-sharp mind and wicked smile. Distance was supposed to eject her from his mind.

No luck. He thought about her more often, and craved her harder, so much harder.

What they'd done in that shower…it had been more than a joining of two bodies. It had been the melding of souls.

Shit. He'd sunk so low, he now waxed poetic?

Well, why not? Since he'd lost his family, he'd had only one purpose: to mourn. Yet, as he'd slid into Ryanne's hot, tight depths, he'd exalted, forgetting the past, focusing on the moment…and all the moments awaiting him in the future.

Damn this! Did he even deserve a future with Ryanne? He was slime. Worse than slime. He'd cheated on his wife's memory.

She's gone. I did nothing wrong.

If that were true, why did guilt plague him? Why had the sweetest pleasure led to the bitterest regret? Why had he gone from the highest of highs to the lowest of lows?

For his own good, he should stop the happy shower time play-by-play running through his mind on constant refresh and pretend it had never happened. He should stay away from Ryanne.

Impossible. Dushku would retaliate for what Jude had done to Anton and Dennis. The only questions were *when* and *how.* Of course, Jude could guess when—soon.

The stress had left him feeling as if his skin were stretched over his bones tight enough to rip. The few times he'd left the bar, he'd gone home only to shower and change.

He'd tried to distract himself with a background check on Savannah. Though he'd used every trick he knew, he'd had abysmal results. Was Savannah her real name? What was her last name? Where was she from? Men like Martin Dushku often shipped in girls from other countries, then hid their passports and visas so they had nowhere else to go. Was Savannah born overseas? If she had an accent, she masked it well.

Yesterday, Jude asked one of the men who worked in the

Oklahoma City offices of LPH Protection to drive down and buy a night with Savannah in order to whisk her to safety, get her a new ID and hide her for good, but Dushku had stopped bringing her around.

So many obstacles. Jude had no idea what to do.

Chatter interrupted his thoughts. Daniel's engagement party had kicked off about an hour ago, but Jude had spent every minute checking his phone, watching—what else—camera feed at the Scratching Post.

Now his attention snagged on the reason for the chatter: Ryanne had arrived.

She stood just outside the tent that had been erected outside the Strawberry Inn, golden light shimmering over her, paying absolute tribute to the deep bronze of her skin. Her dark hair hung in decadent waves, the sides anchored back by two crimson ribbons.

Exquisite.

She wore a skintight black dress with a hem that ended just below her knees. A red bow cinched around her waist. A bow he imagined undoing with his teeth. Four-inch crimson heels only added to her appeal.

She was, without a doubt, the sexiest woman in the world. He knew this for fact. For the military, he'd traveled the world.

Breath caught in his throat when her dark gaze met his. His body vibrated with awareness, and his blood heated. *Touch her...*

Breath seemed to catch in her throat as well, but she quickly turned her attention to Brock, who stood beside him. She smiled and waved, and Brock gave her a thumbs-up.

Jude bit his tongue until he tasted blood. *Going to pretend I don't exist? I'll teach her—*

Nothing.

The entire town had shown up for the party, filling the tent. Twinkling lights hung overhead, interspersed with colored flowers and paper lanterns. A sign that read Gettin' Hitched had been nailed to a white picket fence. Tables were set up in every corner, offering an array of casseroles made by local favorite Brook Lynn Dillon.

In one of the dishes, Brook Lynn had mixed peanut butter, chocolate, bananas and bits of bacon. Jude refused to sample the oddity...only to decide he wasn't leaving until he'd gotten the recipe. Ryanne took a bite and moaned with pleasure.

I know that moan. I've caused it. The fire in his blood reignited.

Reignited? Ha! The flames had never died.

Look at me, shortcake. Want me the way I want you.

The endearment floored him, but the thought shamed him. He'd abandoned this woman immediately after sleeping with her, then pushed her away when she was kind enough to offer him a second chance, and now he expected her to cater to his every whim?

Again she turned her attention elsewhere, exactly what he deserved.

Had she thought of him at all? Did she regret sleeping with him?

Had he taken her virginity?

More and more the question troubled him. Just as soon as he would convince himself she'd been with other men, doubts would surface. Jude's initial entry had startled and pained her, and she'd been so tight, barely able to fit him inside.

Did he *want* to be her first?

Not even a little, he thought, even as a sense of possessiveness grabbed him by the neck and placed him in an undeniable chokehold.

She's mine. No one else is allowed to touch what's mine.

If he'd taken her virginity and abandoned her afterward...

She was someone's daughter. If his girls had lived, and a man had ever treated them so shabbily, Jude would have been killing mad.

I should be shot.

No, I should apologize. He should sweep Ryanne into his arms and carry her to a room in the inn.

Sweat beaded on his forehead and trickled over his spine.

What would Constance say about the man he'd become? A man who'd treated his lover as if she were disposable, unimportant. A man so afraid of impregnating another woman he'd paid a doctor to cut into his testicles.

"Staring like a creeper," Brock said, placing a cup of strawberry lemonade into Jude's hand. "Not cool, dude."

"I've never cared about being cool." He drained half the cup, the coldness of the drink registering more than the sweetness, soothing his dry throat...but not for long.

A tall man approached Ryanne. He exuded the kind of arrogance usually found on Wall Street. Jude's grip tightened on the cup, crinkling the plastic.

Smiling with her customary flirtatiousness, Ryanne shook Wall Street's hand.

Rage burned inside of Jude, driving out every other emotion, leaving no room for guilt, remorse or tenderness. Clearly, she'd taken his words to heart. Sex without commitment. One time only. She was free to enrapture any other man she desired.

"Good. I see you've noticed someone is making a move on your girl," Brock said.

"She's not my girl." *Believe it. Accept it.* "She's my boss."

Wall Street hadn't been to the bar since Jude had started working there. If ever he showed up, he'd leave with a black eye and broken nose.

His dark hair was cut and styled to perfection, and his face shaved. The suit he wore had no wrinkles while Jude's button-down had seen better days—several years ago. No doubt Wall Street had both of his legs, and he could make love to a woman while standing up.

"Do you know what's sad?" Brock's pale green eyes were wary as he confiscated Jude's drink. "I'm a total screw up, it's all I've got going for me, and yet you've somehow turned me into the voice of reason. It hurts, man."

Guilt flared. He'd worried his friend. "Not true." Brock had an off-the-charts IQ, a bank account the size of Texas thanks to a trust left by his grandfather, and a heart of solid gold. "Your problem is your zipper. It's open for business 24/7. The little guy's tired and needs a vacation."

Smiling a genuine smile, Brock flipped him off.

Daniel and his father, Virgil Porter, stepped from the crowd to join them. Through pictures, Jude knew Virgil had once been as tall and strong as his son. Today, not so much. Age had left its mark. His shoulders were slumped, his bones fragile. He'd lost a good deal of hair and had more wrinkles than a discarded prom dress.

Most days, Virgil was grumpier than Jude. But underneath his bluster was a deep love for his son, his town and, really, everyone he met. Which struck Jude as odd. Virgil lost his wife in an accident years ago and had struggled to recover.

Was recovery even possible?

Virgil patted him on the shoulder, saying, "Came to tell you that you're looking at our sweet little Ryanne Wade the way a serial killer looks at his next victim. You planning on locking her in your basement, boy? Maybe wearing her skin?"

"Told you," Brock muttered.

"No, sir, I'm not." His gaze returned to Ryanne, unbidden.

Wall Street smoothed a strand of hair from her face and hooked it behind her ear, throwing new kindling on Jude's rage.

Ryanne took a step back, at least, stopping the guy's next caress. What she didn't do? Walk away.

Who was the man? Besides dead. What was he doing here?

Damn it, Ryanne should know better than to trust a newcomer. What if this one worked for Dushku?

"A little advice from an old man," Virgil said with a sigh.

"Fight for what you want, while you can. If you don't, someone else will win your prize, and you'll have no right to complain."

The old man didn't understand. No one did. Not even Jude.

He wanted Ryanne, but the moment he took her, fresh guilt would raze him. *Worse* guilt, because he'd already been there, done that, and should know better. He would end up hurting her all over again.

"Dad gave me the same advice," Daniel said, "and if I'd heeded him, I would have settled down with Thea a lot sooner. I would have been *happy* a lot sooner."

Jude didn't think he'd recognize happiness if it kicked him in the balls.

"Sorry, boys, but I've got to go. I'm being summoned by my damsel in distress." An eager Daniel rushed off to join Dorothea, who'd been cornered by her mother's book club. The old biddies loved romance novels, and had no qualms asking everyone in town about their preferred sexual positions.

Yeah. They'd once asked Jude if he'd ever tried "that S and M stuff." He'd nearly stepped in front of a bus—willingly, gladly—as he'd made his escape.

His gaze returned to Ryanne. Still with Wall Street, her fingers toying with the bow around her waist. A bow highlighting the flatness of her stomach.

The rubber. It broke. Damn it, I knew the water would be a problem. He'd known, but he'd proceeded anyway, out of his mind with desire and desperate to have the woman before she changed her mind.

The timing is wrong, yes?

Only if you mean I'm ovulating right now.

Ryanne was on the pill, hadn't missed a single dose. There was no need to worry.

So why was he still fucking worried?

"She'll be traveling the world soon." Brock finished off the strawberry lemonade. "Why not enjoy her while you can?"

"Because. Just because," he said. But the idea…had merit. *Enjoy her before her trip. Say goodbye when she leaves. Move on with your life.*

"Want to know a secret, son?" Virgil winked at him. "Love is the answer to every problem on the planet, even yours."

At one time, Jude would have agreed with him. Then his family died and his great love for them hadn't brought them back. Love had failed him. "I'm not interested in falling again."

Virgil smiled a sad smile, his gaze faraway. "I was married to my Bonnie for over twenty years, and they were the best years of my life. When she died—" His chin trembled. "I've mourned her every day since. I've hurt. I've hurt so bad some nights I could only sob into my pillow. But even if I'd known our end, I wouldn't have avoided our beginning. I would have married her regardless. I have a feeling you'd say the same about your wife."

As the weight of the old man's words settled over Jude, he stumbled back. Every muscle in his body tensed. If he'd known what would happen to Constance and the girls, if he'd known their terrible fate, and his own, would he have turned his back on love to avoid loss?

No. Absolutely not. Right? He hadn't known true joy until Constance and the girls. But then, he hadn't known true pain until their deaths, and now he was an empty shell with nothing to offer anyone else.

"Shoot! Edna Mills is headed this way. The gosh dern woman likes to sneak a pinch of my bee-hind. I'm not a piece of meat, you know. I have a brain, and it isn't in my pants." Virgil lumbered off as fast as his arthritic feet would carry him.

Brock's gaze followed the old man to a shadowed tree. "What I wouldn't give to have a father like that."

So true. But why couldn't he answer Virgil's question with a simple yes or no? Jude loved his sweetheart and little sweets, but he would do anything to experience peace. Peace he couldn't have, thanks to his loss. Yet, he also couldn't imagine living his life without his memories of Hailey and Bailey smiling up at him every time he returned from a mission.

Ryanne's laugh drifted across the distance, and his gaze zipped right back to her—and narrowed. Wall Street was in the process of typing into her cell phone. His number?

Limp more pronounced than usual, Jude strode toward the couple. What he would do when he reached them, he had no idea.

"That's my boy," his friend called.

Glaring at Wall Street, he snapped, "I'd like to talk to you privately, Wade."

Like a puss, Wall Street paled and inched backward.

"Hey, Jude," she said with a smile. Not the warm, inviting smile he was used to seeing, but a facsimile, and it gutted him. "This is Glen Baker. We went to junior high together—"

"Don't care," he interjected. Apparently raw possessiveness had stripped away his civilized veneer and strict military discipline. "Let's go inside. Just you and me."

Wall Street blanched. "I, uh, think I see someone I know. I should say hi." He handed the cell phone back to Ryanne.

She glanced at the screen, frowned and latched on to the soon-to-be dead man's arm. "There are only six numbers here. What's the seventh?"

Yep. The bastard had been typing his phone number.

Glancing between them, Wall Street shuddered. "I didn't know you were seeing someone."

"I'm not. Jude is my employee, with zero benefits." To Jude she mouthed, *Go away.* She even made a shooing motion with her free hand.

He ran his tongue over his teeth—and stepped closer to her.

Stiff as a board now, she offered her phone to Wall Street. "Seventh number, please. And remember the manners your momma taught you. It's rude to keep a lady waiting."

Wall Street reached out to accept.

This time *Jude* grabbed his arm, squeezing tight enough to bruise. "Do yourself a favor. Walk away. Now."

"Sure, sure. I'm outta here." Wrenching free, Wall Street beat feet.

Jude breathed a sigh of relief...only to realize this could happen again and again. Ryanne was free to flirt with, call, date, kiss or *sleep with* anyone she desired. Next time he might not be nearby. Or, if he was, he might end up in prison.

Touch what's mine, and die.

There was only one way to stay out of jail. A short-term relationship with Ryanne, as Brock suggested. He would take what he could, while he could.

He and Ryanne could be together every night before she left for Rome. A couple months of blissful sexual satisfaction. Blissful, *exclusive* sexual satisfaction.

As much as he'd suffered in life, he'd earned the right to luxuriate in the woman who tempted him like no other.

He would feel guilt, yes, but that guilt would have an expiration date. The only other option? Walking away and living with long-term regret.

Ryanne glared at him, her chest rising and falling in quick succession. "You had no right, Laurent. Absolutely no right!"

He *so* did not like hearing her refer to him by his last name.

Had he ruined his chances with her? Maybe. Probably. But he'd faced worse odds and won.

First, he owed her a compliment. "You are..." His gaze roved over her, his blood heating. "*Spectacular.* I look at you, and I hunger. As I've proven, I can't stay away."

Her eyes widened as they studied him. Electric currents arced down his spine, and the rest of the world faded. They were the only two people in the world.

He whispered, "I want you, Ryanne. Here, now. I plan to take my time, to savor every inch of you."

Her pupils expanded, a sea of midnight, and her eyelids grew heavy. Tremors rocked her, encouraging his hope. "What happened to once and only once?"

"A mistake. I'd like the opportunity to make you come over and over again." He bent down, kissed the base of her neck, the tip of his tongue grazing the pounding fury of her pulse. "I'm not done with you. Are you done with me?"

"I don't... I can't... Argh! You are like a burr in my saddle, you know that?"

As conversations ceased and multiple sets of eyes focused on them, the world zoomed back into focus. Small-town living. Everyone thought they deserved to know everyone else's business.

"We're drawing an audience. Come on." Jude took her hand and led her through the gaping crowd.

No protests, no attempts to wrench free. His hope continued to magnify.

Inside the inn, he made a beeline for the reception desk, where Holly Mathis, Dorothea's younger sister, was seated.

Spotting him, the teenager set down her phone and crossed her arms over her chest. She always did her best to stand out, and today was no different. She wore a red corset top and a black ruffled skirt. Her neon pink hose were ripped, the tops of her combat boots frayed.

"Why aren't you celebrating your sister's upcoming nuptials?" Ryanne asked the girl.

"Why aren't you minding your own business?" Holly popped a bubble with her gum.

Ryanne smiled with all the sweetness of a rattlesnake. "How about I tell Dorothea about the time you and your friends came to the Scratching Post and—"

"Fine," Holly rushed to add. "I'm grounded. A boy snapped my bra, and I broke his nose. Dorothea congratulated me, but Mom doesn't yet understand the concept of sexual harassment—and the consequences. So why aren't you two losers out there celebrating the upcoming nuptials?"

"We'd like a room," Jude said. "Please and thank you. And did you notice what I did there? Used my manners like a big kid. You should try it sometime."

Pop. "Are you guys going to bone? Because starting right this second we offer hourly rates. One hour is double the cost of an entire night, because it comes with my silence."

He...had no idea how to answer that.

"Depending on how the conversation goes once we're in the room," Ryanne said, "this might be a cold-blooded murder situation."

"In that case." Holly tossed a key at Jude. "The room is free of charge. The press will do us some good. But try not to get blood on the comforter, m'kay?"

Jude rolled his eyes and launched into motion. Thanks to Daniel, the inn had undergone a complete transformation. Gone were threadbare pink carpets, peeling wallpaper with faded strawberries that looked like testicles, and laminate countertops. Every piece of furniture—from the scuffed and stained couches to chairs and coffee tables—had been polished or reupholstered.

Elaborate chandeliers dripped with ruby and emerald crystals shaped to resemble wild strawberries. Different walls had been painted different shades of beige, and the floors were solid wood. The counters now boasted gold-veined marble.

The rooms were being renovated *and* decorated with themes. Well, most of the rooms. The one Holly had given them hadn't yet begun its transformation. At least it had been spotlessly cleaned, and there was a bed...

Jude turned the door lock, an ominous *click* sounding.

"All right," Ryanne said, and sighed. "Let's get this conversation over with so I can be on my way."

He turned and roved his gaze over her slowly, lingering on all the places he planned to touch.

"Jude." She crossed her arms over her breasts, covering the

hardening peaks. "You do realize you're screwing me with your eyes, yes?"

"Yes. But I can't look at you any other way."

She began to soften, then scowled. "Okay, I get it. You're horny, and want to have sex. But why me, the girl you've repeatedly ignored?"

"I haven't ignored you. I *can't*. You walk into a room, and my gaze finds you. You walk away, and all I want to do is follow. You breathe, and my body *aches*."

A gasp. "I... You..."

I've rendered her speechless. Shouldn't smile.

What the hell? I want to smile?

"I want to have sex with you a second, third and fourth time," he said. "Actually, I want to lose count, and I don't want to stop until you leave for Rome."

Her mouth opened, snapped closed. "So you would be my temporary boyfriend?"

A boyfriend was a husband without legal ties.

His skin burned too hot while his blood flashed ice cold, and a clammy sweat formed over his brow. "There's no need for labels."

"So this would be a two-month-long one-night stand? We'd be friends with benefits?"

He nodded: *yes*. He was the speechless one now.

Goose bumps broke out over her arms. One minute passed. Two. She licked her lips, fanning the flames of his desire. "Before I'd ever consider agreeing, we'd need to get a few things straight."

Elation went head-to-head with fear. If she had conditions, he wasn't out of the game. But. Commitment terrified him. Fall into love or even like with a woman, only to lose her? Never again.

Desire eclipsed both the elation and the fear.

He nodded: *continue*.

"Last time, you treated me terribly after sex."

Guilt flared, and finally he found his voice. "You're right, Wade. I was an asshole. I'll try to do better this time."

"Wade again," she muttered.

Hated the use of her last name as much as he did? "Ryanne. Shortcake."

She softened. Another minute ticked by in silence, this one thick with tension. Staring down at her shoes, she toyed with the belt around her waist. Nibbled on her bottom lip.

When next she faced him, her eyes were narrowed, the long length of her lashes fused together like puzzle pieces. "I'm not sure you understand how deeply you hurt me. I gave you my—" Her cheeks flushed a vibrant shade of rose. "Body. I gave you my body, and you—"

"Wait. Stop for a second." Suspicions danced through his head yet again, and his gut churned. Why had she paused? Only one reason made sense. To stop herself from saying *my virginity.* "Was our first time *your* first time?" he asked point-blank.

The color in her cheeks deepened and spread. "What does it matter?"

Oh, shit. Shit! Breathing became an impossibility. Answering a question with a question was telling. "It matters. So tell me true. Was our first time your first time?"

"*Why* does it matter?"

"Because."

"Because why?"

Damn her! "Because you shouldn't have gifted your virginity to a broken man."

She blanched, her arms falling to her sides. "Why do you keep calling yourself broken?"

"And once again you failed to answer my question. Tell me the truth, Ryanne."

Up went her chin. "By giving myself to you, I gave *us both* the gift of an *orgasm.* Stop being greedy, asking for more."

Feeling as if he were choking, he pulled at his tie to loosen the knot. "I will find out the truth one way or another. Even if I have to start asking the good people of Strawberry Valley about your dating history."

"You wouldn't!"

"Oh, yes, I would."

"Fine." Her chin lifted another notch. "Take heart, Laurent, because I most certainly did not give my virginity to a broken man."

He began to sigh with relief...relief paired with—surely not. Surely he wasn't disappointed.

Then she added, "I gave my virginity to *you*. A warrior. A protector. A man who made me feel safe and sexy, who rushed over to help me when I needed him most."

Jude stumbled back, overwhelmed by a tidal wave of shock, anger, more guilt. A *lot* more guilt. More fear and possessiveness. Even...euphoria.

"Why didn't you tell me before?" he demanded.

"I was afraid you'd stop." The picture of feminine pique, she anchored her hands on her hips. "But don't go feeling special. If not for an avalanche of trust issues, I might have a thousand lovers in my past."

Would he have stopped if he'd known the truth?

No need to ponder. No, nothing would have stopped him. "Why did you trust *me*?"

"A moment of insanity."

Hardly. "Why? Tell me."

She huffed and puffed with indignation, but said, "Before I met you, I'd already worked through most of my issues. I'd found a journal Earl had written, and his love for his first wife...well, you reminded me of him."

Thank God for Earl.

Jude scoured a hand down his face. "I'm sorry I hurt you. I *will* do better this time."

"I want to believe you, I really do, but…"

"But," he prompted, gentle now.

"I'm not going to make the same mistake twice."

Needing to touch her, craving a connection, he stepped toward her. "Being with me doesn't have to be a mistake."

She gulped and stepped back. "Maybe, maybe not. I have questions."

"Ask. Quickly." He pushed his weight into his heels, somehow finding the strength to remain in place. "Time isn't on our side."

Her tongue slid over her lower lip, leaving a sheen of moisture. "You mentioned you wanted to be with me every night before I leave for Rome, that we'll be friends with benefits."

"I don't hear a question."

"*Are* we friends? Before, you said—"

"I know what I said." Annnd remaining in place ceased to be an option. He moved directly in front of her, only a whisper away, the scent of strawberries and cream intensifying. "I'll never lie to you, and I'll protect you and yours. When you need help, I'll drop everything. We *are* friends."

She closed her eyes, drew in a heavy breath. As she exhaled, she faced him, her irises exquisitely smoky. "Last question. Will you cuddle me afterward?"

Her meaning crystalized, and a slow smile bloomed. "Yes, I will." Gladly.

"Good. Now take off your clothes."

CHAPTER THIRTEEN

Desire *consumed* Ryanne. She'd been a goner the moment Jude approached her. Oh, she'd tried to hold out. Succumbing to the man's rugged appeal a second time could mean one thing: trouble. She'd even tried to move on and flirt with another man.

Glen had made her laugh, so what better candidate? Except, he hadn't made her burn.

With Jude, she *smoldered*.

So he'd played hard to get for a while. So what. Ryanne was one of only two women capable of shattering his iron control. Whether he admitted it or not, she was special to him.

The fact that he'd just offered her a prolonged sexual odyssey—icing on the cake. How could she send him away?

"I don't see you stripping," she said.

He removed his tie, paused, then took a step back. "Clothes stay on until you answer *my* questions."

Oh, no, no, no, cowboy. You aren't going to be in charge.

Desperate for him, she unzipped the top half of her dress, letting the material fall just under the cups of her bra. "Go ahead. Ask. Meanwhile, I'll be over here making myself more comfortable."

His hands fisted at his sides, and she had to cut off a laugh. "You understand that we are one hundred percent exclusive, yes?"

"Try to see another girl. See what happens."

Satisfaction eased the scar that branched through his mouth, turning his perma-frown into another almost-smile. "I need to hear you say the words." Mimicking her, he said, "'No, Jude, I won't be dating other men. Or looking at other men. Or breathing the same air as other men.'"

Silly, sexy man. "Jude, for me no other man exists. Happy now?"

"Not yet, but I'm getting there." He seemed to steel himself for whatever came next. "That Glen guy. Were you interested in him? Will you regret not going out with him?"

How to reply without ruining the moment? "Glen lost his job in the city, so he moved back to Strawberry Valley to stay with his parents. First, he hit me up for a job. I told him we had no open positions, and he said he was kind of glad because he'd rather date me than work for me." Crap! She was babbling. *Get on with it.* "I told him to call me, and we'd work out details. I wanted to forget about you."

His low snarl—of jealousy?—thrilled her. "Do you want to forget me now?"

"I just want to *get* with you."

A flash of amusement in his eyes. "Glen isn't good enough for you. But then, neither am I." He reached for her, every fiber of her being catching fire. Then he plucked her cell phone from her grip.

"Hey!" Even as her heart hammered against her ribs, her brows drew together with confusion as he plugged in her password—a series of numbers she'd never shared with him—and typed—

No, he deleted Glen's unfinished number. His navy blues challenged her to protest as he returned the phone.

Protest? Please. Her bones threatened to melt.

"You have often demanded compliments from me." He trailed his knuckles down the center of her chest, summoning goose bumps. "Today I expect to be seduced by you."

The air thickened, suddenly charged with electricity. The familiar scent of him—spiced rum, black magic—teased her. "Oh, cowboy, let's be honest here. I breathe, and you're seduced."

"You aren't wrong. But I want more." He rubbed a hand down the long, hard length of his erection, which could no longer be hidden beneath his slacks. "With you, I always want more."

Precioso. "Then more you shall have." With a little push, she sent him tumbling onto the bed. Warrior that he was, he could have remained standing if he'd wanted. Lover that he was, he hadn't.

As she backed away from him, sunlight streamed in from a crack in the curtains, spotlighting him, creating a halo around him. Priest, he'd once been called. Right now, he looked more like an angel. Or a *fallen* angel…

"Come here," he rasped, staring up at her with unwavering obsession.

Love watching this man watch me. "Sorry. I'm busy seducing you."

Lust gleamed in his eyes. "You can give me a lap dance. In fact, I insist on it. I *need* to put my hands on you."

"Oh, you'll get a lap dance all right. Maybe. *If* you're properly appreciative while I perform my very first striptease." Ryanne had been told she danced the way men wanted to screw: with absolute abandon. Why not put her skills to good use?

Possessiveness and exquisite tension emanated from him. "You're gifting me with all your firsts."

"Are you complaining?"

"*Never.*"

Hiding a smile, she opened the iTunes app in her phone and

turned on her favorite playlist. Every inch of her body ached as hard rock filled the air. Her pulse points throbbed in time to the bump-and-grind beat as she placed the cell on the desk.

Facing away from her captive audience of one, she removed her belt and shimmied out of her dress, then kicked the garment aside. Wearing a matching black bra and panty set, as well as a pair of red high heels, she began to roll her hips. Hands in her hair...then sliding down her sides, over the globes of her bottom.

"Ryanne." The torment in Jude's tone caused her knees to shake. "Shortcake."

That endearment! Knowing how important names were to him, how they meant something on a deep and personal level, made it even sweeter.

My man deserves a reward. She gripped the edge of the desk and crouched, sticking out her rump, then straightening while slowly undulating. After a quick spin, she placed one of her red stilettos on the chair in front of the desk, and slid the garter down her thigh. A garter she kicked at Jude.

Reflexes well honed, he caught the little scrap of material without ever removing his gaze from her.

"Seduced yet?" She cupped her breasts before gliding her hands over the curve of her waist...between her legs where she ached.

He white-knuckled the sheets. "Come here," he repeated.

Yes, yes. Need his hands on me. Need my hands on him. Trembling, she sauntered across the room to stand before her man.

Her temporary man. *Never forget.*

Unease pricked at her. *Have I set myself up for heartbreak?* Then his intoxicating scent enveloped her all over again, and her head fogged. This man was sex and candy, and soon, she would devour him.

She'd set herself up for *pleasure.*

After flattening her hands on his thighs, she pushed his muscular legs apart. Hip roll, spin. When she faced him, she rose up to press her breasts into his face, hardness to softness. As his mouth descended, she retreated...pressed, retreated, never allowing him to suck on her nipples through her bra.

She leaned down, nipped his earlobe. "Everyone at the party knows what we're doing in here. Are you scandalized?"

His muscles clenched beneath her hands as he raggedly admitted, "I'm unmanned."

"Oh, cowboy. I haven't unmanned you." Heart pounding, she reached between his legs, cupped the heavy weight of his testicles. "Not yet."

His ragged groan caressed her ears. "Lord help me when you do."

She grinned her slyest grin. "I must be the envy of every woman in town. I remember how hot, hard and large you are."

"I remember every inch of your body, as well. The way you gloved me. You are the prize every man longs to win."

This man...oh, this man.

Tremors escalating, she unhooked her bra. The material fell, and she removed her panties, leaving her body bare to his gaze at last.

A strained breath left him, and he fisted the comforter. To stop himself from reaching for her? "There is no woman more perfect."

For you, only you.

"I've shown you mine." She unfastened the top button of his shirt, the muscles in his pecs jumping up to meet her touch. "Now show me yours."

"I'd rather taste yours." He grabbed her hips and pivoted them both, tossing her onto the mattress. A second later, he loomed over her, a lock of golden hair tumbling over his brow. If not for the wicked desire darkening his eyes, he would have looked boyish.

"Jude." She framed his face. "Yes. Taste me. You'll be the first..."

With a groan, he claimed her mouth in an earth-shattering kiss. Their tongues *mated*, thrusting together, mimicking the erotic rhythm of sex. Her belly quivered. Her blood heated, flushing her skin. Her nipples puckered against his chest, and she cursed his shirt, craving skin-to-skin contact, male to female. Jude to Ryanne.

"Can't get enough of you." Remaining fully clothed, he kissed and licked his way to her breasts. As he plumped and kneaded the tender flesh, he tongued her nipples.

Her hips arched, her sex seeking the stone-hard length of his erection. When he moved—dang him!—she rubbed against *his* hip instead. No matter. Pressure, any pressure, only stoked her need higher, welcoming a mix of bliss and agony.

The music faded, a new song spilling from her phone. A soft, romantic ballad this time. Jude never changed his pace, now out of sync with the melody. She was glad. He played her body as if the world would soon end, and the disharmony thrilled her.

She writhed in anticipation as he kissed his way to her navel. His tongue delved inside, then he paused to look at her through the thick fan of his lashes; his irises were electric, no longer navy but crystalline.

"Before we part, I'm going to take you every way a man can take a woman."

"Yes." *Please.*

Jude drank in the erotic bounty splayed beneath him. Silken strands of ebony spilled over the pillows. Hooded eyes glittered with desire. Ruby red lips were soft and parted, ready—still wet from his kiss. Flawless skin had turned rosy with passion. Plump breasts were crested by coral nipples. A cinched waist accentuated flared hips.

Ryanne Wade was the incarnation of sex.

He'd gone two and a half years without a climax, had very rarely pleasured himself, and now he couldn't go two weeks.

From off to on—*very* on. What had this woman done to his legendary control?

Until this moment, he hadn't realized how completely he'd shut down each time pain and grief had overwhelmed him. Or how he'd numbed-out whenever they'd abated. How he'd felt nothing, utterly dead inside, as cold as ice.

Now I burn, because of Ryanne.

"Delicious."

"Yes. Mmm, yes." She reached overhead, clasping the headboard and arching her back, offering him a sensual buffet of delights. "If you want to give rather than receive, well, we all have our crosses to bear."

As he chuckled softly, marveling that he'd found humor amid such a tense situation, or any situation, the warmth of his breath caressed her stomach and a new flood of goose bumps covered the surface of her skin. *So wonderfully sensitive.* He licked one, then another, working his way down, down, finally reaching the apex of her thighs, where heaven awaited…

As he nudged her legs apart with his shoulders, his erection strained against his fly, throbbing insistently. Beauty personified greeted him—pink, wet and swollen with desire. His control was frayed at the edges, ready to snap at any second, but even still he watched Ryanne's face as he slid a finger deep into her core.

Her eyes closed, perfect white teeth biting into her lower lip. *So magnificently responsive.* The elegant line of her back arched, her hips jolting up. At the same time, her inner walls clamped around his finger, as if to hold him captive.

"Jude! Please…more!" Only Ryanne could turn a plea into a command. "I'm going to come. *Neeeed* to—"

On his next inward glide, he pumped a second finger into her molten depths, and her words ended with a moan.

Hell! The air in his lungs steamed, breathing a nearly impossible chore. "You're so wet for me, so incredibly tight."

"Going to…so close…"

"Shall I forgo foreplay this time, as well? Shall I slide my length into you?"

"*Yes*. Give it to me!"

"Are you sure?" He lifted his head to *liiiick* the very heart of her, causing her next "yes" to terminate with a hiss. Sweet, feminine arousal coated his tongue, a fine wine he would forever crave.

"Changed my mind," she rasped. "Give me the foreplay. Give me *all* the foreplay."

A laugh died in his mouth, killed by a groan of need. Jude devoured Ryanne, licking, nipping and sucking. He ground his shaft into the mattress, desperate to take the edge off the building pressure inside him.

She groaned and begged, driving him wild. He drove his fingers in and out of her while flicking his tongue against her little bundle of nerves. Wet heat soaked his hand.

Incoherent words spilled from her beautiful mouth as she writhed against him.

Not sure how much longer I can hold out...

Damn it, no. He would hold out as long as she needed him to hold out. Whatever he had to do, he would ensure there was no pain for her this time. Angling his wrist, he created makeshift scissors with his fingers, and she screamed, her inner walls instantly clenching and unclenching.

The sight and feel of her...the sounds she made, the sweetness of her taste...

"You're ready for me." Jude jolted upright, severing their connection, and a whimper left her. His hands wet with her essence, he ripped open his fly, shoved his underwear underneath his testicles.

Stripping completely would have taken too much time.

He sheathed his length in a condom, then dove down, kissing her. At the same time, he thrust inside her. Instant bliss, pleasure filling his bones, flowing through his veins, rewriting his DNA.

He pumped in and out, in and out, maintaining a slow but steady pace. Until she began to writhe. Then he moved faster and faster, the bed springs creaking, and the headboard rattling against the wall. Finally he was pounding into her, a man possessed, gentleness no longer a thought, or even an afterthought.

Sharp nails scoured his back, the sting only maddening him further. Ryanne's knees squeezed his waist, her ankles locked over his lower back. They were two halves of a whole, entangled irrevocably. Despite her orgasm, she was as caught up in the moment as he was, ruled by passion-fever.

Frenzied, Jude ripped his shirt down the center. Buttons flew in every direction, but his bare chest pressed against her breasts at last. Her nipples were hard little points…points that rubbed against him as he thrust and thrust and thrust. The friction was rapturous.

"Jude!"

He reached between their bodies, stroking her to a second orgasm. As her inner walls tightened on his length, an orgasm tore through *him*, hot satisfaction lashing from him.

She collapsed onto the mattress, and he collapsed on top of her. When he caught his breath, he slid out of her and rolled to his side to save her from being crushed.

"Congratulations." She fist pumped toward the ceiling. "The condom held."

"It's a miracle." Realizing his prosthetic was exposed, he drew the cover over it before she noticed, also shielding her from the coldness of the metal. In an effort to get comfortable, he shifted.

Ryanne draped her body over his chest and pushed the cover away, resting her foot directly on his leg. He stiffened, then forced himself to relax. She'd seen the prosthesis before, and hadn't seemed to mind.

As one minute bled into two, however, his stiffness returned. The only woman he'd ever cuddled was Constance. She'd been shorter than Ryanne, not nearly as curvy, so she'd fit against him differently. He shouldn't like the differences. Key word: shouldn't.

He wasn't sure he ever wanted to move.

You're giving Ryanne everything that once belonged to Constance. Save something.

"You don't have to snuggle me. It's fine. You can go," she said. "I won't be mad this time, promise. I get that this is difficult—"

"No. A deal's a deal. I'm staying put." He simply needed a distraction. "We're going to do more than snuggle. We're going to talk."

"Okay, I don't mean to be a buzzkill while you're doing your *I am man, hear me bark* thing, but I'm a little sweaty, and you're giving off enough heat to melt the Arctic. Why don't we return to the party? We can—"

"Nope. Now we're snuggling, talking *and* making plans for tomorrow. Suggest we leave again, and I'll add a fourth item to the list."

She snorted. "We don't have time for all that. The party—"

"Snuggling. Talking. Plans. Then we're going to the kitchen and feeding each other whatever Dorothea has in the fridge. Want to protest a third time?"

Now she laughed outright, the sound magical. Every bit of tension drained from him, leaving him lax, practically boneless.

"Fine. But this is your show," she said, "so you call the shots. What is it you'd like to talk about?"

No need to ponder. "You." His curiosity about her knew no bounds.

"Just me?" She gave his nipple a good, long lick, and he decided staying had been a very good idea. "Not you? Sorry, cowboy, but you don't get tit without tat."

"I do like tit. But what happened to me being the one to run this show?"

"Changed my mind. Women have to deal with menstrua-

tion, pregnancy, childbirth and menopause. You can deal with
a chat about your life."

"Well, men have to deal with women, so we're already tied."

She gasped, slapped his shoulder. "You did *not* just say that."

"I did, and I stand by it. Unless you want to give me what I
want?"

CHAPTER FOURTEEN

Ryanne swallowed another laugh. This man had just rocked her world. Her body still hummed with incomparable satisfaction, and she wasn't sure she'd ever be able to walk again. *Totally worth it!*

At first, Jude's discomfort with their position had been obvious, yet he'd stayed put, and insisted they talk, which had kinda sorta tickled her to her toes. They might be temporary, but her contentment came before his anxiety. Then he'd teased her, turning the tables on her.

Affection for him was as soft as clouds, and as certain as rain in spring. She could fall hard for this man. She'd have to be careful. Her future trip—trips—depended on her ability to separate sex from emotion.

"Fine," she finally said, curling into his side. "I'll give you what you want." But she would do everything in her power to get what *she* wanted in the process. "Ask me anything. Just know that I'm a little disappointed you didn't do a full background check on me, like Daniel did for Dorothea."

"A gross invasion of privacy is your idea of a romantic gesture? Good to know. But how do you know I *didn't* look into you?"

Had he?

A normal woman would be upset by the possibility, right?

When have I ever been normal?

Ryanne grinned. "Learn anything interesting?"

"I'm ungentlemanly enough to remind you that you don't get to ask the questions, Wade. I do." Thoughtful, he brushed his finger up and down the ridges of her spine, making her shiver. "What does your tattoo mean?"

She glanced at the lock etched into her wrist. "Earl had a key tattoo to remind him that every decision matters. With a single choice can come success or failure. And since he showed me the true meaning of love, unlocking my heart, I got the lock in his honor. He was the best dad a girl could have."

"What about your biological father?"

"I know his name—Thomas Wade—and that he's from Dallas, Texas. He and my mom divorced while she was pregnant with me. He told her to get an abortion or deal on her own. I didn't believe her...at first."

"You contacted him?"

Stomach twisting, she said, "I got his number, and spent the next few months building my courage while also weaving dreams about him."

His hold on her tightened, an offer of comfort. "Reality can be better than fantasy."

"Or worse," she whispered. "Finally I did it. I called him. He labeled my mother a whore, said he doubted I was his, told me not to contact him again and hung up." The cruelty of his rejection had shocked her, but the fact that he hadn't wanted to claim her had hurt in ways she'd never imagined possible.

"I'm sorry. If the man doesn't want anything to do with you, he's not worthy of you." A pause, then a softly asked, "How old were you?"

"When I contacted him? Thirteen." Selma had been married

to abusive Mr. Scott at the time, and Ryanne had hoped against hope that her biological father would swoop in to the rescue.

Now she could rescue herself.

Jude's blistering curse rang through the room. "Little girls need their fathers."

Oh...crap. Maybe she shouldn't have mentioned Daddy Dearest. Had she just reminded Jude of the daughters he would never again see? Probably. Except, there'd been no pain in his voice, only outrage on her behalf.

Had he finally begun to heal?

Throat going dry, she forged ahead. "Big girls need their mothers, but mine stopped contacting me a few years ago. She was going through her hundredth divorce, and I begged to live with one of my former stepdads. Earl offered safety, security and a chance to finish school with my friends while Selma offered an RV trip around the country, and an endless parade of new men who might or might not be creepers. I hated the thought of leaving her, but Earl was sick and needed someone to care for him."

Jude's hold on her tightened yet again, almost bruising her. "Did any of her men ever..."

"Once or twice," she admitted. When he jumped out of bed, a disheveled fallen angel determined to deliver vigilante justice, she grabbed his hand and rushed to add, "Those who touched me inappropriately, I fought. I also told authorities here in Strawberry Valley, wanting an official record of the crimes, so that the guys would never be able to hide behind a wall of innocence."

The hand she held balled into a fist, but slowly her fallen angel eased back into bed. "Did your mother stay with the men?"

"No. She believed my claims and left every time." Ryanne sat up long enough to tug on his shoulders and urge him to stretch out beside her.

When he rolled to his side, he buried his head in the hollow of her neck and wrapped his arms around her waist, as if he wanted—needed—to cover her body with his own, to shield her from any threat, past, present or future.

The notion melted her…until she remembered they had no future.

Disappointment cut through her.

No, no. Couldn't be. She was excited for her travels. Would never be like her mother and change her plans and goals for a man. Men came and went, but dreams lasted forever.

"I've told you about my parents," she said. "Now it's your turn. Tell me…" What? She should probably start easy, so he had no reason to protest, and could quickly get used to sharing his life with her. "What's your middle name? I can't believe I slept with a man without knowing his full name."

"Walker."

"Jude Walker Laurent, huh. How adorable."

One of his shoulders hiked in a shrug. "My mother said I reminded her of my father. Like you, I never really knew him. I saw him around town, but really only knew what she told me. Apparently he was a walker—always walked away from his responsibilities."

Okay, wow. Ryanne wanted to drop-kick his mother. "You are the most responsible man I've ever met. Therefore, I hereby declare Walker stands for your willingness to walk the extra mile for your friends."

A twitch of his lips. "Sorry, shortcake, but the expression is *go* the extra mile."

"Fine. You're the cock of the walk. Boom! Nailed it."

Another twitch of his lips followed by a full-blown smile. "I'm sold."

Proud of herself, she decided to take the conversation to the next level. "Tell me about your wife. How long were you together?"

He opened and closed his mouth, cleared his throat. "Nine years." With barely a pause he added, "Where's your mom now?"

Ryanne let the change of subject slide without comment, even though she had to add another blast of hurt to the lockbox in the back of her mind. Here she was, sharing everything, while he gave the bare minimum. The scales were becoming unbalanced.

"Last time I heard, she had just gotten another divorce and was packing up to leave Colorado." Determined to try again, she asked, "What about your parents? Where's your mom? Your dad? Still living?"

"Yes, they're both alive," he said. Then, "Do you have any—"

"Nope. Tell me about your parents."

Thick silence.

Oppressive silence.

"My mom lives in Midland, Texas," he said, and Ryanne wanted to pound her chest like a gorilla. Success! "She spends her days taking care of her family farm, the only thing she's ever really loved. Like your mom, she was once known for getting around. My father has a farm of his own nearby—and a family—but Mother became his side slice so he would help her with crops. I have three older brothers and a sister, and we all have different dads."

"Are you close to your siblings?"

Another pause, as if he had to weigh every word he spoke, and her elation drained. "No. All four moved out and never looked back."

Meaning, they'd never contacted him again? "I'm sorry." Their absences must have felt like rejections. "Have you ever tried to track them down?"

"They abandoned me. They don't get a second chance."

Oookay. Jude wasn't the forgiving type. Noted.

"Besides," he added. "I have Daniel and Brock."

"You guys met in the army?"

"Yes."

She waited, but he said no more. Before she could press, Dorothea's special ringtone filled the room. "All right," she said.

"That's Dorothea calling. I think she's going to demand we return to the party."

"Yeah. Let's return."

No longer quite so happy to spend time with her, cuddling and chatting?

Ryanne grabbed a pillow and smacked him in the stomach with it, both aggravated and playful. As he sputtered, she smacked him again. When she tried to smack him a third time, he was ready, the other pillow in hand, the perfect block.

With a laugh, she launched a full-blown attack, nailing him in the face. Because yes, she fought dirty.

"What—" Smack. "Hey!" Smack. "Wade!" Smack. "You're going to pay for that." His growl was fierce, but his eyes crackled with good humor.

I'm helping him! Teaching him how to have fun.

He swung his pillow at her, knocking her to her back. As she laughed, feathers exploded from a tear, raining through the room.

"Stop!" she said, giggling after he delivered a third smack. "You're my sex bunny, not my—"

He stopped, as ordered, his navy blues narrowed and glittering. "Did you say sexy *buddy* or sex *bunny*?"

"Duh. Bunny. You're here for my pleasure and amusement. So, pleasure and amuse me."

"Dance, monkey, dance, is that it?" He dropped the pillow, ripped hers out of her kung fu grip and tickled her until she begged for mercy. In an effort to escape him, she accidentally kicked his leg, and he winced.

Oh, crap! She sobered instantly, saying, "I'm so sorry."

"Don't worry about it." His tone was stiff. So was his body, for that matter.

Having none of that, she crawled down the bed. When she reached his feet, tension radiated from him. Still she removed the sleeve over his prosthesis, then the prosthesis itself, following the same steps he'd taken the night they'd showered together.

"What are you doing?" he asked, looking over her shoulder.

Unable to meet her eyes? "I'm doing exactly what it looks like. Forgetting all about the party and concentrating on my temporary man." She began massaging his leg. She'd done a little research about the best way to help an amputee. Massage could reduce swelling and pain, increase circulation in scar tissue, and lessen muscle stiffness and spasms.

Hissing, he jolted upright and pulled from her grip.

"Did I hurt you?" she asked softly.

He pinched the bridge of his nose. "No, I just—"

"Now don't you go telling me you're embarrassed." Determined to continue, she deftly but firmly placed his thigh atop her lap. "I've seen this part of you before."

"Yes, but…it's ugly, and you didn't get up close and personal before."

The rawness of his tone hurt *her.* "Your wound speaks of bravery and courage. You could have died, but you fought to live. How could I ever find it ugly?"

He remained stiff, and it was clear he didn't believe her. She wasn't going to push the issue. Not yet.

You had to learn to crawl before you could walk. She'd take this one step at a time.

As she kneaded his muscles, she decided not to ask about his tattoos, either. The next topic would be easy, fun. "We need to name the kittens."

His tongue slid over his straight, white teeth. "If you plan on finding homes for them, let their new families name them."

"I do want to find them homes, but I can't keep referring to them by numbers."

"Trust me, you can. If you name them, you'll get attached. You'll end up with eight cats, and everyone in town will call you by your new nickname—Crazy Cat Lady."

She sputtered. "Yeah, well, I *can't* keep them." And she wasn't sad about it. Her heart wasn't leaking acid at the thought of saying goodbye. Really. "I'll be too busy traveling the globe to raise them."

"Give them generic names, then, like Hairy, Furry or Patches."

Or she could name them after something she loved, because they deserved the best, not for any other reason. "Have you met Lincoln West? He's engaged to Jessie Kay Dillon."

"I did a job for him," Jude said, brow furrowing. "Security at his engagement party. Why?"

That's right. One of West's ex-girlfriends had tried to kill Jessie Kay. "He created some of my favorite video games. *Alice in Zombieland, Angels of the Dark,* and *Lords of the Underworld.*"

"You play video games?"

"No. I *win* video games, but only on my days off. I plan to play more while I'm traveling." And she couldn't wait! "*Lords of the Underworld* is my ultimate go-to. Demon-possessed immortal warriors are on a quest to find and destroy Pandora's box. I think I'll name the kittens after them."

"You want to name kittens after demon-possessed men?"

"Why not? Rumor is, all cats are spawned in hell. Besides, the Lords love them some pussies."

He nearly choked on his tongue. "The woman who never curses did not just use the P-word."

She smiled at him, all innocence. "*Pussycat* is not a curse word."

At first, he simply blinked up at her. Then, his mouth curved at the corners as he returned her smile, causing her heart to skip a treacherous beat. "You can play *before* your travels. Just install video-game stations at the bar. Pay to play."

Whoa. Mind blown. "That's freaking *brilliant,* Jude."

"My ideas usually are. Speaking of the bar, how's it doing, now that all the changes are in place? Are you spending more than you're making?"

"If I continue to rent out the bar throughout the week, I'll recoup my losses before I leave for Rome."

For some reason, his smile faded. He glanced at a wristwatch he wasn't wearing. "We should return to the party before Dorothea calls again."

No way. She wasn't ready to part with him. And she wasn't sure how he would treat her in public—wasn't ready to find out. What if he ignored her? What if he didn't want to hold her hand? What if he *did* want to hold her hand? Crap! Could she handle PDA? "You wouldn't strip until I answered a question for you, and I'm not letting you dress until you answer a question for me."

A heavy sigh. "All right. Lay it on me."

Double crap! What was she supposed to ask him? *Oh! I know!* "How would you describe me to someone who's never met me?"

Without missing a beat, he said, "Every man's fantasy come to sizzling life." His head canted to the side, his gaze returning to her...and heating. "How would you describe me?"

"Hold up. Give me a minute to process what you just said." Every man's fantasy come to sizzling life? Pleasure washed through her, warming her, and she savored the sensation. Was that really how he saw her?

She didn't care about being every man's fantasy, only cared about being his—and the notion suddenly scared her.

"Well?" he prompted. "You've had your minute."

Deep breath in...out. "I would say you are so irresistible, you're able to tempt the untemptable, and you're more addictive than my moonshine." Crap! She shouldn't have mentioned alcohol. "I mean, more addictive than kitten kisses."

"Am I, then?" In a flash, he grabbed her hips and yanked her forward, forcing her to straddle his lap. His erection bobbed between them, hard and thick and long. "I'm going to need a little proof."

Purring, aroused beyond belief, she braced her weight on her knees, leaned over and rubbed her puckered nipples against his chest. "Judging by your shaft-o-meter, I'm guessing you're good to go *without* proof."

"With you, I'm always good to go." He cupped her bottom, squeezed. "I'm even willing to—" His cell phone made an odd noise.

A second later, her phone buzzed. A text had just come in.

"Ignore it," she said, rolling her hips. Contact! She sucked in a breath, and he issued another curse.

"The message, whatever it is, is about the bar," he said, his tone grave. "You have special ringtones for your friends, I have a special ringtone for the security feed at the Scratching Post."

Poo on a stick! Sobering quickly, Ryanne hopped off the bed. After throwing Jude his phone, she checked the screen of her own...and her knees threatened to give out.

No. No, no, no.

Absolute, total chaos. Screaming patrons raced for the front door while an alarm screeched. Why? What the heck had happened? Then she noticed the flames flickering over the counter where drinks were usually served.

"Jude," she gasped out.

He grabbed his phone and watched the feed, the color draining from his cheeks.

"Why haven't the sprinklers kicked on?" he demanded.

"I don't know. *I don't know!* But we need to leave. Now."

CHAPTER FIFTEEN

On the mad dash to the Scratching Post, Jude called Daniel to explain the situation. There was no reason to phone 911. With the security system they'd installed, emergency crews had been notified the moment the fire alarm sounded.

Adrenaline surged through his veins as if he were hooked to an IV. His muscles felt bigger, his bones stronger, like steel. His heart galloped toward a finish line he couldn't see.

Ryanne sat in the passenger seat of his truck, as still as a statue. He'd wanted her to stay behind, this woman who'd shared dark pieces of her past, giving him a glimpse of the little girl she used to be, with dark, wavy hair and a mischievous gleam in her eyes. A gleam that slowly faded as loved ones had let her down and moved on, and adults had betrayed her trust. If she were hurt today...

When Jude noticed a fire just outside the town square, multiple fire trucks already on-site, he hung up on Daniel.

What was the likelihood of two fires happening on the same night? Not high.

Over the years, Jude had seen firsthand how terrorists operated. He suspected Dushku had set this fire first in order to keep the firemen busy. Too busy to deal with a second blaze.

Bastard!

One way or another, Ryanne was going to be hurt today. If not physically, then mentally or emotionally. Hell, even financially.

Already pale and waxen, she pressed a hand over her mouth and cried, "Belle and the kittens."

"I haven't forgotten. They are my first priority." Belle could probably escape through a window, if one had been left open, or even through the bar, but she wouldn't be able to carry out all of her babies.

Panic waited at the periphery of his thoughts, but years of situational training and actual combat helped keep it at bay. *Act now, react later.*

"Call Vandercamp," he said. "Let him know we're going to need him at the scene with medical supplies. Just in case."

She obeyed, and ended the conversation with, "Get there as fast as you can, Brett."

Jude glanced in the rearview mirror. Despite breaking speed records, Daniel and Brock had already caught up with him, and now remained on his six.

"If the bar burns down, I'll lose my livelihood, home and every memento I have of Earl." Never had Ryanne's voice sounded so hollow. "All in a single night."

He would sell an organ on the black market, if necessary, to buy her a new home. "Stuff can be replaced. You'll always have your—never mind. I can't believe I was about to tell you the trite things others have said to me. I'm sorry."

Streaks of black painted the horizon, an obscenity in the sky, and Ryanne whimpered, only strengthening his rage. Dushku had done this.

Dushku would pay.

The truck crested the hill, the Scratching Post finally coming into view. Smoke billowed through the windows, and flames crackled along one side of the building. Perhaps most of the structure could be saved?

He drove off-road, speeding toward the bar, his truck's tires flinging dirt and gravel.

The patrons had gotten out safely, their cars already out of the lot. Some of the people had stuck around; they either needed medical attention or morbid curiosity had kept them close. A few stragglers were filming the destruction with their phones. Idiots!

Dushku and his men were there, too, watching...smirking.

There were no firemen on the premises, as Jude had suspected. If the other fire hadn't been raging in town, they would have beaten him here.

He parked, grabbed the blanket from the back and jumped out. Knowing Daniel and Brock would protect Ryanne, he wasted no time, sprinting into the building to rescue Belle and the babies. The adrenaline still surging through his veins gave him strength, dulling any flash of pain in his leg.

"Jude!" Ryanne screamed.

He ignored her. He had to if he had any chance of success—and survival. Just before breaching the front door, he took a deep breath of air, knowing he had to hold it as long as possible, and wrapped the blanket around the lower half of his face. Already his eyes burned and watered, intense heat making him feel as if he were cooking from the inside out.

At the moment, the blaze was somewhat contained. A perfect circle crackled around the bar...where bottles of alcohol were stored—directly beneath Ryanne's apartment.

This had been a targeted strike meant to harm the owner. The property was simply collateral damage.

As Jude raced forward, he narrowed his focus—*get in, get out.* He jumped and dodged, but not quickly enough. Flames lashed his arm, singeing his shirt, leaving a white-hot line of blisters in their wake. He hissed, but didn't slow, taking the stairs three at a time.

Smoke burned his eyes, his throat. *Can't stop. Can't go back without those cats.* Light-headed, a bit unsteady, he punched the code in the lock and shouldered his way past the door.

Soot: everywhere. Temperature: hellish. In the sunroom, an agitated Belle prowled in front of her babies.

A flurry of movement behind him. Brock flew into the room.

"Ryanne—" Jude began. The single word scraped his throat raw; he suspected he'd already sustained esophageal burns.

Between coughing fits, he said, "She's safe with Daniel."

He hated that his friend was in danger outside of combat, but welcomed the aid. Working together as they'd done a thousand times before, they placed the entire fur family inside a laundry hamper, using wet towels to prevent any more smoke inhalation.

Brock led the way out, and Jude carried the hamper. By the time they reached the stairs, the blaze had already spread. Half of the banister was engulfed, plus a few of the steps. Too dangerous. If the wood snapped, they'd plummet. They backtracked, returning to the apartment.

Jude opened the window in the sunroom, and cool night air gusted inside. Droplets of water misted over him, cool and welcome, and he frowned. Why?

The answer clicked. Two fire trucks had finally arrived. Lights flashed nearby, men in full bodysuits working to douse the fire.

"Over here," he shouted, but he knew he hadn't been heard over the roar of the flames and firehoses. No matter. A truck's ladder was already extending up to him, thanks to Ryanne, who was pointing in his direction.

As soon as the edge reached the window, he practically shoved Brock out and handed his friend the hamper. Jude followed him out.

Just a little farther…almost there…

His foot hit land, and someone rushed over to hustle him toward a waiting ambulance. Light-headedness had graduated to full-blown swimming, but the second his gaze landed on the smug Dushku—who hadn't moved from his spot among the crowd—he erupted, pushing his way through the masses to get in the old man's face.

"You think you've won? You have no idea the hell you've unleashed."

Dushku withdrew a linen square from his pocket and wiped his glasses, as if Jude's presence had dirtied them. "You lost, Mr. Laurent. Accept defeat gracefully, and be thankful you and yours survived. This could have ended much worse."

Hard hands locked around Jude—Daniel. "We can deal with him later, after we've watched the security feed and proven he's responsible. Now's the time you take care of yourself."

Dushku revealed no hint of emotion.

Daniel dragged Jude to an ambulance, where he was hooked to an oxygen mask. Then Daniel went to check on Brock while Jude searched the surrounding area for Ryanne. No sign of her.

"The brunette," he said, trying not to panic.

"The Mexican hottie? She's fine, sugar, you have my word," the medic replied. "Like everyone else, she's being kept at a distance for her own safety."

"I need to see her." Had to assure himself that she was all right. He removed the mask and leaped from the vehicle.

"Hey," the medic called. "Your blood pressure is too high and—" His voice got lost in the murmur of the crowd and the roar of the water spray.

Jude found Ryanne with Belle and the kittens, as well as Daniel, Loner and Brett Vandercamp. All four labored furiously, using some sort of suction on the kittens to clean their nasal passages.

Ryanne's cheeks were colorless, her bottom lip swollen. Her front teeth had left two little puncture wounds in the center. She lifted her gaze, spotted Jude and cried out. In a blink, she was flying across the distance. When she threw herself into his arms, he caught her, his eyes burning all over again. Damn smoke. As weak as he was, impact sent him stumbling back, sharp pains lancing through his leg.

"Sorry, I'm sorry," she rushed out. "Are you okay? You're covered in soot and your skin! Your poor skin." Her chin trembled as she looked him over. "So many blisters."

"I'll be fine." He stared at the bar, the flames dying as water from multiple hoses sprayed.

A stray thought hit him: if the bar burned down, Ryanne would no longer be a bar owner. She could walk away, start a new life.

What. The. Hell? He was so prejudiced, he welcomed the destruction of Ryanne's livelihood?

He deserved every blister, and more.

"Jude." Her hand fluttered over her heart. "Did you just… *smile?*"

Did he? "The cats are alive and well," was all he said. A statement of fact.

"Yes," she replied, her tone flat now, "but you weren't looking at the cats. You were looking at my home."

"You did," ryanne said, before Jude had a chance to respond. "You rarely smile. I have to fight you for a single grin, yet you willingly, happily give one while my home burns down. You hate the fact that I sell alcohol. I bet you hate yourself, too, for screwing me."

She remembered the words he'd spoken to her the night she'd discovered Dushku was selling Savannah in her parking lot.

Frankly, I'd rather let it burn to the ground.

It. Her bar. Well, he'd certainly gotten his wish.

"I'm sorry," he said. "It was a momentary lapse of judgment. A moment of insanity."

Maybe he believed that, but he only fooled himself.

She'd fooled herself, too. He hadn't stayed away from her these past few weeks because she'd been a wrecking ball to two and a half years of self-imposed celibacy. He'd stayed away because he'd found her lacking. She finally saw the truth. To Jude, the Scratching Post would always be the bane of his world. *She* would always be the bane of his world.

She was shaking so hard, she felt as if she were seizing. Her cats were alive, at least, some in better condition than others. Jude—their rescuer and her betrayer—had escaped the flames with only minor injuries.

"From the looks of things," she said, "the firefighters will soon extinguish the blaze. Perhaps you'd like to light a match."

"Ryanne—"

"No. I didn't serve the boy who killed your family, but you treat me as if I'm the one responsible." Could she really spend the next couple months of her life with this man?

Tears stung her eyes.

"Ryanne," he repeated, reaching for her.

"No." She leaped out of range. "Don't. I mean it." Not here, not now. She might break down, and she'd rather die than break down in front of Dushku. "We'll talk later." Tomorrow, maybe. Or next month. Or when she returned from Rome. Or never. Her lockbox of hurt threatened to burst open at any second.

"I'm taking Belle and her babies to my clinic," Brett said, snagging her attention. "Will put them all in the oxygen tank." He pointed to Loner, who was covered in soot like everyone else. "You. Can you come with me? Ryanne can't leave, and Jude needs medical attention. My assistant is at home in bed."

Loner nodded, eager to help. "You just have to tell me what you want me to do."

"Carry the hamper, I'll carry the equipment."

The two rushed off, and though Ryanne would have liked to follow, she clasped Jude's arm as he coughed, nearly hacking up a lung.

"You're getting medical assistance. Don't protest," she snapped when he opened his mouth.

As she ushered him to the ambulance, he closed his mouth. Opened it again. Closed it again.

Brock sat on a gurney, a clear mask covering the lower half of his face.

"Well, well." A redheaded medic bustled in the back, searching for another mask. "My other sexy patient decided to return. Couldn't get enough of me, sugar? Understandable. Hardly anyone can."

Jude eased beside Brock, looking anywhere but at Ryanne.

Red anchored the mask around Jude's nose and mouth while saying to Ryanne, "Sorry, honey, but we're taking these two to the emergency clinic in Grapevine, and there isn't room for you. You'll have to follow us."

"No. We're staying here," Jude said. "We can't leave until we speak with the authorities."

Her tremors intensified, a ten on the RW Afflicter Scale. "I'll stay behind, and you'll go." They needed time apart, and she needed time to think. Emotions were too high right now, too raw.

"No. I'm staying with you." He removed the mask despite the medic's protests.

"Yes," she snapped. "Put the mask on. Now."

At the same time, Red said, "If you want to recover in a timely fashion, you'll suck up oxygen like a good boy. Otherwise you'll be knocked on your ass for days, unable to argue with your hottie."

"Don't worry. I'll stay with her." Daniel approached her side, draped an arm over her shoulders. "Go," he told the medic. "Get my boys the care they need."

Red banged on the window that blocked him from the driver, and shut the door. Ryanne's gaze remained on Jude until the last possible second. Anger pulsed from him. No, anger wasn't a strong enough word. *Rage.* Why? Because circumstances forced him to leave…or had he'd realized he couldn't fix what he'd just broken? Her trust, yes, but also the fragile bond between them.

The lights on the vehicle switched on, the siren blaring. As the ambulance pulled away from the parking lot and motored down the road, Ryanne's knees threatened to buckle.

"He'll be okay. He's survived far worse." Daniel looked her over, concern tightening his features. "Will *you* be okay? Let's find you a chair so you can sit down."

No way. Dushku and company still watched, though they'd returned to their side of the street. Afraid of Jude? "There's too much to do."

"Ma'am? Are you the owner of this bar?" A fireman covered in soot stepped up, his gaze focused on her.

"Yes." *I can do this.* "How can I help you?"

"As soon as the smoke clears," Fireman said, "you can check out the damage, but I think you'll be pleased to know the worst of it is localized to a single area."

Waiting to go inside was torture. Was her best friend—her bar—dead or alive?

Finally approval came and she raced inside, alternating waves of relief and dismay hitting her. The counter would need to be replaced, and her liquor supply was history. No, not true. She wasn't completely wiped out. She still had a large stash of moonshine and locally sourced beers in the basement.

Her office and the stairs leading to her apartment would have to be rebuilt, but everything else simply needed a good scrubbing. Soot covered many of the walls, most of the tables and chairs. A layer of ash covered the dance floor, but outside the bar area, the wood planks were in perfect condition.

Jude would be disappointed.

Her teeth ground together.

Different men and women spoke with her. Dazed, she forgot their names. All but Officer Jim Rayburn, who didn't try to hide his smirk, and the arson investigator. The latter asked her a million questions about her whereabouts and maybe kinda sorta looked at her as if she were to blame. Whatever. The truth would come out. And really, she was too shocked to care what anyone thought. In less than an hour, her entire world had been turned upside down.

"There's no question the fire was set deliberately," the AI told her. "An investigation will be launched. If someone was paid to do it, or if they acted alone, we'll find the truth. So, if there's anything you'd like to tell me, now is the time."

"Oh, I know the fire was set deliberately, and I can guess Mr. Dushku over there paid someone. He's wanted my bar since he decided to open a club across the street. Ask Jim Rayburn. I'm pretty sure he's on Dushku's payroll."

As Jim blustered, she pulled her phone from its sheath on her leg, then showed the fireman and Daniel what little security feed had been sent to her in-box.

Thank God Jude had insisted on cameras.

Maybe she'd misinterpreted his smile? Maybe he *had* been thinking about the kittens.

Maybe she was an idiot, trying to justify his actions.

AI's expression softened somewhat. "I'd like a copy of that."

"Sure thing. I'll make sure you receive security feed for the entire day," Daniel told him.

"Much appreciated." AI focused on Ryanne. "If you want to gather some of your belongings, one of the officers will accompany you. I'm sorry to say you can't be in here without an escort until the investigation is complete."

Tears momentarily obstructed her vision. "No, thanks." Everything smelled like smoke, and would constantly remind her of what had happened, and all she'd lost. "I'll be fine." Would she, though?

Jude hadn't even gotten to use the grab bars she and the girls had installed.

Ugh. *That* was her main concern? After everything he'd done? *What is* wrong *with me?*

The guy patted her on the shoulder, an awkward and failed attempt at offering comfort. Then he told her he would be in touch and padded off, leaving her to deal with the wreckage of her life—alone.

CHAPTER SIXTEEN

The next few weeks passed in a blur for Ryanne. She bought a handful of new clothes and moved into a room at the Strawberry Inn with her family of cats. All the little kitties survived without permanent damage, and so did Belle, who seemed to use the fire as an excuse to behave even feistier than ever. Thankfully, there'd been no serious injuries among the patrons, either.

Several days ago, Ryanne had a breakdown. Feeling isolated and abandoned, wishing Earl would magically appear to hug her, desperate for some kind of parental support, *any* kind of parental support, she'd called her mother.

A very big mistake.

The conversation had been short but not very sweet. After telling Selma what happened, her mother had said, "This might just be a blessing in disguise, *cariño*. Now you can let go of Earl."

Let go of Earl? Never! Ryanne had hung up and cried like a baby. She'd wanted so badly to find Jude and throw herself into his arms, but...that smile. It kept playing through her mind, allowing fury to take root deep inside her heart.

He'd smiled, thrilled by the ruination of her bar. His satisfaction had been momentary, yes, but even a single second was too long.

When it rained, it poured. One of her waitresses quit, unwilling to wait for the bar to reopen. She needed money *now*, and Ryanne understood. Then Sutter gave her an ultimatum: *continue to pay me, even though I'm not working, or accept my resignation.* Again, she understood. People needed money to survive.

Ryanne decided to pay everyone out of pocket, under one condition. Her employees had to sign a contract agreeing to return to work as soon as the doors to the Scratching Post opened. Everyone had signed, without hesitation.

Now I'm homeless, jobless and hemorrhaging cash. Yay me.

She'd considered canceling her trip to Rome, but her plane tickets and the villa had been paid for already—and both were nonrefundable. Another mistake on her part. At the time of purchase, she'd feared a way out would be an excuse to lose her lady balls. She'd thought: What if Rome wasn't as magnificent as she'd envisioned? What if her fantasies were better? And yeah, okay, she'd desired Jude even then, and had wondered what would happen to her resolve if he ever showed interest in her.

I will not *become my mother.*

If Ryanne needed the reminder a thousand times, she would give herself the reminder a thousand *and one* times.

Would Jude smile about her departure, happy to be rid of her?

She hadn't gone to the hospital to see him, had only called to check on him. He was released the next day and showed up at the inn, knocking on her door, but she told him to go away. He asked if the cats were okay, and as soon as she confirmed that they were, he left.

Afterward, she'd fumed. *Only cares about my kittens, the* bastardo! He'd even returned the next day and the next, each time asking if the cats missed him.

In fact, she was due for another visit any—

A knock sounded at her door.

She called, "Go away, Jude."

"Talk to me, Wade."

Using her last name again? Jerk!

Behind her, every single kitten meowed. They *did* miss him, the traitors.

"No need," she replied. "You smiled while my home burned down. We're done."

There. She'd said the words out loud. Made it official.

Don't cry. Don't you dare cry.

Where was the lockbox?

Stuff, click, shove.

"Ryanne."

The hurt in his voice…

Stuff. "Much like your siblings, I've abandoned you, and you don't give second chances, remember? Walk away." *Oh, my gosh.* Had she really just said that? She was a witch of the highest order.

There was a pause, thick with tension. Then he said, "You alone can have a second chance. See how forgiving I can be? You try it. Forgive me. Because I'm sorry. I'm so sorry. I'm not happy about what happened. I'm ashamed of my reaction. I wish I could go back—"

"But you can't. You can't go back, and neither can I. I can't unsee that smile."

The knob twisted. Trying to come inside without permission? The lock held.

"Open the door, Ryanne. Please. I'm not smiling now."

A plea from those scarred lips…

A pang sliced and diced her chest. She took a step toward the door, stopped. Took another step, stopped. *Resist!*

"Tell me something, Jude. If I were a schoolteacher like Lyndie, would you have wanted a long-term relationship with me rather than a short-term affair?" *Stuff, stuff.* "You hate bars, and I get it. I do. But deep down you don't think I'm worthy of your affection, and that I don't get," she said, feeling as if she were being stabbed in the heart over and over again. "Just...go away!" *Stuff, stuff. STUFF.* "Please."

Another pause before he rasped, "At least tell me if Belle and the kittens miss me."

Meow. Meow. Meow.

"I don't know," she grated. "They haven't said."

Finally, silence. Then, the heavy thud of footsteps as he walked away.

Part of her wanted to race out the door and shout, "I'll give you one more chance. Don't blow it this time." Truth was, some couples worked, some didn't. She and Jude had had two shots to be together, and they'd failed miserably. One more chance wasn't going to do either of them any favors.

Stuff, click, shove.

The next day, Glen Baker texted her. He'd gotten her number, even though she hadn't given it to him. He offered an apology for the bar, as well as his behavior when Jude interrupted them at the engagement party, and asked if there was anything he could do to help.

Jude should take lessons: *how to treat a woman you want to date.*

In the nicest way possible, she told Glen thanks but no thanks. She wasn't in the mood for masculine company. Men sucked.

The romance ban was back!

Even the arson investigator had failed her. He had combed through video feed, and ruled the fire an accident. Apparently a patron lit a cigarette at the counter. Sutter informed him that smoking was prohibited, and the customer dropped the cigarette in the nearest trash can. Within minutes, flames erupted.

It was all a little too neat and tidy for Ryanne's peace of mind. Who was the patron who'd lit up? He'd worn a hat, shielding his identity from the cameras. And Sutter couldn't remember his face, because, at the same time he'd told the patron about the bar's nonsmoking policy, he'd dealt with two other patrons who'd come close to fist-fighting over a girl.

An elaborate setup? Or was Ryanne simply looking for ways to blame Dushku?

At least insurance would pay for the building's repairs, which had just begun. Since the construction workers would be clocking out at six, Ryanne had decided to open the bar at seven. Well, the patio outside the bar, anyway, since her liquor license permitted her to sell alcohol there. She would erect a tent just behind the patio, where patrons could dance. Sutter and her waitress would work the crowd, selling boxed snacks and pops, ensuring everyone had fun. To provide music, Power Trip would play on a makeshift dais Brock was currently building.

Jude had done nothing to help.

Lockbox!

But come on. What did she expect? She'd pushed him away at every turn.

He shouldn't have given up so easily.

Easily? He'd visited her every single day.

Yeah, but he should have busted down the door. Something!

Ugh. Mixed signals alert. *Make up your mind,* mi querida. *Do you want him to fight for you or stay away?*

She...didn't know.

Another knock sounded at her door, sending the kittens into a chorus of meows.

"Sorry, guys, but it's not Jude." She stole a quick glance at the mirror over the desk. Hair brushed—check. Cheeks rosy—check. Blush could do wonders for ashen skin. And yet, none of her makeup had been able to hide the dark circles under her eyes.

Did it matter? She had no one to impress.

Clothes in place—check. A skintight T-shirt, ripped jeans and combat boots.

When the door opened, Dorothea and Lyndie soared inside, beauty and sexiness personified.

After years of hating her body, Dorothea had finally decided to embrace the lushness of her curves. A bright red dress hugged her from shoulders to just below her knees, making her look like a '50s pinup.

Lyndie usually wore oversize cardigans and khakis—basically feed sacks—hoping to deter masculine appreciation right from the start. Tonight the strawberry blonde wore an outfit similar to Ryanne's: tight enough to guess her religion.

"I know I've said this before," Ryanne began, "but I apologize for unleashing my drama at your engagement party."

Dorothea hugged her before gripping her forearms and shaking her. "Party shmarty. The fire wasn't your fault and—this is probably horrible to admit, but—it gave me an excuse to leave, which I'd wanted to do before the party even started."

Ryanne threw her arms around the girl, hugging her close. "Dang, I love you. And I'm sorry for my behavior lately, too." She hadn't just lashed out at Jude. She'd lashed out at *everyone*.

"I love you, too. And don't worry. I remember my drama with Daniel. I wasn't always the sweetest truffle in the box."

Lyndie wrapped one arm around Ryanne and the other around Dorothea. "You guys love me, too. I know, I know. Now, tell us what's going on with Jude, Rye."

Dorothea nodded with gusto. "Don't think we haven't noticed how many times he's come to your door. I wasn't sure if I should call the police or give him a key."

Desperate for help, she finally admitted what had happened, how Jude had smiled as flames ate her bar. "He said I brought him back to life. But how could he feel that way about me and smile while I lost everything?"

"Okay, here's the reality of your situation." Dorothea led everyone to the bed. Kittens immediately jumped into their laps. "You own a bar, and his family was killed by a drunk driver who'd just left a bar. During the fire, he had an instinctual reaction, probably transferred his hate for whatever bar the drunk driver left onto the Scratching Post. It happened in the heat of the moment—oh, crap, sorry for going there—when he didn't have time to process his emotions. Did you know he's been at the Scratching Post every day since? As soon as the investigators gave him the go-ahead, he began working with the construction crews to fix the damage—on his own dime."

What! She'd checked on the bar every day. How had she missed him? Why hadn't he said anything to her about what he was doing?

Because you refused to speak with him, dummy.

"For that matter," Lyndie said, her tone gentle, so gentle, "if his emotions are only just now coming back to life, everything he feels is new to him and must confuse him."

That...made sense. Dang it, her friends were right. Jude was dealing with his past traumas to the best of his ability. Meanwhile, Ryanne was punishing him for a reaction he'd had no control over. *After* he'd taken a chance on a relationship with her, and *despite* his hatred for her profession.

Still, her hurt sharpened, nearly cutting its way out of the lockbox. She blinked back tears and focused on Belle, petting her soft fur.

Dorothea and Lyndie cooed at the kittens, laughed at their antics. Praise God above, her feline army no longer looked like a *rat* army. Their ears had finally popped out. They were walking, running and had even begun to climb.

Ultimately, Ryanne had decided to stick to plan and name the adorable crew after Lincoln West's *Lords of the Underworld* video game, rather than selecting generic names as Jude suggested. The sweeties had too much personality, and like the Lords, they were feisty. So, the members of her feline family were now called William, Anya, Lucien, Cameo, Strider, Torin and Paris.

"I think I've fallen in love with Torin and William." Lyndie cuddled both males against her chest. "They're the most mischievous of the bunch."

So true. "They'll be ready for a new home in a few weeks, after they've been neutered." And oh, crap, Jude might have been maybe possibly...right. Ryanne wanted to scoop up every kitten and shout, *Mine!*

But she wouldn't. She could share her bounty with her friends. In fact, she'd already promised Anya and Strider to Dorothea.

Yesterday, when Dorothea's pit bulls, Adonis and Echo, had scented the cats and come barreling through the door, Ryanne expected a blood bath. Instead, the canines treated the kittens with tenderness and concern, licking their faces and allowing the cuties to crawl all over them.

Ryanne checked the water and food bowls, making sure everything was in order. "You guys ready to go?" She hadn't wanted her friends to attend the festivities, because really, the entire night was a huge eff you to Dushku. Or Douche Canoe, as she now called him. What if he threw a *mantrum*?

The *bastardo* had come to see her again, daring to approach with a smile, as if he were an innocent Sunday-school teacher. He'd explained that, with all her recent troubles, she should be happy to take twenty-five thousand dollars less than his original offer.

Saying she'd been enraged was like saying the ocean was merely a teardrop.

She'd turned him down, and he'd stormed off.

I might be down, but I'm not broken.

Broken...

The word echoed in her head. Once, Jude had considered *himself* broken. Did he still?

"I'm ready." Lyndie tugged at the hem of her short skirt. "I think. Maybe I should change?"

Dorothea tapped the schoolteacher on top of her head. "You're more than ready. You're smoking!" The color drained from her cheeks. "I mean, smoking in a good way, not in a bar-burning way." She hung her head. "I keep referencing the worst night of your life. I'm sorry, Ryanne."

"Don't be ridiculous." Ryanne waved a hand through the air. "She *does* look smoking."

The pair beamed at her, and she forced herself to return their smiles, despite her growing dismay.

The thought of these wonderful women in any kind of danger sickened her, but both had insisted.

Would Jude show up? How would she react if he did?

Better question: How would she react if he *didn't*?

Jude remained in the shadows and tried not to stare at Ryanne as she served beer and moonshine to a small crowd gathered on the patio in back of the Scratching Post. He tried—and failed.

Strategically placed halogens lit up the night and spilled over her. Raven locks flowed down her back, a glorious fall of ebony silk. As she spoke with a patron, her bloodred lips curled up, unveiling a smile that didn't reach her eyes. The white shirt she wore, so innocent and sweet, clashed with the wildness he'd twice stoked in her.

There were dark circles under her eyes. Obviously she hadn't been sleeping, hadn't recovered emotionally from the bad hand she'd been dealt. Guilt beleaguered him.

He should have been with her, exhausting her with sex so that she *had* to sleep. But she'd made it clear she wanted nothing to do with him. And he couldn't blame her. For a moment, he'd been happy, thinking he'd seen the last of the Scratching Post.

Too screwed in the head for a woman like Ryanne.

He'd hoped the time apart would numb him and help him figure out his next step, but still he ached to hold her in his arms. Today, tomorrow...forever? No. Hell, no. He ached to taste her, and touch her, to hear her cries of abandon, until she left for Rome, that was all.

Fool! Already he missed her more than he missed his leg. *Her,* not just sex. He missed her wit and her laugh. Her care and concern. Her sass.

Damn, he missed her sass.

How would he cope when she was an ocean away?

Three days ago, he'd driven into the city and gotten a strawberry tattooed on his wrist. Now he carried a constant reminder of her—memories were better than nothing.

Tonight, a leather cuff hid the strawberry. He had no desire to answer questions about it.

His phone buzzed, but he didn't have to check the screen to know who had sent the message. Carrie had remained in contact with him, curious about his new life. She'd even invited him to return to Midland to rejoin their family.

He glanced at Ryanne, noticed a brittle aura and flinched. Maybe going back to Texas wasn't such a bad idea.

Of course, he'd have to wait until Dushku moved on, or died...with help. The urge to use the skills Uncle Sam taught him had almost proven irresistible. Also, he had to finish repairs inside the bar. He'd removed and replaced damaged wood from the wall and floors, but needed to finish the new staircase.

When Jude had noticed the grab bars in Ryanne's personal bathroom, he'd dropped to his knees, overcome by different emotions. Even before he'd agreed to date her, she'd made arrangements for him to comfortably use her shower.

If he wasn't careful, he was going to break her sweet heart more than he already had. How could he live with himself then?

Her gaze scanned the parking lot. Searching for someone? She bypassed him, only to zoom back. Between one second and the next, he felt as if a train hit him. Awareness fizzed in his veins, as potent as any drug. Then torment twisted her features. *Then* her expression blanked.

He nearly dropped to his knees in supplication. *Don't ice me out, shortcake.*

Had she gone numb, like him?

The idea of white-hot Ryanne Wade trapped in a deep freeze wrecked him.

A customer snapped long-nailed fingers in Ryanne's face, breaking the hold she had on him.

"Jude? Mr. Laurent?"

The familiar voice came from behind him. He turned on his heel...found Savannah standing just beyond the tent he'd helped Brock erect only a few hours ago. The skin around one of her eyes sported motley bruises, and there was a hand-shaped blue-black imprint on her neck.

"I... You said you'd help me," she whispered, peering down at her feet. "I'm ready to let you."

Protective instincts bloomed—he ignored them. He wasn't sure he could trust her. This could be a trap set by Dushku.

Tread carefully. "What changed your mind?"

She wrapped her arms around her middle. "They have my son. Thomas. I dated Filip Dushku, Martin's son. We moved in together when I got pregnant. Then Filip went to prison, and I gave birth to Thomas in Martin's home. He... I... Martin took Thomas from me. I willingly went to work for him in exchange for being allowed to see my boy once every morning. Today my sweet little boy slapped me. The things he's learning at Martin's hand..." She wiped her tears with a jerky motion. "Filip is supposed to be released in the next year, and I thought I could hold out and he would... Well, it doesn't matter now."

She'd thought Filip would save her, and now, because she'd been with so many other men, she assumed he would wash his hands of her?

"Even if Filip wanted me," she said, "I'll never again want him." A bitter laugh. "I bet that was Martin's plan all along. I just... I just want my son. Can you help me? You're the only person I've met who's stood up to him."

She was the boy's mother? "Why not go to the cops?" Whether Jude could trust her or not, he couldn't send her away. He had to act.

"Are you kidding? You think I haven't gone that route before? Martin is great at paying people off or uncovering enough dirt to blackmail anyone in authority."

That, Jude believed without question. "I can set you up in another town while I—"

"No." Blond locks whisked against her cheeks as she shook her head. "I'm not leaving without my son."

"—investigate your claims," he finished saying anyway. He had to know with 100 percent surety that the boy belonged to her, that this wasn't a ploy to harm Dushku by harming his grandson. "Help me find answers. Is your real name Savannah? What's your last name? Where are you from? Where did you have the boy—what state?"

"Yes, my real name is Savannah. My last name is White. I'm from Dallas, Texas, and I had Thomas in Martin's home there. He paid a midwife to help with the delivery. I don't know her name."

Savannah White. Thank the Lord he now had a starting point. "Come with me." He held out his hand. "If everything you've told me checks out, we'll figure out our next move together."

Her mouth opened, closed. Again, she shook her head and took a step back. "I told you, I'm not leaving without my son. I'll stay with Martin until you believe me. Just…don't tell anyone what I've told you, okay? The fewer people who know, the better chance I'll survive this. Okay?"

His arm fell to his side. "I won't share the details with anyone but the guys who will help me investigate, and Ryanne." She wanted to help, too.

"Swear it," Savannah insisted.

"I swear. You have my word."

Relief added color to her pale cheeks, and she rattled off a number. "One of my…regulars gave me a cell phone." Disgust and shame spilled from her tone.

"As soon as I have what I need, I'll text you, and we'll plan your exit."

"With Thomas."

"With Thomas," he agreed.

She closed her eyes, a tear sliding down her cheek. Then she faced him, hard mask back in place. "Thank you. And in the spirit of full disclosure, if it comes down to protecting you or my son, or hell, even myself, I'll be sure to send flowers to your friends."

"Understood and accepted."

Savannah!

Ryanne caught sight of the blonde. She was talking to Jude, who'd been sulking all evening, ruining Ryanne's peace of mind. Every time her gaze had found him, she'd struggled to keep the hurt inside the lockbox.

Now she asked Sutter to take charge and rushed over. By the time she reached Jude's side, Savannah was gone.

Argh! She and Jude were alone, nothing between them but shadows.

"Hello," he said, all kinds of sadness in his tone.

Sadness? He had no right! He'd done this to her—to them.

Slowly she faced him. Seeing him up close, the fatigue darkening his features, the lockbox began to shake, everything wanting out.

No. Absolutely not. This man had promised her the world, and in the same day, *destroyed* her world—with a smile.

"I can't be here right now." This was too much, and she was still too raw.

She tried to walk away, but he latched on to her bicep, stopping her. When she attempted to wrench free, he tightened his grip.

"Please, Ryanne. Talk to me. Let me explain."

"Let me go."

Again he tightened his hold, as if he feared he would never

see her again if he let go. "I can fix this. You just have to give me a chance."

"Why bother? I'm only a short-term affair."

"You're not *only* anything," he said, and stepped closer to her.

She could have shouted for help. She could have used the self-defense moves she'd learned years ago. Yes, she could have. But the lockbox splintered apart, hurt spilling through her, filling her up, *drowning* her. Hurt Jude had caused. Hurt Earl's death and her mother's abandonment had caused. Hurts from her childhood, things she'd thought she'd gotten over.

Just—like—that. Her control snapped and, with a cry more animal than human, banged her fists into Jude's chest. Not once did he try to protect himself from her wrath. He made himself more vulnerable, wrapping his arms around her waist and holding her close—closer—cooing at her the way she sometimes cooed at the kittens.

If anyone tried to approach, Jude waved them away.

Eventually, Ryanne's strength depleted. With a sigh of exhaustion, she sagged against him, and rested her head in the hollow of his neck.

He combed his fingers through her hair. "I'm sorry. I'm so sorry. I've got you. Everything will be okay."

"I forgive you for the smile, Jude. But..." Every word scraped her now-raw throat. "I don't think you can repair the damage you've done. I don't think we can be together."

Though he stiffened, his tone remained gentle. "I'm going to change your mind."

If only. "Let's not do this. I'm tired of arguing with you. I'm tired of your hot and cold attitude with me. I'm just...tired."

"I'm sorry," he repeated. He toyed with the ends of her hair. "I swear to you, if you give me another chance, I won't be hot and cold anymore. I'll just be hot."

Easily said, harder to do. Besides, she didn't want him staying with her because he'd promised; she wanted him to *want* to be with her, to admire and respect her.

"Why bother?" she said, her tone just as gentle. "Time is running out. Besides, I give too much, and you give too little."

"I'm giving you everything I can."

"I know." But it wasn't enough. Not anymore.

"What is it you want from me? Exactly?"

That, she didn't know. All or nothing? The heart currently in a dead woman's possession?

"All I know is that we're too different," she said, hating herself, hating him. This hurt. This hurt bad. "We want different things, and that's okay. We're not failures apart, we're just failures together."

"No. I don't believe that." His navy blues glittered. "Being without you has been the worst kind of hell. With you, I don't feel like a man defeated by his past. I feel like a man with a future."

Pretty words. "I wish I could believe you." Though she wanted to stay cuddled against his chest more than anything, she straightened and stepped back...freer? Lighter? "I'm sorry I hit you."

"Don't be. I deserved it."

"No, you didn't." *Go. Go now.* "Well. This is goodbye."

Heart thudding against her ribs, Ryanne stalked to her station—before she did something foolish, like accept his offer and ruin *both* their futures.

CHAPTER SEVENTEEN

The next two weeks ticked by without incident.

Ryanne stayed in contact with Jude about the repairs at the Scratching Post. They were friendly to each other, and it was nice, if heartbreaking.

She missed what they'd had before. Sex and laughs. *Communion.*

My fault we're not together. He'd asked for another chance, and she'd spurned him.

Had she made the right decision?

They avoided discussing anything personal, but did meet multiple times about Savannah. Apparently she had a son—Savannah mailed Jude photographs of her pregnancy as well as letters Filip had written her when he was first imprisoned, asking about the boy.

Dushku had been holding the boy hostage all of his life, and Savannah now wanted, needed, help. She'd been horribly used and abused, her little boy raised by a monster. Something had to be done.

Jude had called Savannah late last night, and the two had worked up a plan. He would show up at Dushku's home later this morning, when Savannah and Thomas were scheduled to be together. He would create a distraction, and she would escape with the boy. Daniel and Brock would be waiting just outside Dushku's property—out of range of the man's security cameras—and they would escort the pair to the city, where employees of LPH Protection would drive them to a safe house, and work to get them new identities.

If Jude got hurt...

Sickness churned in Ryanne's stomach. He'd faced more dangerous situations in the military. He would walk away from this one, too.

With a sigh, she petted and kissed the cats before trudging out of her room at the Strawberry Inn. She should be happy. The wounds left by years of hurt had finally scabbed over. All because of Jude. Because, despite everything, he'd been there for her when she needed him. Because he'd held her close, protecting her, as she'd crumbled. Yet...

The thought of leaving him, even for a month, caused a new hurt.

I will not act like my mother. I will not spend my life catering to the needs of an emotionally distant man.

Determined, Ryanne headed to the lobby to meet Dorothea. By some miracle, her friend had convinced her to wake at an ungodly hour and go jogging, promising exercise would clear Ryanne's mind and heart, or some crap like that.

"How in the world do you look like sex while wearing yoga pants?" Dorothea anchored her hands on her hips, trying to hide a wealth of tension behind a smile. Had she fought with Daniel? "I look like five pounds of sausage meat stuffed into a one-pound wrapper."

Ryanne rolled her eyes. "You look like a ray of sunshine. I look like death." She hadn't slept well since the fire. Any time she closed her eyes, she saw Jude rushing into the flames, felt the same sense of helplessness, wondering if she was going to lose her man, her cats and her business all in the same night.

"Sunshine? Score! Now stop flirting with me, and come on."

The first two miles, Ryanne was able to keep up. By the third mile, she was drenched in sweat, panting and wheezing. She stopped in the middle of a dirt road, hunching over to brace her hands on her knees.

"Wait," she managed to call. "Hospital...dying...heart attack."

A laughing Dorothea backtracked and jogged in place. Her breaths were even, only a glimmer of perspiration on her brow.

"You can't be human," Ryanne grumbled, and her friend barked out another laugh.

Except her laughter didn't last long, the tension Ryanne noticed earlier returning. "Okay, I have to tell you something, but please, please, please stay calm, okay? I wasn't sure when to tell you, so I decided to wait until we were away from the inn and you could react the way you wanted, without fearing someone would see or hear."

Panic struck. Acid churned in her stomach, waves of nausea nearly choking her. "What happened? What's wrong? Tell me!"

"Just before you came down to the lobby, I received a text from Daniel. The tent..." Color seeped from Dorothea's cheeks, leaving her waxen. "Sometime after you closed last night, someone shredded your tent and tore up your parking lot, turning the gravel into a giant mud puddle."

Meaning, she wouldn't be able to open tonight or any other night for a while. Probably a long while. She could go without the tent, but she couldn't serve her customers in mud. No one wanted to get dirty while on the prowl for a hookup.

Dushku. He was to blame.

"I'm so, so freaking sorry, Ryanne."

Tears stung her eyes, and glass shards seemed to join the acid, her nausea intensifying until—

There, on the dirt road, she vomited the contents of her stomach. A cup of water and a banana.

With a cry of concern, Dorothea rushed to her side. "Oh, Ryanne. If there's anything I can do…"

Again and again, Ryanne had fought Dushku's underhanded attacks and come out on top. But what had it gotten her? Another devastating blow. Why keep fighting? Why not give up, give in and save herself another defeat?

"I want to go home," she whispered. But she didn't have a home, did she. Her war with Dushku had cost her the apartment, temporarily, and some of her favorite possessions, permanently. The smell of smoke could be cleaned from most pieces of furniture, maybe, hopefully, but broken vases and warped paintings could not be repaired.

Her friend helped her to her feet, but the emotional upheaval proved too strong and her stomach protested again. She threw up one more time before she had the power to head back to the inn.

When they reached the town square, residents were stirring, opening their businesses for the day. Virgil Porter and Anthony Rodriguez were already outside Style Me Tender, playing checkers as usual. Both men smiled and waved, then stood and approached when they noticed her fragile condition.

"Poor Miss Wade," Anthony said. "Did you have yourself one of them heatstrokes?"

"Nah. This girl's in distress," Virgil said. "You tell us what's wrong, and we'll fix it, lickety-split."

"Thanks, guys, but I just need to rest," she muttered.

Finally she and Dorothea reached the entrance of the inn. Dorothea held open the doors, and Ryanne shuffled inside… where her mother waited at the counter, flirting with Daniel Porter, a suitcase at her feet.

Jude parked in front of the Dushku estate. Best property in Blueberry Hill. A fifty-five-acre working blueberry farm with an eight-thousand-square-foot antebellum estate. Armed guards walked the balcony, Anton and Dennis among them.

Considering Jude had spent twenty minutes at the security gate at the entrance, the pair he'd beaten at the Scratching Post had already been notified of his presence. Both males stopped to aim their semiautomatics at him.

Go ahead. Shoot me.

The worst that could happen? He'd die.

Wasn't like death was a big deal. Through no fault of his own, he would join his family at long last. Considering his emotional state the past few weeks, he could use the peace.

I'll never give up.

A muscle jumped in his jaw. *Fight to live.* He couldn't, wouldn't, leave Ryanne to deal with Dushku alone.

If all went according to plan, Savannah and Thomas would be safe within the next half hour. Using Dushku's playbook against him, Jude had created a distraction earlier this morning, sneaking onto the property and setting the blueberry fields on fire. Tit for tat. Any other day, guilt would have slayed him. Today, Dushku had shredded Ryanne's tent, and ruined her parking lot—Jude had thrown the match without a single qualm.

The blaze had been extinguished, but smoke still thickened the air, the perfect cover for Savannah and Thomas. More than that, most of Dushku's men were still in the fields to mitigate the damage.

As Jude emerged from his truck, Dushku opened the front doors and descended the porch steps. The usual smug smile had been replaced by a fierce scowl. "Jude Laurent. To what do I owe this visit?"

Game on. "I'd like to chat about your destruction of Ryanne's property."

"Do you hope to trick me into confessing to a crime while you wear a wire? Too bad. I'm innocent." Dushku pressed a weathered hand against his double-breasted suit. "If I happen to profit from her bad luck, well, she should take heart. The fact that she's alive and well is a true miracle. And if she were smart, she'd sell the bar before things get worse. What if another tragedy befalls her?"

Calm. Steady.

Screw it. *I'm going to kill him.* Rage dotted Jude's vision. As long as this man drew breath, he would be a thorn in Jude's side. He had no respect for women or children, or *life*; reasoning with him was impossible.

With a single strike, Jude could sever his carotid artery. If he got hit by a hail of gunfire in the process, he got hit. Even injured he could dive into his truck and burn rubber past the gate. He'd survived worse.

Remember—can't help anyone if you're in prison for murder.

Right. He settled his weight in his heels, and remained in place. "You haven't met your match—the truth is, I'm way out of your league."

Dushku arched a brow, unperturbed. "Is that so?"

"I tried to tell you before, but you failed to understand. You made the biggest mistake of your life when you decided to go after Ryanne Wade. Without her, I'll be free to end you, damn the consequences. I have nothing else to live for. And without me, my friends will feel free to end you, damn the consequences. They take their revenge seriously. Either way, you're screwed."

For the first time, Jude detected a glimmer of fear in the old man's eyes.

"Brock sees her. She's headed his way." A familiar voice whispered through the piece in Jude's ear. Daniel was keeping track of both Jude and Brock, who'd apparently spotted Savannah.

He smiled.

"What?" Dushku demanded.

The front doors suddenly swung open. Anton came stomping out, menace in every step. "Where is she? Where's Savannah?"

"What are you talking about?" Dushku's brow wrinkled with confusion. "I saw her twenty minutes ago."

The last time he'd seen her, Jude had just reached the security gate. Everything was happening according to plan.

"She and the boy are missing. They aren't in her room." Anton flared his nostrils like a bull about to charge and focused on Jude. "Where is she? Tell me, or so help me, I'll—"

Motion short and jerky, Dushku held up his hand in a bid for silence. "Did you search the house?"

"Not all of it," Anton admitted, his tone stiff.

"She couldn't have gotten far. Go. Search every room, even the storm shelter." Dushku pointed to two other guards. "You, search the surrounding woods."

Leveling his gaze on Jude, he grated, "I know you had something to do with this."

"Me? Go against you?" Jude arched a brow. "Why would I dare?"

Dushku prowled closer to him, then stopped, his nostrils flaring. Realized he'd lose in a physical altercation? "Let's take Mr. Laurent inside. We'll continue our...chat."

As the guards walked toward him, Jude smiled and tapped the small device in his ear. "I don't think you want to touch me right now. For all you know, I have the sheriff of Strawberry Valley on Bluetooth, listening to every word." He didn't; he had Daniel, who had gone quiet.

Dushku popped his jaw as Jude climbed in his truck, unencumbered. His gaze remained on his adversary. *You and I, we aren't done, though.*

The old man *seethed.*

Jude eased down the drive. As he passed the gate, Dushku in his rearview mirror, Daniel spoke up again.

"She betrayed us. Brock trekked the woods, intending to meet her, only to watch her and the boy climb into someone else's car and speed away. He missed the plates, so we have no way to check out the car's owner."

In the end, had she not trusted Jude? Or had she used *him* as a distraction? Perhaps she'd turned to the john who'd given her the cell phone.

A mistake on her part, but there was nothing Jude could do about it now.

"By the way," Daniel added, "Ryanne has been throwing up all morning, and on top of that little sundae, her mom showed up at the inn, causing trouble."

Ryanne…sick…

A virus? Or something more sinister? Had Dushku struck again?

"I'm on my way." Fighting panic, Jude put the pedal to the metal and sped toward the Strawberry Inn.

CHAPTER EIGHTEEN

Can't deal with this right now, Ryanne thought.

She lay in bed, a cool rag draped over her forehead while the kittens used her body as a scratching post—and oh, the irony.

On top of everything else, Jude was at Dushku's house, helping Savannah. As soon as realization had struck, Ryanne had vomited all over again. He was in danger, and there was nothing she could do to aid him. She just had to wait.

Now her mother, who'd followed her to her room, wanted to "catch up."

Selma hadn't aged a day. Her long black hair had no signs of gray, and her flawless olive skin had only a trace of lines. Dark eyes possessed a sensual tilt, and pouty lips promised a thousand delights.

How many Strawberry Valley males would make a play for her?

"My *cariño*," Selma said, sitting on the edge of the bed. As if she hadn't ignored Ryanne for years, and their relationship was no longer in tatters. "How can I help you?"

"You can leave. I feel better now, but I could use some rest."

"You most certainly do not feel better. I hate to break it to you, baby girl, but you look like someone took you out behind a shed and shot you."

Emotionally? *Nailed it.* Ryanne tossed the rag on the nightstand and sat up, glaring at her mother while gently petting William and Cameo. "Why are you here? You disowned me, remember?"

Cheeks flushing with shame, Selma said, "I only disowned you because you betrayed me, choosing that man over your own flesh and blood. But I've forgiven you. We can move on now."

That man. Earl. The best person she'd ever known. "Talk about him with respect, or don't talk to me at all. Are we clear?"

The color in Selma's cheeks deepened, and she shifted uncomfortably. "I'm sorry, *cariño.* All right? Better?" When Ryanne nodded, she grinned. "I admit I was over the moon when you called me."

Too little, too late. When Selma disowned her, Ryanne had sobbed. She'd mourned. Then she'd picked herself up, with Earl's help, and learned to live without her mother.

"Just…go away. *Please.* We'll talk later, okay?" The nausea had finally eased, but the urge to cry had escalated. This was her life. No matter how bad things got, something could always be worse.

"Te he extrañado, cariño." I've missed you, sweetheart.

"Is that why you called, texted and wrote me so many letters?" she snapped.

A soft sigh. "I was hurt and jealous, that's all. You loved that— Earl so much more than you loved me."

"Do we have to do this now?" She had a choice to make. Sell the Scratching Post to Dushku, admitting defeat, and get a normal job, or find a way to open the bar regardless of the problems. "I need to be alone, need to think. The bar is closed for repairs, so I've been opening on the patio, but the parking lot is now a mud lake."

"Ohhh. You should invite men to strip and mud wrestle. I'd pay good money to see that. Well, I'd let a man pay good money for me to see that."

Of course her mother would pay to see people— Ryanne's mind zinged with the possible solution. Mud wrestling. Or better yet, oil wrestling. Oil was sexier than mud, and watching people oil wrestle would give customers a good reason to get dirty.

Pay to play.

They could lay tarps over the ground. A little mud would find its way to the surface, but a little was better than a lot. Or she could do both mud and oil wrestling, filling giant plastic pools with whatever substance she decided, and charging "combatants" ten dollars a match. Plus a cover fee! Food for thought.

If someone got hurt and sued...

Once upon a time, Earl had a mechanical bull. To ride it, patrons had to sign a waiver releasing the bar of any liability, and they had to sign before they'd had a single drink. She could do the same.

"Thank you," she said, reaching for her phone to call Jude. How excited he would be when he found out—

Would he be excited?

Her shoulders sagged, her eyes burned. "You *really* need to go, Selma."

"Selma? I'm your dear momma. You should call me—"

"There's no time to chat. I have a ton of planning to do." She leaped to her feet, careful of the kittens, and propelled a sputtering Selma toward the exit.

Opening the door, she spotted Jude, headed straight for her, and her heart thudded. Thank the Lord! He was alive and looked to be uninjured.

He stopped in front of her, their gazes clashing, brown against blue. Concern tightened his features, and locks of sandy-blond hair stuck out in spikes, as if he'd tried to rip out a hunk or two.

"Are you all right?" he asked. "Daniel told me you've been throwing up. I thought Dushku might have—" His voice cracked.

Might have what? Poisoned her? And Jude had worried about

her health? "No, I'm fine," she assured him, her tone gentle. "How are Savannah and the boy?"

"You're sure you're okay?" he insisted.

"Yes."

Relief brightened his expression. "I'm not sure about Savannah. She chose to leave with someone else."

What! Why? "As long as she's safe from Dushku, I'm happy, I guess."

"Who's Savannah? Who's Dushku?" Selma fanned her face as she looked over Jude. "And just who are you, *hermoso*?"

"No! Absolutely not. Do not flirt," Ryanne barked. Not with him. "He's off-limits *forever*." Not that saying "off-limits" had ever done any good with her mother.

"What?" Selma wiggled her brows. "I'm single, still young, and I appreciate a man with—"

"Stop. Just stop." Please. "You don't want my sloppy seconds, okay?" Oh, crap! Had she really just said that? She cast an apologetic look to Jude.

He looked far from offended. In fact, he studied Selma for several long moments, and his eyes narrowed to tiny slits. From anger—or attraction?

Of course he found her mother attractive. Who didn't?

"Oh! Do tell, baby girl. How was he?" Selma bumped their shoulders together. "Spill. Start with every inch of him covered and end with him naked and exhausted."

Tell her mother about Jude's spectacular bedroom prowess? Gag!

Ryanne gave the woman a gentle push into the hall, at Jude's side. The two looked good together. She gnashed her teeth. "I'll be opening the Scratching Post tomorrow night." Though she would prefer to wait till the end of the week, after she'd done some planning and spoken to her lawyer, she had to capitalize on the town's ignorance of what had happened to her parking lot. Rather than feeling sorry for her, people might think she'd created the mess on purpose. For fun. "If you decide to stop by, wear clothes you don't mind getting dirty. It's going to be oil and/or mud wrestling night."

"You're using my idea?" Selma grinned and clapped. "See, *cariño*. We make such a good team!"

Jude seized the opportunity to enter the room and bid Selma a swift adieu by closing the door in her stunned face. "Oil and/ or mud wrestling?" He cocked an eyebrow at Ryanne before striding to the bed to cuddle and pet the kittens.

Dang it, she'd gone too long without hearing the sound of his voice. Now the huskiness of his tone stroked her ears, and she wanted to purr like the kittens.

And what a glorious picture he made. The alpha male with a clowder of fragile felines. Worse, his scent permeated the room, intoxicating Ryanne, making her body clench with longing. Her blood heated, and her bones seemed to begin the slow process of liquefying. A reaction only he could cause.

Stay strong. "You got a problem with oil and mud wrestling, or just the survival of my bar?"

He flinched. "I thought you forgave me for the smile."

She had. She really had. Ashamed of herself for lashing out— again—she replied, "You're right. I'm sorry. I have no excuse for my behavior. Except for all the excuses I have. My mother, throwing up a million times and Dushku's latest plot against me."

"You're forgiven. And I promise you, Ryanne, I would *never* want your home or livelihood destroyed. If you can't trust me about anything else, at least trust me about that."

The urge to jump into his arms, to hold on and never let go, bombarded her. The urge to use his chest as a punching bag followed. How light and free she'd felt last time. The urge to drop to her knees and cry—no laugh, no cry—came last, and lingered.

What the heck was *wrong* with her?

She'd never been this emotional. It was just, Jude was so sweet, so concerned for her.

Well, she'd decided to resist him romantically, so, she had better freaking start resisting him. Not just when it was easy, but especially when it was hard...so wonderfully hard.

Staring at his fly? Bad, Ryanne. Bad!

Bad *Jude*. That fly grew...and grew...

"I want your bar to succeed," he said, his voice smoke and gravel now, "and I think oil wrestling is a great idea. But you've been sick. You should be in bed, not planning a major event."

"I *was* sick. As you can see, I'm feeling better." Without depression and defeat weighing her down, her energy returned and her stomach fully settled. "And I *do* have a lot of planning to oversee, so..."

"I'll help. Tell me what you want done, and I'll take care of it. You'll rest." As he spoke, he carried the kittens to the bathroom, two at a time. He had a slight limp today, and it tugged at her heartstrings.

"What are you doing?" Ryanne asked.

"Giving us a little privacy."

She gulped. "Because you're afraid the kittens will gossip about our conversation?" Alone or in a crowd, it didn't matter. Nothing was going to happen today. Probably.

"Because I don't want to corrupt their innocent eyes."

"Please tell me you're thinking about murdering me." That, she could fight. If he kissed her...

"Some people *do* consider pleasure a weapon."

Poo on a stick!

"All you have to do is resist me," he said, "and I'll stop."

That. That was the problem. *Could* she?

"We want different things, Jude."

"We want each other, Ryanne." When Belle joined her babies, he shut the bathroom door and approached Ryanne. She lost her breath and stepped back. The exit blocked her retreat. Her heart began to beat harder, faster, and the air crackled with awareness.

Only a whisper away, he rasped, "My body craves yours every moment of every day. Does yours crave mine?"

The hope and heartbreak in his tone tore her insides to shreds. *Resist!* "Cravings aren't always good for us."

Unabashed, he forged ahead. "You always remind me of strawberry shortcake. You are the tastiest treat in town." His cheek nuzzled hers, his beard stubble tickling her sensitive skin. "In the world."

Softening…

Buck up. Stay strong. Ryanne reached out to push him away… but ended up curling her fingers into the collar of his shirt. He was deliciously muscular, tough and hot, and she was weak and needy, tremors prancing along her spine.

Panting, she met his gaze. To her delight, he was panting, too.

"I need you, Ryanne, and you need me. Give me a chance to prove it."

"We shouldn't…"

"Oh, shortcake. We should."

The endearment weakened her knees, as always, but the ragged tone he used…pure, unadulterated desire.

Stay. Strong. "I wanted to… I mean, I should have… I expected… Argh!" Whatever. She'd tried, and failed. Now she would enjoy. "I can't resist you," she admitted, and triumph turned his navy blues into sapphires. "But this is the last time. This is goodbye." Closure for them both.

Now his eyes darkened. "This isn't goodbye. I'll never tell you goodbye. This is hello." Before she could protest, his lips crashed against hers, his tongue thrusting inside her mouth.

She melted against him, welcoming him, kissing him back as if her life depended on it. And in a way, it did. This *was* goodbye. As much as it pained her, they would be better off as friends.

His sweet taste invaded her senses. No, not just invaded. Overtook. He was pure aggression, a conquering warrior, determined to have his woman. His prize.

I'm not his woman or his prize. Constance is. Constance always will be.

But here, now, for this brief, stolen moment, he would belong to Ryanne.

"Don't stop," she rasped.

He required no further encouragement, ripping at the waist of her pants, shoving the material down her legs, along with her soaked panties. On his knees, he devoured her, paying homage or supplication, or both, drawing moan after moan from her. Moans he answered in kind.

Her legs trembled and her nails dug into his scalp as his tongue flicked, working her into a frenzied state, where only pleasure mattered. He reached up to play with her breasts, pluck at her nipples, and drive her far more insane. Just when she was about to break apart at the seams, he stopped, stood.

Argh! "Jude!"

"Not yet." He ripped open his jeans and pushed his underwear underneath his testicles, freeing his massive erection.

A new flood of arousal pooled between her legs. He lifted her, forcing her to lock her ankles behind his waist...

And then he kissed her again, letting her taste herself on his lips. Then, oh, then, he slammed inside her.

Pleasure consumed her; the most intense orgasm of her life. It tore her down and built her back up. Moans and mewls flowed from her lips, practically a song. Something was different this time...something...what? *Can't think.* As he hammered in and out of her, harder, faster, she had to bite the cord between his neck and shoulder to contain a scream.

The orgasm continued to build...and build...until a second exploded through her.

As she clenched and unclenched on his length, Jude joined her, shouting her name, grunting, then shuddering against her while jetting inside her.

His shoulders sagged, and he leaned into her, pressing her

more firmly against the wall. His heart raced in sync with hers, the puffs of their breathing flowing together.

For a long while, neither of them spoke. Too afraid to ruin the moment?

Her legs trembled and eventually slid down, down. Waves of sadness washed over her as her feet rested on the floor. Was this truly the last time she would be with Jude?

He straightened, pulling from her, severing contact, and she finally realized what had been different. He hadn't worn a condom. For the first time, he hadn't been hypervigilant about protection.

Maybe he was ready to take their relationship to the next—

What are you doing? Stop! That line of thought would only set her up for another failure.

"You don't have to worry about your little swimmers, if any still happen to be active." Even though she'd thrown up her birth control this morning, she'd just had a period. It had been lighter than usual, and shorter to boot, but it had been a period all the same.

He sucked in a breath, as if only just realizing he'd forgotten a latex barrier.

See! He wasn't ready.

"I want to stay here with you," he said as he righted his clothing, "but I'll leave if you tell me to go."

Too vulnerable to deal. Trembling, she dressed. "I…yes. Go." *Stay.* "I want to be alone. Thank you for understanding."

"Ryanne."

"No." Unwelcome tears burned her eyes as she gave him a nudge into the hall. "Goodbye, Jude."

As she shut the door, his gaze remained on hers until the last possible moment, his features pale, breaking what remained of her heart. There at the end, she thought she heard him whisper, "Hello, Ryanne."

CHAPTER NINETEEN

Cheers echoed through the night. Three rival towns had come together to engage in the ultimate showdown. Strawberry Valley, Blueberry Hill and Grapevine. In three different plastic pools, citizens challenged each other to oil wars. Others watched.

Jude had donned a special boot in order to protect his prosthesis from mud and oil. He stood off to the side, ready to spring into action if anyone got too rowdy—or Dushku struck. The man had to be fuming about Savannah and Thomas, not to mention Ryanne's ingenious plan. A true lemons to lemonade story.

To Jude's knowledge, the Scratching Post had never drawn such a large crowd. Even Glen Baker, the guy who'd almost given his number to Ryanne at Daniel's engagement party, had come.

Jude had run a background check on him. As Glen had admitted to Ryanne, he'd recently lost his job. What he hadn't told her: he was being investigated for stealing from the company.

If he put his sticky fingers anywhere near Ryanne, he would lose them.

Sutter and the waitresses worked the crowd, while "snack

specialist" Caroline Mills walked around with a basket in her arms, selling sandwiches wrapped in plastic.

Jude was happy for Ryanne and her success. He just wasn't happy for himself.

He'd had mind-blowing, unforgettable sex with her, like a junkie who'd needed another fix. He'd suffered so much for so long; she offered euphoria—then took euphoria away. Now he was twitchy. *Desperate.*

Seeing her every day and not having the freedom to kiss, touch and hold her was worse than taking a knife to the chest.

Hello.

Goodbye.

He'd only been fooling himself. Ryanne might want him, but she didn't want to want him. Their roles had reversed. She fought her attraction to him the way he'd once fought his attraction to her.

He hated it, but what could he do? He'd damaged their relationship beyond repair.

He would be better off returning to Midland. Strawberry Valley offered prolonged torment, nothing more. What would happen the day Ryanne decided to date another man? Jail time, that's what.

So, decision made. As soon as he'd taken care of Dushku, Jude would move back to Texas. Carrie and Russ would be pleased.

Daniel and Brock would be upset, but they would understand.

"You should be in one of those rings, big boy." Selma sidled up to him and wiggled her perfectly plucked brows. "I'd love to see your dirtiest moves."

Flirting with him? *You've got to be kidding me.* She was a beautiful woman, and he could see where Ryanne had gotten her innate sensuality, but the only thing he wanted to do to Selma was shake her. She should have taken better care of her only child.

Like I have room to judge.

"Please don't hit on me, ma'am. I'm kind of dating your daughter."

She wagged a finger in his face. "Don't you dare ma'am me. I'm young. Vibrant."

"And in denial."

"*Anyway.* I know all about your sexual escapades with my girl. But tell me this, macho man. Has she forbidden you from having fun when the two of you aren't together?"

Right on cue, someone in the ring called out, "I got mud on my boots and oil in my butt crack. Gonna need a rubber hose to get it all out."

"Excuses, excuses," someone else shouted. "Admit it. You're just hoping for a little backdoor action."

Snickers and guffaws blended, cutting through the night.

"I gave your mom backdoor action last night," was the reply. "But there was nothing *little* about it."

Hooting and hollering now.

"I'm not interested in having fun," Jude finally told Selma. "I'm here to protect your daughter from very bad men."

She *hmphed.* "Don't act like you care about Ryanne's well-being. I know your type, and I know better. You want her in your bed until you tire of her."

His jaw ached as his teeth scraped together. "A man doesn't get tired of Ryanne Wade. A man gets addicted." And that was the truth.

Selma gaped at him, as if she'd never heard more ludicrous words. "If that's true, why are you *kind of* dating my daughter and not actually dating her? Why haven't you put a ring on her finger? Why does she look miserable every time she glances in your direction?"

"She has a plan for her life, and I'm not a part of it."

Would he travel with her if she asked? He wasn't sure. The thought of seeing the world without his little girls shredded him. But so did the idea of life without Ryanne.

Life? As in, a long-term commitment?

Was he ready for that? It's what Ryanne wanted. At least, he suspected. Some of the things she'd said...

We want different things. She'd mentioned this one twice. He'd wanted a temporary relationship. She'd wanted...a permanent one?

Why bother? Time is running out. Again, he had to wonder if she wanted more time with him.

The last time she'd mentioned their "short-term affair" her tone had been wistful.

"Plans shmans." Selma moved in front of him to pat his cheek. "I've heard gossip about you. The grumpy widower with no family and no leg. Poor you. Boo-hoo. You waste a lot of time feeling sorry for yourself, don't you?"

Anger scalded him. How easily she spoke of traumas that had changed him spirit, soul and body. "I grieve," he snapped.

"Please, boy-o. You fear."

The anger gave way to rage, rushing through his veins, scorching everything in its path. Dark smoke seemed to fill his mind. "You don't know me. You don't know *shit*."

"Please. Enlighten me, then."

Refusing to engage her a moment longer, he pressed his lips together and remained silent, staring off in the distance. Him? Unable to overcome his fears? No. Hell, no.

Maybe.

Damn it, no. He grieved the loss of his family, something this woman couldn't possibly understand.

"I married a man like you, you know," she said, having no idea the beast she provoked. Or simply not caring. "He broke my heart every day, and I wouldn't wish him on my worst enemy. Well, maybe I'd wish him on Edna Mills. We were neighbors once, and she refused to let Caroline play with Ryanne, because she thought I'd try to steal her husband. As if I'd want anything to do with her ground sirloin. I had grade A filet."

"You slept with Ryanne's boyfriends. I wouldn't exactly call you discriminating."

"I most certainly did not sleep with those boys. I tested them by *offering* sex. There's a difference. I never had any intention of following through. I just wanted to make sure they'd remain faithful to my girl. And guess what? They *wouldn't* remain faithful. But I knew Ryanne wouldn't believe me unless she saw their betrayal with her own eyes. She was far too trusting."

Now she trusted no one. "Is that what you're doing to me? Testing me?"

Her next smile had bite. "Just so you know, if you hurt my little girl, I'll cut off your balls and wear them as earrings." Finally, she sauntered off.

"Don't act as if you care about her," he called. "You didn't exactly protect her as a child. What makes you think you can protect her now, after ignoring her all these years?"

Back stiff, she paused and looked at him over her shoulder. "Maybe I wasn't the best mother, but I'm determined to make up for the past. From everything I've heard, you've been good for Ryanne. From everything I've seen, she still wants you. But it's going to take more than physical desire if you two crazy kids are going to get a happily-ever-after."

Happily-ever-after.

Forever.

Selma wasn't done. "She loved Earl with all her heart, and you remind me of him. Crankiest bastard ever born. While she stuck to him like glue, she runs away from you. I wonder why."

For the next hour, Selma's words plagued Jude. Why had Ryanne loved Earl, the "crankiest bastard ever born"? Why had she stayed with him, but not with Jude?

Earl offered safety, security, she'd once said.

Safety. Security. Exactly what Jude offered, too. So why was he having so much trouble pinning her down?

Although, if Jude had offered only a half-measure of safety and security, and only temporarily, he'd offered nothing more than platitudes. In a relationship like theirs, he had to offer all that he was, all that he would be, and he had to offer forever or he had better just walk away.

Forever. Happily-ever-after.

Life. A long-term commitment.

Maybe Selma was bat shit crazy and knew nothing about her daughter. But then, Jude clearly didn't know anything, either.

For a long while, he watched the couples around him. Some held hands. Others laughed together. A few shared passionate glances. Fewer argued about this or that, but all presented a united front. Two made one. Envy cuddled up to him, petting him like a long-lost lover. He'd had that kind of bond with Constance, missed it—her—every day. But the truth was, her loss no longer hurt as badly.

As much as Ryanne had tormented him, she had helped ease him.

Brock and Daniel noticed him, and approached warily, as if they were attempting to tame a wild animal.

"Okay, enough," Brock said. "You can't go on like this. You want your girl, so go get her."

"You have a chance to be happy," Daniel said. "Why embrace your misery when you can embrace your girl?"

Razors seemed to tear through his insides. These guys meant well. They wanted the best for him, but they remembered the old Jude. The guy who smiled and cracked jokes, who used to stare up at the stars, comforted by the fact that the same stars stared down at his girls.

He wished he could be the same man to Ryanne that he'd been to Constance. Any time he'd been home on leave, he'd prepared surprise meals for Constance. He'd given her gifts. Once she'd admired a beaded pillow on a TV show, and he'd had it re-created. Countless times, he'd cut flowers from her archenemy's garden, an old biddy who'd lived in their neighborhood.

He'd never done anything kind or romantic for Ryanne, and the thought suddenly bothered him. She was a prize, and she deserved to be treated as one.

Why had he stopped fighting for her? Because winning her would be hard, if not impossible? So the hell what. Because they wanted different things? Did he even know what he wanted?

Stop trying and start failing.

Actually, stop *doing* and start failing. Trying never did shit for anyone, except give the trier a thousand excuses to do a piss-poor job. If Jude continued doing—fighting—he risked getting hurt again. So. The hell. What. He was hurting regardless. What did he have to lose?

He didn't have to move back to Midland any time soon, or at all. And Ryanne hadn't yet left for Rome. There was still time to romance her.

A spark of excitement burned inside him. He thought about all the times Ryanne had texted him, asking him to do something with her. He thought about words she'd once rasped at him. *Finally we had fun together.*

So. She craved fun—with him. He hadn't made any attempt to amuse her, but that would change. Tonight.

"I'm going after her. If I don't win her, it won't be because I stopped fighting."

"About time." Daniel patted him on the shoulder.

Brock was too busy staring at Lyndie to pay any more attention to Jude. She stood underneath a halogen light, talking to a man Jude had never met. Not in person, anyway. But Dorothea knew the guy. Jonathan Hillcrest. A teacher at Strawberry Valley High. A few months ago, Daniel asked Jude to do a background check on everyone the pretty inn owner had interacted with.

"Take your own advice, you fool," Jude said, patting his friend on the shoulder. Then he propelled into motion, determined to earn his prize.

"I *dream* of the day a man looks at me the way Jude Laurent is looking at you," Lyndie said as soon as Jonathan Hillcrest walked away. She pressed a hand over her heart and sighed.

The sweet girl had opted to stay on the patio with Ryanne, selling towels, pops, beers and CockaMoons. While Ryanne had gotten a catering endorsement that would allow her to sell alcohol in her parking lot as well, she'd decided to stick to the parameters of her license and sell within the boundaries of the Scratching Post—aka the floor plan inside and out. Better safe than sorry with Dushku around.

"How is he looking at me?" *Like he wants me?* Tremors overtook Ryanne as she collected five dollars from the guy in line and handed him a beer. "The way Brock is looking at you?"

"Brock isn't... He wouldn't... Stop trying to distract me. Jude is looking at you like you shine brighter than the stars."

Really?

Don't face him. Don't you dare face him. Not again. Any time she'd snuck a peek, he *had* been staring at her with a mix of longing and regret, hunger and desperation, and the same sensations had risen in *her*.

The madness had to end.

Perhaps she needed to say goodbye again?

Nope, absolutely not. He might want her, but nothing had changed between them. The more time she spent with him, the more it would hurt when they parted. So, no more hello/goodbyes. No more Jude, period.

Whoa! Going too far. He *had* helped her with tonight's festivities. He'd been enthusiastic and tireless, doing anything and everything she asked, all without complaint.

So, more Jude, but no more hello/goodbyes. She'd go cold turkey, treating his carnal appeal as she would any other kind of addiction. Sure, she'd probably have to endure withdrawals. The shakes, unprovoked crankiness, heck, maybe even more vomiting. She'd gotten sick again this morning, but the stomach pains had ebbed when she'd taken a hot, steamy shower.

"Uh-oh," Lyndie said. "Incoming."

Ryanne swallowed a groan as the scent of spiced rum hit her awareness. "Don't you dare leave—"

"I'll just give you two a moment. Sorry not sorry," her friend said, blowing her a kiss and hurrying away.

Traitor!

Doing everything in her power to mentally prepare for the beauty of Jude Laurent, Ryanne turned.

She wasn't prepared.

Blond hair hung in tangled waves around his rugged face, and the golden stubble on his jaw glistened in the light. He wore a black T-shirt, his muscles on perfect he-man display. His ripped jeans molded to his legs. Blue rubber boots stretched over his knees and cinched in tight so that no mud or oil could leak into his prosthesis.

She gulped. "Hey, Jude."

"Hello, shortcake."

Shortcake again. And why hadn't she realized the word *hello* on his scarred lips would forever make her shiver?

"By the way, I prefer cowboy," he said.

Too bad. She'd called him cowboy because she'd planned to ride him into the sunset. "I'm calling you Jude, and that's that."

"I understand. You'd rather refer to me as the praised one."

He deadpanned the line, dry humor at its finest—humor he'd so rarely displayed before—and she had to cut off her snort.

"Do you know why I call you shortcake?" He stood close to her, his head bent so he could whisper in her ear. None of the customers she served had any idea what they were saying to each other.

"Because I smell and taste like strawberries," she muttered, her heart fluttering.

"Because shortcake is sweeter when it's slathered with cream."

Her eyes widened. There was no way on God's green earth Jude Laurent had just referenced her arousal.

"I *really* like your cream," he purred.

He had. He really had. Pleasure flushed her cheeks. He'd also given her a compliment she hadn't had to request. And such a dirty one, at that, nearly melting her bones.

"I meant what I said earlier. We don't work well together?" A question now?

"Thanks for asking. We do, and I'd like a chance to prove it. As your long-term boyfriend."

Boyfriend? Long-term? The words reverberated in her head as her heart kicked into an erratic beat. "Are you a pod person? What happened to my Jude?"

His eyelids hooded in an instant. "Your Jude?"

The flush spread lightning-fast. "Zip it. That was a slip of the tongue, nothing more."

"Well, I always like when you slip me your tongue. I like it *a lot*. By the way," he added, before she had a chance to respond, or melt into a puddle of goo. "I accept your challenge."

Moving faster than her reflexes could block, he draped her over his shoulder like a sack of potatoes.

Ryanne squealed and, going into some kind of erotic shock, beat her fists against his back. "You put me down right this second, you Neanderthal." *Sexy behemoth.* "I'm working."

"I signaled Brock. He's going to sell the drinks and towels." Jude continued striding forward, maneuvering through the crowd. When he reached one of the pools, he bellowed, "Everyone out!"

A new chorus of cheers rang out. Catcalls and whistles resounded. People called:

"Get her wet, Jude!"

"New rules, all clothes must come off!"

"Take him down, Miss Ryanne. Girls rule, and boys drool."

That voice she recognized. Loner. He now worked as Brett's part-time assistant, and he'd come out tonight to show his support.

"Jude," Ryanne intoned. "Don't you dare. If you do, I will personally—"

With a shrug, he dumped her into the oil. Thick slime oozed over her shirt and pants, quickly soaking the material, wetting her skin. Sputtering, she tried to stand, slipped, managed to catch her balance, then slipped again when Jude smiled. Breath exploded from her lungs as her butt hit the ground.

Jude laughed, actually laughed.

Not wanting him to escape her wrath, she acted quickly, hurling two scoops of oil at him. The substance splattered over his face and dripped onto his chest. He spat once, twice, then turned a faux glare on her, but his navy blues glittered with amusement.

First a laugh. Now genuine happiness. Who was this man?

Being without you has been the worst kind of hell.

He climbed into the pool, but Ryanne didn't give him time to gain his bearings. Remaining on the ground, batting her lashes innocently, she smiled a wicked smile—and swiped out her leg, knocking his ankles together. He tumbled to his butt, landing right beside her.

She should hop out and run, never looking back. This was Jude, and bad things happened when they got together...such bad, naughty things. But she had to beat him at *something*.

Gasps of horror sounded outside the pool.

"Did Ryanne kick our Jude?" someone called. "Don't she know he's disabled?"

"He's bigger and stronger than any of you," Ryanne called right back.

Jude smiled at her. A smile without reservation. A *radiant* smile. Inside, she melted.

Resist!

"Just for that," he said, "I'll consider letting you win."

Oh, he would, would he?

Ryanne stood, somehow remaining steady, and walked toward him. He reached overhead and removed his shirt, revealing a chest that would forever star in her fantasies. Female spectators cheered. As Ryanne wavered—and okay, yes, ogled him—he removed one of his leather wrist cuffs, revealing a strawberry tattooed underneath.

"I wasn't going to show you this, but…" He shrugged. "A man has to use whatever weapons he has in his arsenal."

She gasped. A strawberry. Not for the town…but for her?

He cares about me!

"I love it," she whispered.

"Good." He lashed out his arm, using his drenched shirt as a whip. The end wrapped around her wrist, drawing another gasp from her. He yanked, forcing her to slide closer to him. In a flash, he had her wrists tied and draped around his neck.

Before she had time to process what he'd done, he pushed her down. Looming over her, he slapped a palm beside her temple once, twice, three times, splashing oil every which way.

"She's out," he shouted, then gifted her with another smile.

Cheers. An announcer calling, "Ding, ding, ding. We have a winner. Jude Laurent, everyone!"

"Jude, you gotta teach me that move," Cooter Bowright pleaded.

Ryanne glared up at her beautiful captor. "I thought you were going to let me win."

"No, I said I'd *consider* letting you win. I considered it, and figured it'd be a bad idea. You're already too pretty and too bossy. We don't need to add cocky to the mix."

Seriously. Who was this man?

Well, whoever he was, he needed to learn a valuable lesson. Mess with the bull, get the horns.

Ryanne slid her legs up between their bodies, an easy task considering they were both covered in oil, and flattened her feet on Jude's chest. Holding his wrists to maintain control, she kicked her legs straight and sent him soaring over her head. Only then did she release him, laughing as he landed on his back behind her. She scrambled to her knees and crawled over him.

One, two, three, she slapped her hand beside his temple, splashing oil over his face.

"*He's* out," she said with a smirk.

First he gaped up at her. Surprised she had such devious moves—and that his spine was still intact? Then *he* laughed. A full on, nothing held back laugh. His eyes crinkled at the corners, and his entire chest rumbled. He was so beautiful, like a work of art epitomizing happiness. She remained on top of him, utterly stunned. He'd always been sexy and beautiful, but now also...*devastating.*

His gaze met hers, and though his laughter faded, his smile remained. "Thank you. I haven't laughed like this in...ever."

"You mean you didn't laugh like this with Constance?" As soon as the question left her, she bit her lip, wishing she could take back the words.

He answered after the slightest hesitation, scratching his chin and saying, "Well, she never beat me up."

"Hey! I didn't beat you up."

"My relationship with her was different from my relationship with you," he continued. "We were parents so young, the bulk of our attention devoted to our kids. You and me are all about *fun.*"

Her jaw dropped, realization striking her with the force of a baseball bat. Jude Laurent had just shared personal information about his wife, without reservation or regret. And he'd admitted he had fun with Ryanne.

He placed a soft, sweet kiss on her cheek. "Do you want to tell me goodbye? I've grown fond of your method." As she sputtered for a response, he gave her another kiss. "You're important to me, shortcake. You and I...we want the same thing, and I'm going to prove it."

CHAPTER TWENTY

By noon the next day, Jude had created a nest in bed. Everything he needed surrounded him. Pillows. Bottles of water. A bag of hand-cut chips he'd taken from the bar. Baby book. Pen. Laptop. He was home. His real home. The one he shared with Brock, but had so rarely visited lately, instead choosing to spend his nights at the Strawberry Inn, where he could be near Ryanne, even if they were separated by walls.

Last night, after oil wrestling with her, he'd returned to the cabin to give Ryanne time to think about everything he'd said. Because he was a gentleman. Sometimes. And because he'd been hiding from life far too long.

He'd tossed and turned all night, his mind in turmoil. Finally, he'd known what he had to do.

Today, he would slay his demons and become the man Ryanne needed him to be.

He leaned against the headboard, his laptop at his left, feed from the bar constantly playing—all was still and quiet. The baby book Carrie sent him rested on his lap. He'd already flipped through the pages once, but he'd done it quickly, simply glanc-

ing at every photo without reading what Constance had written underneath.

Miraculously, he'd survived.

Now he flipped through the pages slowly, reading every word,
studying the minutest detail on every picture. In fact, he'd been
staring at a picture of Constance and the girls for over an hour,
misty-eyed. His beautiful wife had been blessed with silvery
white hair and a smattering of freckles, and she'd hated both.
As a child, she'd been teased mercilessly, called Ghost Girl and
Freckle Face. Jude had loved running his fingers through her
silken mass of curls, and tracing his tongue over her freckles.

She'd been adorably short and naturally thin, so delicate he'd
sometimes suspected a strong wind would knock her over. He'd
felt like a giant in comparison, but also invincible. Protecting
and defending her had been an honor and a privilege.

He ran his finger over the photo, tracing the length of her
arm, before shifting his gaze to the girls. They'd had his hair,
sandy-blond with a slight wave, but they'd had Constance's eyes,
as green as emeralds. In the picture, they were three years old,
full of life, love and laughter. The princess and the tomboy, two
halves of a whole.

The caption read: Daddy is overseas and had to miss the girls'
birthday party. While he couldn't be there in body, he made sure
to be there in spirit.

In Constance's hand was a photo of Jude wearing a birthday
hat. He'd had the photo printed, glued it to cardboard and cut
out his image, then anchored feet to a popsicle stick and mailed
the whole thing home. How he'd hated being away, missing important events. Some nights he'd lain awake, eaten up with guilt.

He flipped to the next page—a picture of him with the girls.
He cradled a plastic baby doll in his arms while Bailey and Hailey played doctor, checking the doll for a rash and giving her a
shot of water, aka medicine.

This caption read: Time for a checkup!

He remembered holding his newborns in his arms, counting their fingers and toes and rubbing his freshly shaved jaw against their chubby baby cheeks. The girls had smelled like heaven… until they'd dirtied their diapers. Then they'd smelled like hell.

Jude chuckled and once again admitted Virgil was right. He wouldn't have given up his years with Constance and the girls to save himself from the agony and anguish he would suffer later. Not for any reason. He cherished every second he'd spent with his sweetheart and little sweets.

But all too soon, his laughter turned to sobs. Life wasn't supposed to be this way. Daddies weren't supposed to lose their children. Husbands weren't supposed to lose their wives. So why had he lost both? A simple case of bad luck? Fate? No. Hell, no. Fate hadn't forced a frat boy to go to a bar, drink too much and drive home. Fate hadn't led Constance to put the girls in the car at night and drive…who knew where. He could only guess. Both girls had suffered with a cold. They must have run out of medicine, and Constance, who hadn't had a babysitter, had felt she had no choice but to take both girls with her to pick up more.

The same pang he'd felt since their deaths sliced through his chest yet again, but it wasn't quite as sharp this time, and the pain didn't linger. He'd lost his family because of choices. The choice made by Frat Boy. The choice made by Constance. Every decision mattered, because in the end, there was no changing the past.

I can *change my present and my future.* He could have forever—with Ryanne.

The loss of his family had knocked him down hard. He'd stayed down for two and a half years. With Ryanne's help, he'd finally found the strength to stand.

He wasn't sure when or how it had happened, but at some point, he *had* risen. He was no longer defeated, but ready to fight for better. No longer despondent, but hopeful. He had a purpose again. A life with Ryanne Nicole Wade.

He could make her happy. And in turn, she could make *him* happy.

Who was he kidding? She was *already* making him happy, even though she was nothing like Constance. She wasn't shy, but bold. She wasn't fragile, but strong. Strong enough to knock him on his ass. She wasn't subdued, but witty. Her warped sense of humor was a perfect match for his own, now that he *had* a sense of humor again.

He couldn't live without her.

He'd have to tell Carrie and Russ he wouldn't be moving to Texas, ever. He would be staying in Strawberry Valley, and he would be fighting for his happily-ever-after.

A knock sounded at his door, echoing through his bedroom. "Hey. You spanking the monkey in there?" Brock called.

With a snort, Jude climbed from the bed and hopped to his desk to place the baby book in a drawer. "No monkey spanking. You can come in without burning your corneas."

His friend marched inside, dark circles under his eyes and a week's worth of black stubble on his jaw. He had a smile as wide as ever, but for the first time in a long time, this one appeared genuine.

"What?" Jude demanded, instantly suspicious. No one had a more warped sense of humor than Brock. "What did you do?"

"Only the best thing ever. You're about to fall to your knees and thank me for being the best friend you've ever had, will ever have, *can* ever have. I put Daniel to shame, and I'll expect you to tell him so."

Jude fought to maintain a stern expression. "What did you do?" he repeated.

"Called in the best crews throughout the US and offered the most obscene amounts of money for quick, quality work. As soon as the oil wrestling ended last night, we started. You and your crews had already done the bulk of the work, but we were able to clean up the parking lot and create a brand-new one. It's red brick, with a yellow brick path—details don't matter right now, you'll get to see for yourself. Anyway. It's the coolest parking lot you've ever seen. Also, we finished up the repairs inside the bar. Crews worked all night and all morning. Just finished up, in fact."

His brows drew together as he wavered on his foot. He hadn't anchored his prosthesis in place. "I've been watching the camera feed. No one—"

"I hacked your feed, because I wanted to surprise you," Brock said, his grin widening. "Ryanne should be able to open tomorrow night, after the mortar dries. Go ahead. Tell me I put Daniel to shame."

The reality of what his friend had done began to sink in, and he reeled. For the past two and a half years, he'd mourned and grieved and, though he'd loved his friends, he'd been gruff and grumpy with them. Yet they'd adored him, anyway. Helped him, anyway.

Jude hopped forward to wrap his arms around Brock, holding the guy captive in a bear hug. "Thank you."

"No big deal," Brock said, even as he hugged Jude back as if he were holding on to a lifeline. When they parted, Jude would swear a tear glinted in the corner of his friend's eye. "Just doing what superheroes do. I've even got an army of men surrounding the place, ensuring Dushku can't do shit without serious consequences."

From the lowest of lows to the highest of highs.

A good friend was worth more than a thousand acquaintances. "I freaking adore you, man, but if Ryanne decides to date you instead of me because of this, you had better run for your life."

Brock wiggled his eyebrows, all creepy landlord here to demand rent be paid between the sheets. "I'm surprised she didn't choose me from the beginning. You've seen this face, right?" He patted his cheeks. "Every woman's wildest dream."

"I have seen it. Which is why I'm surprised *I* didn't choose you from the beginning."

"I know, right."

"Does Ryanne know about the repairs?" Jude asked.

"Not yet."

Good. He wanted to be with her, wanted to witness her expression. "I have a few errands to run before we take her."

"Uh, buddy. I don't mean to tell you how to romance your girl, but are you sure you want me tagging along? She's going to cream her jeans when she sees—"

"I'm not afraid to hug you and junk-punch you in the same day. But yes, you're going with us." If he showed up on his own, she might not go with him. They might have called a truce during last night's festivities, but he had a long way to go before his woman—his girlfriend—would take him back.

Ryanne floundered.

Twenty-five minutes ago, Jude and Brock had shown up at the Strawberry Inn. They'd put a blindfold over her eyes and driven her to the Scratching Post. She'd sat in the back of Brock's SUV, Jude pressed against her, his body heat enveloping her, his arousing scent heady in her nose. Keeping her hands to herself had been difficult.

She'd wondered what was going on. When she'd opened her door, he'd been grinning. Grinning! Jude Laurent, with the corners of his lips lifted, his straight white teeth on dazzling display. He'd never looked sexier. And, as if the grin hadn't been confusing enough, he'd radiated excitement.

Now Ryanne stood in the middle of a delicious beefcake sandwich—Jude on one side, Brock on the other—gaping at the beauty before her. The Scratching Post had been transformed. Outside, the parking lot boasted red brick with a yellow brick path leading to the front door. Inside, handcrafted steel latticework covered each of the windows. The floorboards had been replaced, and so had the walls. Strips of sinuous mahogany now extended to create hand-carved nooks along the bar, where patrons could sit.

In back, someone had resurrected Earl's mechanical bull.

Since her postcards had burned to ash, someone—Jude, most likely—had framed pictures taken from all over the globe. The pyramids in Egypt. A temple in India. What looked to be a mountain in Hawaii. Huts built above the bluest water she'd ever seen. Victoria Falls in Zambia. The Amazon River. The Rainbow Mountains in China.

The doors to the bathrooms were no longer plain and utilitarian but decorated with elaborate iron bars. The stairs leading to her apartment were no longer rickety wood but pink-veined marble.

So much work had gone into the changes. So much time and money.

Tears burned the backs of her eyes. She'd cried so often lately, over so many things, she'd begun to feel foolish, but this...this was...she had no words.

Jude walked over to the pictures behind the bar and tapped the glass of one. She gasped. Inside the frame was a picture of Jude carrying her over his shoulder, headed for a pool of oil. Someone must have snapped a photo with their phone. Halogen lights revealed every nuance of his satisfied smile.

He'd grinned while he'd carried her?

"This is my favorite," he said. "You can take it down if you don't like it. I'll understand. I'll put up a new one, but I'll understand."

"I..." Still had no words.

"Don't even think about bringing up money," Brock told her, his voice low enough that Jude wouldn't hear him. "You made my boy laugh. No gift in the world could top that one."

One of the tears escaped, cascading down her cheek. She hadn't slept last night. She'd tossed and turned, remembering the soft, gentle kiss Jude had given her before he'd left her in the pool of oil.

"You love him," she said, finally finding her voice.

"I do. Do you?"

She…didn't know, but she'd never been more obsessed with a man. Had never been twisted into so many knots or been so confused by one person. Did *he* love *her*? Did she want him to?

She'd always thought he had two settings: ice cold and passion-fever hot. She'd rarely seen this third side, tender and romantic. But…what side would she see when he found out…

Just say it. Say. It.

When he found out…she was pregnant. Maybe. Probably.

Only an hour before, she'd gotten sick again. After she'd eaten a few saltines, the nausea had gone away. Suspicions had begun to twirl in her head. About six weeks had passed since they'd had sex the first time, and the odds of pregnancy were astronomical, but not impossible. The condom had ripped, and her birth control could have failed. His vasectomy hadn't yet ended the march of his little soldiers.

As a child, she'd wanted a large family. Now? Not so much. She liked her life. But she did kinda sorta melt over the idea of *their* children.

Tonight she would take a test. If it was negative, great. She would breathe a huge sigh of relief. Right? Of course. Definitely. She wouldn't have to reevaluate her future, or tell Jude the life he'd wanted had gotten popped like her cherry.

If it was positive…

Different emotions coagulated inside her. At the forefront? A mix of excitement and dread. Mostly dread. Jude absolutely, positively did not want children. His vasectomy was proof of that.

Tremors racked her as he returned to her side. "By the way," he said. "I saw the grab bars in your bathroom. Had to do a few repairs in there, but I made sure they remained."

A roundabout way of saying he wanted to shower with her again?

Her heart raced with new purpose, and she wasn't sure how she'd resisted him these past few weeks. Especially yesterday, when he'd declared he wanted a long-term relationship with her.

"Get out of here," she said to Brock, not bothering to glance in his direction.

Brock laughed and patted her shoulder, then strode from the building like a good boy. The moment the door closed behind him, Jude clasped her hands in his, held on as if she were a balloon destined to fly away.

He peered deep into her eyes, rooting her in place, a magnet to her metal. "I want to be with you, now and always. A month or two isn't long enough. I don't think a lifetime will be long enough. I know I've messed up again and again. I know you think we can't go the distance. And if I were the man I was yesterday, I'd agree. But I'm new. You've made me new. For you, with you, I can do anything."

Her eyes widened, and her breath caught. And he wasn't even done!

"If you have a question about my past, ask. Ask *anything*," he added. "I'll answer. If you want to travel the world, go for it. I'll be here when you get back. While you're gone, I'll take care of your bar. I won't let any harm come to it."

As if his words weren't enough, he gave her a look...

She'd never seen this one before. Not from him, not from anyone. A wealth of tenderness mixed with unabashed adoration. This man *yearned* for her.

The tremors settled in her knees, and remaining upright required a concentrated effort. Maybe...maybe a baby wouldn't be such a bad thing? Maybe he wouldn't freak out. Maybe he'd even be happy? After all, the guy had practically *proposed* to her just now.

Unless a baby would ruin absolutely everything?

No, of course not. He'd said *now and always*. He wanted forever with her, come what may.

"What are you saying, exactly?" she asked softly. "You want to get married?"

He flinched, just a little, but enough to notice. "I'm not sure I'll ever want to get married again, but I'm not closed to the idea. I do know I want you in my life and home, and I want to have a place in yours."

"We'll live together?"

A nod. "I would like to, yes. And I know you once said you weren't interested in anything long-term, but I'm hoping you've changed your mind."

The moisture in her mouth dried. She licked her lips, astonished by his one-eighty. "What about children? Will you ever want to adop—"

He shook his head, stopping her before she could finish the sentence. "Children will never be part of my future. As much as you want to travel, I thought…hoped…they wouldn't be part of yours, either. If you think you'll want a family, I'll understand, and we can go our separate ways once and for all." His tone hardened more with every word. "But, Ryanne, I don't want to go our separate ways. I want you more than I've ever wanted anything."

Again, she licked her lips. "This is all so new. I don't know what to say." And that was the unvarnished truth.

"Say you'll think about it. *Please.* I know I can make you happy. No, actually, don't say anything else," he rushed to add when she opened her mouth to tell him…she wasn't sure what. "While you're thinking, I'm coming after you." He brought her knuckles to his lips, kissed each one. "You spent the first part of our relationship romancing me. Now it's my turn."

CHAPTER TWENTY-ONE

Ryanne sat on the lid of her toilet, in her newly rebuilt apartment, a pregnancy test in hand. In one minute forty-six seconds, she would know the truth, and the truth would set her free… or doom her budding relationship with Jude once and for all.

He'd kept his promise. He'd begun to woo her.

Yesterday, after dropping his *I want to be with you now and always* bombshell, he'd driven her back to the inn, where he'd ensured a romantic lunch for two waited in her room. They'd eaten and petted the kittens, and he'd told her all about his years with Constance. He'd even talked about his daughters. Once or twice he'd gotten choked up, but mostly he'd laughed about their childhood antics. Playing "salon" and cutting each other's hair. Coloring the walls with permanent marker. Tearing up Constance's clothes to design their own "high fashion line."

He'd left Ryanne with another tender kiss, not once attempting to get her into bed, though she'd known he desired her. The blue-ribbon prized hog behind his fly had given him away. And she'd desired him, too. She'd ached. She'd burned.

She still ached and burned! She wanted him more than ever before, but she also wanted things settled between them.

This morning, she'd found a gift box at her door. Inside was a second control for her game station. The accompanying note had read: *I would love to play with you. Loser gets naked. Winner gets off.*

Part of her desired the old, morose Jude, but oh, wow, the other part of her adored the new, seductive Jude. But still she resisted agreeing to a permanent relationship with him. What if they crashed and burned yet again? Her emotions couldn't take another round of *he's with me, he's with me not, oh, wait, he's with me.* Especially considering life had never been more complicated or chaotic.

The grand opening of the Scratching Post was tonight, and earlier today her mother had announced, "Guess what? I'm going to work for you! I'll be your best waitress, *cariño*, I promise. All the men will go crazy for me in my uniform, and they'll spend all their monies." As she'd spoken, she'd held up a sequined bra and super-short shorts.

"Selma," Ryanne had said on a sigh. "My employees wear white button-downs and jeans."

"I noticed, which is why I'll be in charge of the staff uniform from now on. And the staff! Don't you worry, baby girl. There's no need to thank me with words. Thank me with a raise."

In the end, Ryanne had given in to her mother's "request." Selma had saved the bar with her mud wrestling idea, and even had ideas for future events. An indoor rodeo with the mechanical bull. A foam party. A glow-stick party.

Actually, most of her ideas involved wild parties.

A knock echoed inside Ryanne's bathroom. "Anything yet?" Dorothea asked through the bathroom door.

"We're dying to know," Lyndie said.

Living in a small town, Ryanne had had to make arrangements to get a pregnancy test without alerting the local gossips. Meaning, she'd had to confide in her friends. Dorothea and Lyndie had driven into the city, allowing her to stay at the inn, vomit repeatedly and plan the bar's reopening.

The girls were waiting in her room, probably pacing the floor.

Deep breath in…out… Enough time had passed, surely. Ryanne looked down at the stick and—

Gasped as shock gut-punched her. A flood of acid immediately rained into her stomach, and she jumped up, dropping the test. She threw open the toilet lid and started a new round of vomiting. Her friends heard her retching and pushed inside the room to rush to her side.

Dorothea held back her hair, and Lyndie picked up the test.

"Oh, Ryanne," Lyndie said with a wide smile that soon wavered. "I'm happy for you? Congratulations?"

"It's positive?" Dorothea asked, jumping up and down and clapping. "We're going to be aunties!"

Lyndie nodded, and Dorothea hugged her, saying, "Yes, absolutely, one hundred percent. We're happy for her."

Ryanne detected a slight thread of envy in her friend's voice and wanted to kick her own butt. Dorothea had been pregnant once, but she'd lost the baby in her fifth month when she'd fallen down a flight of stairs. She'd named the stillborn little girl Rose Holly. Now, her reproductive organs were too scarred to have another child.

Ryanne flushed the toilet and fell back to her haunches, then wiped her mouth with a shaky hand. Cool air kissed her clammy skin, making her feel chilled and overheated at the same time.

"How?" she croaked. How was she pregnant? How had his little swimmers and her little hatcher found each other, despite two (seemingly) unbeatable obstacles?

I'm going to have a baby.

A miracle baby.

Jude's baby.

A baby Jude absolutely, positively did not want.

What if he asked her to abort, the way her father had asked her mother?

Ryanne reacted without thought, pressing her hands against

her flat belly. Never! She might not have planned to have a baby, and she might not have known if she wanted one any time soon, and yes, okay, a baby might ruin the plans she did have in place, but she loved the kid with every fiber of her being.

Not just Jude's baby—my baby.

Another gut-punch of shock. The fact that she felt so strongly, so soon proved the little girl who'd wanted a big family had never really died.

At first, whenever Selma had dated a man with children, Ryanne had been over the moon, excited to have playmates. Not all of those playmates had been kind, but those who had, she'd adored. Every time Selma moved on to a new man, Ryanne lost touch with the kids, and it had hurt; eventually she'd stopped allowing herself to bond with the new members of her family.

No one could take her child away from her. She would be the kind of mother she'd never had. Protective. Loving. *Involved.*

And whoa, back up a sec. She'd gotten it wrong. The baby wasn't going to ruin her plans. Ryanne could travel while pregnant, and later, she could travel with a child in tow, though maybe not in the same style.

Jude had said he wanted to wait for her return. Would he still want to wait for her—for *them*—when he learned the truth?

Perhaps he'd want to travel *with* them.

Dream on. Tears poured down her cheeks. She had to tell him, wouldn't keep it from him. Would his romantic gestures stop?

Forget poo on a stick—pee on a stick!

She *had* fallen in love with him, hadn't she? She'd fallen in love with the brave soldier who'd overcome debilitating anguish, the loss of family and a limb, who'd helped a woman in need even when he despised her occupation. That was why Ryanne had given him her virginity, why she'd slept with him after he'd treated her so poorly. Why she'd considered taking him back after he'd smiled while her bar burned.

"Jude lost his daughters," she whispered, her voice ragged. "He's adamant about never having another child."

"No, he fears *losing* another child. There's a difference." Dorothea crouched and petted her hair, her features solemn. "The pain fades with time, but if left unchecked, the fear only grows."

And Ryanne couldn't fight his fear for him. No one could. He had to do it on his own.

Could he?

Word had spread about the grand reopening of the Scratching Post, and the bar filled to the brim, excitement crackling in the air as people lined up to ride the mechanical bull.

Ryanne put Sutter in charge of drinks and didn't try to stop Selma as she worked the tables, or rather, the men. Ryanne stayed in the kitchen with Caroline, making cube steak and cheese sandwiches with red pepper sauce. A grand opening required grander food than usual.

Also, she liked being in the kitchen. She avoided the photos on the walls behind the bar—the constant reminder of Jude's thoughtfulness. And okay, okay, she wanted to hide from Jude himself. Just for a little while. She would tell him about the baby, absolutely, most definitely...later. She just, she wasn't ready for his thoughtfulness to end. Losing his attention and affection would destroy her. He would no longer look at her with adoration but disdain. He would no longer pull her close but push her further away.

"What's wrong with you?" Caroline popped an olive into her mouth. "Your bar is open and better than ever, but you look like you could barf blood at any second."

"First, gross. Second, your employee review just went from most improved to most likely to be fired."

"Yeah, right. You've either got the worst luck of anyone on the planet, or you're cursed. Fights, fires and mud floods, oh my. I doubt anyone else would sign on for this job."

Well. She wasn't wrong. Ryanne wondered what Dushku would do next.

Muffled footsteps. A gasp from Caroline. Ryanne stiffened, expecting something horrible, because why not. Things had been going so great. She turned—

And came face-to-face with a smiling Jude, his hair tousled, his jaw dusted with stubble. He wore ripped jeans and combat boots, and a leather cuff on one wrist, proudly revealing the strawberry tattoo on the other. This was his usual attire. Only difference was, tonight his T-shirt read The Scratching Post.

He was supporting a bar...because she owned it.

"Hello, beautiful," he said.

I prefer the way you said hello with your mouth and hands and thrust after delicious thrust...

Argh! He was the best man she'd ever met, and she was about to ruin his life, and yet she couldn't stop thinking about him naked, which sucked because he wasn't already naked and she wanted, needed more from him, and oh, crap she was babbling inside her own head. Tears stung her eyes. How she hated her tears. They'd come too frequently lately.

His smile fell. He barked at Caroline to leave, and as soon as she'd hit the bricks, he closed the distance to draw Ryanne against his chest. "What's wrong?"

The longer she put it off, the harder it was going to be to tell him. To maybe probably have to let him go...

"Jude, I... I have to tell you something." She wrung her hands together, her palms damp.

He cupped her cheeks, forcing her gaze to remain steady on his. "Did someone hurt you?" Rage simmered in his tone. Scary rage. If someone had hurt her, that someone would die.

"I'm okay." Kind of. She gulped. *Do it. Say it.* "Do you re-member the first time we had sex?"

He frowned but nodded. "I remember *everything* about our first time. How tight and wet you were. How sweet you tasted."

His thumbs caressed the rise of her cheekbones. "Why? Do you want a do-over? I promise I'll stick around afterward."

Could he *be* any sexier?

"No. I mean, yes, I would like that, but that's not the point of this conversation. Do you, uh, remember how the condom broke?"

His frown deepened, his thumbs stilling. "What *is* the point of this conversation?"

Say it. SAY IT. "I don't know how it happened. I mean, I do know, but we took every precaution, did everything right. It shouldn't have happened, but somehow...it did."

"Ryanne," he snapped. Tremors rolled through him, rocking him against her. "I'm sure I'm misunderstanding you. What are you saying? Spell it out for me."

"I... I'm...pregnant," she whispered. "I took a test this morning."

His arms fell away from her, and he stumbled two steps back. The color drained from his cheeks. "The test was wrong. It had to be wrong."

"I've been getting sick every morning." Still she whispered, and she didn't know why. "I had a period, or thought I did. It was lighter than normal. A *lot* lighter. Apparently that can happen early on."

"A baby." He shook his head. "I can't be the father. I had the vasectomy."

Oh, no, he didn't! "You yourself said your swimmers would remain active about two months after the procedure, and we had sex—what? A week later? And sometimes the pill fails. It happened. It's a miracle. *This baby* is a miracle. Our baby."

"I don't... I can't..."

"If you don't believe me, go get your load checked." Her voice rose with every word. "But I *am* pregnant, and the baby *is* yours."

"I know it's mine. I wasn't saying… I'm just shocked and… I'm having trouble wrapping my head around this."

"If you think I planned it…"

"Did you?" he demanded now, his eyes narrowed.

"No! My goal was to travel the world alone, not start a family with the man who continually dumps me."

His shoulders rolled in, and for a moment, he looked utterly dejected. Then his spine straightened, as if it had just fused with steel. "It's not too late to…we can go to the city in the morning…you can—"

Ryanne slapped him. His head whipped to the side, a bead of blood welling at the corner of his lower lip. He'd pushed her past her emotional limit and awoke momma bear instincts. *Must protect my cub.*

"I *knew* you'd go there," she spat, "but I prayed I was wrong."

He opened his mouth.

"I can't believe you used to guard our country. You can't even guard a womb!" As she stood there, staring at him, panting, her hands balled. Disappointment blended with the rage simmering inside her. "I told you my father wanted my mother to abort me. What would have happened if she'd listened to him? You never would have met me. Is that what you wish for, Jude? No Ryanne, no baby. No family, no pain."

He flinched as if she'd slapped him a second time.

Deep breath in, out. *Knew this wasn't going to be easy.* "Look. I didn't expect you to take the news well, and I understand why you're upset."

His expression hardened. "No, Ryanne. You don't understand." His tone hardened, too. "You can't possibly understand."

"You're not the only one who's lost a loved one," she reminded him softly.

"Yes, but I'm the only one who's lost a child."

"And yet that is exactly what you want me to do—lose my child."

Another flinch. He almost looked feral as he pressed a hand against his chest and stumbled back another step. "I'm sorry. I am sorry. I still want to be with you, but I can't deal with..." He waved a hand toward her stomach. "I just can't."

Pain, so much pain. A dagger in her heart. "So that's it, then? We're done?"

"According to you, we were done already."

"According to you, we were going to have *now* and *always* because you weren't going to give up on me ever again."

Yet another flinch. She wasn't pulling her punches tonight. Couldn't. Her future, her *baby's* future, were at stake.

"I...don't know. I need to think. You've had time to process this, I haven't. So give me a few days, okay. *Please.*" That said, he turned on his heel and strode out of the kitchen, leaving her alone—something he'd promised never to do again.

CHAPTER TWENTY-TWO

Jude felt as if he'd come full circle. From the lowest of lows to the highest of highs not just once but twice—and now he was lower than the lowest of lows. Because yes, he'd somehow dug deeper.

He stumbled out of his truck and fell to his knees. He'd done this before, soon after Ryanne had begun to tempt him with her beauty and charm. He'd railed about the travesty of his life that had been spinning out of control.

How could he have known things could get worse?

He'd just begun to crawl out from the muck of his past. He'd begun to heal, had even found moments of humor, sorrow unable to intrude.

Now, grief was a razor in his chest, as strong as the day Constance and the girls had died. That razor slashed his heart to ribbons, causing a slow hemorrhage of any hope he'd managed to cultivate.

Ryanne was pregnant with his child. His baby.

A baby he would inevitably love.

A baby he could lose in a million different ways.

He'd always known death was too powerful to stop, but he'd never suspected life was, too.

How could this have happened? They'd taken every precaution.

He'd been prepared to open himself up to Ryanne, to spend the rest of his days with her. But a baby—a baby he couldn't protect twenty-four hours a day, seven days a week...

Abject fear grabbed his heart and squeezed. A vise-grip he couldn't escape. Thorns seemed to grow inside his throat, snagging every breath he managed to take, leaving him gasping. He wouldn't survive the loss of another child. He would finally, blessedly—gladly—break his promise to Constance and give up.

Not just broken anymore. Twisted. Shattered.

His ears twitched as tires squealed. A car door opened, slammed shut. Rushed footsteps pounded into the ground. He didn't turn, didn't care who'd intruded upon him. Didn't care—until someone dropped beside him, strong arms wrapping around him. Brock. Brock had come for him.

"Ryanne told me," his friend said. "I'm sorry. I'm sorry, man."

Jude clung to him, so grateful for the bond they shared. A bond stronger than blood. Brock was his brother in every way that mattered, and by some miracle, the man seemed to absorb the worst of Jude's grief, leaving him cognizant enough to realize no one should ever have to apologize for the miracle of a new and precious life.

He remembered the joy he'd experienced when Constance had showed him the pregnancy test. Remembered how they'd laughed and held each other, talked long into the night about possible names, guessing which of their features the baby would have. He'd done none of that with Ryanne. He'd snapped and snarled at her, made horrible accusations, then left her to deal with the wild flux of emotions on her own.

"A baby," he croaked.

"Yeah. I think you've got the most potent sperm in history,"

Brock replied, his tone dry. "Face it, your troopers are determined to become people."

Jude barked out a laugh, surprised he could find humor in the situation. Finally he released his friend and fell back into the grass, peering up at the night sky. Without clouds to obscure the light, the stars glittered like diamonds on a bed of black velvet.

"I'm going to be an uncle again. This time, I want to be called Uncle B. Wait. No. Uncle Bro has a better ring to it." Brock thought for a moment, nodded. "Yeah. That's the winner. And okay, okay, if you want me to step up and be the daddy this go-round, I'll jump on that grenade. The thought of Ryanne in my— Umph."

Jude elbowed his friend in the chest, shutting him up.

A chuckling Brock rubbed the spot where a bruise would most definitely form. "What Virgil said to you…"

"Yeah." He already knew he would endure the worst future imaginable simply to have a past with Constance, Bailey and Hailey. Was the same true for Ryanne and her baby? *Their* baby.

If he lost Ryanne tomorrow, would he regret the time he'd spent with her? No need to ponder. No. Absolutely not. She'd shown him how to laugh again. She'd breathed new life in his deadened soul.

And what about their baby? Would he regret a single second of time he spent with their child?

Hell, no.

His fingers plowed through the grass, reaching cold, hard dirt. Why torture himself about the possible death of the child when nothing bad had happened? Most children in this part of the world survived infancy and adolescence, going on to live long, productive lives. Why not deal with the present, as if everything would turn out okay? In the meantime, he could defend Ryanne and the baby from any threat. With his life, if necessary.

Protective instincts surged, almost too strong for his body to contain. *Ryanne and the baby are mine. I protect what's mine.*

Whatever the cost.

Decision made. Tension and dread drained from him, though he knew tough times were ahead, but with Ryanne at his side, he could face anything. That meant winning her back, no ifs, ands or buts about it.

No more taking things slow. From now on, he would stick to her side as if he'd been surgically attached.

"Let's get married."

The softly spoken words reverberated in Ryanne's head. She'd tossed and turned all night in her brand-new bed, tortured by thoughts of Jude's pain, and her mom's salvo.

I couldn't help but overhear your confession to Jude because I was eavesdropping. I'm too young to be a grandmother, cariño. *Did I teach you nothing? This is not how you keep a man. Trust me.*

I didn't do it on purpose, Ryanne had snapped.

Selma had sighed. *I'm sorry, but this is not going to end well for you. You picked a runner.*

Not even Belle and the kittens had been able to soothe Ryanne, but finally, around noon, exhaustion set in and she'd fallen asleep. When next she'd opened her eyes, she'd found her baby daddy standing beside her bed, staring down at her, demanding to…get married?

Stomach churning, she leaped to her feet and raced to the bathroom, where she vomited the contents of her stomach. Jude followed and held back her hair, a kind gesture, and one she appreciated. Didn't mean she no longer wanted to twist off his nuts.

Weakened as she was, she didn't care about vomit-breath, or how sickly she appeared. She flushed the toilet and rested her clammy temple on the seat she'd cleaned last night, knowing this would happen. The vomiting part, not the Jude part.

Light entered the small bathroom through a crack in the blinds, highlighting the harsh lines around his eyes and mouth. He'd had a little trouble sleeping himself, hadn't he?

"Good morning to you, too," she muttered.

Silent, he shuffled around the bathroom, gathering and wetting a washrag. After cleaning her brow and the corners of her mouth, he exited…returning with a glass of water and two saltine crackers.

"Thanks." As she sipped the water and nibbled on the crackers, her stomach began to settle.

He sat in front of her, his expression tight with determination. Finally, he spoke. "I'm sorry I reacted poorly when you shared the news about… I'm sorry. I lost Constance and the twins, and the thought of losing you and…" He shook his head.

He couldn't even say the word *baby* anymore? "The thought of losing me destroyed you, so of course you ran away…thereby losing me. Seems like the perfect plan."

"I never claimed to be the sharpest tool in the shed. Let's get married," he repeated.

Irritation gave way to anger. "Yesterday you couldn't get away from me fast enough. Now you want to marry me because I'm pregnant. Do you know how insulting that is?" How soul-crushing. On her own, she wasn't good enough. Now that she would give birth to his spawn, she could share his last name.

"I'm not allowed to change my mind? And just so you know, I want you *for you*. The baby is a…bonus."

He'd gritted the word *bonus*, as if both syllables had been pushed through a wood chipper. "Look. I don't want to end things with you—" *I don't?* "But there's no need to rush into a commitment."

"We're already committed," he grated.

"No, we *would be* committed if you hadn't freaked out over the baby."

"Ryanne—" He scrubbed his hand down his face. "I made a mistake. One I regret with every fiber of my being."

Stay strong. Resist him. Otherwise she would only set herself up for a major heartache.

"I'm not saying no to your oh, so romantic proposal." *I'm not?* "But I'm not saying yes, either." *Better.* "I need time to think, just like you did."

A long while passed before he nodded, a single, stiff incline of his head. "Take all the time you need. Think." A calculated gleam appeared in his eyes. "In the meantime, you don't get sex until I get marriage."

What! "You're *blackmailing* me with sex I can get somewhere else?"

"No, I'm ultimatuming you with sex. And you will not turn to someone else. You try, and the guy, whoever he is, will end up in the hospital."

The outlaw is back.

Knees, weakening…

"While I'm making threats," he added, "I might as well go for gold. I want you to stop working in the bar."

What the what! "Excuse me?"

"Just for a little while. When Dushku is no longer a threat, you can start again. Also, I don't want you living here. You'll move in with me, where I can keep you and…our child safe."

So he wanted—no, expected—her to give up her livelihood and home? "No way, no how. I'll work, and I'll stay here. And guess what? I don't need to think about your marriage proposal any longer. My answer is no, no, a thousand times no. Take your orders and shove them, Jude Laurent."

He remained undeterred and unaffected. "Your safety is important to me, Ryanne Wade-soon-to-be-Laurent. If you won't move in with me, I'll move in with you."

She'd known the man was stubborn, but come on! This was spectacularly ridiculous. "You can't just decide to move in with me," she said, the words straining past clenched teeth.

Ryanne Laurent.

Ryanne Nicole Laurent.

RNL.

Argh! Even her mind was against her!

"I can. I did. I will," he said. "If you change the locks, I'll just break in."

She opened her mouth to blast him, only to decide against it. Why fight him on this issue when she planned to war with him on others? Besides, she could use him for sex—because yes, if she wanted him in her bed, he would end up in her bed. In the meantime, she would have a few demands of her own. Like, he would be cooking her meals, doing her laundry and any other chores she opted not to do in order to punish him for refusing to give her space.

And okay, yes, it might be nice having him around. A little Laurent resided in her womb, and she already loved the little booger. Why not make the best of the situation for his or her sake?

"Are you going to insist on accompanying me to Rome?" she asked, out of curiosity...and desire. She *wanted* to travel with him.

A muscle jumped beneath his eye. "You're still planning to hop on a plane and travel halfway around the world?"

"For now. Later, I'll be traveling *all* the way around the world. That dream hasn't died."

The muscle *really* jumped beneath his eye. "You've got a few weeks before you're scheduled to leave for your first trip. We have time to discuss the details."

Oh, we do, do we?

First, he had a few hard lessons to learn. "Let's get something straight, cowboy." Her strength returned, and she sat up. "Pregnancy hormones haven't caused my lady balls to shrink. You won't be making my decisions for me. Ever. If you keep trying, I'll kick you to the curb faster than you can beg me for another chance I'll refuse to give you."

He studied her for an eternity, his navy gaze boring into her. Just when she shifted, growing uncomfortable and impatient, he broke the silence and said, "Why did you love Earl so much? Why did you move in with him rather than stay with your mother?"

Uh, what had caused him to think about her stepdad?

"I hated the way she changed for her men, the way she expected me to change, in order to make them happy. Earl let me be me. Why? What does it matter?"

He nodded, as if she'd just explained the mysteries of the universe. Then he stood and helped her to her feet. "I'm going to the cabin to pack my things. I'll be back in a few hours."

Oh, goodness gracious. "You're moving in *today*?"

"Today."

True to his word, Jude moved into Ryanne's apartment that day. He took half the closet space, half the drawers in her dresser, and mixed his toiletries with hers. While she'd helped him unpack, she'd found a baby book filled with notes from his wife and pictures of his children.

When Jude had noticed her with the book, he'd walked out of the room. But he hadn't ordered her to put the book away, so, progress.

He waited on her hand and foot, and she soaked up the attention. Back ache? No problem. Jude would give her a massage. Sick? Hold tight. Jude would warm up a bowl of chicken noodle soup. Need the litter box cleaned? Jude to the rescue.

He played video games with her, washed her clothes, made the bed and vacuumed the floor. Not once had he complained. The only thing he wouldn't do was talk about the baby. Or have sex with her. She'd tried to seduce him, oh, about a million times, slinking around the apartment wearing little to nothing. The most he'd done was cuddle her while she napped.

At night, he slept on the floor of her bedroom, refusing to move to the couch in the living room. The sweet man wanted to be close to her. And torture her.

Some days she wanted to slap him. Other days she wanted to hug him.

The poor guy was eaten up with fear, but as much as she continued to wish otherwise, she couldn't fight the battle for him.

When it came time to open the bar, he stuck to her like glue. He hulked around in the shadows, always nearby, glowering at everyone who dared approach her. She'd lost customers, even the regulars who'd once referred to her boyfriend as "our Jude." His attitude stressed everyone out, and tips were becoming nonexistent.

At this rate, she was going to go broke, and good ole Douche Canoe wasn't going to have to lift a finger.

Speaking of Dushku, he hadn't made another move against her. Had he given up?

Had she?

She missed the heat of Jude's body. The *feel* of his body. She missed his kiss and his touch. His possession.

Even now, desire hummed inside her, a siren song. If she didn't experience relief soon, she was going to spontaneously combust.

"I know that look." Selma set her tray on the bar and leaned on her elbows to perfectly display her cleavage that had kept Ryanne in business, despite Jude's attitude. "You need to get laid, baby girl. See that guy in the wifebeater? I think he's the perfect remedy for what ails you."

Jude, who stood behind Ryanne, stiffened. "*I'm* the remedy for what ails her."

"You're the *cause* of what ails me." To her mother, she said, "I'll consider it." *Consider, and trash.*

A low growl sounded from Jude. Served him right!

Needing a break, she raised her chin and marched into her office. Time to blow off a little steam—with paperwork.

As she sat at the desk, Selma rushed inside. When Jude tried to enter, she slammed the door in his face, calling, "We need a little girl time. Go take care of customers. And flirt—I would."

Mumbling. Footsteps.

Selma plopped into the only chair in front of the desk. "Talk to me, baby doll. I know you love your man. So why are you giving him such a hard time?"

"Because." No way she would spill her guts to her mother. She hadn't even talked about it with Dorothea or Lyndie. For good reasons.

Dorothea might grow to resent Jude for his attitude about the baby. And Lyndie had her own troubles. A few days ago, she'd had a panic attack for the first time in years. Ryanne had rushed to her side as soon as she'd heard, and even though her friend had calmed down, something had changed for and with her. Something was wrong. But pushing for answers had only made her friend worse.

"Because why?" Selma insisted. "Do you not trust him? Well, let me put your mind at ease. I tried to seduce him, but his reaction was nothing like your old boyfriends." She air quoted both "seduce" and "boyfriends." "You remember those boys?"

"Are you insane? Of course I remember. And what do you mean, you tried to seduce Jude?" Ryanne could see the headline of tomorrow's paper: Pregnant Girl Murders Her Mother with a Letter Opener!

"Don't worry. Jude said no, and I've never been so proud. I'm surprised he didn't mention this."

She wasn't surprised. He'd hoped to save her from unnecessary pain.

Always protecting me. Unlike my mother, who's never tried to do so.

"I'd hoped your high school hotties would say no when I told them I'd rock their worlds," Selma continued. "Alas, they found me irresistible, the two-timing *bastardos*."

Ryanne gripped the edge of the desk, her white knuckles threatening to pop out of her skin. "I don't care about the past. You came on to Jude?"

"Aren't you listening? I did, but only as a test. I never would have touched him, just as I never touched the others."

Wait. "So...you didn't sleep with my boyfriends in high school?"

"No! Gross!"

Deep breath in...out...

She thought back, images playing through her mind. Boyfriend One naked in bed. Selma, wearing a crop top and short skirt, busy tying his wrists to a bedpost. Ryanne had walked in. The boy had shouted while fighting to free himself, and Selma had stood there, calm but sad and also a wee bit satisfied.

Ryanne had assumed she'd just climaxed and had run off, angry, grossed out and feeling betrayed. Selma had chased her down and said, "I'm sorry, sweetness. But you're so stubborn. I knew you needed to see the truth for yourself."

She'd scoffed and refused to listen to anything more about it.

Fast-forward to Boyfriend Two. Once again Selma had worn a crop top and short skirt. She'd stretched out on the living room couch while the guy performed a sexy-not-sexy strip-tease in front of her.

Ryanne had walked into the house and her gaze had locked with Selma's. Just like before, her mother had radiated sadness. Only, the satisfaction had been replaced by a hefty dose of... relief?

That time, Ryanne had stayed put and kicked out the guy. Selma had tossed up her arms and said, "Why do you pick so many losers and force me to do this?"

"Force you? Ha!" Too clouded by hurt, Ryanne had locked herself in a room and by morning, the subject had been dropped and had never come up again.

Now realization settled in her chest, a little warm, a little cozy.

For the first time, Ryanne believed her mother's claims. And okay, yes, the fact that Selma even propositioned her old crushes sucked hard-core, but in the woman's twisted way, she *had* helped. And having watched her work, Ryanne had noticed something she'd never before noticed: a hidden core of honesty.

On the other hand, Jude had a very obvious moral compass. He was a good—no, *great* guy.

Forget paperwork. She stood on shaky legs, rounded the desk, soared past her mother and entered the bar, where Jude was emptying the last jar of moonshine into a mug.

He was actually...no way, impossible...but the image remained the same. He was serving alcohol to a patron.

What the what! He wasn't just protecting Ryanne and her establishment. He was actively participating in the sale of alcohol. For her. Because he cared.

Beautiful, heart-breaking, heart-mending man. *Stick a fork in me, I'm done.* She wrapped her arms around his waist and squeezed.

He turned, his eyes wide with hope. "What brought this on?"

"I like you." She clasped his hand, lifted and kissed the strawberry etched into his wrist. "A lot."

The corners of his mouth twitched. "I like you, too, shortcake."

"Good. Now that that's settled..." She raked her knuckles over the stubble on his jaw before backing up a step. "You keep working. I'll grab another jar of moonshine from the basement."

He offered no protest as she reached for the door handle concealed among the shelves of liquor. As she moved into the entryway, she tugged the string hanging from the ceiling. Light flooded the dark corridor, illuminating the concrete steps. The lower she went, the cooler and danker the air became. At the bottom, shelves were covered with glass jars. Some of those jars were filled to the brim, others were empty.

She lifted a full one, but someone latched on to her wrist, stopping her. Jude! The calluses on his palm sent shivers whisking down her spine.

"*I'll* carry it," he said. "You shouldn't be lugging heavy objects."

"I remember a time I had to heft an entire box of moonshine up the basement steps, all on my own. I asked you for help, and you asked me if I was testing you."

"I was a jackass. Thankfully, you've trained me better."

"Or you're worried about me because I'm pregnant."

"That, too."

"Too bad, so sad. I can handle a single jar."

"I know you can." His gaze bored into hers, currents of electricity arcing between them. "But I'm here."

Here…ready to be seduced…

"You certainly are." With her free hand, she traced her knuckles down his muscled chest, not stopping until she reached the waist of his pants. "How about you put yourself to better use and give me an orgasm? Just a quick one? Then I won't have to take my mom's advice and go after the guy wearing the wifebeater."

Despite everything, she wanted a future with Jude.

He sucked in a breath—and stepped closer, pressing her against the wall. "I'll give you an orgasm, nice and slow, if you'll agree we can be married in the morning." Down, down he leaned. He plucked her lower lip between his teeth, nearly singeing her with lust. "All you need to do is say yes, and I'll do the rest."

CHAPTER TWENTY-THREE

Hunger clawed at Jude's insides. His body trembled with need. Ryanne stood before him, hair a dark, silken cloud that framed her exquisite face. Her rich brown eyes glittered with arousal. Pregnancy had given her olive skin a radiant glow. She wasn't just a part of his life; she *was* his life.

Every day his desire for her strengthened.

Every day his determination to win her intensified.

Every day, more and more, she became his reason to breathe.

"Say yes," he whispered, his lips hovering over hers. His arm snaked around her waist, holding her. The hold wasn't gentle, either; it was more of a demand to stay put. "*Please*, say yes."

Tremors rocked her against him. "I admit, I kind of want to," she said, "and that's huge for me. I hadn't planned on this, on you, but I think I could get on board with the whole hubby-wifey thing. Maybe. Probably. I've liked having you around, and I certainly do like the idea of you being legally required to wait on me."

He brightened—

"But," she added, and his mood darkened. "My answer is no,

and it will remain no until you've beaten the fear of losing me and the baby."

A flash of cold. "What makes you think I fear losing you?"

"Jude, you follow me everywhere I go. Fear is stress, and stress is bad for your health."

"Maybe I like watching your ass as you walk."

"Maybe? Ha! Definitely. But you can't deny you're stressed 24/7."

No, he couldn't. "I have fears, yes, but so do you."

"What? Me? No."

"You're afraid of losing your identity, changing for a man."

"I… I…" The color in her cheeks drained.

"Don't try to deny it. It's true. The only difference between us is your fear won't cost me my life. But what if I fail you? What if I can't keep you safe? I'm missing part of my leg and—"

With a scowl, she gripped his shoulders to shake him. "You are the strongest man I've ever met. And maybe you're right. Maybe I am afraid of losing myself. But either way, I've realized I can take care of myself."

"I know you can. I don't think I would have let myself risk falling for you otherwise."

Her eyes widened, becoming windows of amazement. "You've fallen for me? I mean, duh. You've fallen for me, and your heart is filled with rainbows and unicorn tears. It's obvious." She brushed an invisible piece of lint from her shoulder. "But this is the first time you've said the words."

"Do you need the words?"

"Do *you*?" she challenged.

Perhaps more than he'd ever needed anything. "I do."

Though she melted against him, she didn't tell him she'd fallen for him, too. She simply tightened her grip on his shoulders, her nails digging into his shirt to ensure he remained in place. As if he would ever leave her side again.

"Fight the fear," she said, "and you can have me."

You can have me...

The hunger inside him rubbed a fork and knife together, ready to feast. "I want you *now*. Say you'll marry me."

"I've set my terms. All or nothing."

Stubborn woman. "I notice begging for forgiveness isn't among those terms. You've exonerated me for everything I've done in the past?"

"Don't get me wrong. You've messed up big time. Over and over again." As he glowered at her, she added, "But you're the father of my child, and holding a grudge against you would be counterproductive. I mean, I have no idea what to do with a baby. You do. You can help me."

The words *child* and *baby* were becoming easier to hear.

"How do I fight the fear?" If it were the only obstacle in their way, he would overcome it. He would overcome anything in order to spend his life with this woman.

She pondered his dilemma, came up blank. "How did you fight fear in the army, when you had to go on dangerous missions?"

"I focused on the task at hand. Rescue. Kill. Or both. But then, I knew my enemy and my objective. With you, everyone is the enemy. Everything is an accident waiting to happen—waiting to take you from me. My objective is to protect you from everyone and everything."

She sighed. "Life happens, and in the end, we only regret the chances we didn't take. When worries do rise, don't feed them by running negative scenarios through your head, force yourself to think of something else. Something good. Like how I might reward you for your bravery..."

"I like the sound of that." He rubbed the tip of his nose against hers. "I'll talk to Daniel, too. Maybe he has a few secrets." Having lost his mom as a boy, and watched multiple friends and soldiers die from explosions, enemy gunfire and even friendly fire, the man had once suffered similar fears. For a future with Dorothea, he'd somehow overcome.

"Baby girl." Selma's voice echoed through the cellar. "You might want to come up. Someone's here to see you and your pretty boy. I put her in your office. Oh, and you might want to hurry, because she looks like the five-fingered discount type."

Pretty boy?

"Coming," Ryanne called.

Not yet, but she would be. "I'll figure out how to beat my fears," he whispered to her, "and then you'll be mine." He kissed her, a brutal meeting of lips. A *brief* meeting of lips, far too brief, before he took her hand in his to lead her upstairs.

Her panting breaths made him smile—and groan. He wasn't sure he would survive another night sleeping on the floor.

Up top, Jude entered the office first, a hand on the gun sheathed at his waist. He drew up short.

Savannah. Savannah and a dark-haired little boy. Thomas.

The blonde was ashen as she paced in front of the desk. Her son watched her from a desk chair, spinning, spinning.

"Savannah," Ryanne gasped out, rushing around him. "What happened? What's wrong?"

Savannah wrung her hands. "Only everything."

"Who the hell are you?" the boy demanded with a royal tone, as if the world existed for his delight.

A groan from Savannah. "Thomas, please. Hell isn't a nice word. Okay?"

"You're not the boss of me." The boy spit at her, and she cringed. "Hell, hell, hell."

"I'm sorry," she said to Jude. "I should have gone with you, but I wasn't sure I could trust you. I've just... I've been through so much and decided to pay a customer to get me out of town. He claimed to love me, but he only wanted... Anyway, Martin's been on my trail and almost caught me." Chewing on her bottom lip, she stepped closer and whispered, "He wants to punish me, *kill* me, and keep Thomas for himself. I didn't know where else to go."

"You can stay here, with us," Ryanne told her. "I know you'll be close to Dushku, and that isn't ideal, but our security is top notch."

Savannah's presence would endanger Ryanne and the baby.

Already endangered. True, but this would give Dushku *another* reason to attack.

Jude's pulse raced, and his chest burned. The fear he was supposed to fight overtook him, and he knew he'd just failed a very big test. But here and now, he didn't care. He wouldn't negotiate or second-guess his instincts when it came to Ryanne's safety.

"She can stay at the cabin with Brock," he said. "Security is just as tight there, and she won't be exposed to customers coming in and out, or be seen by people at Dushku's work site."

As he spoke, Savannah nodded. "Yes. The cabin. We'll stay there."

Ryanne surprised him when she, too, nodded.

He must have gaped at her, because she said, "What? I know a better plan when I hear it."

Not kissing her proved impossible. A warm blush stormed her cheeks as he pressed his mouth against hers, lingered for a moment, only a moment. Savannah watched with raw envy in her eyes, and Thomas pretended to gag.

"I'll get Brock, and we'll head out the back way." He strode from the office, holding on to Ryanne's hand until the last possible second before stalking through the club to find his friend.

Brock sat at a table in back, shrouded by shadows. Empty beer bottles littered his table. He'd stopped shaving his head, the strands now sticking out in spikes as a woman combed her fingers through. His eyes were bloodshot, and there was no sign of his usual smile.

Jude knew he'd heard from his parents early this morning. The pair had a way of blackening his mood. Not exactly a shock.

They referred to him as a disappointment, and pushed him to return and take over the family business.

At the moment, he was busy glaring at the bar…at Lyndie, who sat with Dorothea and Daniel, laughing as Selma mixed drinks.

Daniel and I aren't the only ones battling fear.

When a man approached Lyndie, Brock jumped to his feet, the woman on his lap forced to straighten or fall.

Jude swooped in, apologizing on his friend's behalf before sending her on her way. "Need your help," he said to Brock.

Without hesitation, his friend focused on him. "Of course."

On the way to the office, he explained what had transpired. In seconds, Brock transformed from moody civilian to fierce soldier. A man capable of any dark deed. Jude had witnessed the transformation a thousand times, and it was one of the reasons he'd gravitated toward the male during training. Like called to like.

Savannah had Thomas in her arms, resting on her hip. Ryanne was the one pacing now.

"Savannah, this is Brock. Brock, Savannah."

Thomas stared at Brock with eyes as wide as saucers. "You're big."

"I eat lots of broccoli," Brock muttered.

"Stay here," Jude said to Ryanne. Daniel would watch over her.

"Nope. No way." She shook her head, dark hair caressing her cheeks. "I'm going with you."

What would Earl do?

Though Jude wanted to argue with her, he decided to shut his stupid mouth and let Ryanne do what she thought was best—fighting fear, trusting the mother of his child.

He waved to the door, indicating she was to follow Brock, who had taken the lead.

Chin high, Ryanne wrapped her arm around the blonde's

waist and, together, they swept out of the room, heading for the back alley entrance, near where he'd parked his truck.

Outside, cool night air wafted over him. Wind whistled.

The alley was empty. Usually homeless men and women waited for Ryanne to serve leftover food.

Apprehension pricked his neck, combat instincts flaring. Must have pricked Brock, too; he stilled.

Then he heard a gun being cocked.

"Get down!" he and Brock shouted in unison.

Jude shoved Ryanne, Savannah and Thomas to the ground, while Brock dove in the other direction, unsheathing a semi-automatic.

A shot rang out, and a sharp pain sliced across Jude's bicep. Warm liquid spilled down his arm. He twisted midair, taking the bulk of the impact upon landing. Then he turned, tucking Ryanne underneath his body.

Brock jumped to his feet and gave chase. Despite the pain in Jude's arm, he ushered the women and child into a corner and palmed his .44. Savannah was crying, but Ryanne was silent and pale. Thomas was smiling, as if they were playing a game.

No game. This was life and death.

Judging by the location of Jude's wound, he suspected Ryanne or Savannah had been the target.

Had he not pushed the women out of the way...

The bullet could have hit Ryanne. He could have lost her and the baby.

The baby! How was the baby?

"You're bleeding," Ryanne gasped out. "Jude, you were shot."

"Just a flesh wound." He'd been shot and grazed enough times to know the difference. "How are you?"

"Fine, I'm fine, but...you're bleeding," she repeated.

"This is nothing. You're sure you're okay?"

His fear must have proved contagious. No longer simply pale, she was chalk white. "Why? Do you know something I don't? Could impact hurt the baby?"

A cursing Brock returned, saving him from having to reply. "Shooter got away." He sheathed his weapon and drew the small flashlight he always carried. "You got lucky. Just a flesh wound."

"Told you," he said to Ryanne.

"Get him to a hospital," she cried. "And me! Now. This second."

The top of Jude's prosthesis dug deep into the underside of his knee as he stood, Ryanne cradled in his arms. "I'm taking her to the city," he told Brock. And then…it might be time to end Dushku once and for all. He'd warned the man. Hurt Ryanne, and pay.

"Put me down." She uttered the command without moving, clearly too concerned about his well-being to risk hurting him. "Please. I'll walk."

"I'll take care of the others," Brock said. "Go."

Jude hurried to the truck.

"Jude," Ryanne said, resting her head against his chest, her fingers tangled in his shirt. "Be honest. Do you think something happened to the baby?"

He blocked her voice, unable to reassure her—unable to reassure himself. *Get her to the hospital, listen to reason later.*

CHAPTER TWENTY-FOUR

Ryanne perched on the bench in her shower, hot water raining upon her. She was alone. A good thing. She wanted to punch Jude in the throat and hug him, all at the same time. Her heart hadn't stopped fluttering; the organ reminded her of a butterfly with clipped wings.

Tonight she'd had an ultrasound. Her first. It had been a rushed job to assure fearful parents their baby was alive and well. She'd hated and dreaded every moment—until at long last the heartbeat was found, strong and sure.

Jude's fear had fed hers and vice versa. And afterward, even though she'd been limp with relief, she'd still been tense, because Jude had refused medical attention until after the ultrasound.

What if he'd bled out during the wait?

Trembling, she drew her knees up to her chest, wrapped her arms around her legs and rested her forehead against her knees. What a horrible night. Attempted murder. Jude injured. A taste of the terror he'd once lived with on a daily basis.

No, he didn't live. He *couldn't* live like this, with fear cemented in his heart, forming an impenetrable wall, and in his mind, shredding every joyous memory and leaving only despair. He simply existed.

After leaving the hospital, they'd visited with the chief of Blueberry Hill PD, as well as the sheriff of Strawberry Valley PD. Both men had appeared genuinely upset, and had promised to look into the shooting, but she doubted anything would be found. Men like Dushku knew how to cover their tracks.

Tears burned her cheeks as different facts bombarded her.

Jude had taken a bullet for her, and no one would be punished.

At least her baby had a strong heartbeat.

Jude could have died.

Her baby was the size of a grain of rice.

Dushku was capable of murder. What if he decided to end Jude? The baby?

Jude wasn't her husband, so the doctors and nurses hadn't given her any updates when he was taken to a private room to have his wound stitched.

Her baby could have perished in between one blink and another, and there would have been nothing she could do to stop it.

Ugh! The back and forth thoughts were giving her whiplash. And really, this was another helping of the torment Jude lived with—existed with—on a daily basis.

If he continued on this path...

Only destruction awaited him.

He had to fight and defeat the fear. Not just for Ryanne, not anymore, but for himself. Fear wasn't healthy. Mentally, emotionally or physically. He would put himself in an early grave, his life filled with pain and regret.

But how could she help him? He'd coexisted with the monster for so long, he might not recognize himself without it.

What's more, tonight had only exacerbated the problem. He'd barely spoken to her on the drive home, had asked her the same question three times. *Are you okay?*

The stall door opened. Jude reached inside and shut off the

water. "Let's dry you off." He offered his hand and helped her stand. His gaze remained just over her shoulder as he wrapped a towel around her. "You'll be happy to know Belle and her lords and lordettes are asleep in the sunroom."

He was shirtless, a bandage on his arm, wearing only a pair of boxer briefs. After wringing out her hair, he pulled one of his T-shirts over her head, gently tucked her arms through the holes.

Radiating a quiet but savage tension, he carried her to bed.

"I'm not exactly a lightweight, and your arm—" she began.

"Is fine. Just a little sore. And you *are* a lightweight."

When he pulled away, she tugged on his arm, careful of his wound, urging him to lie beside her. "Stay with me tonight," she beseeched. "Please."

A pause. A twitch of the muscle under his eye. Then he removed his prosthesis and curled into her. As one minute bled into another, she waited for the tension to drain from him.

It didn't.

"Talk to me," she begged. "Tell me what's bothering you."

"I keep replaying the shooting inside my head. How close you came to... How quickly I could have lost you."

"But you didn't."

"I want to kill him," he admitted.

"No. If you were locked away—"

"I wouldn't be caught. I promise you, no one will ever find the body."

"No. You won't just risk your freedom, you'll risk your heart." She dug her nails into his chest. "Besides, someone else would simply rise up in the ranks and take Dushku's place."

"Ryanne—"

"No, I don't want to talk about Dushku anymore." She wanted Jude. No ultimatum. No thought for any moment but this one. "Kiss me. Make me forget tonight ever happened." *Let me do the same for you.*

He required no further prompting. With an animalistic groan, he slanted his lips over hers, his tongue seeking entrance. No, *demanding* entrance. He kissed her with fervor and heat, nothing held back.

He was passion unleashed. "Tell me I'm your boyfriend. Say it. At least admit that much."

Love for him consumed her. Love and need. Being without him these past few days had been hellish. Now she had a fever, and he had the cure. Was Jude perfect? No. Would they have their fair share of problems? Probably. Did she want to live without him? Never. Was he perfect for her? Absolutely.

"You're my boyfriend, Jude Laurent."

Brutal satisfaction tightened the muscles in his face. "And you, Ryanne Wade, are my girlfriend."

His big hands kneaded her breasts. As her nipples puckered for him, he grazed his thumbs over the aching peaks, his touch almost desperate. But then, her touch was just the same. Perhaps even more so. *Almost lost him*. She attempted to caress, savor and brand every inch of him all at once; she failed, but enjoyed every second as she reaffirmed he was here, he was well and they were together.

Now and always?

He kissed a path down her body, sucking on her nipples through her T-shirt, then rucked up the cotton and tongued her navel. With no panties to impede him, he slid a finger deep inside her, wringing a cry of bliss from her.

"Spread your legs," he rasped. "That's it. Wider. I need another taste of you."

Cool air met the fiery heat of her core, and she shivered. Again he kissed a path down…down…his head hovered between her thighs, the warmth of his breath incendiary, sweeping her up in a maddening frenzy.

"Jude." Her back curved and her hips lifted, as she tried to force his mouth on her. "Do it. Please."

One second passed, two. The agony of anticipation only intensified her need for him.

"I love your sweet pleas." The bed tilted as he leaned over and switched on the lamp. Light spilled over them both.

Beautiful Jude. Savage pleasure glittered in eyes no longer navy but black, the pupils blown. The scar that bisected his lips only added to his brutal appeal, reminding her of his strength, his will to survive no matter the blockades. The muscles in his chest bulged, covered in her scratch marks.

"So lovely," he said, his voice thick—and then he licked between her thighs.

A sound—half moan, half scream—left her as her arms shot overhead, her fingers curling around the headboard. Her spine arched, a thousand tremors moving through her at once. He devoured her until she writhed against him, begging incoherently for release. Then his fingers joined the play. First one, then another. They worked in tandem with his tongue, his wicked, wonderful tongue.

"You like this," he rasped. "You've never been so wet."

The moment, the very second, he licked her again, she shot off like a rocket. The orgasm tore through her, her tremors rocking the bed. As she collapsed onto the mattress, limp, she expected him to glide his massive length inside her. He rolled to her side instead.

Their panting breaths blended as she climbed on top of him, ready to ride him to release.

"No," he grated, his hands on her waist, holding her still. "I meant what I said. No sex until you agree to marry me."

He thought to deny her the pleasure of *his* pleasure? "Oral is sex," she pointed out.

"All right, I'll rephrase. No *penetration* until you agree to marry me."

"You sure?" She cupped her breasts, and his gaze lowered,

suddenly riveted on her nipples. "Your fingers had no problem penetrating my—"

"I know what my fingers did." His grip on her tightened as he flashed his teeth. Sweat glistened on his brow, and a passion-fever flushed his cheeks. This man wanted her. Wanted her bad. The knowledge electrified her.

"Well. Blue balls is a serious condition. I'm sure it must claim the life of at least one male every year." With her coyest smile, she inched down his body, tucked his underwear beneath his testicles and let her mouth hover over the glistening head of his erection. "If you'd rather wait for marriage, feel free to stop me any time…"

A vein throbbed in his brow. His hands fisted on the sheets as a strained sound left him.

"I'll take that as a *please, darling Ryanne, keep going*," she said—and gobbled him up.

Jude held a sleeping Ryanne in the crook of his uninjured arm all night and deep into the morning. Sunlight seeped through the window curtains, but didn't reach the bed. Unable to rest, his mind too chaotic, he'd gotten up a few times to ensure she would have everything she needed when she awoke. A glass of water and a handful of saltines; he'd also reattached his prosthesis in case she was too sick to walk into the bathroom on her own.

What was he going to do about Dushku?

Ryanne was right. Killing him would do no good if some-one else—someone worse—took his place.

At first Jude had wondered if Savannah had set him up. *If it comes down to me or you, I'll send your loved ones flowers.* Then he'd smartened up. She adored her boy, and would never willingly place him in a dangerous situation.

As Ryanne began to stir, Jude hid his emotions behind a men-tal wall, a difficult feat but one he just managed. He'd done it many times for missions, allowing him to focus on facts. This time, he needed an answer to his questions: Why? Why had Du-shku opted for such a public attempt on Savannah's life? Why not follow her, sneak into the cabin and shoot her while she slept? Perhaps Brock or Jude could have been framed for the crime.

Had someone other than Dushku wanted her dead?

To Jude's knowledge, she had no other enemies.

Had one of Dushku's employees taken it upon himself to re-move his boss's problem?

Possible, but not likely. The consequences for disobedience had to be steep.

Perhaps Dushku had acted on emotion rather than logic?

The idea had merit, but it would mean Savannah's defection with Thomas had pushed the old man past his limits. Perhaps he truly loved the boy. Though why risk the boy getting hurt accidentally?

A soft sigh drifted from Ryanne as she stretched, her body rubbing against Jude's. Air hissed between his teeth. Last night she'd wrung him dry, sucking on his shaft as if it were her fa-vorite candy. He'd enjoyed every second, and yet, denying his body's need to sink inside her, to fill her up and brand her, had left him…sensitive.

"Morning," she rasped, her lashes fluttering open. As he grazed his fingers over the ridges in her spine, a sweet smile played at the corners of her lips.

Every day, every second, this woman grew in beauty.

And someone nearly took her away from me.

In a rush, his emotions scaled the wall he'd erected, so swift and ravenous they reminded him of zombies he'd once seen in a movie; those zombies had crawled on top of each other, each one like a rung on a ladder, until someone finally reached the top of the wall and *every* zombie spilled over. An apt comparison. His emotions *had* risen from the dead. All the fear, all the dread, all the rage. Each flooded him, stronger than before; perhaps they'd been pumping iron and shooting up steroids. He'd lost so many things in his young life, but Ryanne and their child would not be added to the list—no matter what measures he had to take.

"How do you feel?" he asked.

"Surprisingly well. My stomach is calm." She draped her arm over his chest, resting her chin on top of her hand. "But yours isn't, is it? You're all worked up again."

Silence would serve him better than truth.

"Do you need another tongue-lashing, cowboy? Or perhaps you'd like to take me for a morning ride?"

The desire that had simmered in his blood now began to boil. *Resist!* Marriage was too important to him. Ignoring her question—barely—he said, "Let's talk, get to know each other better."

The flash of a grin. "All right. What do you want to know?"

Everything. "If you could trade lives with someone for an entire day, who would you choose?"

Her brow wrinkled with confusion before she laughed outright. "Why would I want to trade places with anyone? You look at no one else the way you look at me."

Boiling hotter…

He kissed her temple, barely resisting the urge to claim her lips. "How did I ever resist you?"

"Don't know. It's one of life's greatest mysteries. But what about you? Who would you want to trade places with?"

"I think…you. I'd seduce myself again and again."

She snorted. "If I hadn't already lo—liked you, I would have started just now."

Lo—liked. Had she almost said she loved him?

"Next question," he said. The more he learned about her, the more he lo—liked her, too. "If you had to spend the rest of your life on a deserted island, but could only take three men with you, who would you choose? One has to be from a book, one from a movie and one from real life."

A slow smile spread over her face. "My fictional man would

be Owen Perkins from *Naked Pursuit* by Jill Monroe. He would be my silver screen hottie as well, since the book was made into a Lifetime movie. And my real life man would be…hmm…let's see…let me think…"

Jude smacked her butt. "First, what's so special about this Owen guy that you need two of him, and second, you have to think about the one from real life? Seriously?"

"First, Owen is a sexy fireman and I have a new appreciation for his line of work. Plus, he's very good with handcuffs—something else I'm beginning to appreciate. I'd like to keep you trapped in this bed forever. Second, I *guess* I'd pick you as my real life hero."

"You guess? And I hope you're serious about the handcuffs because I will be buying a pair."

She giggled, an adorable girlish giggle that caused his chest to ache.

The phone on the nightstand suddenly buzzed, letting him know the security feed from the Scratching Post had just hit his in-box. They stiffened in unison, all thoughts of love and sex gone.

He swiped up his cell and opened the video, dreading what he'd find. Another fire? Another gunman?

Instead, he watched as his in-laws knocked on the front door.

CHAPTER TWENTY-FIVE

How had Ryanne gone from almost being shot to wanting to be shot?

Easy: the arrival of Jude's former in-laws, Russ and Carrie Jones.

After checking the security feed, Jude dressed in a hurry and *gently requested* Ryanne do the same. *Get your ass in gear, shortcake. I don't want you out of my sight.*

As she'd donned a lace blouse and a pair of unripped jeans, wanting to look her best, curiosity had gotten the better of her, and she'd willingly trailed Jude downstairs.

First introductions were made. Names only. Then the couple had fawned over him, worried about his injury, wanting every detail.

"Your message last night scared me to death," Carrie said. "Someone shot you, but you don't want us to worry about it if we hear gossip, because you're fine. Well, we're worried. We need more information, Jude. We hopped in the car first thing this morning. Your friend Brock told us where you were staying, so here we are."

They'd peppered him with a million questions about the

shooting, and when they were satisfied—if a bit frustrated because he wouldn't tell them anything about why or who—they asked him about his life. Ryanne stood in the background, wanting to duck behind the bar every time Carrie tossed her a weird look, like *who the eff are you, and why are you still here?*

These people had lost their daughter and grandchildren. They wouldn't be happy when they discovered Jude had found a replacement family. Not that Ryanne could ever replace Constance.

Jude offered only the barest of answers, mentioning the security business he'd started with friends, and how he was protecting Ryanne from the new bad guy in town. Only then did Carrie relax.

Nope. She wouldn't be happy to learn Jude and Ryanne were dating.

Perhaps I should slink away, leave the family to their reunion? That way, Jude wouldn't be tempted to confess he was in a relationship, and inadvertently hurt the couple.

The front door suddenly burst open, and Jude reached for his gun. He relaxed when Selma stalked inside, even though her expression was all kinds of fierce. "What's this I hear about my girl being shot?"

"I wasn't shot, Jude was," Ryanne replied.

"Oh. Well." Selma wiped her brow, in the universal sign for *that's a relief.* "I'm sure he's fine. He's got all those delicious muscles to slow down a bullet." Today she wore a beaded tank top and a pair of short shorts, her legs on spectacular display. At fifty-two, she looked better than most women in their twenties. "So who do we have here?"

Jude inhaled deeply, exhaled slowly. Obviously he suspected what Ryanne knew: Selma could destroy these nice people with a few careless words. If he didn't admit he and Ryanne were dating, the truth could come out in other, less gentle ways.

"Selma, meet my in-laws. Carrie, Russ, this is Selma, Ryanne's mother." He stretched out his arm to beckon her over. "Ryanne and I are dating."

Seeing no way out of this, Ryanne reluctantly took his hand and moved to his side.

Carrie blanched. "I... I didn't realize you were dating anyone." She looked to be Selma's age, but life hadn't been as kind to her. Grief had aged her, the loss of her loved ones evident in every line on her face. She focused on Jude, desperation in her eyes. "You haven't been in town very long. Aren't you worried about rushing into a relationship? And what about your plan to return to Texas?"

Ryanne gasped. "Texas?" He'd made plans to move?

"I'm staying in Strawberry Valley," Jude said, kissing Ryanne's hand.

"And they're doing more than dating." Selma settled her hands on her hips. "They're practically engaged. Jude put a bun in my girl's oven."

Carrie jolted; Russ gaped.

Ryanne groaned, wishing the floor would open up and swallow her. This. This was what she'd hoped to avoid.

To Jude's credit, he handled the abrupt announcement well, not apologizing to his in-laws, thereby insulting Ryanne, and not yelling at Selma. "We just found out."

Russ recovered from his shock first. The tall, thin man with adorable bifocals shook Jude's hand. "Congratulations, son. You picked a stunner."

Wheezing now, Carrie pulled at the collar of her cardigan. "But you haven't been in town very long," she repeated.

Laughing, Selma elbowed Russ in the stomach. "Only takes one night. Isn't that right, handsome?"

"Sure is," Russ said with what looked to be a genuine grin. "This calls for a celebration."

Seriously. The woman could charm anyone with a penis.

"Our Coni would be glad to know you're happy again, Jude."

Carrie's posture changed—stiffened—as she turned her attention to Ryanne. "She was such a good girl, kind to everyone. She was a teacher, you know. Her students loved her to pieces."

"They were blessed to know her," Ryanne said. "She certainly enriched Jude's life in the best of ways."

Carrie adjusted the strap of her purse. "What is it you do, Ryanne?"

"I own the bar." *Schlepp drinks.*

"Oh. I see."

Ryanne gave Jude's hand a squeeze. "If you guys don't mind, I'm going to steal Selma and hole up in the kitchen so we can plan tonight's foam party."

Jude gave her a squeeze right back. "Don't—please don't leave," he said. "Stay indoors."

Hello, fear. Never far from the surface.

"Very well," she said, making a concession. "But do not, under any circumstances, return without Chips Ahoy!"

"I won't." *Thank you,* he mouthed.

She nodded and waved goodbye to Carrie and Russ and dragged her mother into the kitchen.

As soon as Daniel arrived at the Scratching Post to watch over Ryanne, Jude took Russ and Carrie to lunch. A hasty meal at Two Farms, located in Strawberry Valley's town square, where he did his best to sidestep questions about Ryanne. He'd hurt his in-laws today. Unintentionally, yes, but hurt was hurt, and it didn't sit well with him.

He'd planned to tell the truth, anyway, but he'd wanted to dole out the information slowly, not drop it like a bomb.

The moment he'd realized Ryanne understood his dilemma, there'd been no more denying just how deeply he'd fallen for her.

After lunch, he drove Russ and Carrie to the Strawberry Inn, because they'd decided to stay a few days.

He got that they were disappointed. Constance had been an only child, and Jude was all they had left. The fact that he was moving on, starting a new family, had to devastate them. But he wouldn't let Ryanne go. Not now, not ever. Somehow, he would make Carrie and Russ understand that he wasn't just starting a new family, he was adding to theirs.

He walked the couple to their door, but when he turned to leave after they'd said their goodbyes, Carrie grabbed hold of his wrist. "I'm concerned, Jude. Did you get that Ryanne person pregnant in an attempt to replace your girls?"

For the first time in years, he craved a beer. "She's going to be the mother of my child," he said, and Carrie blanched. "Please talk about her with respect."

The color drained from her cheeks, but she nodded. "You're right. I'm sorry."

"No," he finally answered. "The pregnancy wasn't on purpose." But it had happened, and he wouldn't change it. "I'm not trying to replace Constance. I can't, and besides that, I don't want to. She's a part of me, and she'll always have a special place in my heart. But I realized just how impossible it is to hold on to someone who isn't here while trying to hold on to someone else who is. I had to let go of what should have been and grab hold of what could be with Ryanne."

"I just… I think you need to think this through. You were eighteen when you married Coni. Now you're jumping into a long-term relationship? Shouldn't you… I don't know…play the field or something, now that you're ready to date again? Make sure you're not going to regret settling down?"

As if any other woman could compare to Ryanne. She'd obsessed and possessed him from moment one, somehow taking the worst of his pain and giving him a reason to wake up every morning. She'd given him pleasure, erasing his grief.

And, really, he'd played the field in high school. Had no interest in doing so again. He'd watched Brock and the other soldiers who'd slept with anyone willing; picking up strange women had never made any of them happy. Only more miserable.

"I love her," he said, and with the intensity of a lightning strike, he realized the truth of the statement. He didn't need to think about it. Love was there, a light inside him. A brilliant beacon of hope.

He loved Ryanne Wade with every fiber of his being, and he hadn't fallen slowly, or gently. He'd leaped off a cliff and plummeted at warp speed, entrusting her with the fragile remains of his heart.

He loved her more than life. Loved her wit, her sassy mouth and tell-it-like-it-is attitude. Loved her sex kitten playfulness and the bold passion she displayed for him.

Carrie backed down, but he suspected she was far from satisfied. "I'm sorry," she said. "I didn't realize..."

He hugged her and kissed her cheek. "I'll be working at the Scratching Post tonight, but I can come by in the morning and take you to breakfast. We'll talk then, okay?"

She looked away from him, nodded. He bid Russ goodbye and took off, heading to the store to pick up a bag or twelve of chocolate chip cookies.

Along the way, a text from Brock came in. You get that this girl's name is Savannah "Vanna" White and mine is Brock "Rock" Hudson. It's freaking me out. Other than that, all is well here.

When Jude returned to the bar, he found two officers from Blueberry Hill as well as two from Strawberry Valley arguing over jurisdiction while searching the alley for the bullet and shell from last night's attack. He left them to their work and headed inside.

Jude still hadn't decided what to do about Dushku.

With straight-up murder taken off the table, his options were limited. Threats hadn't sufficed. Fighting fire with fire had only heralded more violence.

Fight fire with water.

Having dealt with criminals in the past, he had a feeling Dushku would respond to only one thing: losing every penny he'd ever schemed to earn. As an added bonus, no one else could rise in the ranks to take his place if he had no money. Win–win. Problem solved.

Selma puttered around in the kitchen. Jude snuck past her and headed for the apartment. As soon as he reached the hallway, he heard…crying?

He burst past the door to find a sobbing Ryanne sitting on the floor of the living room, clutching one of the kittens to her chest.

"What happened?" he roared, rushing to her.

Daniel, who paced in front of the bay windows, held up his hands, palms out. "I only mentioned Dorothea's excitement about adopting two of the cats. Then the waterworks started, and they haven't stopped."

Had to be pregnancy hormones. Before this, Ryanne had never cried. And that might have been a good thing. She cried like she did everything else: with her whole being. Red blotches painted her face, her eyes were swollen, her nose running and her shoulders shaking.

"I'm going to miss my kittens so much, and all I wanted to do was eat Chips Ahoy! but I ate the last one and you weren't here with a new pack and I considered eating the bag of chocolate chips but they aren't the same and I want the same and do you think the lords and lordettes will miss me when they're gone, and what if they get depressed?" Sniffle, sniffle.

Took him a moment to unpack her statements, but when he did, he rushed to assure her. "We can keep the entire litter, love. In fact, I insist on it."

"Don't be ridiculous," she said between sniffles. "I promised Dorothea and Lyndie kittens, so they are getting kittens."

"There are plenty of kittens in shelters throughout the state. Who says we have to give anyone *our* kittens?" Filled with tenderness for this woman, he petted her hair, kissed her temple. "Also, I brought more cookies. See?"

"Why did you bring me cookies? Dang it, Jude! What if I get fat, and you stop wanting me?"

"The more you gain, the more of you there is to lo—like." She might not be ready for his profession of love, and he didn't want to scare her. Or have a witness. But, uh, he'd just called her *love*. He'd have to be more careful. "I promise, I'll never stop wanting you."

She leaned into him, and to his delight, her tears gave way to a hearty chuckle. "I'm sorry I overreacted. I don't know what's wrong with me lately. Well, I do know. I'm baking your bun. I'm also sorry I snot-cried on you. How embarrassing."

Damn, he loved this woman with all his heart, and he wanted her happy, always. *Can't lose her. Ever.* "Tonight I'll burp and fart in bed. Then we'll be even."

"Okay, it's official. You guys disgust me," Daniel said, clearly trying not to laugh.

Ryanne gave him a double-birded salute before batting her lashes at Jude. "That would be delightful, thank you. By the way, I hope you weren't joking about the cookies. I'm totally into a trade. Your cookies for mine."

He barked out a laugh. Silly, wonderful woman.

His tasks for the day changed. Get rid of Daniel, get inside Ryanne.

No, no. Can't lose sight of the endgame. Lifelong commitment before temporary pleasure. Even mind-blowing pleasure.

He gave her temple another kiss before he straightened. "I need to speak with Daniel about tonight's security." Among other things. "Do you mind if we use your office downstairs?"

"Go, go," she said, waving to the door and tearing into her newest bag of cookies. "I'm now too busy to deal with you." Crumbs fell out of her mouth. "But don't you dare worry about me. I want to get laid sometime in this century."

Daniel covered his mouth with his hand, but the dude wouldn't stop chortling like an idiot.

Jude stayed silent as he led his friend downstairs. Once they were enclosed in her office, where no cameras could relay their conversation to Ryanne or anyone else, he asked for Daniel's thoughts about draining Dushku's accounts.

"It's doable. Illegal, but doable. If he gets wind of our plans before those accounts are cleaned, he'll unleash hellfire."

"I'm not worried about the legalities. No one will be able to prove we did anything wrong. More than that, we won't be taking the money for ourselves. We'll be giving every cent to an organization that helps fight against sex slavery." And in the meantime, he'd be able to get rid of Dushku for good, protecting Ryanne long-term.

Speaking of long-term...

Pacing in front of the desk, he massaged the back of his neck. "Forget Dushku for a minute. You once feared losing Dorothea the way you lost your mom and so many of our friends. How did you stop?"

"Stop...fearing?"

A clipped nod.

"I didn't, not at first. Eventually I realized I couldn't have both. Couldn't keep Dorothea and the fear. When I tried, I drove her crazy. And myself!"

"I've had the same realization," he admitted, "but it hasn't done me any good. I'm at the driving-us-both-crazy phase." And wasn't it ironic. All he wanted to do was keep her close, but with his words and actions he only pushed her away.

"Now, my friend, you have to make a quality decision. Stay with her, even though she could be taken from you at any moment, or let her go. Since we both know what you'll decide, we can skip to the next part. Your thoughts dictate your reality. Think about something, and pretty soon your feelings follow. Every day we make choices, and those choices define our future. Even the smallest decision can have a big impact. The butterfly effect. Thoughts and actions create ripples of energy.

Energy creates motion. So start treating fear like the enemy, and one day your feelings and everything else will catch up."

"Fear *is* the enemy." It was the only obstacle in the way of his relationship with Ryanne. "But I don't yet grasp how to treat it as such."

"Start by killing one thought at a time."

"And?" He needed more, wanted an instant miracle cure.

"Force your mind to think about something else. Something good. About your woman, maybe. Her smile."

In other words, no instant miracle cure. "Ryanne suggested the same thing. So far, I've failed."

"Perhaps you're being too gentle. Any time fear rears its ugly head, beat it to a bloody pulp by doing what it tells you *not* to do."

CHAPTER TWENTY-SIX

Cowboy: Where are you?

Ryanne: Why do you want to know? So you can have down and dirty sex with me?

Cowboy: Wade.

Ryanne: Aw! You spent the night with me and still remember my name. You must be a unicorn.

Cowboy: I will find you.

Ryanne: Like it's hard. Is it, though? Is it hard? Are you planning to demand I give you an orgasm? I bet you are. The real question is: Do you want me to use my hands, mouth or body?

No other text came in, and Ryanne smiled. Teasing Jude had become the highlight of her day.

That, and the updates Brock sent her about Savannah and Thomas.

Brock: The kid just shouted that he needs an ice-cold beer. How am I supposed to respond to that?

Brock: Vanna hid the remote control so I can't change the channel. She's watching Say Yes to the Dress. I really hope Dushku sends someone to kill ME.

Once, Savannah stole his phone to send a message of her own.

Brock: Savannah here. Is there any way you can spare Jude for the evening? I don't want to steal your man, I swear. As if that would be possible! The way he looks at you, well, I know men and I know he's all yours. But this isn't about sex. I just like him better than Brock the Cock. (Please excuse my language.) But Brock sucks!

If only Jude would overcome his fear!

Ryanne: I can spare him, but he's afraid of losing me, and won't let me out of his sight. It's driving me crazy. You say you know men—what should I do?

Brock: Girl, the time to worry is when he can't stand to have you IN his sight.

Good point.

The kitchen doors suddenly burst open, laughter and a hundred different conversations from behind the door assaulting her ears as Jude strode inside, glaring when he spotted her.

"You're irritating," he grumbled.

"No, I'm preorgasmic. And you are, too. That's why you're so irritable."

His next step stumbled, but he quickly righted himself. The tension he radiated changed in an instant, from stressed to hungry.

Doing her best not to gloat, she lined up the necessary ingredients for bacon, jalapeño and jelly sandwiches. Serving meals instead of just snacks had been a big hit at the last event, so she'd decided to continue in that vein. Caroline had been helping her, but the flighty girl had taken a five-minute break ten minutes ago and had yet to return.

"How's the battle with fear coming?" she asked.

"It's coming," Jude said.

"Sadly it's the *only* thing coming tonight." Last night's loving had been an aberration. He was still determined to resist her until she said yes to his "proposal," and she was still determined to resist him until he'd conquered his fear.

That fear had proven to be more contagious than ever; it kept trying to get her, too. What if the gunman came back?

However, Ryanne refused—absolutely refused—to let her mind play the worst-case scenario game. Worry leached happiness and calm, and both Jude and the baby needed her happy and calm.

"Must you turn everything I say into an innuendo?" he grated.

"Yes. What can I say? It's my superpower. And if you were getting laid regularly, you'd be thrilled about it."

With a grunt, he poured himself a glass of water, minus the lemon, and plopped onto the chair at the end of the counter, where he set up his laptop. Great. The kitchen had just become his new workstation.

He'd hired off-duty officers from Strawberry PD to guard the Scratching Post, inside and out. If Dushku *did* make another move against her, he'd be in for a surprise. And really, if Ryanne could wait him out, succeed despite his best efforts, maybe he'd finally give up and move on.

A girl could hope, anyway.

"If you stay away from me the rest of the night," she said, "not texting me or watching me on camera, I'll believe you're ready to receive my hand in marriage."

He didn't look up from the screen. "Even when Dushku is gone, I won't want to spend a night away from you. Give me another task."

Danged stubborn man. "There will always be a threat. A virus. Bacteria. Bad drivers. A robbery gone wrong."

She thought he muttered something like, "If you and our kid die, I die."

"Jude," she said, stomping her foot. "You better mean those words figuratively because—"

"I could use a little peace and quiet, Wade." *Type, type, type.* "I'm working."

She rolled her eyes. "Do you have a new client?"

"You're my only client. The rest of the team is handling the others. By the way, I'm no longer accepting your money. Your security is now free of charge."

What! "No way! You run a business, and if you're going to provide for me and Ryanne Jr., you need to make money."

Finally he glanced up. One brow arched. "Are you saying I need to take *your* money in order to make money to provide for you?"

"That *is* how commerce works. Also, you owe me two dollars and fifty cents for the water."

He pinched the bridge of his nose, his shoulders drooping. Poor guy. He'd never looked wearier. "Use the money for the baby, instead of your trip. Problem solved."

Caroline rushed into the kitchen, stopping her reply—not that she knew what to say. "Sorry, sorry. I didn't mean to take so long."

The buttons on her shirt were no longer aligned, and her hair had come out of its ponytail to tangle around her flushed face.

"Make out on your own time," Ryanne told her, now grumbling like Jude.

Why would he not want her to spend money on her trip? Did he want her to stay in town with him?

Did *she* want to stay in town with him?

No! Won't be like my mother. No man—not even her man—would stop her from living her dreams. If Jude wanted to come with her, great. If not, fine.

Please, please want to come with me.

Poo on a stick! She better not start crying again.

"I will." Caroline moved to Ryanne's side and took over the jalapeño jelly. "I got carried away, I'm sorry. It's been a while, if you know what I mean."

"Who's the guy?" Ryanne asked.

"Someone we went to high school with. Glen Baker. Remember him?"

"I do. Did he find a job?"

While Jude's attention remained on his laptop, he suddenly radiated all kinds of satisfaction, clearly happy Glen had found someone else.

"He did, though he won't tell me where," Caroline said. "He's working on a trial basis and doesn't want to jinx it."

Jude muttered, "Idiot."

"Ignore Mr. Laurent," Ryanne said. "If he were a gentleman, he'd leave us in peace."

Caroline's lips quirked up at the corners. "Honey, if you want a man to leave a room, you've got to start talking about tampons, menstrual cramps or yeast."

Jude looked more likely to smile than run.

"Now," Caroline said, "why don't *you* take a break? You work too hard."

"Only so I can play hard later. I'll be leaving for Rome soon," she said with a little more volume than necessary.

"Well, *I* work too hard, then." Caroline pouted. "Everyone

from Strawberry Valley is out there having fun with foam, and we're stuck in here making sandwiches."

"Making sandwiches *and* money. And FYI, making money is more important than fun." Once again, she increased the volume of her voice for Jude's sake.

He ignored her. Or pretended to.

One of the waitresses peeked her head through the doors. "Got another order. And where's the food for Vandercamp and his assistant? They're getting restless."

"Here." Caroline rushed two plates her way.

Knowing Jude's gaze continually sought her, just to make sure she was okay, Ryanne decided to torture him for his money-for-the-baby comment by cleaning the counter around him, brushing her breasts against him at every opportunity.

His tension redoubled, and his breath hitched, the air between them suddenly crackling.

The muscles in her belly contracted, warmth pooling between her legs. Beneath her bra, her nipples beaded and ached for a touch. His touch. Only ever his.

Talk about a plan backfiring! She'd ended up torturing *herself*.

This was going to be a long night.

Jude trailed Ryanne as she visited with one customer after another. Though he remained in the shadows, he still managed to make everyone uncomfortable. Whenever he approached, people stopped laughing, spraying foam and drinking. Conversations died.

Ryanne kept tossing him death-glares over her shoulder, but he refused to back down. He was on edge, his leg sore and his body primed. He *needed* her in his arms, but had to settle for keeping her close.

Worse, he'd woken up plagued by a feeling that he was going to lose her, sooner rather than later, and with every hour that had passed, the ominous feeling had only magnified.

Damn it, he knew the source of the feeling, and so did she. What else? Fear. The enemy he'd once treated as an old friend.

Any time fear rears its ugly head, beat it to a bloody pulp by doing what it tells you not to do.

Daniel's words played through Jude's mind on constant repeat. Fear told him to enfold Ryanne in plastic bubbles, lock her inside the Scratching Post and never let her leave. He'd even started to think up ways to stop her from traveling. What if the plane crashed? What if she were abducted, or raped?

Argh! He wanted to bang his head against the wall. He had to do the opposite—no Bubble Wrap, no locking her in the bar, no commanding her to stay in Oklahoma.

Shit. If she insisted on going to Rome, he would insist on going with her. He would have suggested it sooner, but he hadn't wanted to face the memories of his travels without his girls, and really, he'd hoped to talk Ryanne out of going altogether.

Whether he stayed or went, he needed to face his memories.

"If you stick to me any closer, cowboy, you're going to smother me. And the customers! They've stopped spending the money I was planning to leave on the dresser for you, so that you could spend it on me."

He heard the exasperation in her voice, knew he should back off. Then a chant of her name erupted—*Ryanne, Ryanne, Ryanne.* People wanted her to sing with the band.

Backing off ceased to be an option. She would be the center of attention, and vulnerable, without shield or defense.

"Stay off the stage," he commanded. "Stay here. Where you're safe."

"No way, no how. My admiration for you might be unconditional, but my temper is another story. I'm doing this. You made everyone uncomfortable, so now I've got to make them happy." She smiled and nodded at the crowd.

When she headed for the dais, he grabbed hold of her wrist,

stopping her before she got very far. A single tug, and she was pressed against him.

"Don't do this," he said, speaking straight into her ear in order to be heard over the chanting. He wrapped his arm around her waist to better keep her in place, his fingers curving over her perfect ass. "Up there you'll be an easy target." How could she overlook the danger?

Leaning back, she studied his face, and whatever she saw merely darkened her mood. She framed his face with her precious hands and rose on her tiptoes to speak directly into *his* ear. "Down here, I won't be living my life on my terms. I'll be caving to fear—just like you."

His heart thundered against his ribs, cracking the bone, surely. The pain...the ache in his chest.

Damn it! How was he supposed to get through to the most stubborn woman on earth? "Be smart about this. Stay safe." What if one of Dushku's men was hiding among the crowd, armed, ready to take her out for helping Savannah escape? "Please, shortcake."

The use of the endearment could be classified as a manipulation tactic right now, but he didn't care.

For once, she didn't soften. "We've had this conversation before, Jude, and I'd rather not have it again in front of an audience." Multicolored strobe lights spilled over her, vanished, only to spill over her again, highlighting a beauty too pure for mere mortal men. "Now let me go."

"Never!"

While the fevered response softened her, it didn't soothe her. With a gentleness that agonized him, she said, "Keep this up, and you're going to regret it."

His chest bowed in challenge, his hand sliding down her ass to actually cup her cheek. "Threaten to leave me all you want, but I would rather watch you walk away than carry you to your grave."

"I wasn't threatening to leave you, you foolish man, and I'm insulted you would think so. You should know me better than that."

He flushed, but still maintained his hold on her.

"Fight this, cowboy. For me. For *us*."

In a moment of raw honesty, he croaked, "I don't think I can." Her life meant more to him than his own.

"You're giving up? Just like that?" What remained of her good humor vanished. "Well, you can go screw yourself, because I'm not going to!" Smiling again for the crowd—a smile that didn't reach her eyes—she wrenched free, sidestepped him and marched onto the stage.

All eyes focused on her, the chants finally dying down as cheers rang out. Jude had to plant his booted feet in the floor to stop himself from stalking after her and dragging her off that stage.

When she moved to the mic, the band spread out behind her. Within seconds, a soft ballad filled the air, and her whiskey-and-smoke voice followed. The battle with fear ended then and there, the giant slayed. At least for the moment. Jude stood frozen, utterly transfixed. He'd heard her sing before, but he'd forgotten how sensual she sounded. How sensual…and irresistible. Every word contained a note of heartbreak and longing, hope and regret, and he knew soul-deep *he* was the one who had caused the heartbreak and regret, not Dushku.

Jude's shoulders rolled in. He kept messing up with her. Would he ever get things right?

Well, he was going to have to, because he couldn't tolerate the alternative. Life without her.

Maybe he'd start faking a sense of calm?

Whoa. Fake it? What was *wrong* with him? He would actually consider lying to the mother of his child?

No. Absolutely not. He refused to sink so low.

Fear was an obstacle, remember? Obstacles could be overcome.

Fight this, Ryanne had said.

I don't think I can, he'd replied, but he'd lied to *himself.* He could. He would. He would fight until he died, if necessary, but he would win. Surrender wasn't an option, would never be an option.

He needed to talk to her, but decided to hang back when she left the stage and give her a little breathing room at last. It was difficult to stay away, but he did it, patrolling the crowd, searching for anything or anyone out of the ordinary.

Finally, it was time for the Scratching Post to close. He spotted Carrie and Russ among the dissipating crowd and closed the distance. "Hey. I didn't expect to see you guys tonight."

Carrie hugged him, her familiar perfume enveloping him. For a moment, his mind flashed back to his wedding day. *Take care of my little girl, Jude.*

I will. Always.

Then I'll always be in your debt.

"I know you said we'd have breakfast in the morning, but I really hoped to speak with you tonight." There was a tremor in her voice. "If you're not too busy?"

He suspected the talk would include advice to dump Ryanne. *Never going to happen.* "I can't. I'm sorry. I made a mess of things with Ryanne, and I've got to fix it." Somehow. She came first. From now on, she would always come first.

Carrie surprised him, smiling a half sad, half apologetic smile and saying, "That's fine, but I'm here, you're here, so I'm going to say my piece, anyway. I don't want you hung up on my wonderful but passed daughter for the rest of your life, and I'm sorry I acted the way I did. So tell your sweet Ryanne you're sorry for whatever you did, because we both know you're at fault. You're a man, and sometimes you guys don't have enough oxygen in your brains."

The support absolutely floored him, and he croaked, "I'll tell her." Though he doubted another apology would smooth things over. "I love you, you know."

"I love you, too. You're a good boy with a good heart, and I'm looking forward to being a grandma again. Don't keep us in the dark anymore, all right? We want to be a part of your life."

"You are… Mom."

She beamed at him, some of the grief she'd carried around like a second skin suddenly falling away.

Russ stepped up to hug him, too. "You've got a baby on the way. Why aren't you happier?"

"I've been too worried to be happy," he answered honestly.

"About?"

"Life and death." Mostly death.

"Son, there isn't life without death. It happens to all of us at some point or another. I just hate to see yours happen while you're still alive."

Jude had no reply for him, because he'd just been sucker punched. If you didn't take time to enjoy your life, to make others happy rather than miserable, did you have a life worth living?

As the couple headed for the door, he scanned the bar, at last finding Ryanne. Pangs of longing and regret left him grasping at his chest. She was vital, beautiful beyond imagining despite the dark circles under her eyes. Dark circles he and his fear had caused.

Never again.

She and her employees were cleaning the foam from the floors.

"You guys can take off," he told the employees. He would finish up himself—after he'd chatted with Ryanne.

She stiffened but didn't contradict him as her people filed out of the building. He checked all the locks and turned on the alarm. When he finished, he remained in the shadows, watching her work for a moment. Her motions were jerky, her annoyance on full display as she sanitized the saddle on the mechanical bull and anchored a brand-new cover on it.

Determined, Jude stepped toward her. "I'm sorry. I had no right to treat you the way I did."

"I've heard a version of those words before." She pressed her forehead against the saddle, her back to him. "I'm not breaking up with you, Jude, but I need space. A lot of space."

Going to lose her, despite everything.

No! Damn it, no.

Rage roared to life. Rage for what he'd lost and suffered. Rage for his foolish behavior. Rage for all the times he'd hurt the woman he treasured.

A single spark can start a wildfire.

Those sparks spread, grew, heated. One second Jude stood in place, perhaps the picture of calm, the next he erupted, punching the wall again and again, his fist pummeling at rapid fire.

Wood crushed beneath the force. Splinters rained. A thick cloud of plaster formed around him. He didn't care. Today he'd stalked Ryanne, a predator tormented by his past. Of course she wanted to take a break from him. He wanted to take a break from himself!

He punched and snarled until the rage and grief, sorrow and worry drained at long last, leaving him empty. A vessel to be filled.

Out with the old, in with the new.

He was panting, his hands bleeding, and the pain...it was physical rather than mental, and thus manageable.

He turned on his heel, only then realizing he'd just ruined a wall in her bar—her home. His stomach sank. Did she fear him now?

"Ryanne—" When his gaze met hers, he had to do a double take. She watched him with eyes full of wonder and relief.

"Feel better?" she asked.

"I do." With his mind stripped of emotion, only truth remained. He hadn't feared for Ryanne's life, not exactly. He'd feared what *his* life would be like without her in it.

There isn't life without death. It happens to all of us at some point or another. I just hate to see yours happen while you're still alive.

Russ was right. Jude had been a walking dead man, eating everyone's joy.

Fear will only ever hurt you. Hope will save you.

Ryanne was right, as well. Jude couldn't protect her from everything. Bad things happened in the world. As she'd said, anything could kill her—a virus, a car accident, someone other than Dushku. People made bad decisions and evil existed.

If Jude always expected the worst, would it soon become a self-fulfilling prophecy?

Absolutely. Look at where he'd taken their relationship already. By fearing her loss, he had succeeded only in driving her away.

Today's space was tomorrow's goodbye.

Did letting go of his fear mean he could no longer do everything in his power to protect her? No. Hell, no. He could. He should. He'd decided to let go of fear, not sever an entire lobe of his brain. But he should also trust her to make the best decisions for herself, which meant he had to stop peering into the darkness of what could be and start looking for the light in what was.

What was—he had her, here and now. He had to spend his time enjoying her rather than continuing to torment them both.

Your thoughts dictate your reality. Think about something, and pretty soon your feelings follow. Every day we make choices, and those choices define our future. Even the smallest decision can have a big impact. The butterfly effect. Thoughts and actions create ripples of energy. Energy creates motion. So start treating fear like the enemy, and one day your feelings and everything else will catch up.

He had to give himself permission to experience the happiness she gave him, come what may.

I'll never give up… Ryanne.

Even as his heart stuttered inside his chest, he rasped, "You don't need space. I'm a changed man, and things will be different from now on, I swear it. I finally know how I'm going to fight fear."

Hope glimmered in those rich, dark eyes, even as the muscles in her shoulders bunched. She was being tugged in two separate directions, he would bet. "I'm happy for you, Jude. I really am. But you'd be doing it simply to keep me, and as we've seen, that doesn't work well for either of us."

"I'm not doing it for you, well, not only for you, but for me, too. I refuse to live with fear a second longer. I'd rather live with you."

The hope brightened, but it was tempered with dread, as if she didn't *want* to put too much stock in his claims. He took another step toward her; she remained in place. Unfazed, he kept going, until he'd pressed her against the mechanical bull.

Little panting breaths left her.

She licked her lips. "How are you going to fight it?"

"Not *going to*. Fighting *now*. One day at a time. One thought at a time. I'm done treating you like glass. For all I care, you can carry your own jars of moonshine from now on."

She snorted, as he'd hoped.

"If you want to travel, we'll travel," he continued. "Unless you'd rather travel alone?"

A little gasp left her. "You'd be willing to go with me?"

"Not just willing, but happily. And if you want to sing in the bar tomorrow night or the next, I'm not going to protest. If you want to run errands around town, I won't try to stop you."

"Even though Dushku is still a threat?"

"Even though. I'm not saying I'll be perfect from now on, because I might shadow you if you leave, and by *might* I mean I *will*, but I'm going to be better."

Her eyes widened, different emotions playing in their depths. More hope. Less dread. Excitement. Arousal. Happiness of her own. Her body softened against his. Melted, really, and he had to contain the urge to bang on his chest. If this were his reward for fighting fear—her willing surrender—he'd gladly remain on the battlefield for the rest of his life.

"Yes," she finally said, smiling up at him as if he'd just made all her dreams come true. "I will do you the great honor of becoming your wife."

The acceptance shocked him, even as satisfaction heated him from head to toe. "Damn right you will. But tonight the two of us are going to be *dis*honorable. So strip down to your panties and climb on the bull, shortcake. I'm going to do bad, bad things to you."

CHAPTER TWENTY-SEVEN

Shivers cascaded through Ryanne. Bad, bad things? Yes, please. All evening she'd vacillated between arousal, anger and uncertainty, all courtesy of Jude. Now arousal won the battle, consuming her.

This man was a natural born conqueror, a trained seducer, and he was giving this relationship his all, nothing held back. Except maybe his heart. Did he love her? He must. Look at how hard he'd fought to keep her.

"Still giving me orders, cowboy? Well, good news. This one I happen to like."

Trembling with desire, she stripped down to her panties and hopped onto the bull.

His gaze roved over her, heating—heating *her*. "Turn around—face the other way."

"Sir, yes, sir." She turned, as commanded, sitting on the bull backward.

He typed into his phone, stripped to his underwear and climbed in front of her, his delicious scent enveloping her.

With the push of a few buttons, the machine jolted into

motion, nearly tossing her off. They both had an app on their phones that synced with the bull's controls.

"Jude," she said with a laugh.

"Don't worry. I won't let you fall." His arms snaked around her, holding her in place. Holding her where she belonged—against him. "You've been begging me for a ride all night, and I'm going to make sure you get one."

Another laugh bubbled from her. "Someone has learned how to innuendo. I've been a terrible influence on you." As the bull continued to buck and swing, she said, "What about the cameras?"

"No one can see us. The feed is now streaming exclusively to my phone."

"So we can watch the video later?"

"Exactly."

"How naughty of you." Smiling her most wicked smile, she flattened her palms on his chest. His heartbeat raced, the organ practically jumping up to meet her touch. "Just so you know, I want a ring."

"You'll get one. Probably a tattoo of one, too. The world will know you're mine."

Again he pressed a series of buttons in the app, this time slowing the bull to a crawl.

His navy eyes lightened, glittering like sapphires, the warmth of his breath fanning over her breasts as he rested his forehead on her shoulder, drawing goose bumps to the surface.

Dang, she loved this man. Loved him with every fiber of her being. She'd already realized the truth, but her love had grown since then. She loved every part of him.

"The highlight of my day," she rasped, "is when Jude the Ice Man melts for me, only me." And oh, crap, the gentle back and forth motion was turning her on, the stiff leather rubbing between her legs. A moan escaped her.

His head whipped up, his attention fixed on her hammering

pulse. He smiled a wicked smile. "I see my evil plan is working. Now, prepare for every day to be your favorite."

Ooh la la. "What is your evil plan, hmm?"

He leaned forward, grazed her earlobe with his teeth. In a blink, the tone of their connection changed, humor fading, leaving only the sweet burn of arousal.

"Making you beg for me," he said.

The bull tilted, and another moan escaped her. "I haven't begged yet."

"Silly shortcake. You will."

Anticipation flooded her as he cupped and kneaded her breasts, the bull continuing to rock slowly, so slowly, back and forth.

"I have wanted you for so long." He played with her nipples, white lightning streaking to her core. "Now I'm going to have you."

"But we're not married yet." *Protesting? Seriously?* She ran her tongue over her lips. "What happened to waiting until I'm Ryanne Laurent?"

"I love you, whatever your name happens to be. Tonight, that's enough."

Shock. Amazement. Wonder. Each emotion flooded her. He loved her. Jude Walker Laurent loved her back.

Overcome, she threw her arms around him. "I love you, too. So danged much."

"You'd better." His mouth slanted over hers, drugging her, his taste as intoxicating as an entire bottle of whiskey. Though a sense of urgency had claimed her, Jude took his time, his tongue rolling with hers, as if savoring every second. No matter how she attempted to speed him up, scratching at him, biting him, frantically rubbing against the hard length of his erection, he maintained that slow, steady pace.

The air heated, beads of sweat popping up on her brow, between her shoulder blades and every place Jude's skin touched hers. When finally she yielded to his leisurely seduction, he flattened his hand between her breasts and urged her backward.

"Lie down as best you can," he croaked. "You're going to be my buffet of sensual delights."

"Wicked…romantic…what happened to the Ice Man?"

"He met the Fire Queen."

With her back resting on the neck of the bull and her spread thighs on top of Jude's, her body was completely vulnerable to his every whim. First he toyed with her nipples, stoking the fire inside her. Then he dragged his fingertips along the still-flat plane of her belly. Then, oh, then, he traced the outline of her panties. The waist, the sides…the center seam.

Moaning and groaning, Ryanne writhed, seeking more, everything he had to give, getting lost in his touch, in this man she loved. This man she trusted. Getting to this point might have been a challenge, but their tests and trials had only made their need for each other stronger. An unbreakable bond had been forged, the darkness of the past eclipsed by the brightness of the future.

"Jude…my cowboy."

One of his fingers snuck past her panties and slipped inside her. Air hissed between her teeth, the exquisite feel of him destroying what remained of her control. Her hips lifted, sending him deeper.

"So wet. So tight," he praised. He wedged in a second finger, only driving her need for him higher. A need that would never be quenched. "So mine."

Still the bull rocked on, Jude matching the thrust of his fingers to its languid rhythm. Pleasure became agony, agony became pleasure. All she could do was enjoy.

"Every day, in a thousand different ways, you undo me, love. You're my world."

Despite the slow pace, a swift and brutal orgasm ripped through her. His actions, his words—too much! As she shouted her rapture to the ceiling, her inner walls clenching, Jude drew her to a sitting position. Rather than collapsing against him, weakened by the pleasure, she revved up.

Need him. All of him. Now.

"Get inside me." Ryanne shoved his underwear out of the way, his shaft springing free. The head already glistened with moisture. Desperate, she hoisted herself up as best she could, moved her panties out of the way and poised him at her entrance. "Please. I'm begging."

Jude took her by the waist, stopping her from sinking all the way to the base. "There's no place I'd rather be than inside you, but I'm going to take my time getting there."

With his gaze locked on hers, his hands on her bottom and her nails in his shoulders, he continued to move with the bull, entering her one torturous inch at a time. Hours seemed to pass until she was finally, blissfully, seated on him. And oh—oh! He'd touched a sensitive spot inside her, fueling the ravenous ache in her core...and her soul.

Again and again and again he rolled his hips in a counter-clockwise motion. Not once did he increase his pace. The friction! The heat! She cried out. Her chest was flush against his, sweat causing a succulent glide. He was the flame, and she was the match. Together they burned.

It was the most romantic moment of her life, his love for her as palpable as his desire. Two had become one, and the knowledge pushed her closer and closer to the edge.

"Almost...there," she said between panting breaths, then ran his lower lip between her teeth. "Please. Please!"

He was panting, too. His beautiful, scarred fingers traced a path of fire around her waist, slipped past her panties and pressed against the little bundle of nerves soaked with her arousal.

Ryanne erupted, shuddering against him, screaming, her entire being caught up in a raging storm of pleasure and satisfaction.

"Can *feel* you coming," Jude rasped. His thrusts increased, until he hammered inside her—until he roared her name and poured himself into her.

True to his word, Jude stopped shadowing Ryanne's every move. For the next few days, as he and Daniel unsuccessfully scoured records of different shell corporations and dummy companies in an attempt to find Dushku's pot of gold, he'd even left the Scratching Post without having a full-blown panic attack. Of course, he'd still monitored security from his phone.

He'd had breakfast with Carrie and Russ, as planned, and when he'd told them about his engagement to Ryanne, they'd expressed joy. Carrie encouraged him to move forward without guilt or fear. Russ mentioned how wonderful it was to see the sparkle had returned to his eyes.

They'd said their goodbyes, and he'd promised to visit. His child would have the best grandparents in the world.

Today, he'd left the Scratching Post for a different reason. One all his own. He'd spent over four hours inside a tattoo shop in the city, getting a surprise for Ryanne etched into his chest. He'd also bought her a ring. A large center pearl with four small diamonds on one side; each diamond was set in platinum and had a small hook at the end, making the ring resemble a cat paw.

Nontraditional, yes, but so Ryanne.

Now he couldn't stop smiling.

Life was good, and if all went according to plan, it would only get better.

Ryanne worked in the kitchen alongside Caroline, preparing cookies and cakes for the bar's next event. The glow-stick party. She'd found edible glow in the dark frosting, and decided to go with sweet treats versus savory tonight.

As Caroline rambled on about Glen Baker—*When he kisses me, I see stars, but any time I try for more, he stops me and I swear to goodness gracious he looks like he's going to vomit, but I'm wrong, right, he can't look like he's going to vomit because he's totally into me, why else would he keep asking me out, oh, you know what, I bet it's his new job, all the stress of performing well causes undue stress on another type of performance, if you know what I mean*—Ryanne tried not to miss Jude. Had she seriously complained about having him around all the time?

I suck.

The man was the puzzle piece that had been missing from her life. And he loved her. The greatest guy ever born loved her, exactly as she was. He worshipped her body every night, teased her, took care of her, and looked forward to more days, months and years with her.

"Glen?" Caroline said.

"What about him?" When no answer was forthcoming, Ryanne looked up, her gaze landing on her frowning employee.

"What are you doing here?" Caroline asked, staring past Ryanne.

Glen? Here?

Confused, Ryanne turned…and found Glen standing a few feet away. He was pale and waxen, sweat dotting his brow, dirt staining his clothes. He had his hands behind his back as he rocked from one foot to the other.

This wasn't the confident but struggling businessman who'd flirted with her at Dorothea's party. This was someone else entirely.

A better question: "How did you get in?" The bar wasn't open, so all the doors were locked. Jude had double-checked before he'd left, and had probably checked a thousand times on his phone, too. He had to know an unauthorized male had breached the premises.

"I'm sorry," Glen said, peering at Ryanne. "I had no money, and lots of legal troubles."

"What does that have to do with—"

"He offered me enough money to start my own company *and* he ensured the embezzlement charges against me were dropped," Glen interjected, a tormented expression on his face. "All I had to do was get rid of the whore and make sure you understood the same would happen to you if you interfered again, but I messed up and... I can't go to jail, Ryanne."

There was only one "he" that made any sense in this situation. Dushku. Her heart skipped a beat. "Whatever you're here to do—"

"I'm sorry," he repeated, striding forward. He extended his arm, and she caught sight of the Colt .44 clutched in his grip.

Caroline whimpered. "How could you do this, Glen? You told me you—"

"Shut up," he snapped. "Just shut up. This is hard enough."

Ryanne stepped in front of her trembling employee and tried to back him away, but the counter stopped her. Caroline moved beside her to present a united front.

"Glen," Ryanne said. "You need to think about this, okay. You're only inviting new legal troubles."

"You don't understand. He owns me now. If I don't do what he says..."

No talking sense into him. Noted. "I'll help you. Jude will help you, but only if you let Caroline and me walk out of this kitchen."

"You can't even help yourself," he spat.

No offering aid.

Very well. Ryanne bent down, grabbed her own gun and straightened. But she was too late.

Before she could take aim, he slammed the butt of the Colt into her temple. Pain exploded inside her head—and then the world went dark.

CHAPTER TWENTY-EIGHT

A dull ache in her entire body woke her, or maybe it was the persistent throb in her temple.

With a groan, Ryanne blinked open her eyes. Hazy eyesight, surroundings a blur. What the heck had happened? Morning sickness?

Possible. Her stomach churned with a toxic mix of acid and what seemed to be nails.

Had Jude carried her to bed? Her ears twitched, detecting the sound of shuffling footsteps and muffled voices. No way. He wouldn't have let people inside their apartment.

Blink, blink, blink. At last her vision began to clear. She reached up, or rather, tried to. Her hands were stuck.

Stuck?

She struggled, and the sound of jangling metal rang out. Chains?

Her hands were bound behind her back, but not with metal. Plastic, maybe. The plastic *was* hooked to a chain, the other end of the chain anchored to the far wall, giving her room to walk around but not enough to leave the area.

As she increased her struggles, something warm and wet dripped into her eyes. Blood?

Why would—

Memories broke through whatever wall had held them back. Glen had snuck into her bar. He'd pistol-whipped her, knocking her out.

She jolted upright. Dizziness struck with a vengeance, and she would have collapsed if not for a large wooden crate that halted her descent. When she attempted to brace against it, her arms, still bound behind her back, refused to cooperate. The plastic—zip ties.

Her heart hammered wildly. She was in a warehouse? The building might just span the length of a football field.

Boxes abounded throughout, and at least five cars were parked along one side—a Hummer, two Jeeps and two vans. In the corner, a foldout table had papers and different office supplies scattered across the top. There were other rooms nearby, a half wall cordoning each. Dust mites whirled through the air.

Had Glen carried her out of the Scratching Post himself, or had he gotten help from Dushku's men? Where was Caroline?

Caroline!

A few feet away, her unconscious friend lay on a dirty concrete floor. Like Ryanne, her hands were bound behind her back with a zip tie that was looped through a chain. She had a bruise and knot on her temple.

How much time had passed? Jude had to have seen what happened on the feed. Maybe he'd followed Glen and would fly through the door…any…second…

The shuffle of footsteps grew louder, the voices no longer quite so muffled.

Urgency driving her, Ryanne contorted in an effort to reach for her gun. Dang it! The holster in her boot was empty. She had no other weapons on her.

As quietly as possible, she scooted to Caroline's side and performed the world's most awkward pat down. No weapons on her, either.

A pained moan left the girl as her eyes blinked open. Then she gasped and jerked upright. "Glen," she said. "I'm so sorry. I had no idea—"

"Shhh." When Caroline pressed her lips together, Ryanne whispered, "How did Glen get into the bar?"

Shame flushed her cheeks. "Last night, when I was on break, we kissed in the alley. He was the reason I was late. He must have watched me punch in the code."

So they'd both played right into his plan. Okay, whatever. What was done was done. Now they had to find a way to break their bindings and sneak out before Glen came back.

"We can't stay here," she said as quietly as possible. The voices were so close their words were almost distinguishable. She pushed to her feet and raced to the desk, careful not to let the chain clink against the floor. Pens, pencils and rubber bands. She grabbed a few of everything.

If she could, she would pick the locks on the chain. If she couldn't, the pens and pencils could act as daggers. The rubber bands...she wasn't sure yet, but better safe than sorry.

Next she returned to Caroline's side. Remembering Coot's story about his wife, she attempted to break her zip ties. Failed. Wait. What had he done, exactly? *Come on, come on. Think! Stop letting panic cloud your thoughts.* He'd dragged his arms—

Two men stalked around a half wall. Glen and Cigarette, the muscled giant who'd once squired Savannah around Strawberry Valley. Cigarette wore a smug smile and held a .44. *Ryanne's .44* to be exact. She recognized the mother-of-pearl handle.

Glen wrung his hands. He took the lead, rushing to Caroline and Ryanne. "I'm sorry. You should have left town after the shooting in the alley. I wasn't trying to hurt you."

Cabrón!

"Bastard," Caroline spit at him. "I hope you contract a flesh-eating bacteria in your tiny penis!"

Cigarette laughed. "She's feisty. I like her."

The way he leered at her... Ryanne shuddered.

"*You're* the one who shot Jude?" she demanded, glaring at Glen.

Everyone's attention returned to her.

Glen was the one who had almost harmed her baby. He'd admitted to the shooting before, but the truth hadn't yet crystalized. Now it took everything she had to remain in place and not drive her fists into his face.

"So you're a criminal *and* a lousy kisser?" Caroline said with a sneer. "I should have listened to my mother. You aren't worth two shits and a giggle."

"All right, ladies. Fun times are over." Cigarette lifted the gun, aimed at Ryanne. "Here's what's going to happen. We're going to call Jude. If he wants you two to survive the hour, he'll bring us Savannah and Thomas. Until then, you're going to keep your mouths shut. Understand?"

Tremors of fear swept through Ryanne as she nodded. Caroline hissed.

Cigarette peered into Ryanne's eyes—gloating. "If Dushku weren't on his way, you and I could have a little fun. But lucky for you, orders are orders, and you aren't to be harmed...yet."

He walked away, and Glen followed.

"What are we going to do?" Caroline whispered as soon as the guys disappeared around the corner. "They won't let us leave, even if Jude makes the trade. We've seen too much. We'll be... be..." She whimpered, her bravado deserting her.

First of all, Jude wouldn't make the trade. He wouldn't allow Savannah to be harmed. Second, there was no way Ryanne was staying put, her sweet baby in danger.

"We've got to escape before Jude arrives," she said quietly. "Follow my lead, okay?"

Wasting no time, she contorted her body, nearly pulling her

shoulders out of their sockets as she worked her arms under then over her legs. With her hands in front of her, she easily performed Coot's infamous move—raised her bound hands over her head, and swiftly swung her arms down, her elbows spread to bypass her hips, pulling her hands apart—argh! The ties didn't break. She tried again, then again and finally achieved success, the plastic ripping, the chain falling to the ground, useless.

Caroline managed to do the same, and Ryanne dragged her to her feet.

If they could make their way outside, they might survive this. But as they moved through the building, ducking behind boxes, checking the cars for keys, she only managed to make her way deeper inside.

Thud!

Her ear twitched. The slam of a door? Had to be! They were close to an exit, then, but not close enough. As she and Caroline wedged themselves between two boxes, Ryanne's heart drummed so loudly against her ribs she feared someone would hear her before spotting her.

Pounding footsteps registered. More than one person approached.

"Tell me." Dushku's voice rang out, autocratic to the extreme.

As Cigarette explained the situation, the footsteps lessened in volume. Ryanne peeked over the box in front of her, only to duck. Two guards had remained behind. They stood at least fifty yards to her left—by the door?

Caroline trembled and pressed a hand to her mouth. They stared at each other, waiting, dreading what would happen next.

"Where are they?" Dushku shouted. "Find them!"

The guards rushed forward but stopped when a series of loud bangs rang out.

"Sir," one of them called. "The man you contacted is here."

Jude?

No, no, no. He would be walking straight into the lion's den for no reason!

★ ★ ★

Jude approached the entrance of the old steel mill located on the outskirts of Blueberry Hill, his rage barely contained. When he'd reached the Scratching Post, he'd gone in search of Ryanne, desperate for a kiss. He'd found a splatter of blood instead.

He'd been watching the security feeds like a madman, obsessed and possessed. Just when he'd decided to prove he'd kicked fear to the curb and give Ryanne a little breathing room, Dushku attacked.

Irony was a stone-cold bitch.

Jude had tried not to panic as he'd played back the security feed. Then he'd seen Glen Baker using the correct code to enter through the back door. The very reason Jude hadn't been alerted about an intruder. *Then* he'd watched the bastard pistol-whip both Ryanne and Caroline.

A text from an unknown number had come in with this address and the message Bring Savannah and the boy, and come unarmed. He hadn't needed a number to deduce the identity of the sender. This was Dushku's chance to get Thomas back, and also kill Savannah, Ryanne and Caroline, all while blaming Jude.

The man was counting on Jude's upset to cloud his judgment.

Two days ago, it would have. Today, the opposite happened. Despite his rage and, yes, even a bombardment of fear, Jude maintained razor-sharp clarity. *Save Ryanne and the baby, whatever the cost.* He'd contacted Daniel and Brock, who'd followed him here, leaving Savannah and Thomas with Strawberry Valley's incorruptible Sheriff Lintz.

Jude had a small transmitter in his ear, allowing his friends to hear what was going on around him and respond.

Need all the help I can get.

Jude had come unarmed, as commanded, certain he would be frisked at moment one. But no matter. He didn't need weapons to win this war. As soon as he'd verified Ryanne's well-being, he would attack—and he wouldn't stop until Dushku and every single one of his men were neutralized.

"Got you in my sights," Brock's voice whispered in his ear.

"Ditto that," Daniel said.

"Tell me you've found Dushku's money." Jude needed leverage, and he needed it now.

Daniel's sigh crackled over the line. "It'll be done by the time you're inside."

"It had better be." Ryanne's life depended on this.

As Jude approached large metal doors, he drew in a deep breath, held it…released it.

He raised his fist and knocked.

To his left, a garage door big enough for a semitruck began to lift. Two armed guards swarmed him, patted him down. He was a little surprised he wasn't just shot on sight, which he'd kind of expected.

He'd worn Kevlar underneath his shirt. That Kevlar wouldn't help him if he was shot in the head, but it *would* protect vital organs if he were shot in the chest.

"Kevlar?" One of the males laughed.

"At least he's clean," the other said.

They pushed him forward. He tripped, his leg unprepared to support his weight. Through sheer strength of will, he managed to remain upright.

Dushku, Anton, Dennis and Glen Baker waited several yards ahead. And so did Officer Jim Rayburn. *Knew it.* Boxes, crates and metal storage units acted as decor.

Dushku smiled a smile that didn't reach his eyes. For some reason, he wasn't gloating. He actually appeared…unsettled? "Where are Savannah and the boy?"

"Where are Ryanne and Caroline?" Jude snapped. "I want proof of life. Now."

CHAPTER TWENTY-NINE

Ryanne swallowed a cry of distress. Jude was here, but he was unarmed, danger surrounding him at every turn. Jim Rayburn was here, too. As an officer of the Blueberry Hill PD, his word of today's events would be believed above everyone else's. More than that, he wouldn't want anyone spilling tales about his allegiance to a gang. He would want Jude, Ryanne and Caroline killed, wouldn't he?

So badly Ryanne wanted to jump up and shout, "Here I am!" Heart leaping, she pressed her lips together and peeked over the boxes.

Jude had never been more beautiful to her. His hard features were tight with tension, making his skin look as if it might tear at any second. Determination radiated from him. His sandy hair stuck out in spikes, and his eyes possessed a wild gleam, his lips a harsh line.

In that moment, she knew he would do anything, absolutely anything, to save her. There was no line he wouldn't cross. The very reason she and Caroline had to stay put. If they distracted him or startled the others, he might be shot. And so might she and her baby! She needed to gain Jude's attention stealthily, let him know she was okay, and that she and Caroline could sneak out with him…somehow.

"Proof of life," Dushku said, only the slightest bit of unease in his tone. "Very well."

Ugh, just how was the guy going to provide proof of life when he had no idea where she and Caroline were?

Caroline squeezed her hand, a clear request to stop peeking over the box.

"Get the girls." Dushku snapped his fingers, and Snake rushed off, disappearing around one of those half walls. "I must admit, I'm a little surprised you came at all. You had to know how this would end."

Ryanne's stomach threatened to rebel. How easily he spoke of death.

"I knew you'd keep the women alive until you had what you wanted. Afterward, I'll kill Ryanne, Caroline and Savannah, and then myself, right? That's the story the world will hear, anyway."

"No, Mr. Laurent. I'll let your Ryanne live, as promised. I'm not a monster," Dushku replied. "Besides, she's a pretty piece. I could make use of her."

Jude unveiled the coldest, meanest smile she'd ever seen. "You're right about one thing. Our war will end today." He'd been pushed past all civility, his humanity stripped away. "I'm going to kill you."

Dushku laughed.

Ryanne needed to divert everyone's attention, like, now. She looked down at the supplies she'd stolen, her mind whirling. Simply throwing a pencil or pen would do no good, considering she couldn't lift her arms without gaining everyone's attention.

An idea bloomed and, hopeful, she got to work as quietly as possible.

What are you doing? Caroline mouthed.

You'll see, she mouthed back, as she attempted to assemble Coot's infamous crossbow.

"You're going to be sorely disappointed," Dushku said. "I always get what I want, and I want your blood spilled over my floor. You and yours have been more trouble than you're worth."

"Pouting?"

"This is your fault, you know. You displayed your weakness the day we met. Love for another will *always* stop you from doing what needs to be done. If you want to succeed, you have to look out for yourself."

"You're the one who's going to be disappointed." Jude took a step forward. "Love makes a man stronger. Gives him a solid foundation on which to stand. Love takes the guesswork out of his choices and makes his path clear."

Such beautiful words. Ryanne wanted to hug him.

When Jude took another step forward, everyone but Dushku aimed a gun at him.

"That's close enough," Dushku snapped, obviously unnerved by Jude's lack of fear.

Jude unveiled another smile, this one smug. "Check your bank accounts. You're about to discover you're broke, not a cent to your name."

Dushku laughed. "Hardly."

"You don't know me, so let me clue you in. I never bluff. Go ahead, check. And when you realize I'm telling the truth, you'll let Ryanne and Caroline go. Otherwise you'll never see a dime." His gaze moved over the guards. "And you guys won't get paid."

A moment passed, tension crackling in the air. Then, "Bring me a laptop. Now!"

Cigarette hurried off.

All right. With two guards busy elsewhere, there would be no better time to use the crossbow. But Ryanne was trembling, a rush of adrenaline giving her strength while also screwing with her agility, and she failed to finish the weapon's construction before Cigarette returned with the laptop.

Dushku's fingers jabbed at the keyboard. He grew stiffer, then shouted the darkest string of curses she'd ever heard. "Where's my money?"

The guns aimed at Jude were cocked.

Ryanne finished the crossbow at last. Now or never. She took aim—and fired off a shot. The pencil soared past a row of boxes and thumped into a far wall. Dushku, Glen, Jim and Cigarette turned. Without a moment's hesitation, Jude leaped into action, spinning, grabbing the barrel of the gun held by the guard standing behind him. With his other hand, he punched the guy's wrist, putting himself out of striking range, at the same time forcing the man to relinquish his grip on the weapon.

Boom! Boom! Boom! Boom!

Jude shot the guards, Jim and Cigarette in swift succession; she knew he'd chosen Jim and Cigarette versus Dushku because they had weapons of their own. All four males collapsed within milliseconds of each other, unable to fire off a shot of their own.

While Jude had nailed the guards and Cigarette in the heart, he'd only hobbled Jim's shoulder, preventing him from retrieving and lifting the gun he'd dropped during his fall. All purposeful actions on Jude's part, she suspected. He was a military hero with skill, and he wouldn't miss what he aimed at, even if it happened to move.

Ryanne had never witnessed a death before, and even though these men were mean and nasty—*had been* mean and nasty—they were still human, and watching them die was surreal and horrible, and made her stomach churn.

With the biggest threats out of the way, Jude kicked Jim's gun farther away and focused on the pale and trembling Dushku.

"Where are the girls?" Jude demanded.

"Put the gun down, Mr. Laurent." Dushku couldn't mask his fury—or his fear. "Let's talk about this. I have other men inside the warehouse. Any second they'll come barreling this way, and if you're aiming at me, they'll take you out. You'll never see Miss Wade again."

Glen dropped to his knees, tears running down his cheeks. After every terrible thing he'd done to avoid prison, he must realize his actions today had earned him a far greater sentence than he would have gotten for embezzlement.

"Where. Are. The. Girls?" Jude insisted.

"We're here." After a brief pause, making sure she wouldn't be shot at, Ryanne stood to quaking legs. "We escaped our bonds and have been hiding. We're unharmed."

Caroline raised her arm to wave while keeping the rest of her body hidden behind the boxes.

Abject relief emanated from Jude, rage from Dushku.

"Can you make it to the door without leaving the safety of the boxes?" Though Jude spoke to Ryanne, his attention remained fixed on his target.

"We can't," she said, after scrutinizing the route they'd have to take.

"Then stay where you are, okay? I'll escort you out after Daniel and Brock make sure there's no one else in the building."

Before she could reply, Snake peeked around a wall and, aiming haphazardly, frantically hammered off a series of rapid-fire shots—at Jude. One of those shots hit him.

"No!" she screamed as he crumpled. Horror punched her so fiercely she lost her breath, a second scream dying a brutal death inside her throat.

Before anyone could move, two more shots boomed, but it was Snake who toppled, blood pouring from his forehead to pool around his motionless body.

Another death, but this time, she had no sympathy. Daniel and Brock rushed up from behind him, even stepping over him, their guns trained on the remaining threats. Mud covered the two from head to toe.

Moaning, Jude sat up and shook his head as if his ears were ringing. He patted frantically at his chest, but no blood coated his hands. He was unharmed?

Thank you, God! Thank you, thank you, thank you!

"It's safe to come out," Daniel announced. "We took out the other men. They never saw us coming."

With a cry of relief, Ryanne rushed to her man. Halfway there, she dropped to her weakened knees and skidded. She threw her arms around him, quickly losing sight of the rest of the world.

"Are you okay? Please tell me you're okay, cowboy, before I lose it."

"I'm okay, love. Wearing Kevlar." He drew her closer, enfolding her against him. Shudders rocked him back and forth, and she figured his adrenaline was crashing, now that the worst was over. "You?"

"I'm not wearing Kevlar, but I'm fine." Tears filled her eyes and flooded her cheeks as she beat her fists against his shoulders. "I had this in the bag, you foolish man. Escaped my chain, was sneaking to the door. Why did you come and risk your life?"

"Without you, I don't have a life."

"They could have killed you."

"But they didn't, and now the war is over. Without money, no one will be willing to take Dushku's place."

"What if the money is retrieved?"

"Impossible. It's already been dispersed to different charities."

"Revenge—"

"Won't be a problem, either. He has too many enemies. He won't last a week in prison. You're finally safe. Savannah, too. The war is over," he repeated. "With Dushku, and with myself. Fear didn't win. *Fear didn't win.*"

She hugged him again, unwilling to let go now or ever. "I'm so proud of you, and I love you. I love you so much."

"I love you, too." He kissed her temple, her cheek. Her lips. Then they stared into each other's eyes, basking in a beautiful reunion.

Seconds, minutes, an eternity passed, before the rest of the world came back into focus. Daniel was trying to comfort a distraught Caroline while also talking on the phone with…a 911 operator? Must be. He was explaining the situation. Jim, Glen and Dushku had their noses pressed against a wall as Brock paced behind them. Jude told her that Jim wouldn't be a problem, either. The guys would hack into the security feed and prove his involvement with Dushku, who was trying to talk his way free, making promises he couldn't keep.

At some point the cops arrived, shocked by the turn of events, especially with Jim. Then the medics arrived. Uniformed men and women packed the warehouse. Pictures and statements were taken, and arrests were made. Ryanne, Jude and Caroline were escorted to an ambulance outside, their vitals checked. The sun was shining, and in the parking lot different vehicles were flashing multicolored lights.

Jude removed his shirt and vest, revealing two black and blue knots on his chest. A chest that looked slightly different than before, and not because of the injury. The reason escaped her, however.

At least he was given a clean bill of health. And so were she and Caroline.

"You ready to go home, love?" Jude now crouched in front of her, his hands cupping her cheeks.

"Yes, please."

In his truck, she rested her head on his shoulder. "I'm so glad you and Daniel met and became friends. If you hadn't, we might not have ever hooked up."

"I firmly believe we would have hooked up no matter the circumstances. Let's face it, love, you were meant to be mine. How else could two people less likely to fall for each other—a man who wished he were dead and a woman full of life—have come together?"

After a hot, steaming shower, Jude carried Ryanne to bed and held her close, making no move to seduce her. Right now, cuddling her—cherishing her—meant *everything*. He clung to the woman who had won his heart. The woman who'd taught him the death of his family hadn't heralded the end of his life.

His love for Constance and the girls would always be with him. Love never died. Love endured. Now he had a second chance to love again, and he wouldn't waste a moment of it.

"Are your fears trying to resurface?" Ryanne asked, her tone groggy.

"Not even a little. I've got them locked down, and I doubt they'll ever be able to escape again. Today you broke your zip ties, hid from a mobster and distracted his goons, overcoming abysmal odds for survival. You're a fighter, you'll always be a fighter, and I'll always have your love, no matter what happens."

She kissed his chest—and gasped. "Oh, my gosh! I finally realized what's different about you, you darling man. You tattooed my name in a circle around the heart and daggers."

"More than that," he said with a grin.

She studied his chest. "And a banner...?"

"For our baby's name."

A new batch of tears welled in her eyes. "Jude."

"I wanted to surprise you."

"Cowboy, I'm not just surprised, I'm honored and humbled. And turned on! You've never looked sexier."

He smiled at her, tenderly smoothed a lock of hair from her face. "This future thing? We've got it in the bag, love. We're going to get our happily-ever-after, guaranteed."

EPILOGUE

Unable to go another minute more without being legally wed, Ryanne married her man in a small, informal ceremony held at the Strawberry Inn. She wore a skintight red dress—because why not?—and he wore a pin-striped suit and tie.

Dorothea and Lyndie acted as her maids-of-honor, and her mother gave her away. Daniel and Brock stood with Jude, and so did Carrie and Russ.

Ryanne would forever cherish the memory. They'd overcome so much to be together, she truly believed nothing would ever be able to tear them apart, and she drew a great measure of peace from that.

After the ceremony, she and Jude decided to use the trip to Rome as the world's best honeymoon. At first, it was difficult for him, because the last time he'd traveled to Italy, he'd been with Constance and the twins. But as the days ticked by, he'd begun to share stories about the girls, who were here in spirit.

Ryanne and Jude were now swinging on a hammock anchored to the terrace of their villa, bathed in moonlight and water. A cool breeze drifted scents of pine, clay and dewy grass.

"We've been here two and a half weeks," she said. "I know you've been missing home."

"I have you. I'm good."

"Yes, but you're ready to return. Admit it."

"Love, we can add another month to the trip, if you want."

Argh! "You really churn my butter and butter my buns, cowboy. I didn't want to be the only one to feel this way, but oh, well. I'm ready to go home to our cats." Living her childhood dream was better than she'd envisioned, but also not always as fun as she'd hoped. Having to pee a thousand times during their flight had sucked balls. And throwing up all the pasta and gelato hadn't been a blast, either.

Besides, the cats—their extended family—had to be missing them something fierce. She and Jude had decided to keep all seven kittens, plus momma Belle. Over the years, they'd suffered enough losses. No need to suffer any more. Since Ryanne had promised Dorothea and Lyndie two kittens each, she'd paid the adoption fees for her friends to find their new family members at a nearby shelter. Win-win.

"Brock promised to take care of the cats, love. They're fine."

"Yes, but what about your cat baby books?" Jude was making one for each of the kittens. "What if Paris climbs on the fridge for the first time and we miss it? What if Anya and Cameo tussle again and we aren't there to cheer them on?"

"Brock is—"

"Constantly distracted by other pussies. I know."

Jude barked out a laugh. "I can't believe you said that."

"What? It's true!"

"What about your dream of traveling the world?" he asked.

"It hasn't changed. Well, it has, but for the better. I once wanted to see the world on my own, because I didn't know I could trust a man and take him with me. I also didn't know how special a good home could be, but now I do, and I miss it. Don't get me wrong. I still want to visit every country and state, with my husband and our baby at my side. I want us to make wonderful memories together, but only a week or two at a time. We can see the sights, experience the atmosphere, eat all the food and return to the Scratching Post without feeling like I'm—we're—constantly plagued by homesickness."

His hand settled over her belly. "The little miracle Laurent will enjoy seeing the world. I know Hailey and Bailey loved the places Constance and I took them. They always felt as though they were on a grand adventure."

Nowadays he mentioned his first family with ease, and it thrilled her heart. Those girls would always be a part of him, and Ryanne would always be grateful for the love they'd given him, and the man they'd helped him become.

She kissed the corner of his beautiful, scarred mouth. Even in the moonlight she could make out the fierceness of his features...the hungry gleam in his eyes. A hunger that was never sated. Always he wanted her, and always her body responded in kind, starved for this man who had won her trust and heart.

"We're going to make so many wonderful memories together," she said.

"This is a magnificent start."

So many things had happened in the weeks since her abduction. Dushku had been charged with a wealth of crimes, and because he was broke, he couldn't afford to pay for fancy lawyers, or pay the judge to let him go. He would be serving a life sentence with men he'd betrayed and blackmailed. Glen Baker and Jim Rayburn had been arrested on multiple charges, as well. As Jude had promised, the security feed from Dushku's warehouse had proven Jim's guilt.

Ryanne could breathe easier now, and so could Lyndie. Jim wouldn't be causing trouble anymore.

Savannah and her son had officially moved to Strawberry Valley. She now worked as a maid at the inn. What she would do when Thomas's father was released from prison, no one knew.

"Plus," Ryanne said, returning to their conversation about heading home early. "Don't you want to get started on your new duties at the Scratching Post? I hear your boss is a real dragon lady."

"Good thing I know how to make that dragon lady purr. But what, exactly, are my new duties?"

Last night, as they'd laid snuggled together in bed, they'd chatted about *Jude's* hopes and dreams. He wanted to remain in charge of the bar's security, making sure no drunk drivers got behind the wheel of a car. He also planned to have his vasectomy reversed, so they could one day add to their family. A fact that pleased her greatly. They had a lot of love to give.

"Well," she said, "on top of running our new nightly security team, you're going to have to make sure I'm pleasured at least once a day, and to help facilitate that, you're going to have to work with your shirt off so I can admire your chest any time I want."

"Your terms are acceptable. I'll change our flights," he said. "But we're not heading back tomorrow. I don't want you regretting leaving early, so you're going to give Rome two—no, three more days. There are still places you haven't seen."

"You mean places we haven't made love."

"Exactly. But in the future, we'll plan shorter trips."

"Sounds fair, O wise one. Poor Selma, though. She's been in charge of the Scratching Post, and she's going to hate giving up the reins of control early. And poor Brock. He's not going to be happy, having to move out of our apartment sooner rather than later."

"I wouldn't worry about him. I'm sure Lyndie will distract him some way or another. She always does."

So true. Ryanne was rooting for those two crazy kids to work out their problems and start dating; they obviously wanted each other. "Why hasn't he asked her out?"

"Other than the fact that she's terrified of him?"

"Yes."

"She's former Junior League, right?"

"Mmm-hmm."

"That's why. Or one of the reasons. She's almost everything his parents would love."

"Almost?"

"Her divorce. They'd give him shit for it. If he ever brought her home, that is. Which he would never do. They'd eat her alive, and his protective instincts would surge. He'd react violently, as he tends to do, and probably scare the piss out of her."

"So what's wrong with his parents?"

"Imagine living in a ten-thousand-square-foot house with two people who find fault with everything you do and say, and an older brother who never does anything wrong. You'd have plenty of places to hide from the people, but no place to hide from the sting of their disapproval."

Ouch. "So Brock goes after different women to find the approval he didn't get as a child, if only for a night."

"In part. Sex isn't something he and I have discussed, but I suspect the less time he spends with a woman, the less she learns about him, so the less she has to dislike, allowing him to leave her with the memory of having her world rocked, nothing more, nothing less. Besides, PTSD registers differently for different people, and I've noticed Brock's causes him to do whatever it takes to make the people around him fall in love with him, if only for a little while, since he can't love himself." Jude lazily toyed with the ends of her hair. "That's my opinion, at least. I could be wrong."

Well, if Brock ever decided to go after Lyndie, he'd have his hands full, that was for sure. And vice versa!

Maybe Ryanne would give one of them a push? Lyndie desperately needed to experience a relationship free of abuse, with a man strong enough to help her fight her panic attacks, at the same time soothing the scared little girl within. To know that she was worth more than her father and ex-husband let her believe. To understand that she was a treasure and—

Nope. Bad Ryanne. No matchmaking. Brock wasn't one for commitment. If he were to break Lyndie's heart, Ryanne would have to break his face.

But then, to help him overcome a past mired with rejection, he desperately needed to experience a relationship full of acceptance and adoration. Lyndie's fear of him might push him too far.

Or force him to do better, helping him find what he was looking for.

Stop! Just stop. The fallout could be devastating.

"Me and my boys… I'm not sure why we fight our happiness so hard," Jude said, his voice fierce. "I'm sorry for every moment I gave in to fear, love."

If she were honest, part of her had expected that fear to return at some point and stomp all over his new zest for life. Oh, how wrong she'd been. He'd learned that fear left unchallenged could control him. And, as a soldier dedicated to achieving victory, ceding the minutest bit of control had rankled, so he'd taken the reins and held on with an intractable grip.

He hadn't broken a sweat when she'd wandered off in the Vatican, and he hadn't panicked when he'd woken in bed alone after she'd gone in search of a chocolate chip cookie.

Life was pretty much perfect.

"Do you still feel like you're broken?" she asked, petting his chest.

"After you picked up my pieces and put me back together again? Not even a little."

Darling, romantic man. She held up her hand, a gorgeous pearl-and-diamond cat paw ring glinting on her finger. The best engagement and wedding ring ever. "Are you happy?"

"Ecstatically so. And you?"

"Magnificently so." She wasn't just happy, she was gloriously satisfied. Amazingly content. "I never thought I could feel this way." A feeling she was certain her mother had searched for all these years, as she'd moved from man to man.

Gonna be nicer to that woman from now on.

"I'll do anything for you. Anything." Jude cupped the globes of her bottom. "You know that, don't you?"

"I kind of figured it out when you jeopardized your life to save mine." And she loved him all the more for it. He'd put her and the baby first—something she would forever do for him. "You won me, body and soul."

"As you've won me. You shattered my resistance, frayed my control and flooded light into my darkness. You are the key to my shackles. You set me free." As he spoke, he traced a finger over the lock on her wrist.

Right then, she made a decision to get another tattoo. A key on her other wrist. A constant reminder of this moment and the beautiful words her husband had just uttered.

No matter how many days, months, years they had ahead of them, Ryanne would forever rest in the knowledge that she had been—was—well loved. This shortcake–crazy cat lady had experienced the best of life, the thrill of adventure and the all-consuming power of a great man's adoration. Her cowboy, her honey buns. Her praised one. Her *precioso*.

She *so* looked forward to whatever came next.

★ ★ ★ ★ ★

If you liked Jude and Ryanne's story,
don't miss the next book in
THE ORIGINAL HEARTBREAKERS *series,*
Brock and Lyndie's sizzling tale,
CAN'T GET ENOUGH.
The playboy meets his match. Coming soon...

If you're a fan of hot contemporary romance,
look for Lori Foster's next sizzling book,
CLOSE CONTACT,
from HQN Books.
For the men of the Body Armor security agency,
the only thing more dangerous than the job they do
is the risk of losing their hearts.
Read on for an exclusive sneak peek…

Miles rode the private elevator in the Body Armor agency to his boss's very upscale office. The early-morning summons left him confused and he didn't like it. He'd been in the shower when she'd called at 7:00 a.m. Her message had said only that he was to get there as quickly as possible. She had a *surprise* for him.

Of course he'd called her back, but she'd told him she'd explain everything once he made it to the office.

He'd finished his extensive training only a few weeks ago, learning enhanced computer skills and practicing his shot with a variety of guns. He'd settled on the Glock as his preferred weapon, but carried a few other toys, as well.

So far he'd had two cases, both of them pretty routine. He'd helped to control pushy fans at a sporting event for a baseball player during a PR stint, and then escorted a big-time author with a new movie deal to some local signings around the area.

Easy peasy.

He missed competing, damn it. Missed the cage and the physical exertion. If fate hadn't played him a dirty hand, he'd be at it still, fighting his way to a championship belt.

The loss of his fight career was only one of many regrets he suffered lately, and as usual, he shoved it from his mind, determined to live in the here and now.

The elevator opened and he stepped out, going straight to Sahara Silver's posh office. As he passed Enoch Walker, Sahara's personal assistant, he said, "She's expecting me."

"Indeed she is," Enoch said without looking up from his PC screen. "Go right on in."

Did he detect an unusual note in Enoch's voice? Hard to tell when Enoch stayed focused on his task.

Miles liked Enoch a lot. He was a little dude with a will of iron and mad organizational skills. Always friendly, incredibly smart and damned reliable.

Because the door was closed, Miles knocked, and a mere second later it opened, almost as if Sahara had been waiting for him.

Oozing satisfaction, she smiled. "Miles."

He paused, suddenly on guard. So far, his boss had been something of an enigma. On the outside, she was a real looker, a shapely five foot eight inches of sass with glossy mink-brown hair, direct blue eyes and the demeanor of an Amazon. On the inside, she probably wrestled alligators and won. Always polished, always in killer heels and always sporting attitude.

"That's a different smile for you," he noted. "Why do I feel like I'm about to be offered as a sacrifice to angry gods?"

The smile widened, then she stepped back to allow him to enter. "Thank you for getting here so quickly."

"You didn't leave me much choice with that cryptic message."

"I'm never cryptic."

"No? Then what was so urgent that I—" That was when Miles saw her. His eyes flared as he noted her huddled position in a padded chair, a steaming cup of coffee held in both hands. "Maxi?"

When he said her name, she straightened but didn't look at him.

"What are you doing here?" For two months, he'd waited for her, hoping she'd get in touch again.

She hadn't.

From the start, she'd made it clear that he was a convenient booty call and nothing more. That should have worked great for him, but instead, it had driven him nuts.

He'd finally—well, *almost*—put her out of his mind with the job switch and move to a new apartment. Now here she was, at Body Armor of all places.

A slow burn started, making him blind to Sahara standing close, at least until she said, "Your friend has had something of an ordeal."

"And she came to me?" Umbrage churned, made sharper by other losses at the same time. He fashioned a sarcastic grin. "Surprising, since she walked away without a goodbye."

Maxi looked at him then. Those dark eyes he'd always found so mesmerizing were now glazed and somehow troubled.

And they stared at him like a lifeline.

It dawned on him that she looked terrible when he hadn't thought that possible. One of the very few things she'd ever revealed to him was her occupation as a personal stylist, a job that seemed to suit her since the lady had always looked very put together.

Not now, though. Dried leaves clung to her long, tangled blond hair. Gone were the trendy clothes; instead she wore an oversize flannel shirt, faded cutoffs and bright green rubber boots dotted with yellow ducks. The ridiculous clothes made her look endearing.

Concern sharpened his tone. "What the hell happened to you?"

When she didn't answer, he went to one knee in front of her, resting his hands on her slim thighs. A few months ago they'd been in a similar position, both naked. But she hadn't looked wounded then. No, she'd been soft and hot, moaning his name.

Blocking that memory seemed imperative. His tone didn't lose the edge. "Maxi?"

Pale slender fingers curled around the cup of steaming coffee. She swallowed audibly, met his gaze again and muttered, "I'm not sure."

"What does that mean?"

Sahara strolled up behind him. "Sometime before dawn, Ms. Nevar woke up in her yard, feeling very sick and with no memory of how she got there."

Miles looked back at Sahara, his voice stern with surprise. "What are you talking about?"

"She was a fair distance from her farmhouse but made it to the back porch. Needless to say, she wasn't keen on going back inside, not without knowing what might await her. The house was dark and her property is isolated with no close neighbors."

Miles sat back on his heels in disbelief. He didn't know jack shit about her property, but he put that aside for the moment. "Drunk?" He hadn't figured her for a big drinker, but then, what did he really know about her—except that, for a time, she'd enjoyed using him for sex?

As if to convince him, Maxi stared into his eyes. "I'd only had one glass of wine. At least, that's all I can remember."

All she remembered? "Could you have drunk enough to black out?"

She took that like a physical hit, flinching away from him and making him feel like an asshole.

Brisk now, Sahara said, "Despite being disoriented, she had the forethought, and guts I might add, to enter the unlit house to get her purse, car keys and those adorable boots."

Adorable? They belonged on a ten-year-old, not a grown woman.

"Staying there was out of the question, and she wasn't sure where else to go." Sahara propped a hip on the desk. "Since she remembered that you work here, this is where she came."

So she finally had a use for him again? No, he wouldn't be that easy, not this time. But he had questions, a million of them.

Looking back at his boss, Miles said, "Give us a minute, will you?"

She smiled down at him. "Not on your life."

He recognized that inflexible expression well enough. Sahara Silver did what she wanted, when she wanted. The lady was born to be a boss. In medieval times, she probably would have carried a whip. Still, he tried. "If she's here to see me—"

"She's here to hire you."

Hire him? He turned back to Maxi and got her timid nod. Skeptical, he clarified, "As a bodyguard?"

"Yes."

Since when did a woman need to be protected from a hangover? Did he want to be involved with that?

Now that he worked at the Body Armor agency, did he have a choice?

Sahara ruled with a small iron fist and she, at least, seemed taken with Maxi's far-fetched tale. If Sahara took the contract, he might not have much say in it.

And who was he kidding? As much as he'd like to deny it, territorial tendencies had sparked back to life the second he saw Maxi again. In his gut, he knew he was happy—even relieved—to again have her within reach.

Maybe because she was the one who got away, or the one who hadn't been all that hung up on him in the first place.

His ego was still stung, that was all.

It didn't help that her disinterest had piled on at a low point in his life, making her rejection seem more important.

She'd come on to him hot and heavy and they'd gotten together three separate times, had phenomenal sex that, at least to him, had felt more than physical, and then she'd booked. She'd guarded her privacy more than her body, and other than her name and occupation, he hadn't known much about her—not where she worked, or lived, or anything about her family...

As to that, maybe getting smashed and passing out in her yard was a regular thing for her. If so, he'd count himself lucky that she'd cut ties when she had.

Yet, somehow, that didn't fit with his impressions of her.

First things first. He had to get a handle on what had actually happened. "Where is this farmhouse?"

"In Burlwood."

"Never heard of it."

"Few people have. It's a really small town forty-five minutes south of here, close to the Kentucky border."

With that answered, he went on to other details. "So you woke up outside?"

"Yes."

"In your front yard?"

She shook her head. "A good distance away, on the far side of the pond."

"Like a little decorative pond?"

"It's two acres."

Wow. Okay, so not close to the house then. "How long were you out there?"

Her brows pinched together and her hands tightened. "I honestly don't know. The last thing I remember is opening a book to read." She drew in a deep, shaky breath. "That's it. Just reading. Then I woke up with a splitting headache, some bug bites and gravel digging into my spine."

"What were you doing before opening the book?"

Staring down at her hands, she gave it some thought. "I remember cleaning the kitchen."

"Before that?"

She shook her head. "It was an all-day job."

Who spent all day cleaning one room? He didn't know Maxi's habits, but maybe she'd never done any cleaning if tidying up dinner felt like a big chore to her. Hell, all he really knew about her was that she made him laugh, he enjoyed talking to her and she burned him up in bed.

Yeah, not a good time for that particular memory.

"Did you have company?"

"I don't think so."

"You don't remember?"

"I can't remember much of anything."

"Then how do you know—"

"No one comes out to the farmhouse," she snapped. "But I already told you, if someone did, I do *not* remember it." Temper brought her forward in her seat. "I can't remember *anything*. Especially not how I ended up sleeping on the ground in the middle of the night!"

Okay, so he had to admit, all in all that sounded like more than alcohol. Hell, had someone actually drugged her? If so, how and when?

Don't miss
CLOSE CONTACT
by New York Times *bestselling author*
Lori Foster!